G000300675

CATHERINE ROBERTSON'S novels have all been number one New Zealand bestsellers. Her fourth novel, *The Hiding Places*, also won the 2015 Nelson Libraries' Award for New Zealand Fiction. Catherine reviews books for the *New Zealand Listener* and is a regular guest on RNZ's The Panel and Jesse Mulligan's Book Critic slot. She is married with two grown sons, two Burmese cats, two rescue dogs and a powerful vacuum cleaner. She divides her time between Wellington and Hawke's Bay.

What you wish for

CATHERINE ROBERTSON

BLACK
SWAN

BLACK SWAN

UK | USA | Canada | Ireland | Australia
India | New Zealand | South Africa | China

Black Swan is an imprint of the Penguin Random House group of companies, whose
addresses can be found at global.penguinrandomhouse.com.

Penguin
Random House
New Zealand

First published by Penguin Random House New Zealand, 2019

1 3 5 7 9 10 8 6 4 2

Text © Catherine Robertson, 2019

The moral right of the author has been asserted.

All rights reserved. Without limiting the rights under copyright reserved above,
no part of this publication may be reproduced, stored in or introduced into
a retrieval system, or transmitted, in any form or by any means (electronic,
mechanical, photocopying, recording or otherwise), without the prior written
permission of both the copyright owner and the above publisher of this book.

Design by Rachel Clark © Penguin Random House New Zealand
Cover photograph by alex_tok/iStock
Author photograph by Russell Kleyn
Printed and bound in Australia by Griffin Press, an Accredited ISO AS/
NZS 14001 Environmental Management Systems Printer

A catalogue record for this book is available from the National Library of New Zealand.

ISBN 978-0-14-377281-1

eISBN 978-0-14-377282-8

penguin.co.nz

MIX
Paper from
responsible sources
FSC™ C009448

To Lesley, Nigel and Noah, with all my love.

A few readers have asked for a cast of characters, so here they are:

Dr Ashwin Ghadavi: newly arrived, rather anxious town GP

Devon Pohio-Ladbrook: barman, horse wrangler, currently not in a good mood

Emma Reid: eco-warrior daughter of Jacko and Mac

Patricia Weston: wife of Bernard, carer for children in need

Sidney Gillespie: mother of Aidan and Rory, jam-maker, assistant beekeeper

Vic Halsworth: farmer whose life is up the proverbial

Barrett Tahana aka Brownie: handsome, well spoken, recently out of jail

Bernard Weston: will do anything to ensure Patricia doesn't leave him again

Bronagh Macfarlane: chatty mother of Kerry, holidaying from the UK

Casey Marshall: town police officer, Corinna's sister

Charles Love: adored retired town GP

Corinna Marshall: lawyer, activist, married to Tai Te Wera

Douglas Macfarlane: not at all chatty husband of Bronagh

Gene Collins: Jacko Reid's best friend and professional mischief-maker

Jacko Reid: large, forthright owner of the Boat Shed restaurant

Jan Dundy: Gabriel's Bay Primary School principal

Kerry Macfarlane aka the Ginger Joker: chatty partner of Sidney Gillespie

Loko: eco-warrior, mansplainer

Mac Reid: short, forthright wife of Jacko, office manager for Dr G

Magnus Torvaldsen: recluse, Scrabble enthusiast

Moana: Devon's colleague at the Lightning Tree stables

Oksana: vigorous house cleaner, partner of Magnus

Otto Visser: farmer, mate of Vic's

Reuben Coates: small boy temporarily in Patricia Weston's care

Ron Hanrahan: property developer, Gene Collins's nemesis

Tai Te Wera: lawyer, husband of Corinna Marshall

Titus Phipps: beekeeper

Darius, Rua: Wood Sprites

Ianthe, Bea: plant collective volunteers

Immy, Jason, Mrs Dickens: Lightning Tree stables crew

Meredith Barton: Kerry's former employer

The moose: a moose

SBA25771
13.50 como

The Moose

The moose could not explain why only a few humans could see it. For one thing, it was two metres tall and weighed four hundred kilos. And for half the year it had antlers so wide that it could not avoid crashing into branches or leaving trails of tree fungus and epiphytes dislodged from a height that should have raised the eyebrows of those familiar with the second-largest bush dweller, the red stag. Or, as the moose liked to call him, *Tihkoosue*, which, roughly translated, meant Short-Arse. The red stag did not like his nickname but there wasn't much he could do about it.

Perhaps the human mind was to blame, not their eyes? In the moose's deliberately limited experience, humans spoke with a loud conviction that increased in parallel with their consumption of alcohol. If your status among your peers depended on you being right, then your brain had to reject all evidence to the contrary. 'There are no bloody moose left here, you berk — they died out decades ago' was a phrase the moose had more than once overheard. If moose could not exist, then, ipso facto, neither could the evidence. Human self-worth depended on it.

The moose felt it could not judge humans for this. It had questioned its own existence many times, prompted by an instinct lodged deep in its DNA that kept insisting it lived in entirely the wrong place. Its ancestors had not eaten these permanently green trees! They'd grazed on trembling aspen and sweet deciduous maple! All right, they *had* consumed the same dandelions and pondweed, though the pondweed here seemed also out of place, too vigorous in its growth, overwhelming the other water plants. The moose sensed it might be doing its foreign home a favour by consuming pondweed, roots and all. Besides, it was delicious.

Delicious, too, was the food offered to the moose by one of the humans who did choose to see it. The man who did not wear clothing. Who lived in the glass house on the edge of the bush with the woman who wore clothing only when she went out. Pink clothing, mostly. With sparkles.

The moose always waited until the woman left the house. She was strong and fierce, and occasionally swore in a language that seemed vaguely familiar to the moose. The man, by contrast, was mellow, welcoming. The first time the man had seen the moose peering over his balcony, he'd shown no surprise. He'd smiled and held out his hand. In it was a roundish brown object that smelled sweet, like the memory of maple bark that lingered in the moose's DNA.

'Vatrushka?' said the man. 'A traditional Russian bun, filled with sweet cheese and jam from our own raspberries. Very good.'

The moose extended its lips and took the bun. It wasn't pondweed, but it was, indeed, very good.

'I'm Magnus,' said the man. 'Nice to meet you.'

The moose did not know that its own name evolved from the Proto-Algonquian word, *mo-swa*, meaning 'it strips'. If it had, it would have spotted that it and the man had something in common. The man was always naked, even on colder days, because, unlike the woman, he never went out. Which meant he was happy to provide a snack no matter the hour. The moose was grateful. It had developed quite a taste for Russian buns.

The man seemed happy also to accept the existence of the moose. Of course, the animal was right there in front of his eyes, taking a cheese and jam-filled bun from his hand, but even given that weight of evidence, there'd been no guarantee the man would believe it. The moose had once appeared before two hunters in a glade. By accident; it was mating season and it had been distracted. The two men blinked at the moose, but all their other body parts remained fixed, as if constrained by invisible straitjackets. The moose decided it would be politic to quietly amble back into the bush, walk for a bit and then run. The hunters did not follow it. Later, the moose wondered how they'd reacted to its mating call, as it knew how far away the deep grunting could be heard. Probably attributed it to the red stag, whose own mating call was laughingly called a roar. The moose's memory contained the sound made by an irate grizzly bear. Now *that* was a roar.

Bears, wolves, cougars; the moose's instinct still urged it to be wary. But in this place, the one that never felt quite right, it was bothered only by the red stag (soft as well as short), wild pigs and the odd pig dog that it could scare off with only the threat of a kick. The dogs were not used to ungulates that could kick in all directions, but they learned fast. They were only smaller wolves, after all, and in the moose's memory, wolves were sent howling with a swift, sharp hoof to the guts.

In its memory, humans were the real danger. There was a dreadful story that the heads of dead moose were mounted on wooden shields and hung on walls of human houses, though most moose believed it had been made up by their grandparents, whose cautionary tales, as is universal to all species, were always heartily seasoned with ghoulishness.

Here, in this aspen-free land, those who observed the moose were gentle. Naked Magnus, the old man with the bees, and his wife, who'd loved hiking alone, and who'd fallen one day and not got up again. The moose had nudged her into the stream, hoping the water would revive her. It did not. When her body had been removed, the moose visited the old man to pass on its condolences. Death was natural, but that did not mean it was always welcome.

Those with guns — perhaps the moose had just been lucky with them? The two hunters weren't the only ones who'd ignored the evidence of their eyes. The farmer whose land led down to the river — he'd seen one of the cows and her calf crossing the water. But instead of reaching for his rifle, he'd sat heavily down on a rock and buried his head in his hands, as if the sight was too much to bear. If the cow had not had her calf with her, she told the moose, she would have asked the sad man, 'Sa kir winkan?' Are you OK? But the calf's safety was paramount. By the time the man lifted his head, he would have seen only stones in the river.

'How many more of you are there?' Magnus had asked once, though his smile said he did not expect an answer.

Four. The moose, two cows, one pregnant, and the last surviving calf, a young female, seven months old, not yet ready to leave its mother. Before them, many had died because this place, it was not right. The moose was the only male, and he was nineteen years old. He would live six more years at most. If the cow was not pregnant with a bull calf, or it, like others before, did not survive, he had six more years to produce another male. Or else . . .

But that was tomorrow. Today, there was pondweed and bark. There was the freedom of moving through the trees unfettered by mating-season-sized antlers. There was the red stag to bring down a peg or two. And if the moose timed its visit to naked Magnus to coincide with his afternoon break, there would be a fresh-baked Russian bun.

Today was a good day to be a moose.

CHAPTER 1

Ash

'There are no bloody moose left here, you berk — they died out decades ago.'

After four-and-a-bit months in Gabriel's Bay, Ashwin Ghadavi knew that, when uttered by Jacko Reid, the term 'berk' was tantamount to an endearment. Jacko often called his friends 'berks', also 'dickheads', 'retards' and 'nongs'. When he was mildly irked, he called them 'bastards'. No one knew what he said when he was seriously irked because an angry Jacko had the same effect as a Brazilian wandering spider emerging from a bunch of bananas in the fruit bowl — cleared the room in seconds.

Jacko owned the restaurant they were currently drinking in, and it was clear that people came to the Boat Shed not only for the excellent food, but also for the opportunity to be glared at by Jacko. Ash guessed it induced the same flirting-with-death frisson that a person might feel at the top of a bungy jump or with chopsticks poised over slivers of Japanese blowfish. Even in relaxed mode, Jacko was formidable — six foot seven, white blonde buzz-cut hair, hands that could crush a watermelon. Not that Jacko would ever crush a watermelon; he did not believe in wasting food. But Ash had no doubt that if he wanted to crush one, he could.

'But there is photographic evidence.' In the last month, Ash had become bold enough to venture the odd rebuttal. 'A cow and her calf, from which we can conclude that they were successfully breeding.'

'That was in the 1950s,' said Gene Collins, Jacko's best friend despite being the all-time most-awarded recipient of the 'bastard' epithet. 'Moose live for — what, fifteen years?'

'Up to twenty-five,' said Devon, cleaning glasses behind the bar.

Devon Pohio-Ladbrook worked five evenings at the Boat Shed, and weekday mornings at a horse rescue centre and training stables. In between, he was studying for a Bachelor's in Biological Science via distance learning. Devon was twenty-three, and made Ash feel like he'd taken the easy road by spending the last decade training to be a mere doctor. He should have taken helicopter-flying lessons as well, or, at the very least, scaled the world's major peaks.

'There you go,' said Gene. 'So any moose born in the 1950s would have been dead by the end of the '70s. You're forty years too late, mate.'

'People are convinced they still exist today,' said Ash.

'People are convinced that fluoride in the water allows the government to control our minds.'

'Government,' muttered Jacko, as if envisaging it as a water-melon.

'Easy tiger,' said Gene. 'Speaking personally, our beloved leaders have been bumped down my own shit list ever since our new enemy arrived, grasping hands outstretched, wreathed in the toxic stench of capitalism.'

'You're a business owner,' said Devon. 'You make money off the sweat of others. How are *you* suddenly a socialist?'

Gene Collins ran a concrete pouring company, which kept him, his wife and three daughters in relative affluence, even though, as far as Ash could tell, his head office was the Kozy Kettle café over the hill in Hampton. Ash supposed it saved on overheads.

'I provide a valuable service and pay a fair wage,' said Gene. 'And I'm not proposing to blight our waterfront with a shitty industrial park.'

'You tendered for the concrete, you hypocrite,' said Jacko. 'And got it, too.'

'Naturally,' said Gene. 'Keep your enemies close, that's my motto.'

'So close you can reach into their wallets?'

'Well, since I hit a wall preventing the bloody project getting this far, I figured if you can't beat 'em, join 'em . . .'

Gene was short and round, with a neat salt and pepper beard and a penchant for Pasifika-patterned shirts. When Ash had first met him, he'd thought him a cheery kind of bloke. He now knew that Gene's smile was the equivalent of the click heard when your foot came down on a landmine — a signal that you were in mortal peril and there wasn't a single thing you could do about it.

Gene smiled. 'And once you're on the inside, then you can wreak some *proper* havoc.'

'I thought Liz threatened to shiv you if you got in any trouble?' said Jacko.

'Incorrect. My darling wife said she'd come at me with a machete.'

Gene sipped his beer. It was the only kind the Boat Shed served, and came in a plain brown bottle with the word 'Beer' handwritten on it.

'That's what happens when white chicks marry us half-Samoans,' he added. 'They assimilate too thoroughly.'

Devon was shaking his head.

'Just because you're half brown doesn't mean you can make crappy racist jokes,' he said to Gene. 'If you tried that in *my* family, you'd get your arse kicked.'

'Come on,' Gene protested. 'You can't tell me that *no* one in your whole entire whānau has ever made a Māori joke?'

'Our priority is respect, man. In deeds and words.'

'And if you don't watch your mouth, you'll get a smack round the chops from your aunties?' said Gene, with a grin.

Devon cast a look at Ash, who wished he wouldn't. Ash had not yet got over his embarrassing first encounter with the young man, even though others had assured him that he was not the first to make that mistake. (The others were laughing quite heartily as they said this, which Ash felt lent a somewhat equivocal edge to their support.) The mistake had arisen because, despite being born to unambiguously Māori parents, Devon had milk-coffee skin, brown eyes, long blonde hair, a slender physique and the face of a model. A female model. Folk conjectured that he was a throwback to non-Māori ancestors, who included Scottish whalers, Dutch cheesemakers and Polish refugees. Whatever the reason, Devon was a striking genetic anomaly in a family that treated him no differently to any other member. It was only strangers who went, in Devon's words, 'all weird on him'. Ash had indeed gone 'all weird', and the memory still made him cringe with shame.

'See?' said Devon to Ash. 'Attitudes like this is why our society can't progress.'

'Well, I'm not sure that is the entirety of factors as to why—'

'You make Indian jokes in your family, Dr G?' said Gene.

Ash's first thought was to say that humorous banter arose in his family home about as often as ice-cream vans drove around Mars piping 'Greensleeves'. His father had founded a merchant banking firm in the Ghadavis' home city of Ahmedabad and, having successfully employed his two oldest sons, could not understand why his youngest had no head for finance, and why, if he insisted on becoming a doctor, he did not aspire to be a Harley Street consultant or celebrity cosmetic surgeon. His mother ran their household and was involved in good works. Ash did not know what these were, and any enquiry would only invite derision to be poured upon him. His mother was very certain of everything and had no patience with those who were not — a significant subset of

16

humanity that had always included Ash. His brothers did laugh on occasion, but Ash rarely joined in owing to being most often in a corner, crying — which was the reason his brothers were laughing in the first place.

However, none of the above felt like an appropriately jovial response to Gene's question.

'I cannot claim to know any good jokes,' said Ash. 'But what do you call a Hindu man going backwards?'

'OK, what?' said Gene.

'Rever-Singh.'

'Fucking terrible,' said Jacko.

'That was the pick of the bunch, I am sorry to say,' said Ash.

'Never fear.' Gene had turned to face the door, where the creak of salt-dried wood announced the arrival of another in their midst. 'The Ginger Joker is finally here.'

Into the Boat Shed stepped the now familiar red hair of Kerry Macfarlane, who until Ash's arrival had been the most well-known foreigner in Gabriel's Bay. He didn't have far to walk to join them because the restaurant was, indeed, a renovated boat shed. Jacko preferred names that were simple and literal because he could see no point, as he explained, in 'pissing about'. The décor was equally redolent of Jacko's personality. On display were objects that included a carved wooden rifle, a lampstand made from deer antlers, a ukulele, a pair of scuffed cowboy boots and a taxidermied weasel.

Kerry skirted the tables and brightly painted folding chairs, and arrived at the bar, where Gene and Ash occupied two of the four stools. From his, Ash could look into the lean-to kitchen, and through the panes of the back door to the ocean. In the last of the July daylight, the water was choppy and slate grey, and the few gulls on the kelp-strewn sand had hunkered down to avoid the wind.

Kerry took the stool next to Ash, and followed his line of sight.

'Just think,' he said. 'If you and I were back home, we could be fighting for a spot on Brighton Beach with fifty million others, all thrilled that the temperature had reached its projected high of seventeen degrees.'

'I travelled to Brighton only once,' said Ash. 'With a fellow medical student who insisted we cycle from there to Rottingdean.'

'And there we have it. How to put the blight in Blighty.'

Jacko thumped a beer down in front of Kerry. 'You're late.'

Ash would have trembled inwardly if Jacko had addressed him in that accusatory manner; he felt that he was still very much in a trial period and should watch his step lest he be summarily rejected. Kerry had been in Gabriel's Bay for not much longer, less than a year, and yet he had a steady girlfriend, a well-paid IT job in Hampton, and everyone seemed to like him. Ash felt a twinge of envy that Kerry, who did not hold any position of actual responsibility, had been so easily accepted by the Gabriel's Bay community. Then again, Kerry had not supplanted the town's beloved, nay revered, doctor, who had cared for its inhabitants for the last forty-five years. And although he, too, was foreign, Kerry was also white. Ash did not want to think it made a difference, especially in a town whose braided ancestries included Māori, Samoan, Russian, Welsh, Norwegian, Dutch, Polish, Scottish and, rumour had it, the blood of a Cheyenne chief. But he suspected it might. Either that, or he simply did not have Kerry's knack of endearing himself to people. Ash wasn't sure which option depressed him most.

Kerry picked up his beer. 'I was delayed by an accident on the hill.'

'Anyone we know?' said Gene. 'Better still, anyone we don't like?'

'An overturned truckload of carrots. By the time I arrived, most had been crushed. It looked like the footpath outside the Crown on Saturday night.'

Gene raised his beer in salute. 'That's why we drink here.'

'You could eat here, too, once in a while, you cheap git,' said Jacko.

'And miss sharing meals with my family?' said Gene. 'Where else would I find out about Justin Bieber's tattoos? Or that I can't say "bae" any more because it's, like, totally uncool, and that "stanning" is a thing?'

'What kind of a thing?' Kerry said.

'No idea.'

'It means being a fan,' said Devon. 'You know, as in: my mum stans John Rowles.'

'New Zealand crooner,' Kerry explained to Ash. 'Handsome devil. My own mother is more of a Rory Gallagher fan, God rest his loud, Irish soul. The neighbours would have been much happier if she'd preferred Chris de Burgh.'

'Aren't your folks turning up here any minute?' Devon asked Kerry.

'Could you not have waited?' Kerry slumped onto the bar top. 'Two more beers and I'd have forgotten.'

Ash had early on worked out that any complaints Kerry made about his parents were entirely fictional. The Macfarlanes adored each other, and were looking forward to being reunited for the first time in two-and-a-half years. It was Bronagh and Douglas Macfarlane's first proper holiday overseas, if you didn't count their honeymoon on South Uist. According to Kerry, they usually vacationed in cheap beachside camping grounds in a caravan called Adventure Before Dementia, though Ash could not be entirely convinced of that last detail. Kerry liked to embellish and he was good at it. It was one of the traits that endeared him to people, and one that Ash could not hope to emulate.

'Where are they staying, your parents?' said Gene. 'With you?'

'God no,' said Kerry. 'My house is a demolition zone thanks to my cack-handed attempts at DIY. Last weekend, I gave up and called every builder within a hundred miles, but turns out they are all booked up until the end of the next millennium.'

'Yep, lots of work out there at the moment,' said Gene. 'It's all these rich people buying up our land. I can put in a word for you, if you like?'

'I do like, thank you. Won't help my parents, but fortunately they've found affordable lodging at some farm-stay close to the river.'

'Willow Cottage?' said Jacko.

'Sounds right,' said Kerry, and added, 'why are you frowning?'

'He always looks like that,' said Gene. 'It's the natural cast of his face.'

'That's Vic Halsworth's place,' Jacko said to Gene.

'Ah.' Gene nodded. 'Gotcha.'

'Why are you frowning?' demanded Kerry. 'Will my parents be forced to doss down in my barn?'

'Nah,' said Jacko. 'Should be right.'

'Yeah,' said Gene. 'Should be . . .'

'You know, I have a spare room in my house,' said Ash. 'Your parents would be very welcome to it.'

Kerry blinked, startled, then smiled and clinked his beer bottle against Ash's.

'That is a most generous if foolhardy-bordering-on-lunatic offer, Dr G. Let's hope you never have to make good on it.'

Outside, a car braked on gravel. Its doors opened and shut. Voices approached. Devon slipped out from behind the bar, and went to greet the group coming through the door.

'Show time.' Jacko slung a tea towel over his shoulder. 'First proper customers of the evening.'

'Harsh but true.' Gene slid from his stool. 'I'll be off then. Home to dazzle them with my new-found knowledge of "stanning". Though by the time I get there, it'll probably be out of date.'

Kerry upended his beer. 'Me too,' he said. 'I'm cooking for Sidney and the boys tonight.' He clapped Ash on the shoulder. 'See you, Dr G.'

'Good night,' said Ash, but the two men already had their backs to him.

Devon was taking coats from the five who'd arrived. Mother and father, and three teenage children. Cheerful in each other's company. Just as they all sat down, another group entered. Six friends, in their twenties, ready for a good night out.

'You staying?' said Jacko.

Ash often ate at the Boat Shed, but tonight he did not feel like dining alone. Of course, if he went home, he would be entirely alone, but he wouldn't be surrounded by people who weren't.

'Thank you, but no.'

He felt conscious of the formality of his phrasing, but could not yet bring himself to use the vernacular. Cheers, mate. Ta, bro. It wasn't his style. It wasn't his native tongue.

'See you tomorrow, Dr G?' said Devon, as Ash opened the door onto a cold, dark evening.

'Of course,' said Ash.

Where else did he have to go?

CHAPTER 2

Vic

The calves were due in five weeks, the lambs in seven. His guests were due in two days. And his wife had moved to Coonamble to be with a man she'd met on the internet.

To be fair, she'd met Vic on the internet, too, so he could hardly accuse her of sleazy practices. But they'd both been single then, so it wasn't the same. At least he'd been pretty certain she was single. If she'd had other suitors, it seemed unlikely she'd have picked him. Donna was what his late father would have called 'comely'. Whereas no matter how many times he re-took it, his profile shot made him look like he'd just been bitten on the arse by a miniature pony.

They'd connected three years ago, when he was forty-two and had never been kissed. That wasn't true, but it had felt true back then. Donna's previous marriage had lasted twelve years, but Vic's longest relationship had run its course in eighteen months. All two of the women who'd tried living with him had left for the same reasons: the farm was too remote, too hilly, too damp. The house was too old, he worked too many hours, he earned too little. He needed more than two shirts. His Swanndri stank. The K-Tel hair-cutting comb hadn't worked in 1973 and it didn't work now. No man under eighty-five wore white Y-fronts. It was not actually illegal to allow meat and vegetables to touch on the plate. Yes, eggplant was a vegetable. Two thirds of the world's seven billion people ate rice every day, so would it kill him to try it?

Donna had been so nice in their online chats that Vic had felt compelled to list every complaint he'd ever received, including all the ones he felt were manifestly unjustified (one third of the world did not eat rice, and he was happy to be counted among them). Donna had always wanted to live on a farm, she'd assured him. She liked peace and quiet, and small towns without many people. She liked cattle and sheep and old houses. She had a foolproof method of laundering white Y-fronts.

All of this proved to be true. Donna quit her job as a dentist's receptionist in Papakura, and moved in with Vic. A month later, they were married. Two weeks after that, she announced a plan to supplement their income — buying one of those prefab Victorian-style cottages and plonking it on a piece of ground out back whereupon it would transform into a B&B. This involved felling a stand of macrocarpas that had been there for over a hundred years. But as Donna rightly pointed out, they were ugly trees and harboured the magpies that dived on you like Messerschmitts, skimming so close that their beaks had, at times, drawn blood. Vic's command to 'Bugger off!' had, on every occasion, been ignored by the swooping sods, but when the trees came down, off they were forced to bugger. He didn't miss the need for permanent vigilance, but he'd enjoyed their gargling call-out from high up in the branches. Other farmers he knew would have reached for their gun, but Titus Phipps once told him that magpies remembered who was good to them. Old Phippsy had trained a young one to talk. It could say the words 'quardle ardle wardle doodle', which confused a lot of people. The magpie loved Phippsy's wife, Mary, and when she died suddenly while out tramping, it pined away until Phippsy put it out of its misery with a pad of ether.

So, anyway, the macrocarpas went, the magpies moved, and Willow Cottage opened for business, with the new Mrs Halsworth as your host. It was a bit of a trek to get there. First you had to tackle the hill over from Hampton, and even Vic didn't like doing that too often; the old ute handled like a cow teat-deep in mud. And then you had to find the farm turn-off — Vic made Donna a sign from a slab of macrocarpa (waste not, want not) — and drive two kilometres over metal to the main house. Willow Cottage was another half a k' up a path that Vic laid over with macrocarpa planks to make a kind of boardwalk. It got slippery in winter, so he covered it in chicken wire. Did the job, as long as you wore flat shoes. And watched your step.

Willow Cottage wasn't exactly overrun with guests from day one. Donna spent a lot of time online, and quite a bit of money, placing advertisements and connecting with tourist sites. Vic had hoped she might help with calving — he'd had a bad run with rotavirus last season, requiring hands-on twenty-four-hour care of calves that were simultaneously starving and shitting out everything inside them. There was a vaccine, he knew, but what with a drought for three years and that outbreak of facial eczema, and then the fert costs went through the roof so he couldn't afford to boost the pasture growth, so the stock finished underweight and he made a whacking great loss, and he had to cut his sheep numbers by over a third and not replace a bunch of his breeding cows and heifers, and for the last two seasons he'd been pretty much on his own because he couldn't pay for a full-time farm assistant, and the shearers had got a bit toey with his payments being in arrears, so he'd had to cut his drench and 5-in-1 budget, and the summer before, he'd lost ten of his best beef animals to blackleg. Then all that rain they'd had — they said better late than never but they were morons, because the hills were slipping like buggery and those fences down towards the river were rotting in the now too-damp ground, and he'd had one mob break through and end up in the drink, and the Regional Council had already sent a letter warning about fines for run-off into waterways, and then they'd called about the folk living wild down by the river and implied they were his responsibility and Vic had got shirty, which in hindsight was stupid because you didn't want the Council on your back . . .

He didn't tell Donna any of this. He didn't tell her that some nights he woke in panic, and that even outdoors, doing the work he loved, his mind would sort of dissociate from his body and he'd looked down at his misty real self and wonder if he could leave it behind for good. He certainly didn't tell her about the hallucination. Besides, he wasn't sure he'd seen them, anyway. Could have been a really large deer and fawn, or two extremely odd-shaped Angus cattle.

He didn't tell her because she was so happy. Her investment in advertising paid off and they were getting a booking every couple of weeks — albeit with a bit of a fallow patch over the worst of winter. She set the cottage up with fresh flowers, tea and coffee, clean sheets and towels. For the morning, she'd provide a basket of fresh-baked bread and jam, and her own breakfast cereal made of seeds and nuts, which Vic said she shouldn't waste on him. If her guests wanted a cooked breakfast, she'd bring it up to them on a tray with one of those metal covers, just like in a flash hotel. She loved talking to everyone, finding out where they were from, giving them tips for touristy stuff to do in the area. Vic knew where to go hunting, but most of their guests turned out to be a bit squeamish about dead animals, even those that had died of natural causes. Donna told him to skip the offal pit next time he took people around the farm.

The guests who were arriving in two days, a couple from London, had been a last minute booking because their original accommodation fell through. Donna marked out their stay on the calendar in the kitchen — nearly four whole weeks, unheard of.

And the following day, when he was out shovelling a slip off a track, she packed her bags and drove to Hampton airport, from whence she caught a domestic flight to Wellington and an international one to Sydney, where the man from Coonamble was waiting to drive her five hundred and thirty-five kilometres to her new home.

Vic googled Coonamble and found it was in many respects very similar to Gabriel's Bay. Except that it was in Australia, and contained one thing that Gabriel's Bay now conspicuously lacked: his wife.

His longest relationship had lasted eighteen months. His marriage had broken that record by three months and four days. Their two-year anniversary would have been this October. Cotton was the traditional gift. What he'd had in mind to get her was an embroidered hanky. Or maybe a new striped tea towel to put over the guest's fresh bread. Now he guessed he could scrub that off his to-do list.

She'd left an explanatory note on the fridge under a Minion magnet. It ended with the word 'Sorry'. Vic had scrunched the note up and opened the fridge. He found eggs and bacon behind another note that said 'For the guests!' Vic scrunched that note up, too, and fried his dinner.

That was Monday. It was now Thursday night, and he was no closer to working out what to do when his guests arrived on Saturday. He couldn't ring them and tell them they had to find somewhere else to stay because he knew Willow Cottage was their only option. Their son lived in Gabriel's Bay, apparently, and they wanted to be near him, but the only other accommodation they could afford was the old camping ground, and that didn't open until November. Vic might be a sad bastard but he wasn't an actual bastard. He couldn't turn them away.

With luck, they'd be happy to fend for themselves. With luck they wouldn't ask him any difficult questions. With luck, he'd be able to hand them the cottage keys and then see neither hide nor hair of them for the whole four weeks.

If he had that kind of luck, he'd buy a Lotto ticket. Because right now, the goddess of fortune was not smiling on him. Right now, she was making him assume the position and cough, and the smile she did have on suggested this was only the first examination of many.

It was eight o'clock and Vic hadn't yet made dinner. He'd used up all the eggs and bacon and all the bread Donna had stored in the freezer. In the pantry was a click-top container full of seed-nut mixture, numerous dry ingredients and little boxes of herbs and spices. Up high was a can of sardines that predated Donna and (Vic read the date stamp on the side) had expired in March.

The can looked intact, no dents. Vic opened it and ate its contents while watching *Project Runway* on the only channel his TV could receive.

CHAPTER 3

Patricia

'Bernard, may I have a word?'

The expression on her husband's face filled Patricia with guilt. First, a flash of alarm, then a smile that was cautious but eager. What she might be about to say filled him with terror but he was determined to do whatever she asked to keep her happy. To keep her, full stop.

Last year, Patricia had temporarily removed herself from her marriage, and gone travelling, roaming really, for two months. She'd needed time to find out what it felt like to be on her own, and to decide if she wanted to return to a husband who, for their entire thirty-nine year marriage, had held a candle for someone else. Someone more beautiful and elegant, and with more class. A slender Hepplewhite side table next to her chunky Welsh dresser.

Bernard's infatuation was not her sole reason for leaving. At sixty-three, the scales had fallen from Patricia's eyes and she'd been appalled to see how extensively she'd let her sense of self erode. Because it had occurred gradually, over decades, she'd been conscious only of the outer changes — the ballooning of her girth, the greying of her hair, the thickening of her ankles and facial features. She had not observed a corresponding accretion of despair and self-loathing, had not felt their murky sediment build up, intent on smothering and extinguishing what had been once a vibrant light.

When Patricia met Bernard, they'd both been twenty-four. Her full figure was out of date, the magazines favouring twig-like women in pantsuits. But Patricia knew what suited her, and she did not care that it was unfashionable because it lent her a quality that had once been known as 'va-va-voom'. Red lipstick and heels, a cinched-in waist and full skirt, an only-just-modest neckline. Occasionally, she stuck a fake beauty spot just above her lip to emulate Marilyn Monroe, even though her own hair was dark. She frequented the local rock 'n' roll club, and jived energetically. She had no shortage of male attention.

Why then, had she chosen Bernard? He was small and bespectacled, and had no sartorial style. He was no dancer, though having been drilled in it at boarding school, he could execute a passable Gay Gordons. He was shy to the point of being mute so, of course, it had been she who'd made the first move. Patricia worked in a book shop. Bernard worked for a publishing firm and, as Patricia found out, considered books to be his best friends.

They were dissimilar in almost every way back then, so why had Patricia been drawn to him? During her time away from her marriage, Patricia utilised fully the benefits of hindsight in order to better understand her life to date. What could she see? Bernard was intelligent and, once he overcame his shyness, talkative, and Patricia was tired of men with limited conversation. He was kind, and too many of the men she'd danced with were bullies, in the main because they held outdated attitudes towards the role of women (hence why they clung on to the rock 'n' roll era). Bernard's upbringing had been a conservative one, but apart from insisting on holding doors open and standing when a woman entered the room, he had no chauvinistic tendencies. It had been Patricia who'd settled in to the traditional role, taking on the housework and gardening, wearing more acceptable, practical clothes, and giving up her job because, surely, she would soon become a mother . . .

Is that where it started — the erosion of self? Was it set off by that disappointment, which began as a trickle — not everyone conceives first go, you're young, you've got plenty of time — but became a steady flow beneath the surface of her life, a hidden river gradually hollowing her out. No, it was foolish to lay the blame at that door — at any door. The blame lay solely with her. She'd let herself go, in all senses of that phrase. She'd let her light go out, and not raged against its dying. She'd let Bernard remain infatuated with another, even though the hurt cut deep. She could have protested, could have striven to compete. But instead, she'd given in, given the race up as lost before she'd even made the start line.

That was what she'd decided during her time away — it was down to her. The success of her marriage, the quality of her life, her appearance — all within her control, should she choose to act.

She did choose. She returned to Bernard on New Year's Eve, and he welcomed her back with tears and embraces because it was Patricia whom he really loved. She got a flattering haircut and bought clothes that made her feel happy. She resigned from some of her volunteer work, and began investigating other ways she could feel valuable and productive. Recently, she'd found one in particular that both excited and terrified her. And it was about this that she needed to have a word with Bernard.

Her husband was gazing at her with trepidation. Patricia doubted she'd be able to reassure him, but this was important to her. Possibly even necessary. She sat in the armchair across from his, in their comfortable living room with the fire in the hearth. Their comfortable, tidy living room with its good furniture and collection of quite valuable objets d'art. Was she mad? No, they were just things. They could be replaced.

'Bernard,' she said. 'I've applied to the government to become a caregiver for children.'

He stared at her, uncomprehending. Fair enough, poor old boy.

She may well have been speaking in Yoruba for all the sense those words made to him.

'Not for fulltime foster care,' she explained, 'but short-term or respite care — taking children in for anything from a few days to a few months, until their families are ready to have them back.'

'Taking them in?'

Bernard's scrambled brain was perhaps confusing children with clothing that required alteration.

'Yes, into our house,' said Patricia, ignoring the blip in her confidence.

'Here?'

'Yes, Bernard, here. In our house.' She prepared to repeat herself yet again, but it had finally sunk in. Much as an axe sinks into a log.

'Dear God, are you in earnest?' said Bernard. 'Strange children in our house? Sleeping in our beds? Eating at our table? Touching our—'

He jerked upright, as if someone had attached a live wire to his spinal cord. 'Not my books. They can not touch my books.'

Patricia held up a pacifying hand. 'Your library will be out of bounds, that will be made clear.'

'Yes, but . . .' Bernard was now wriggling around in his chair, his every instinct rebelling. 'They'll be difficult children, won't they? With issues . . .'

'Very likely,' said Patricia. 'But that does not mean they will be vandals. Or thieves. It means they need a safe, warm place to stay, food to eat and kindness. All of which we can give them.'

Bernard slumped in his chair, gripped both its arms for support.

'We're sixty-four,' he said. 'Surely, we are far too old?'

'Not at all,' she told him. 'Caregivers are often grandparents.'

'How did you . . .?' His voice was almost a whisper. 'How did this . . .?'

'How did this cockamamie idea come about?' Patricia smiled ruefully at him. 'Yes, I know how it sounds, and I apologise again for springing it on you. But let me assure you I am not going into this blindly. I have done my research.'

'You've spoken to someone?'

'Several people. But I spoke first to Corinna, who in the course of her work as a family lawyer has had experience of children in care.'

'I see. And what was her advice?'

Patricia knew that Bernard considered Corinna Marshall as one of the forces to be reckoned with in his life. She was young, attractive and outspoken about issues she believed in, particularly those that affected Māori. Bernard had none of those qualities, but he was learning to be more assertive. Except with Patricia, of course, for whom he'd currently do anything. Though with this latest request, Patricia did feel she might be pushing her luck.

'Corinna believed that I should meet the government's requirements, and gave me the names of three caregivers in the district to telephone and find out first hand what the role might demand.'

'Sensible.'

'Yes, she is. Very,' said Patricia. 'And so I telephoned the first of them, and almost changed my mind.'

'Will you tell me why?'

'Absolutely not. I went to see Corinna again and expressed my doubts, and she very patiently suggested I defer my decision until I'd talked to everyone on my list. She also suggested I talk to her sister, Casey, who is, of course, also involved in assessing care arrangements.'

'I imagine Casey would be exposed to the worst situations,' said Bernard. 'If the police need to be brought in, the circumstances must be dire.'

'Not always, she told me,' said Patricia. 'Not every child is a victim of neglect or abuse. Sometimes, the families are doing a decent job, but become overworked or ill and simply need a break.

Casey keeps an eye on several such families, in conjunction with social services. She said if a child was sent to us, that's from where he or she would likely come. They do aim to match children and caregivers appropriately.'

Bernard removed his spectacles and dug the heel of his hand into one eye. Patricia's heart went out; she could see his anxiety and reluctance vying with his earnest desire to please her.

'I'm so sorry for springing this on you,' she said again. 'But I didn't want to say anything until I, myself, was convinced. If I'd spoken to you when I was still unsure of the idea, I suspect you could easily have persuaded me out of it.'

He hooked his glasses back over his ears, exhaled.

'And you are convinced?' he said.

'Utterly. We can do this — I can do this,' she said. 'I will do the bulk of the work. You need only support me.'

'I don't know how to talk to children.'

'I imagine they'll teach you.'

'What if they ask me difficult questions? What if they have tantrums in public? What if they can't read?'

Patricia came and sat on the arm of his chair, bent her head and kissed the top of his.

'We'll be part of a team,' she said. 'We'll have support and advice and help. And if it proves impossible, I'll say we tried, and I'll move on.'

'When is this all likely to occur?'

'My application hasn't yet been accepted.'

Her husband smiled up at her. It wasn't the widest of smiles, but he was doing his best.

'It will be,' he said. 'Because you are wonderful.'

'I may also be stark raving mad,' said Patricia. 'And given what I've been told about the need for caregivers, it might not be terribly long before we have that confirmed.'

CHAPTER 4

Sidney

'Are you ready for the descent of the in-laws?' said Mac.

'Ah, ha, ha,' said Sidney. 'Not even a little bit.'

Mac held out her standard sweet offering, a packet of Krispies. Sidney took two. Coconut was the new super-food, wasn't it? Despite the fact coconut water tasted like fresh armpit sweat. That said, it didn't taste as bad as wheatgrass juice, which surely was better suited to inducing vomiting in dogs after they'd ingested chocolate. Sidney's new pals in the Gabriel's Bay plant collective were fans of biodynamic fluids, including something called colloidal silver, which apparently boosted the immune system by disabling fungi and bacteria, but which you couldn't store near any electrical appliance because its properties degraded when exposed to magnetic fields. Sidney suspected she might have not have grasped its benefits in their entirety, but it didn't matter because the only alternative wellness-enhancing liquid she could afford was her own wee. With that, she drew a firm line, even though, in about ten minutes' time, it would be ninety per cent pure PG Tips.

'I'm only grateful they didn't ask to bunk down in my lounge,' Sidney said. 'I mean, what was Kerry thinking, trying to renovate? The name "skill" saw should have been a clue as to what he needed before commencing.'

'They still might need to bunk with you,' warned Mac. 'Jacko said Vic Halsworth's wife's left him.'

'Oh, shit, poor Vic!' said Sidney. 'Not that I know him well. He pops in to see Mr Phipps occasionally, so I've fed him the odd crumpet. Limited vocab. Terrible haircut. But seems nice enough. Do you think he won't be up for being *mein host* at Willow Cottage?'

'Well, we'll soon find out,' said Mac. 'Is Kerry picking his folks up from the airport?'

'Aye. Tomorrow at eleven. Back to my place for lunch because Kerry's gas stove is as well behaved as sensitised nitro-glycerine. No idea what I'll feed them.'

'Do you want to bring them here, instead? Jacko can cater.'

Mac and Jacko had been together since he was seventeen and she fifteen. She was now fifty-four, with fluffy brown hair pulled back in a rough ponytail, and a pragmatic attitude to fashion — i.e. she paid it no mind whatsoever. She was also fifteen inches shorter than her husband, a fact that had led more than one unwary unfortunate to discover, when they pointed it out, that such a height discrepancy was not the comedy gold they might have thought.

'That would be *magnificent*, thank you,' said Sidney. 'Thank Jacko, too, when you break it to him.'

Then because she felt compelled to double-check (perhaps she'd been some sort of heading dog in a past life, needing to keep an eye on everyone), she added, 'Are you sure?'

'I like Bronagh,' said Mac. 'She amuses me.'

Sidney had a mental image of a person dancing while bullets ricocheted between their feet. But in this case, Mac was quite sincere. Kerry's mother, Nurse Bronagh, had helped Mac find a replacement for her long-time and (though Mac would part with fingernails before admitting it) adored employer, Dr Charles Love. Sidney hadn't checked in recently to see how Mac was getting on with the handsome if high-strung Dr Ghadavi. Her only comment after he'd been there a month was 'Tolerable', which meant he hadn't tried to suggest Mac do anything differently and had not objected to her driving a busload of old folk over the hill to Hampton every Monday morning, so they could do their shopping and banking, go to the library, and have tea and a bun at the Kozy Kettle. The new doctor spent Monday mornings making house calls, because that's what the old doctor had done, and Sidney was sure that Mac had left Dr G in no doubt that breaking with tradition would be akin to converting the swing set in the children's playground into a gibbet and stringing up Father Christmas.

Sidney had taken Rory to see him with an infected throat, and Dr G had been kind, calm and professional. In social situations, though, he had the twitchiness of a flightless bird that's got whiff of a weasel. It could be a consequence of working with Mac — there were people who'd sought PTSD counselling after a single encounter with her. Or it could be that the good doctor was so worried about fitting in that he simply couldn't relax enough to fit in.

'Should we invite Dr G to lunch, too?' Sidney said.

'Why?' Mac said.

'I don't know. Because he has no friends?'

'He drinks with the guys at the Boat Shed.'

'Yes, but what does he do in between that and doctoring? What's he doing this weekend, for instance?'

'How should *I* know?' Mac sounded aggrieved.

'You work with him nine hours a day, five days a week!' Sidney protested. 'You spend more time with him than any of us!'

'That doesn't mean I'm interested in him as a person!'

Mac saw Sidney's expression, and screwed up her mouth. 'Oh, very well — invite him to lunch. But if Jacko wants to cook cow, he'll have to like it or lump it.'

Sidney did not know whether Dr G was the kind of Hindu who practised vegetarianism, or indeed whether he was Hindu at all, but she made a mental note to bring an extra large potato salad.

'How are things financially?' Mac asked.

Sidney recognised the tactic. Mac was getting back at her for making her feel guilty.

'Borderline,' she admitted.

Sidney had managed for the last ten years to support two boys on the sole parent benefit, and meet the government's requirements for part-time work. She did one evening at the Boat Shed and filled in if Devon couldn't make it. She made jam and chutney from her garden produce and sold them at the Hampton farmers market, and had recently begun potting up seedlings for sale via the plant collective. She earned a few more dollars tutoring high school students, and helping Titus Phipps with his hives. When there wasn't a lot of bee work, he paid her the same amount to bring food for him and do a few chores, for which she was grateful, doubly so because while the amount he paid her was small, it was still far too much for what she did.

Last year, through a well-intentioned but frankly mental attempt to help another child, Sidney had dug herself into a financial hole and been forced to sell her car. Determined never to revisit that hell-place-of-shame, Sidney had stuck to her budget with the obsessive zeal of a cross-fit junkie, and was now back in the black by a hair. It helped that Kerry cooked for the four of them three times a week with food he insisted on going halves for, and that he'd been able to lend her his old station wagon because his salary had allowed him to upgrade to a newish four-wheel drive.

'I live in the country now,' he said. 'Though if I start talking about getting an Irish setter, feel free to slap me.'

It would be nice, Sidney reflected, if two steps forward didn't inevitably lead to one step back. But recently, the boys had taken up extra after-school activities. Both of them played football, and Aidan, aged eleven, had been offered free kung fu lessons with

Casey Marshall's boyfriend, while ten-year-old Rory had joined the library book club. A lifelong bookworm herself, Sidney had despaired of her boys picking up any reading matter beyond Lego instructions and Weetbix cards. But a month ago, to her astonishment and delight, Rory had brought home Deltora Quest, series one, from the school library, and read all eight books in two days. Tentatively, Sidney pointed him at her own bookshelf, where sat the Moomintrolls, Diana Wynne Jones and *Ramona the Pest*. He chose Ramona and didn't seem to mind that it was a) written one million years ago and b) about a girl.

'If I can get him to read *Anne of Green Gables*,' Sidney told Kerry, 'my life's mission will be complete.'

So Sidney had been very happy for Rory to join the book club, and pleased enough that Aidan had been offered another outlet for his energy. Her eldest had veered a tiny bit off the rails last year and Officer Marshall had stuck him firmly back on with words chosen to inspire lasting terror. However, Casey was a realist and knew that, just like trains, boys needed regular releases of steam, hence the favour of free kung fu lessons. When Sidney expressed concern about Aidan demonstrating his new-found 'Hi-yaa!' powers on others in the school ground, Casey reassured her that her boyfriend, Logan, was a *mens sana in corpore sano* kind of guy and put equal emphasis on mental as well as physical discipline. Sidney privately wished him good luck with that.

The downside was distance. Last year's football coaching had been taken by Kerry at the local primary school, but his full-time job had put an end to that. Now, football coaching, kung fu *and* book club were located forty kilometres away in Hampton. This meant additional petrol costs, and clashed with the times she'd arranged to tutor her two students. As neither was keen to come to her place during the weekend, it looked like she'd have to give up this small but vital income stream.

And hanging over all of this was the fact the previous government had believed that only women in formal relationships could be stay-at-home mothers, and the current government hadn't got around to fixing it. If you didn't have a partner to support you, then you were a welfare sponger and needed to get your butt back into employment. No matter that you were doing twice the work because you were on your own. No matter that you were contributing to the betterment of society by raising decent human beings. Every year, Sidney had to re-apply for the benefit, and every year, there was less chance she'd be approved. The financial abyss had opened once before — twice if you count when the boys' father left her — and Sidney had no wish to gaze into it a third time. The prudent decision was to find a way to ditch the benefit altogether. Which would be ideal, except that she had no qualifications except a scrap of paper that said it was an art history degree, and no skills except an ability to remove tight lids from jars.

'Know of any part-time work going that can preferably be done at home between the hours of nine and three?' Sidney asked Mac. 'And that doesn't involve pyramid selling or scamming old people?'

'Why don't you sell up and move in with the Ginger Ninja?' said Mac. 'Wouldn't that be the simplest way to take the pressure off?'

'We've been going out for three seconds!' said Sidney. 'What happens if it all turns to custard? And, besides, why should *I* sell up and not him?'

'Because he's got the barn that'll house Littleville.'

'The barn that needs proper loos, a wheelchair ramp, a ticket counter and a security system that's more than tin cans on a string?'

'I thought Doc Love was on the trail of funds?' said Mac.

'He is,' said Sidney. 'But the trail is breadcrumbs, distantly spaced. At this rate, Littleville will be our posthumous gift to the town. Our names will be engraved on a memorial plaque, and I guarantee they'll spell mine with two "y"s.'

'And I suppose your man is too busy now with his high-powered job to put time into his own project?'

It was a good thing Sidney knew Mac well, she thought. If it was your first encounter, you might think she was being plain insulting. But Mac was simply being plain. She believed sugar coating and equivocation unnecessarily complicated human communication, and thought 'euphemism' was a piston-valved brass instrument. And she had a point; Littleville had been Kerry's vision — an attraction to bring visitors into, and thus begin to revive, Gabriel's Bay. When he'd come up with the idea, he'd been working part-time, and so had been able to get the project to the starting line. He'd persuaded his former employers, the Bartons, to relinquish their fabulous model railway and dollhouse, and Mac's former employer, Doc Love, to donate his detailed and historically accurate war dioramas. Kerry had rallied the community to get behind the project, and even found a site, only to lose it again when it was sold to developers. For a while, it looked as if Littleville — and Kerry, too — was goneville, but he'd surprised everyone, not least himself, by committing to stay. He'd gone back to his old career in data management, sold his house in England and bought a farmhouse, which came with the new site for Littleville, a mostly intact barn. And he'd declared his love for Sidney, who, after initial resistance, had declared hers back.

Well, perhaps 'initial' wasn't an entirely ingenuous choice of words. Resistance was still very much present. Which was why Sidney had bridled at Mac's suggestion that she and Kerry co-habit, and was now searching for an opportunity to change the subject.

Too late.

'It's all going well, isn't it?' said Mac. 'You and the Ginger Man? The boys like him, and he's great with them. So why not shack up?'

'Because it's barely been eight months!'

'I knew Jacko was the one after eight minutes.'

'Whereas *I* messed up big time with my last man!' said Sidney. 'So if it's all right with you, I'd rather be *really* sure.'

'Keep your hair on,' said Mac, mildly. 'And you *are* sure, you're just too scared to admit it. You've had ten years to get clear about what went wrong with Dickwad. You know full well what you want and don't want in a partner.'

Sidney took another Krispie. Biting down hard on a crunchy biscuit was a poor substitute for swearing but it'd have to do.

Though arguing was pointless, Mac was wrong. Sidney had spent three whole years with Dickwad, aka Fergal, and his departure, when Aidan was thirteen months old and Rory only two months, had been a complete surprise. Kerry knew all about Fergal, and how Sidney felt. He'd once referred to him as 'He who shall not be named' but that had led Rory to form the traumatic conclusion that his birth father was Lord Voldemort, so now they didn't refer to him at all.

Sidney had trusted Fergal enough to move all the way to Gabriel's Bay, buy a house and have two children with him. She'd believed they had no secrets — and a future. If she hadn't even *glimpsed* the real Fergal in three years, then how could she tell who Kerry was after only eight months?

And, barring the recent blip, she'd managed perfectly well on her own for a whole decade, hadn't she? Why did she suddenly need to be rescued by a man?

'I'll ask around,' said Mac. 'See if anyone's hiring.'

'Bless you,' said Sidney.

Mac might wield honesty like a pool ball inside a sock, but she knew how to be a true friend.

'And tell Dr G to arrive at twelve-thirty with a bottle of good red,' Mac added.

Sidney knew this would involve a trip to Hampton because the only red wine available for purchase in Gabriel's Bay was dispensed from two-litre cardboard boxes via a plastic spigot. Sidney knew Mac knew this, too, and on her mental list, under *Extra large potato salad*, added: *Kerry to buy pinot*.

Sidney might not want Kerry's help for herself, but she had no qualms about insisting he do favours for someone else.

She got up from Mac's kitchen table, went round and hugged her friend from behind, the kind of physical gesture of affection Mac hated, but too bad. Mac's grown children, Harry and Emma, were both overseas, but Sidney remembered that one of their favourite teases was to yell 'Group hug!' and crush their resistant (but secretly delighted) mother in a dual embrace.

'See you tomorrow,' Sidney said. 'I'd say we're visiting, but it'd be more accurate to call it an invasion.'

'In that case, get Dr G to bring two bottles.'

'Two bottles it is,' said Sidney. 'And to be safe, I'll ensure one of them is whisky.'

CHAPTER 5

Devon

People sucked. Tinder sucked. People on Tinder sucked *balls*. Swipe right — she likes horses, lives in Hampton, is only a year younger. Get a message back: 'OMG WTF r u a lez?'

No point in putting her right. If she used 'OMG' in a message, she'd drive him batshit after ten seconds.

No point in looking at other potential matches, either. Even the Tinder-bot kept asking if his gender information was correct. Probably the same programme that rejected photos of breastfeeding as obscene, but let alt-Nazis freely spew hate speech. He shoved the phone in his pocket. It could stay there.

Devon wasn't so naïve as to hope people would ignore his appearance. He'd been getting stares since he was fifteen, the year he morphed from gangly mop-haired kid into his current self. When he was sixteen, some New York modelling agent saw a photo of him riding his horse on the beach, tracked him down and offered him a contract. They'd promised a huge amount of money, tossed potential earning figures casually into the air like they were autumn leaves, but Devon had heard the rattle of chains behind the blandishments, seen the hook beneath the lure. He'd be their creature. He could kiss his own aspirations and independence goodbye.

When he turned the agency down, a lot of people thought he was nuts, but not his family.

'You know your own mind,' said his Koro Tama. 'You know what life you want. And you know about hard work. Mā mahi, ka ora.'

Then Koro had ruffled Devon's hair. He knew his grandson was vain about his crowning glory, and did it on purpose as a way to tell him not to get too big for his boots. Devon's family encouraged ambition but they were religious about staying grounded. As Devon's mum said over and over, usually accompanied by a sing-song chorus of whānau: 'Handsome is as handsome does.'

But he wasn't handsome, was he? He was beautiful.

Devon had few spiritual leanings. His rational, scientific mind knew full well that he was the product of a luck-of-the-draw combo of recessive DNA. But occasionally — OK, more than occasionally — he lifted his head to the heavens and demanded to know why. Why had he been singled out for this genetic fuckery? Why did his looks have to be completely at odds with his sexual orientation? He could have been his cousin Kris, now Krystal, who hadn't had the full op but who was living very happily as a chick, and earning stonkingly good money as a burlesque dancer in Sydney. He could have been a pretty make-up wearing gay, like Julian Clary or Adam Lambert or that dude from *Orphan Black* — and he would have killed it, no end of dates! There were so many other more fitting combinations that the nature deities could have effected; his family wouldn't give a shit if he were gay or trans or whatever — and neither would he. But no — the gods chose to make him an entirely (and, yeah, he was sure, thanks for asking) heterosexual male with the face of a Disney-fied effing princess. He couldn't even grow a beard past a few wisps that made him look like he'd sneezed into a dandelion clock.

All right, so keeping his hair long probably didn't help. Devon only tied it up when he was working in the Boat Shed — hygiene rules — but otherwise he wore it down, even when riding, which was, he knew, a bit douchy, but hey, it was a free country. And over and above his own personal preference (OK, call it vanity), cutting his hair would feel like he was — capitulating. Giving in to the pressure of bullies and bigots and all the normies in society, who were threatened by the way he stood out. Thanks to another part of his genetic inheritance, he was goddamn stubborn. He refused to let others dictate how he lived his life.

But, shit, times like these with fuckfaces on Tinder, it seemed like the fight just wasn't worth it. He was twenty-three and had never had a lasting relationship. Hadn't had a date in — yeah, too long. And maybe that was it. Now he was getting older, women weren't interested in curiosities anymore; they wanted normal guys they could settle down with, breed normal babies with. Maybe it was over red rover? He'd never get a date ever, and he'd die alone, a crazy old bioscientist whose only friends ate hay.

'Like you, eh, Wally?'

Thirty years old, ugly as sin, Wally was Lightning Tree Horse Rescue's oldest inhabitant. He'd ended up there because his owner had died, and the family all lived overseas. He was too old to be ridden, but he'd make a good paddock mate. Wally was happy with company, and the gentlest horse they had by far, mainly because, unlike most of the others, he hadn't been abused. When Devon felt blue, he'd seek out Wally, under the pretence of checking his ancient teeth and feet, which needed regular attention. In truth, Devon just liked that the old horse was glad to see him. What a sad bastard he was.

'What's with the long face, man?'

It was Moana, one of the three other young people who worked for Lightning Tree's owner's Mrs Dickens. Moana, amazingly, was not related to Devon, having come from somewhere in the King Country. She was tall as him, and super cute in an outdoorsy, *au naturel* way. No makeup, hair in a rough ponytail, never shaved under her arms — not that Devon had a right to critique how people chose to look. Plus, it suited her. Fitted her slightly rough-around-the-edges personality just right. Unlike him, who was the frog prince in reverse.

'Ha, horse jokes,' he said. 'Funny.'

'Only the best for you. Hey there . . .'

The old horse nuzzled her ear, and she smoothed his bristly nose.

'What's up with grumpy here, Wall-o?' she said. 'Why's he hiding out with you when there's work to be done?'

'I'm working!' Devon protested. 'Giving Wally his warrant of fitness. Need to get the farrier in next week. Give his crusty old feet a trim.'

A quick, amused look was accompanied by, 'Sure, whatever.'

She saw right through him, didn't she? For a moment, Devon was tempted to spill his guts, ask her advice. But work was work, and personal was personal. Besides, knowing Mo, she'd probably just tell him to suck it up and move on. Which was exactly what he should be telling himself.

'So what do you need me for?' he said.

'Got a Shetland stallion and a donkey coming in. Donkey kicks, and the little guy'll have your hand off quicker than you can say "evil". Mrs D wants all of us to help unload them.'

'All' meant the two of them, plus Imogen, known as Little Immy because she was five feet nothing, or Nitro because she was strong enough to lift fifty kilograms' worth of hay bales without breaking a sweat, and Jason, known as Spacy Jase for reasons that became obvious after five seconds of conversation.

'Great,' said Devon. 'Fun times.'

'Better than wallowing in Wally's stable,' said Moana.

'I wasn't *wallowing*,' he said, as he followed her out.

'Doesn't matter if you were,' she said. 'But don't let whatever's on your mind distract you. Because I tell you, if this evil little bugger does bite you, you'll *really* have something to cry about.'

Devon's phone had stayed untouched in his pocket all day. But now he was at job number two, Jacko was out on an errand, and, as yet, the Boat Shed had no custom. He'd done all his prep, and the phone was burning a hole in his jeans. So against his better judgement, he checked it. Idiot. Idiot. Troll. Troll. Idiot. And *another* troll. Troll-lol-fucking-lol.

The front door opened. Devon shoved his phone under the bar.

'What's that slapped arse expression for?' Gene commandeered his usual bar stool. 'They give you the two-trains-leave-a-station question in your maths test again?'

Second time he'd been caught looking grumpy. But on the plus side, he'd had years of practice dealing with Gene's BS.

'Actually, we're studying concepts of chemical equilibrium,' he said.

'What a coincidence,' said Gene. 'So am I.'

'Uh huh.'

'I intend to study how the chemical components of the beer you're about to serve me will affect my own equilibrium — for the better is my hope.'

Devon took the cap off a beer and slid it across to Gene, who peered through to the empty kitchen.

'Five o'clock on a Friday and I'm Billy No-Mates,' he said. 'Where's your boss?'

'Collecting eggs from the Chicken Man,' said Devon. 'He and Mac are putting on lunch for Kerry's folks tomorrow. Jacko's

47

decided on egg and bacon pie — good Kiwi staple. Got Sidney and the boys coming, too, and Dr G.'

Gene frowned. 'Can he eat bacon?'

Devon rolled his eyes. 'He's Hindu, not Muslim. And though some Hindu have a strict belief about minimising damage to other life forms, Dr G was getting stuck into a lamb sandwich the other night, so I'd hazard a guess he's not one of them.'

'You taking an elective on Hinduism?' said Gene.

'Nope,' said Devon. 'But when I was at school, I did a stint as kitchen-hand at the Indian takeaway in Hampton.'

'Curry Up?'

'Good name for a fast food joint, huh?' said Devon, with a grin. 'Plus an accurate description of what happened after you ate one of their meals. Customers can't say they weren't warned.'

The Boat Shed front door rattled, but it was just the wind. The weather had been wet and blustery for a few days now, and Devon hadn't been exercising his horse as much as he'd like because Tiu hated the rain. Was perfectly OK about running through the surf, and didn't mind fording rivers. But rain? You'd think it was acid, and he was melting like the Wicked Witch of the West.

'Something up, Dev?'

Gene sounded and looked completely sincere, which was unsettling. When you were used to someone taking the piss 24/7, then that became the norm, and any other mode a suspicious variant. But Devon supposed he should give the guy the benefit of the doubt. Gene and Jacko had been best mates for donkey's years — and if Devon didn't entirely trust Gene, he *did* trust Jacko. Both he and Mac had an infallible instinct for the shonky and shady, and zero tolerance for bombast and pretention.

'Ah, just—'

Devon felt his face begin to colour. But he'd begun now, had to finish.

'Sick of being single,' he said. 'Sick of being too freaky to date.'

'Gotcha.' Gene nodded slowly. 'Aren't you being a bit harsh on yourself? I mean, if a short, fat bloke like me can attract a beauty like Liz, then obviously looks aren't everything.'

'So I just have to find the right one for me, is that it?'

'Well—'

'In a place where I'm related to every second person?'

Gene said, 'Surely, you're not first cousins with *all* of them?'

'Course not,' said Devon. 'But even so, who'd take the risk? If *I* came out of that gene pool, then who knows what other weirdness is lying dormant?'

'Again, harsh,' said Gene. 'And unhelpful. If you're so down on yourself, all people will pick up is those negative vibes. You've got years to become a grumpy old man — no need to hasten the process.'

Devon knew Gene was right. But he didn't usually waste time wallowing in self-pity, so he figured he was allowed a moment. Customers would be here any minute, and he'd have to paste a smile on then. Until the door opened, he'd indulge in the righteous pleasure of being a grouch.

'Maybe what you need is a bigger pool of potential candidates,' said Gene. 'Ever thought of moving to the city?'

'Hate the city,' said Devon.

'Internet?' said Gene. 'Cinder or Linda, or She-Came-In-Through-The-Bathroom-Winder — whatever it's called?'

'Tinder. Sucks.'

'All righty-then.' Gene was smiling now. 'Cardboard sign by the side of State Highway One.'

Devon had to smile, too. 'Yeah, OK, so I should probably try to be a *bit* more flexible.'

Gene chewed on his bottom lip, and Devon could tell something was brewing. Devon had his own pretty good sixth sense about people who made him uneasy — Gene called it his 'woo-wah' — but Devon couldn't pinpoint what was beneath the surface here. Knowing Gene, it had big jaws and was closing in fast on his dangling legs.

'How about if you had a buddy up the same gum tree?' Gene said.

Devon's eyes widened. 'Liz divorcing you?'

'No! At least, I don't think so . . .' Gene sipped his beer. 'No, the missus and me are tight. I meant a buddy closer to your own age.'

Devon felt sharp teeth brush his toes. 'Oh-kayy . . .'

'Jeez, Dev, I'm not asking you to sign up for a cult. Or even life insurance! Hear me out before you run for the hills.'

'Fair enough,' said Devon. 'OK, shoot.'

'You know young Barrett Tahana's out of jail?'

Yep, Devon had heard. Barrett, known for not-the-immediately-obvious reasons as Brownie, had got himself in strife by moon-lighting as a drug courier for the local branch of a big, bad gang. There'd been mitigating circumstances — his mother had died suddenly and, immediately after, his dad had become seriously ill. Not even twenty, Brownie had been faced with massive emotional and financial responsibilities, and when the money got short, he'd been too proud to ask for help. Nature abhorring a vacuum and all that, the gang stepped in with their own brand of budgeting assistance.

Devon knew he shouldn't judge — who was to say how *he'd* behave in high need — but in his private opinion, Brownie had been an arrogant dick to think he could enter that world without paying a price. Devon had said no to modelling because the cost to his quality of life outweighed any gain, and that had been with *some* contractual protection. The only gang word you could trust was when they said you were dead meat.

Brownie had spent six months in jail, his sentence reduced for said mitigating circumstances and also for cooperating with the police — so obviously he wasn't top of the gang's BFF list. However, although Brownie's mum had been from an iwi up north, Millie Tahana had been a much-respected social worker whose impact on the community had been immensely positive — and so the hardcore contingent of Devon's whānau had put the word out that they expected no harm to come to her son. And so far, Brownie still had all his body parts. Devon's respect for his family knew no bounds, but he suspected the real reason Brownie remained unscathed was that the gang had more pressing priorities. The police had smashed their whole operation, put some heavyweights away for years. It was power grab and rebuild time for the local drug merchants. And once they were back in business, they might turn their attention again to the boy who'd narced.

'Are you asking me to hang out with Brownie?' Devon said.

'Look,' said Gene. 'I know you didn't approve of him going over to the dark side, but the lad's paid his dues. All three of his best friends have moved away, though I say good riddance to the obnoxious little turd whose father happens to also be my bitterest enemy. Barrett's father's in full-time hospice care now but that meant the family home had to be sold, so he's bunking down in my shed; Liz is happy to have him because he's incredibly tidy and does the dishes. I've also given him work because he's not eminently hireable right now, and—'

Devon opened his mouth. Gene held up a hand to forestall him.

'And *all* I'm asking of you, Dev, is to invite him out for a drink — or whatever you like — so the poor sod isn't forced to sit with my girls and watch the *Step Up* movies one through five for the third straight week in a row.'

'Could be worse. Could be *Pitch Perfect*.'

The back door into the kitchen squeaked, groaned and then

twanged, a sign that the top hinge had come loose again. Cursing began.

'What do you say, Dev?' Gene asked, quickly. 'Help the boy out?'

Devon lifted his hands in the what-the-hell gesture. 'It's not like I've had any better offers. Oh wait — a guy yelled out a car the other night and asked if I wanted to—'

'Screw!' yelled Jacko.

'Same ballpark.'

Devon rummaged in the drawer under the till, drew out a handful of screws and the screwdriver.

'So I'll take that as a "yes" then?' Gene called, as Devon took the tools through.

'Yeah, yeah,' agreed Devon — ungraciously, he knew, but he wasn't quite done with being pissed off.

When he got back out to the bar, Gene had scrolled through the ancient iPod that comprised Part A of the Boat Shed's sound system, and Primal Scream's 'Jailbird' was pounding out of Part B, the speaker next to the stuffed weasel.

Devon was about to scorch the smirking shit with a well-phrased burn, but, of course, a group of customers chose that moment to enter.

So he settled for a middle finger raised behind his back, and stepped forward to greet them, smile firmly pasted in place.

CHAPTER 6

Ash

The importance of punctuality had been drilled into Ash by his mother, who saw no inconsistency in the fact that her own rule did not apply to her. People knew she was doing them a great favour by agreeing to meet, and would therefore be happy to wait. The only person she was ever on time for was Ash's father, and solely because he had more than once ordered their driver to leave the house without her, giving her no choice but to call for a taxi and pay for it with her own money.

Ash's first extended experience of treating patients had occurred in the accident and emergency ward of a large London hospital. He had anguished about the wait times, tried to be as efficient as he could without seeming to be callous or (worse) diagnosing in error. But it was like that sequence in the old Disney movie *Fantasia* where trainee wizard Mickey Mouse ends up creating an army of water-gathering brooms, who keep coming, keep coming, toting buckets and flooding the castle. For every patient Ash saw, by the time he re-entered the waiting room, four more had appeared. A more experienced physician had a quiet word in his ear about setting realistic goals, although her actual words were, 'If you continue to give a shit about this, you will be under a bus by the end of the week.'

He'd done his best to heed her, and now, while at work, he no longer felt compelled to rush or apologise. But as if nature had to maintain a balance, in his private life, he'd become even more obsessed with being prompt. Which was why he was currently sitting in Mac and Jacko's kitchen, sipping nervously on a glass of water and praying that all the other guests would arrive soon.

His discomfort was the more so because Jacko was busy preparing food, and, if you did not count King, the large chocolate Labrador sleeping under his chair, Ash's only companion at the big wooden table was Mac. He could not think of her as his employee as most of the time it seemed the other way round. And as for considering her to be a friend, that assumed attaining a certain level of intimacy — a prospect that was, quite frankly, terrifying. Having Mac share his workspace was hard enough on his nerves. Just imagine if she gained access to his head?

'Did you have a girlfriend back home?'

Mac delivered this with a slight frown, as if trying to picture what manner of woman, if any, might be attracted to him.

'Home, as in Ahmedabad?'

'Do you consider that home? You've been gone over ten years. Do you visit much?'

Ash knew these were fair questions, and that any reproach he sensed was in his imagination. If Mac wanted to criticise, she would do so directly. Why waste time with snide jabs, when you can finish the job with one solid right hook to the jaw?

'I hardly visit at all,' he admitted. 'My study and work commitments have left little time for travel. The last time I was there was two years ago, when I went to my cousin's wedding.'

'There was a full on Indian wedding over in Hampton a while back,' said Mac. 'Looked like it cost a bomb.'

'Indian weddings are often extravagant affairs, yes,' said Ash.

'And usually arranged, right?'

'Well, er, it depends . . .'

Ash was starting to sweat. At his cousin's wedding, his mother had expressed a wish for all her sons to be married within the next five years. Reading this accurately as less a desire for their individual happiness and more a ploy to control their lives, Ash's brothers had laughed, and promised that they'd get hitched to a suitable girl by age forty, but right now, they were going to continue shagging around. They'd paraphrased this, of course, but the gist was clear. Ash had muttered some excuse about work, and then spent the next two days hiding behind garlanded sculptures of elephants and a metre-high tiered cake. To Ash's immense relief, his mother had not re-stated her intention to cement her social status by pairing him off with a complete stranger. But that did not mean she had given it up, and even though there were currently seven-and-a-half thousand miles between him and his mother, Ash was quite convinced that certain subjects sped like homing missiles along the airwaves. He needed to change this one directly.

'My, er, family are relatively modern,' he said. 'And I have two older brothers, who would take precedence.'

Mac gave him the amused, knowing look that Ash always dreaded, as it usually preceded an accurate if rather brutal observation.

'You can't stand your family, can you?' she said.

Filial disloyalty was another subject that most certainly carried on the airwaves. Once, when a little drunk, he'd confessed his true feelings for his family to the group he was with, and the next morning received instructions to return home for said cousin's wedding. It was clearly a punishment for his loose-tongued treachery, and this time he would choose his words with more care.

'We have different interests,' he said. 'And personalities.' He tried to make his shrug look nonchalant. 'That is how it is in some families.'

Mac's smile suggested she knew *exactly* how it was, and in his family specifically.

'Jacko's one of six,' she said. 'They all get on because his dad banged their heads together when they didn't.'

'Too right,' said Jacko, slicing a radish with a speed that made Ash surreptitiously scan the room for a first-aid kit. 'You grow up rural, everyone needs to pull their weight. No time for squabbling or being precious.'

'There must have come a time,' said Ash, 'when your father could not reach to bang heads?'

'Yeah, but by then we'd learned respect,' said Jacko. 'And we weren't stupid — we knew what'd happen if we shirked or cut corners.'

He swept the pile of radish slices into the salad bowl. Not one fell on the floor, Ash noted. He wouldn't dare fall, either, if he were a radish sliced by Jacko.

'No effort, no reward.' With one blow, Jacko hacked the hairy white roots off a bunch of spring onions. 'Don't care was made to care.'

'You reap what you sow?' said Ash.

Ding, ding. Mac chimed a spoon on the side of her water glass.

'I call time on this round of *So You Think You Can Proverb*,' she said. 'Let's get back to my earlier question about girlfriends.'

Oh, let's not, was Ash's instant, fervent prayer. And, behold, it appeared some deity was actually listening because right then, a smallish boy Ash recognised as Sidney's youngest burst in through the back door, whereupon the sleeping King leapt up and trod heavily on Ash's foot as he raced, woofing in full voice, to meet his friend.

'Shut it!' bellowed Jacko, a dual-purpose order directed at both dog and boy, who'd left the door wide open.

'Rory, outside please,' said Mac, more quietly and therefore much more effectively.

'Yes, out!'

Sidney ushered them past her. Rory's older brother, Aidan,

was already kicking a ball in the back garden and the trio became boisterously entangled.

'Hi, gang. Hi Dr G.'

Sidney placed a large bowl of what looked like potato salad on the bench.

Her face was slightly flushed, and the high colour enhanced what Ash had taken time to realise was really a very pretty face. Why he hadn't noticed earlier Ash put down to the fact he was still, at age twenty-nine, embarrassed to give any woman his age more than a cursory glance, and that Sidney was Kerry's girlfriend and therefore out of bounds, even if he'd had the courage to stare at her for longer than point-three of a second. She was also a mother and though this did not diminish a woman's sex appeal, it did affect how much attention she could claim for herself. In Ash's experience, the majority of children, boys and girls alike, were loud, boisterous and permanently on the edge of physical calamity. Parents and caregivers were reduced to an anxious background burble.

'The folks are right behind,' she told Mac and Jacko. 'Bronagh insisted on seeing the beach.'

'Not a patch on Cleethorpes?' said Mac.

'But at least as bracing as Skegness.'

Voices could be heard outside the back door.

'God, here they come,' Sidney murmured. 'I'm not sure I'm ready.'

'Don't sweat it,' said Mac, rising to greet her visitors. 'First mention of wedding bells and I'll set the tablecloth on fire.'

Ash hung back during the introductions, wondering if anyone would notice if he made a break for it. Kerry's mother was a petite woman in her late fifties, with chestnut hair in what Ash had been informed by old waiting room issues of *Grazia* was a pixie cut. The magazine had also stated that this style should not suit anyone over thirty-five, but it did suit Bronagh Macfarlane, whose resemblance to a denizen of fairyland did not end with the hairstyle. Her features were elfin, and her smile impish. Ash knew better than to be deceived by her slender proportions. Even the tiniest nurses he knew had grips like iron and were not shy of clamping down on sensitive spots if a patient insisted on being difficult.

Her husband was tall, sandy-haired and with the look of a man who wasn't entirely sure where he was or how he got there. If Ash hadn't known that Kerry's father was a secondary school science teacher, he would not have got it wrong if asked to guess. He also recognised Douglas Macfarlane as an employer of his own favourite tactic in social situations — the old smile, nod and fade into the background ploy.

Unluckily, Ash was unable to fade, owing to both his hands now being in the fine-fingered (but at any moment vice-like) clasp of Nurse Macfarlane.

'Well, well, look at you,' she was saying. 'Even more handsome than your photo.'

'God, Ma,' said Kerry. 'Could you limit the people you embarrass in this room to me? I'm used to it.'

Ash was perturbed. Had he got seriously drunk and posted on a dating site, only to have no memory of it come the morning?

'When did you see my photo?'

'I asked her advice when you applied for the job,' said Mac. 'She gave you and your cheekbones the tick of approval.'

'Beer, Doc?'

Jacko, no doubt sensing intervention was required, handed him a cold bottle. Ash resisted the urge to press it against said cheekbones, which must surely be glowing like embers.

'And how are you liking it so far?' said Nurse Bronagh, in the same smiling way she'd say, 'Just a little jab.'

He knew he was too flustered to make a response sound sincere, but pausing any longer would have the same effect. Once again, Jacko saved him, with the simple expedient of shouting out, 'Lunch!' — and in the ensuing commotion of people finding seats, boys being summoned and forced to wash their hands, dogs being banished, and drinks being re-filled, the moment to answer was mercifully lost.

Mercifully, too, he had become the least interesting topic of conversation at the table. First, the Macfarlanes were warned that their accommodation might not be up to par.

'Vic's a decent bloke,' said Jacko, 'but you might need to make your own breakfast. And wash your own sheets.'

He paused, perhaps picturing the man, and added, 'I wouldn't advise trying to converse, either.'

'Not a problem,' said Bronagh. 'At least we'll have four walls around us, and not one-and-a-half.'

That signalled the opportunity for all to roundly deride Kerry's attempt at home renovation. If Ash's failings had been targeted in that way, he'd now be trying to crawl under his plate, but Kerry laughed right along with everyone else.

'I did sort out the gas oven,' was his only defence.

'The one possessed by the Balrog?' said his mother. 'How'd you manage that?'

'I bought a new one and paid the deliveryman twenty bucks to take the old one away.'

'I could have fixed it,' said his father, in a soft, disappointed Scottish accent.

'No, you couldn't,' said Bronagh. 'I mean, you could have but I wouldn't have let you. We haven't come all this way to tinker. We're here to do new and exciting things!'

'You were keen on a bit of New Zealand adventure, weren't you?'

Mac said this to Ash at the exact moment he was forking a piece of curly lettuce into his mouth. Curly lettuce, like spaghetti, was a foodstuff Ash believed should be consumed only in private, owing to its infallible ability to humiliate. Like now, when he had all eyes upon him and the piece halfway in his mouth, leaving him with two choices: fork it out again (disgusting) or attempt to swiftly poke the rest in, knowing that it would be about as effortless as wrestling a king-size duvet into its cover. It took him three tries to get the lettuce in his mouth. Everyone watched, apparently fascinated.

After what felt like eight hours of chewing, Ash managed a reply.

'Indeed I was keen on experiencing the Kiwi outdoors,' he said. 'I brought over my camping equipment, and even my kayak.'

'And?' Mac persisted.

'They are as yet unpacked,' he admitted. 'Settling into the job has been more time-consuming than I had anticipated. Although I have managed to make the occasional short exploration of your bush.'

In unison, Sidney and Kerry snorted, the synchronised nature of their response prompting them to chortle more. Sidney covered her mouth with her hand and sent an apologetic glance Ash's way, while Kerry received an elbow in the ribs from his mother.

'Why are you laughing?' said eleven-year-old Aidan, with a frown.

'Because the pair of us share a pathetically puerile sense of humour,' said Kerry. He took a deep breath, wiped his eyes. 'Sorry, Doc. Carry on.'

Ash knew that when he was nervous, his grasp of English suffered, while at the same time, helpfully, he became more voluble. Replaying his statement, he saw now what the joke was. He also saw, with despairing certainty, that it must soon wend its way to the ears of Gene Collins, meaning Ash would be ribbed about it until the day he died. Odds were high that it would be quoted at his funeral service.

'As I recall,' said Mac, with the inexorability of a Stasi inquisitor, 'you expressed an interest in learning to hunt.'

'That true, Doc?' said Jacko.

Oh, well, he was neck-deep in the pond of humiliation now. Why not have a little swim?

'It is,' Ash replied. 'I have been shooting, which in England means game birds, but I was not given a chance to go stalking, which is the English word for your hunting.'

'Which is the English word for posh feckers on horseback with dogs,' contributed Bronagh.

'Little pitchers, Ma,' warned Kerry.

Fruitlessly, as it turned out, because Jacko's next words were, 'I'll take you hunting, Doc. First weekend it stops pissing down.'

'That sounds like a great gas,' said Bronagh. 'Doesn't it, Douglas?'

Her husband's startled blink suggested he had given the subject scant consideration.

No matter, because Nurse Bronagh pressed on.

'And have you found yourself a girlfriend, yet?' she said to Ash. 'Handsome fella — the local ladies should be flocking.'

Ash waited, but three times was not the charm. Jacko did nothing to save him.

'Well, no, I've—' he began.

Immediately (thank you, mystery deity) he was drowned out by an eruption of ecstatic whining and yelping from outside the back door. King had obviously seen someone he knew well.

Jacko rose, anticipating the knock on the door. But there was none — the visitor barged straight in, and shouted 'Hey!' There were corresponding shouts of recognition, laughter and hugging, while King bounded in circles, delirious with delight.

The visitor was tall and slender, with long blonde hair and a face of surpassing beauty. Ash had a moment of doubt — he'd made a grievous mistake before . . .

Pink-cheeked, beaming, Mac put her arm around the visitor's waist. She had no option — she could not reach the shoulders.

'Bronagh, Douglas, Kerry, Dr G — I'd like you to meet our daughter, Emma.'

She — Emma — smiled right at him. And Ash forgot how to breathe.

CHAPTER 7

Emma

Emma didn't know whether to be glad or disappointed that nothing had changed in the two years she'd been away. Gabriel's Bay was still a shit-hole — same wild, wonderful beach, but the town as shabby as ever, despite that weirdo idea for a tourist attraction her mum had written to her about. Model railways and doll houses? Not to mention Doc Love's war games. Kudos to the old man's eccentricity but, seriously, who else was interested in that stuff?

The family home was *exactly* the same. Sitting now at the kitchen table, it felt like Emma had never been away. When she'd rocked up unannounced during lunch, the conversation was in full swing, so for the last hour she'd sat back to listen and observe. Find out what was going down in the old home town.

Her folks — first priority — were in fine form, which Emma was *definitely* pleased about. A few of her friends had already lost parents to cancer and heart failure. None of them even sixty years old — too young, even if sixty seemed *way* old when you were twenty-three. Her mum had seemed a bit worried about her dad last year, but the man was a ten on the Mohs' scale, hard as diamonds. On her travels, Emma had visited Mt Rushmore and the Sphinx of Giza, and both had reminded her of her dad, in scale and sense of permanence. Those Māori myths where people turned into mountains — that was Jacko Reid. He was sitting back, drinking an aprés lunch beer, still wearing his usual striped frilly apron. Emma and her brother Harry had given it to him as a joke when he'd opened the Boat Shed, but he'd been genuinely thrilled. Her dad didn't give a shit about what was or wasn't supposed to be 'manly'.

Her mum — now interrogating the new doctor, poor bastard — was equally a force of nature — but more like one of those Arab dust storms that arises with no warning and hurls sand in your face at a hundred kilometres an hour. Or a honey badger, small, sturdy and bad-ass enough to fight lions off their own kill. *And* she'd actually given Emma a hug — woo-wee! She must have had a couple of wines beforehand.

Nice to see Sidney again, and the boys were so *big* now. Emma was chuffed that they'd recognised her — she'd babysat them a lot, but two years was an epoch in a kid's life.

And across from Sidney, her new man (about time) — Kerry the Talker. Nice looking, with that dark red hair and brown eyes combo that's pretty killer. He seemed OK. The boys obviously liked him, and the fact he was here breaking bread with her parents meant he'd already been put through the Reid pressure-test and pronounced acceptable.

Yep, her folks had good people instincts. She wondered what they'd think of—

No, too soon. He didn't even know she was here yet. And she didn't know how he'd react when he found out . . .

Laters. Right now she had things to meet, people to do.

The Macfarlane seniors were a hoot. Soon as Emma had been introduced, 'Call me Bronagh' had immediately spilled all the family history. Douglas was born and bred in Aberdeen, and she in London — Dalston, one of those London burbs that was becoming 'desirable', i.e. priced out of reach of ordinary workers. But apparently a few generations back, Bronagh's family were wealthy Northern Irish landowners. Protestant land robbers, in other words, imports from England, abandoning the Catholic peasants to the potato famine, dividing the country. Suppose white New Zealanders couldn't diss others for stealing land, but Cromwell perpetrated some seriously bad shit. You couldn't blame the Bead Mumblers for holding a grudge. Emma decided not to say any of that out loud on her first meeting with Bronagh.

Husband Douglas had barely spoken two words since Emma arrived, but you could tell he had some fight in him. All Scots did, even the geeky ones from Aberdeen. Bronagh had been quick to point out the humour of the fact that she and Douglas shared the same surname. Guess that was an easy way to solve any feminist objections about adopting your husband's surname. No way Emma would give up being a Reid, and she wouldn't hyphenate, either. Only middle-class wankers did that.

And the new doctor, at the head of the table. Hard to get a fix on him because up that end, her mum had him pinned to the spot, and next to Emma, Bronagh and Kerry were currently vying for gold in the chat Olympics. The Doc was super cute, but looked a bit too soft for Emma. And was his name really Ash? Emma had travelled loads in India, but had never met an Ash. Maybe it was short for something, like Ashley? Maybe his parents wanted to pretend they were more English than the English. Sad not to be proud of your own culture.

Which reminded her — she must catch up with Dev. Her brother from another mother. Her best mate from school, though she hadn't been too good at staying in touch. He was the local horse whisperer now, she gathered. And — what a laugh — following in her footsteps with his study. Although her degree was in environmental science, not biological. And she never finished it. Call of the wild proved too enticing.

Dev would finish, even if it took him years. He'd always had drive and focus. He should get out of Gabriel's Bay, though, see the world. Let the world see him — plenty of places he'd be welcome. Embraced, not judged. Hashtag: smalltowns-smallminds.

The new doctor was excusing himself from the table. Things to meet, people to do.

'See you Monday,' Emma's mum said to him. 'The instructions for getting to the Torvaldsen house are on your desk. Don't forget to set the alarm when you head out this time.'

So familiar. Don't forget to do this and that. Don't forget your shoes, hat, coat and [insert other item that only a mother believed was necessary].

Ha, his expression was exactly like a chastened kid's, too. Emma's mum had never needed to resort to the wooden spoon. She had natural authority. And the zero-fear attitude of the afore-mentioned honey badger. You're a thirteen-foot hissing cobra? Bring it on.

'God, poor Dr G,' said Sidney, after the front door had shut. 'I think we drove him away. He'll probably spend the rest of the afternoon curled up under a duvet in a quiet, dark room.'

'How *is* he getting on?' Bronagh asked Emma's mum. 'You were worried he might be a bit of a Mamaji's boy?'

'He's a capable GP,' said Emma's mum, almost reluctantly. 'Knows his stuff. Can handle our worst — the skivers, hypo-chondriacs, no-hopers. Majority of our clientele, in other words. Sounds like London was tough, so I guess he's had his trial by fire. Gabriel's Bay is more of a walk on hot coals — as long as you don't dither, you'll be fine.'

'I'm worried that he's lonely,' said Sidney. 'Any attractive young women we can set him up with?'

'Don't look at me,' said Emma, as they all did exactly that. 'And besides, how do you know he likes girls?'

'Good point.' Sidney raised her eyebrows at Kerry. 'Given out any clues in your after-work beer sessions?'

'Like saying, "Phwoah, look at the tits on that"?'

'I sincerely hope none of you lot has uttered anything *remotely* that crass,' said Sidney. 'But, yes, that's the general direction.'

'Let me see . . .' Kerry stared up to one side. 'We've discussed Gene's failed plan to scupper the waterfront development, Gene's hatred of Rob Hanrahan, chief instigator of the waterfront development, Gene's *new* plan to scupper the waterfront development, and his side-plan to humiliate Rob, whom — did I mention — he hates.'

'And moose,' said Emma's dad.

'And moose,' agreed Kerry. 'We definitely discussed moose.'

'What on earth did Dr G have to say about moose?' said Sidney.

'He's a believer,' said Kerry. 'Thinks they might still be around.'

'Moose,' said Mr M senior, with his rolling burr, 'are not native to this country.'

'Spot on, Pa,' said Kerry. 'But a small herd, or whatever is the correct collective noun, was imported from North America in the nineteen-twenties and released into the wild.'

'They died out decades ago,' said Emma's dad. 'If they were there, we'd know.'

'They thought the takahē was extinct for fifty years,' said Sidney.

'The takahē is the size of a small dog,' said Emma's dad. 'Not the size of a Bedford truck.'

'Is a tacka-hey a New Zealand dog?' enquired Kerry's mother.

'It's a birrd,' said her husband. 'Rresembles a larrge moorr-hen.'

God, Scottish accents were sexy. Even when coming from old guys who wore maroon jumpers and spectacles nerdier than Elvis Costello's.

'So there are definitely no moose left?' said Sidney. 'Just checking because, you know, that would be awesome.'

'No moose,' said Emma's dad, in his way that always put an end to argument. 'If there were, somebody would have spotted them by now.'

'And shot them!' said Emma, cheerfully. ''Cos that's how we roll round here.'

'Nice to have you back, hun,' said her mum. 'We've missed our eco-warrior. How long are you staying for?'

'Not sure,' said Emma. 'I'll see how things pan out.'

Which was true. She just wasn't about to elaborate on what she meant by 'things'.

'I'm considering going back to uni, finishing my degree,' she added, because the odds of her mum currently forming a request for elaboration were high. 'But I want to hang here for a bit, if that's OK? Maybe do some volunteering — be a woofer, something like that.'

'Take down the establishment?' said her mum. 'Stick it to the man?'

'Yeah, yeah.'

As always, better to ignore to her mum's jibes . . .

'Gene could use your help in scuppering the waterfront development,' said Kerry. 'Did I mention he has plans?'

'Gene is all hot air,' said Sidney. 'You should report him for harmful emissions.'

'Like a fart!' said Rory. 'A hy-uuuuge fat FART!'

He and his brother dissolved in a fit of raspberry noises and hysterics. Emma grinned. It'd be cool to be a kid again.

'Right, out, the pair of you!' said Sidney. 'I'll apologise for your horrible manners on your behalf.'

Out the boys went, totally unfazed, cackling and zooming.

'They've been remarkably well-behaved,' said Kerry's mother. 'At their age, this one wouldn't sit still for five minutes unless you tied him to the chair.'

'My therapist was quite adamant I should have reported you for that,' said Kerry.

'Joking,' he added, for Emma's benefit.

'Only about the therapist,' said Bronagh, with a wink.

She put her hands on the table. 'Well, Douglas, I think we've trespassed on these good people long enough, and it's time to see just how dire our holiday digs are.'

'The cottage will be fine,' said Emma's mum. 'It's cute and comfortable. Exact opposite of Vic.'

'Where you staying?' Emma asked.

'On Hillworth Farm,' said her dad. 'You know. Borders the river.'

Emma nodded. What a coincidence. Maybe she should cadge a lift? No, too many questions. And besides, she hadn't seen her parents in the flesh for two years. Skype was a poor substitute, despite the comedy of watching her mum and dad try to fit on the screen together. So many conversations with her mum's forehead and her dad's chin.

Everyone was outside now, saying their goodbyes. Emma started gathering plates. She'd do the dishes in return for a night in her old bed. Her folks would be happy for her to stay as long as she wanted, she knew, but it could make things tricky. Tomorrow, she'd have to get her brother's car up and running again. She should call Dev, as well, get together for a drink, catch up.

Friends, family — they were so important, weren't they? Should be her priority, now that she was finally back home. But there was one impulse — instinct, whatever — that overrode everything else. The apex predator of emotions, the strongest of all. She hadn't even bothered to resist it — came across the world without hesitating. She was probably an idiot, but you know what? She didn't care. Life was about taking risks, getting stuck in, boots and all. Those who hesitate are lost.

Tomorrow, she'd fix Harry's old bomb and take a drive to the river. And find out what was waiting for her there.

CHAPTER 8

Patricia

On weekday mornings after breakfast and before he emerged for morning tea at ten-thirty, Bernard shut the door to his library and attended to any correspondence pertaining to the commercial properties he owned in Hampton and Gabriel's Bay. Bernard had invested in property after the publishing firm he had shares in was acquired. At the time, his family sneered, because they were, in Patricia's opinion, a pack of hideous snobs who considered that the only acceptable way to make money was to inherit it, or steal it from the poor. Fortunately, Bernard was an only child, and his father, uncles and aunts were all dead now. His mother, Verity, was in a retirement home in Hampton, still alive only because she refused to give anyone the satisfaction of being able to dance on her grave. Either that, or God and the Devil had tossed a coin for her and were still debating who had lost.

The property portfolio was relatively straightforward to manage, with most leases being long-term and the tenants reliable. There were two vacant retail spaces in Gabriel's Bay, but those were unlikely to be filled any time soon. Now that he and Patricia were both nudging sixty-five, Bernard had been making noises about hiring an assistant, but as far as she could tell, had done nothing about it.

Possibly because he was distracted by challenges facing the Gabriel's Bay Progressive Association. Bernard was Chair, and a Committee member by the name of Elaine Pardew was intent on undermining him at every turn. Elaine, out of sheer spite, had done her utmost to scupper the Littleville project, which Bernard had championed, and now that it had survived (barely), was actively dissuading locals with influence to support it. This had made Bernard even more determined to get the project off the ground, and he had regular meetings with Littleville trustees, Charles Love, who had time now that he'd retired as town GP, and Tai Te Wera, Corinna Marshall's husband, who was also a lawyer. Tai worked in Hampton and kept tabs on the rise of Elaine through the council ranks. He said she was building a reputation as a councillor with zero tolerance for anything she considered antisocial, including vandalism, loitering and general untidiness, and could well be in line to be the next Hampton mayor.

A part of Patricia admired Elaine's steel and tenacity in pursuit of her own aggrandisement. Patricia, by contrast, had relinquished hold on too many goals, and had trailed in the slipstream of others for far too long. But making oneself big by making others feel small — that did not sit well with her. Complete self-abasement was helpful to no one, except perhaps devout monks, but letting your personality sit quietly in the background meant you could be of service to those who struggled to be heard or acknowledged. Patricia hoped that if a child did come her way, he or she would respond to a calm presence, an unhurried routine. If there was one thing Patricia knew how to be, that was steady. And from what she'd been told, that was a quality manifestly lacking in these children's lives.

The phone. Although Bernard had never specifically requested that he be uninterrupted, Patricia had always assumed he would prefer that, and so if she were home, she would take the calls. Most often, it was Bernard's mother, Verity, who insisted on speaking to him though she knew full well that he wasn't free. Patricia was always polite in her refusal, and had more than once said goodbye and replaced the receiver with sound still emanating from it — an enraged, defiant hissing, such as a hooded cobra might make when pinned by a mongoose.

Patricia squared her shoulders and picked up the phone. Twenty minutes later, she put it down, and knew her world had changed forever.

It was nine fifty-seven, and she could find plenty of tasks to fill the next thirty-three minutes until Bernard finished his morning's work. She could — she *should* — be patient; that was a practice of steady people. But right at this particular moment, steadiness could go hang. Patricia marched to the library, tapped on the door.

'Bernard?'

Instead of the 'Come in' she expected, the door immediately opened, as if Bernard had been waiting.

'Was that the retirement home?' he said, a little breathlessly.

'Ah,' said Patricia, divining the source of his expectancy. 'No, I'm afraid it wasn't. You know she won't shuffle off until she gets her telegram from the Queen. Though, of course, she'd celebrate it as a personal triumph if Her Majesty pre-deceased her.'

Bernard sagged and then stiffened upright again, as if a puppeteer had yanked on a string attached to his head. His thought process was obvious: if his wife had interrupted his work then she must have news that was both urgent and important, and to Bernard, those factors were harbingers of, if not actual doom, then considerable inconvenience.

Patricia decided not to hedge. 'A child is coming to stay. This Sunday. For four weeks.'

'What kind of child?'

The kind who needs our help, Patricia was tempted to respond. But poor Bernard — his voice had risen at least an octave. She knew full well that he'd been wishing the whole idea would never manifest, that they'd remain forever a comfortable twosome, in their comfortable home. After almost losing her, he may not yet be prepared to share her with another. She hoped his natural compassion and courtesy would override any jealous impulses, and that she would not have *two* childish natures to manage.

'His name is Reuben Coates,' she said. 'He is nine years old. His parents live in that wreck of a house on the road out, and are both on the sickness benefit. For the last five years, his older sister has taken on the burden of caring for both her parents and her brother.'

'His sister? How old is *she*?'

'Nineteen. It seems Reuben was somewhat of an after-thought. There are two older brothers in their twenties, long since left for parts unknown, and no other relatives nearby. Maree, the sister, has managed, Lord knows how, to feed and clothe the family, put herself through secondary school and, for the last two years, hold down a full-time job. She has been supported by social services, and Casey Marshall has kept an eye on her, so she has not had to manage entirely on her own. Mostly, but not entirely.'

'Good grief,' said Bernard. 'Sickness benefit, you say? Both parents?'

Patricia could see him trying hard not to judge. He had her sympathies; when she'd been informed by the case worker of Reuben's situation, her impulse had been to march to his house and slap sense into the adults who had abandoned so completely their parental responsibilities and handed them, seemingly without compunction, to their daughter. But the Coateses were an unfortunate pair. In the year Reuben turned four, his mother had been diagnosed with fibromyalgia and his father, just seven months later, with chronic fatigue syndrome. As a result, both were now also being treated for clinical depression. Patricia had sought out her old friend, Charles Love, who'd assured her that these physical conditions were, indeed, horribly debilitating. Even if the sufferers tried their best, they could find it nigh on impossible to function normally. Every day was a struggle — once-simple tasks became mountainous obstacles. Depression was a common side effect, as they became beaten down with pain, exhaustion and despair.

'No matter what the positive-thinking brigade may claim, human beings do not have endless reserves of willpower or emotional resilience,' Charles had told her. 'If we are not given the opportunity to replenish, we run dry — our spirit becomes a casualty of constant battling. And once our spirit has gone, unless our circumstances change, it is unlikely to return. Our world becomes shrunken, grey and joyless.'

The Coateses lived in a dilapidated house on the rural outskirts of Gabriel's Bay, which they had no hope of leaving. Patricia knew the place, and had previously judged its owners for letting it decline so badly. The paint was worn down to the undercoat, the roof was rusted and lifting, and where there might once have been a garden lay piles of hard rubbish smothered by weeds. Wildly overgrown shrubs sprawled over outer walls, blocking access and light, and broken windows were covered with taped-up cardboard. Yes, Patricia had once tut-tutted as she drove by; but now she knew that the house's parlous state was no fault of its owners. It wasn't that the Coateses did not care — they *could* not. That ability had abandoned them.

And now their daughter was also abandoning them. If only for four weeks. The stalwart Maree, who had kept her family together for the last five years, had one more special quality.

'Reuben's sister works for your favourite place, The Book Nook in Hampton,' Patricia told Bernard. 'She needs our help because she's won a scholarship to the United States to attend some kind of advanced bookselling course. It's very prestigious, and hotly contested.'

'*That* Maree!' said Bernard. 'I know her! A most capable young woman, and remarkably knowledgeable for her age . . .'

Patricia could almost hear her husband's mental gears grinding. In Bernard's opinion anyone who cherished books was immediately elevated above lesser mortals. Gainfully employed book people were not the kind to live in dilapidated houses with welfare bludging parents. Capable young women did not foist their siblings onto other people.

'Maree did not expect to win the scholarship,' Patricia explained. 'She initially intended to turn the opportunity down. But her support team, including Casey, persuaded her to take it. Social services will provide respite care for the parents, and we will look after her little brother.'

Bernard's frown signalled his struggle to decide whether the family dragged Maree down, or whether she lifted them up. Patricia had no doubt it would be the latter. In his mind, book people were a breed beyond reproach.

'Why on earth has she not chosen to leave home?' Bernard asked. 'For a bright young woman, the situation must be an absolute penance.'

'I've not had the opportunity to speak directly with her,' said Patricia. 'But from what I've been told, Maree has always been the purposeful type. Living at home allows her to save money, and her aim is to buy a house of her own within the next three to four years, one with a granny flat for her parents. Reuben, too, will live with her until he chooses to leave. The Coates house will be sold, or the land, really, as that is all that now has value. Apparently, Maree detests living in the house, but she is not prepared to deplete her savings to pay for repairs. As I said, a purposeful type.'

'But what if she wants to start a family of her own? Won't it be rather — crowded?'

'I imagine Maree will ensure any suitor knows that living with her extended family will be a non-negotiable part of their relationship. I rather hope I do get to meet her,' added Patricia. 'She sounds formidable. No doubt a reason why she won this scholarship.'

Bernard's mental gears ground again, as he tried to make the contradictory fragments coalesce into a sensible whole. Fair enough, thought Patricia. It was the kind of tale that made you revise upwards your estimation of humanity, while simultaneously downgrading the opinion of your own worth. Would she or Bernard ever have been prepared to live in near squalor to fulfil a single-minded plan that ensured the whole family would be looked after? Would they, at nineteen, have had anywhere near the same mettle, grit or generosity?

Now, of course, all those qualities were about to be tested. Reuben, despite Maree's heroic efforts, had behavioural issues. He was behind in class, inarticulate and prone to lash out physically at other children. Jan Dundy, the principal of Gabriel's Bay primary school, had always been sympathetic to Reuben's situation, but the news that his sister would be leaving — Maree broke it to him over the weekend — had resulted in a day's worth of disruptive outbursts. One teacher had been bitten, and a child kicked in the face. The principal had requested that Reuben stay away from school until Maree was back in his life. Reuben would be with Patricia and Bernard on Sunday, driven by social services straight after breakfast, and would remain with them for twenty-eight days.

Patricia had intended to take on the bulk of the work caring for the child, but right now, that prospect loomed impossibly large. Yes, she would have support from social services, from Casey Marshall, who took a personal interest in the Coates family, and from Jan Dundy, who had provided simple lessons to bridge the schooling gap. But that support would be mostly remote, via phone. It would not be here in the house, by her side, every hour of the day.

'Bernard,' said Patricia. 'I think this might be an ideal time to advertise for that assistant.'

CHAPTER 9

Vic

Even though Bronagh Macfarlane was only fourteen years older than he was, she reminded Vic of his mother. If pressed to say exactly why, he couldn't have. His mother died when he was six, and his memories were few and disconnected — a remark here, a gesture there, stripes on a skirt, flour on hands. He had some photos but the whole person they showed did not match the snippets in his head. Had her hair been dark as in the snapshots, or grey? If she'd been that skinny why had her lap felt so soft? Were those her arms that had hugged him? The ones in his memory were pretty sinewy, the arms of someone who could lift a cast sheep or a hay bale, split logs for firewood. But his dad had not been one to hug or offer a lap to sit on.

Vic realised that since his mother's death, the only embraces he'd received were from women he'd dated. Or married; Donna had been a hugger. When she moved in with Vic, she'd brought a teddy bear from her childhood, Mr Miffles, worn furless and with one wonky eye. Mr Miffles probably appreciated his lack of fur now that he was living in Coonamble. It could get to over forty degrees there in summer.

The best answer Vic could come up with was that Bronagh Macfarlane gave him the same sense of brisk reassurance that he remembered feeling in the presence of his mother. Bronagh spoke and moved quickly, and with purpose. Things got done and though you knew she was behind them, you seemed to have missed the actual moment of doing. Suddenly, there was food in his fridge — he vaguely remembered giving her a wad of cash, which would explain the notes and coins on the kitchen table, in an envelope marked 'Change'. On the table there was also a pile of folded, clean laundry, with the socks in matching balled pairs, one of those arcane domestic skills that Vic admired but had no hope of mastering, like ironing the shoulders of shirts. Vic recalled explaining that his Swanndri shouldn't be washed because it destroyed the wool's natural protective coating. Judging by Bronagh's expression, if he hadn't gone out every morning wearing it, he suspected it, too, would now be folded on the table.

And a swag of broken things had been fixed. The TV got a whole three channels now, thanks to some magical adjusting of the aerial. The dud burner on the stove worked, and the fridge now shut properly. Everywhere, screws had been tightened, gaps sealed, leaks stopped and moving parts that had been stuck fast now slid like silk. Even the old ute ran better. You could turn the steering wheel almost forty-five degrees.

This wasn't Bronagh's work, but that of her husband, Douglas. Vic liked Douglas because he said very little. Mind you, he didn't have much choice. Bronagh had decreed that they should both keep Vic company of an evening. On the upside, she and Douglas took turns cooking dinner. But the price for that was being asked questions by Bronagh. A *lot* of questions. With no prize for getting them all right. It was like that old show, *The Money or the Bag*, when the contestant chose the bag only to be told it contained a clothes peg. So much effort, only to have old whatsisname Toogood haw-haw in your face.

It was getting close to question time now. Dinner was over, and Douglas was clearing plates. Bronagh had roasted a leg of lamb that she'd retrieved from Vic's freezer. Vic hoped it wasn't past its use-by. Donna had refused to cook any meat from his farm. She said it felt like cannibalism, like eating family. Vic wasn't sure how being personally acquainted with an animal made any difference — when in chop form, the original beast was hard to recognise — but she couldn't be persuaded. Despite Donna's professed love for the farming life, Vic couldn't help harbouring a suspicion that her view pre-marriage had been a touch sentimental. Lambs cavorting in fields of daffodils, pigs scrubbed with buttermilk, calves on show day. Chickens that weren't intent on pecking your eyes out, that sort of thing.

He'd mentioned Donna's reluctance to use the frozen lamb to Bronagh, who'd made a 'tch' sound.

'Never turn down free food,' she said. 'Though I'd have been happy to buy it — it's so *cheap* here compared to home. You'd think they fed the gambolling buggers gold-plated grass.'

She and Douglas had an outing planned for tomorrow — a bicycle tour of the Hampton wineries.

'I'll make sandwiches from tonight's leftovers,' Bronagh said. 'I'll take the scrapings from the roasting pan, too — Douglas does love his bread and lard, bless his demented Scottish heart. Besides, fat soaks up alcohol and we don't want to get thrown in the slammer for cycling under the influence, do we?'

This was not one of the questions Vic was expected to answer. Those were brewing like Douglas' post-dinner pot of tea. The tea was so strong, Vic was convinced that when he'd surreptitiously chucked his down the sink, it had cleared the blocked drain. Tonight, he would pour his own, and fill the remaining half-a-mug with milk.

'I'll pack our waterproof ponchos, too,' Bronagh continued. 'Forecast is for a ten per cent chance of showers, which in England would translate to a ninety per cent chance of torrential rain.'

'You're not cycling to Hampton, though, are you?' said Vic. 'Not over the hill?'

'Now, Vic, you've known us for three days. Granted, we may lean towards the barmpot side, but have we struck you as actually insane?'

He probably *should* know the answer to this. Fortunately, Bronagh had prepared her own.

'I'm sure a heartier breed of folk, like the Dutch, for example, wouldn't blink at pedalling that distance,' she said. 'But us being pale and soft, we're hitching a ride. Our son will drop us at winery number one on his way to work, and we'll bike from there. Or we'll stay and drink until we fall over, whatever takes our fancy. At day's end, Kerry will pick us up. Literally, possibly. I hope he's practised his fireman's lift.'

Douglas set down the tray between them. Mugs, spoons, a jug of milk and a big, metal pot containing a liquid that could drill a hole to the centre of the earth. Vic made sure he commandeered the milk jug first.

Then he braced himself: tea time was question time. Over the past few nights, Bronagh had started with his present situation and worked backwards. Evening one had featured his failed marriage, swiftly followed by his previous failed relationships. He'd done a lot of blushing and stammering, but Bronagh was relentless and also (which was harder to resist) kind and understanding. And Vic supposed it was good to get the worst over with early. As not a lot of note had happened outside of his so-called love life, they'd flown rapidly back through his thirties and twenties, and had come in to land on the bumpy field of adolescence.

Judging by her opening questions, Bronagh had a particular interest in this time. After Vic's mother's death, his father had taken his six-year-old son to Wellington. Vic had no idea why — his father never went on holiday. Maybe he had legal or business stuff to sort out, or maybe it was meant to be a treat for young Vic. All he remembered was going to the old museum and opening a drawer to find it full of beetles, including an enormous one, bigger than his hand, called a Goliath. Vic could not be enticed away, and so his father sat on a nearby bench and read the paper. Vic suspected that his adolescence was Bronagh's beetle drawer.

'You left school at fifteen?' she was saying. 'Why? You don't strike me as a thicko.'

'Had to,' said Vic. 'Dad got sick. Had to help with the farm.'

'Sick with what?'

'Lung cancer. Chain smoker.'

'That'll do it. How long did it take him to die?'

Vic was taken aback by her matter-of-fact tone, until he remembered that Bronagh was a nurse.

'Three years. Give or take.'

'So you were an orphan at eighteen?'

She already knew about his mother. Eagle eyes had spotted the photo album, noted none of Ella Halsworth and her son past a certain point.

'A lot of responsibility for a young man,' said Bronagh. 'Did you ever consider selling the farm?'

Another question that took Vic aback. Or, rather, what startled him was that he'd never, not once, asked that question of himself. It had never occurred to him to do so.

'Dad left it to me.' He'd said those words many times before, but to his ears right now they sounded new, and uncertain, as if he was testing them for validity. 'His dad left it to him. And so on, back to my great-great grandfather.'

Bronagh nodded. 'Family,' she said. 'Heritage.'

'Duty,' added Douglas. 'And pride.'

All of the above, Vic agreed. All sound, fine, even noble, reasons to stay. But when you boiled them down, the main reason he'd never considered giving up the farm was that he'd never imagined he had the choice.

'If my Irish family hadn't been a load of feckless, drunken wastrels,' said Bronagh. 'I'd be living high on the hog in a mansion, surrounded by thoroughbreds and faithful retainers. Douglas is Scots through and through, right back to the tattooed Picts. Though the sandy hair is likely courtesy of a pillaging Viking.'

'The Macfarlane clan is at this time without a head,' said Douglas. 'We are officially armigerous.'

'Good thing we bought that cream to rub on your cycle shorts, then,' said Bronagh. 'What do *you* have planned for tomorrow, Vic?'

To be frank, Vic would rather answer more questions about his adolescence, including ones pertaining to his sexual awakening. He was not looking forward to tomorrow, but it had to be done. The Council had told him that he could face prosecution if he didn't act. Vic felt they should do their own dirty work, but apparently, according to the official records, he owned the land, so it was his problem. Of course, it was. He could hear the snap of latex as the Goddess of Fortune donned another glove.

But Bronagh might worry if he told her the truth. Or worse, might want to help.

'I've got a bit of a clean-up job down by the river,' he said. 'Dead trees and what-not.'

'A farmer's work is never done,' said Bronagh. 'Well, as we'll be up early tomorrow, why don't we come over for breakfast? I'll whip up some eggs, and Douglas can brew us all a nice, fortifying pot of tea.'

They called themselves the Wood Sprites. Vic wasn't sure when they'd first appeared. Eight months ago, maybe? It seemed like the camp went up in no time, and now there were ten or twelve living on the riverbank, more men than women, in huts they'd built from sticks, rope and old tarps. Workmanship was better than Vic would have expected. They'd be dry enough inside, but bloody freezing, surely, over these past winter months. He'd thought about lending them his possum skin rugs. Donna had hated the rugs because you could still (kind of) see the shape of the dead possums, so he'd removed them from the house and boxed them up in the shed. But the Wood Sprites had blankets, sleeping bags, woollen rugs of their own. They also had a communal fire pit, vegetable garden and food store. They weren't in need.

When he realised they meant to stay more than a few weeks, Vic had introduced himself. At first, they'd eyed him askance — big man in a Swanndri, carrying a rifle, accompanied by dogs. But once reassured he was harmless, they invited him to sit, offered him tea made from some kind of greenery, which he politely refused. When he'd asked them why they wanted to live like this, they'd laughed.

'Why would you want to live any *other* way?' said a young bloke with dusty dreadlocks, whose name, apparently, was Rua. 'In peace with the birds, trees, river.'

'There's a housing crisis, in case you haven't heard.' This from an older man, Darius, cheeks pink with veins, and a big, grey beard, like a hobo Father Christmas. 'People like us, we're shut out and no one gives a shit. This is our way of fighting back — if society doesn't want us, then fuck 'em, we'll build our own.'

This got appreciative murmurs from a couple of others, but the majority responded with tolerant smiles, shaken heads. Vic figured the Wood Sprites fell into two types. Most were pro-nature, living off grid, in their idea of heaven. A few, like Darius, were here to raise two fingers to the establishment. They were all concerned about Vic's intentions, but he'd assured them he had no issue with their presence. After all, no one owned the riverbank, did they?

Cue sound of Selwyn Toogood haw-hawing. It's the booby prize for you, Vic — seems you *do* own the riverbank! And now you have to serve a trespass notice, on people who're just trying to live a peaceful life, who are no burden on anyone. They don't even use soap when they wash in the river, because they care about the water. Because they want to tread softly on the earth.

As he hiked down to the camp, dogs at his heels, Vic tried to work out what he'd say. Maybe he could just give them a warning, leave it to the Council to enforce any eviction? He was one man — how was he supposed to shift a dozen people? Point his rifle at them and yell 'Scram!'?

Vic wasn't a frequent visitor to the camp. Though the Sprites were now friendly enough — even Darius would grunt a greeting — he still felt like he was the outsider. To them, he was part of a world that was set in its ways, old-fashioned in attitude and behaviour. A world that had strict rules for belonging, and punished or banished those who diverged from the accepted norm.

Vic had always known what was expected of him, and had done his best to comply. He farmed like his father had, and his father before him. He supported the national game, his drink of choice was beer, his pastime hunting, he was one of the lads at the local rugby club. He respected the land, and took pride in his animals. He worked hard. He had calluses on his hands.

All that should mean some kind of reward, right? Money, comfort, family, status — that's what they always said was due to those who played by the rules, gutsed it out, gave it a hundred-and-ten per cent.

Yet here were the Wood Sprites, owning bugger all, living simply, communally, content. And here was he — on paper a landowner, a man of means, but worried, worn out, cash poor, alone. It had gone wrong for him, and Vic wasn't sure how or when.

Maybe the concept of Karma had something in it? Maybe Vic was paying for past sins — not even his, but his father's and forefathers', like in the Bible? Or was it asking for more trouble to conflate two different religions like that?

He could smell the fire from the camp. And bread — they baked it in a cast iron Dutch oven, covered in hot embers, like the old bushmen used to. So far, so familiar, but as Vic approached, he sensed a change. Instead of mellow, the atmosphere felt prickly.

'Stay,' he told the dogs. Normally, being gentle and obedient, they were welcome in camp. But they were big animals, huntaway-ridgeback crosses. To those who hadn't met them, they could give the wrong impression.

He found the Wood Sprites sitting in a circle around the fire pit. He knew them all now, by face, if not by name, and so it was easy to spot the two newcomers. A bloke in his late twenties, olive-skinned but Vic wouldn't hazard a guess to nationality, dreadlocks pulled up in a fat ponytail, one silver hoop in his ear, like a pirate. Wearing a homespun jersey with holes in it, canvas pants, combat boots. His companion had long, blonde hair, and for one moment, Vic mistook her for the kid who worked at Jacko Reid's place, the one who looked like — well, like this girl. Beautiful. Disconcerting.

The new bloke spotted Vic. He was at the head of the circle, as if he'd been appointed — or appointed himself — leader. When his gaze moved towards Vic, everyone else's did, too.

'Nau mai, brother,' he said. His accent, surprisingly, was English. 'Your ears must be burning.'

Vic decided to stay at a distance, even though it forced him to speak up. 'Why's that?'

'News is you're here to kick us out. Kick us off your riverbank, Brother Farmer.'

How the heck had they heard? And who *was* this bloke? He spoke politely, but Vic wasn't fooled. In fact, he'd bet fifty bucks the bloke had a knife in his belt, or, more likely, side of his boot.

The Sprites, whom he'd promised to leave alone, were all staring at him. Vic read some anger in their faces, but mostly sadness, and fear. The blonde girl's mouth was curled in disgust. The dark bloke was amused. Waiting for Vic's response. Enjoying watching Vic dangle, helpless, on his hook.

What should he say? He couldn't truthfully give them much comfort. The Council had decreed.

'Your structures are unsound,' Vic said. 'They break health and safety laws. They have to come down.'

'Will you destroy our homes, Brother Farmer?' The bloke's voice was soft, the challenge in his words implicit.

'I don't want to,' said Vic. 'But the powers that be say I've got no choice.'

'A difficult position to be in.' Didn't sound like he meant the Wood Sprites.

'I can give you a month.' Vic hoped he hadn't just made another promise he couldn't keep.

'Then what?'

The bloke knew full well Vic had no idea. And suddenly, Vic was angry. The world and its dog thought it could boss him about, beat him down, walk all over him, laughing. Haw, haw, haw.

He lifted the rifle, aimed it square at the bloke's head.

'Then,' he said, 'you get off my bloody land.'

CHAPTER 10

Devon

Dr G hadn't a hope, poor bastard. Not a one. If Emma was interested in a guy, she didn't hide it. Emma was more like a dude in that respect. 'Hey, you and me — how about it?' was her approach, although unlike most dudes, she didn't take offence if they said no.

If she wasn't interested, there was no ambiguity either. She'd either tell the guy to piss off — no tolerance for douchebags — or she'd say, 'Thanks, but no thanks.' Nicely enough, but no room for doubt. And anyone who had trouble with the concept of 'No' meaning 'No' never had trouble for long. Emma could take care of herself fine, but it didn't hurt that her dad was Jacko Reid. His presence loomed in the background like a giant *Struwwelpeter* bogeyman who wouldn't cut off just your fingers.

Point was: with Emma, direct was the name of the game. You'd never get her attention with sidelong, moony glances and lovelorn silence. If Dr G wanted her to notice him, he'd better speak up. Or at least sit close enough so he was in her line of sight. No use pining away on the farthest barstool. Shove Gene or Brownie out of the way and get in there, man!

But Devon wouldn't say anything; poor guy didn't need the added humiliation. Fortunately, Devon was the only one who'd noticed Dr G crushing on Emma. Which was nothing new — woo-wah or whatever you wanted to call it, his antenna had always been more finely tuned than anyone else's. Definitely more finely tuned than Emma's, who thought 'nuance' was a pop band from the 1980s. There were only ever two choices in Emma's life — do or do not, yes or no, black or white. And she made her choice quickly, because why muck about? Life was short. In her words: she had things to meet, people to do.

If Devon's woo-wah was not mistaken — and it never was — she was doing someone now. And she didn't want anyone to know, not yet. Devon couldn't guess who the guy was, but he had to be the reason she'd come back. Last time Devon and Emma had connected online, she'd been all about the amazing time she was having volunteering in a sustainable commune for people with mental health issues, in Wiltshire or Someothershire in England. She loved the owners, loved working with the inhabitants, whom she'd described in typical Emma-form as 'full-on cray-cray — druggies, ex-soldiers with PTSD, schizos, kleptos.' The owners were training her up as a counsellor, and giving her opportunities to learn animal husbandry, eco-gardening, etc. She'd given Devon the firm impression she meant to stay on. So what had happened? Who'd she met?

No use grilling her. Emma had inherited stubbornness from both her parents, which meant hers was probably at a level of interest to science. Any case, it was none of his beeswax who she was banging. He shouldn't even begrudge that she *was* banging someone — he was well used to Emma outdoing him in sexual conquests. OK, he did begrudge it, but he shouldn't. When you came down to it, she was probably his best mate.

Unlike Brownie, who he barely knew and had doubts about, but thanks to Gene, was being forced to buddy up with. Couple years back, Devon's sisters had tried to set him up with a date, and that hadn't gone well, either, but at least his date had the merit of being a girl. Not a handsome-and-knows-it, silver-tongued smarm-merchant who acted as though all that gang and prison shit had washed right off him, leaving him smelling lemon-fresh.

Gene had given the impression the guy was struggling, but Devon saw no sign of that. Brownie was joking and laughing, contributing to the banter as if he aimed to lift Gene's title of Archbishop of Banterbury. After Devon finished work, he, Emma and Brownie were supposed to go to a nightclub in Hampton. Not much of a drinker, Devon had volunteered to be designated driver. Given how well Emma and Brownie were getting on, seemed he'd be gooseberry, too.

Shit. He was getting too wound up. He should chill out, or it would be a *looong* night.

Jacko from the kitchen. 'Order up!'

Devon was grateful for the distraction. The Boat Shed wasn't all that busy, so he'd been mostly hanging round behind the bar, polishing glasses, restocking the booze. Getting shitty.

As he took the plates out, he heard the text sound of Emma's phone. An owl hooting. More socially acceptable than her ring-tone, which was some British comedian, saying 'Fuck off, yer nosy bastard.'

On his return, she said, 'Hey, Dev, few of my mates from school are going to be at the rugby club tonight. Got a band playing. How about we skip the drive to Hampton?'

'Sooner die,' he replied.

The regulars at the rugby club were threatened by him, the sad wankers. Devon had stopped going years back because he knew that if the level of abuse he experienced got too bad his whānau would step in. And when certain of the Pohio-Ladbrook men were riled, people ended up hurt, in jail, or both. Devon didn't want any of his family getting in trouble just because some arseholes couldn't handle a bit of gender ambiguity.

'Could be time to face your fears, Grasshopper,' said Gene.

'Now you've got a few more miles on the clock, you might find the ogres have shrunk.'

'They're not so bad,' said Brownie. 'They let *me* back in.'

'You were one of them to start with,' said Devon. 'They protect their own.'

Brownie wouldn't hold his gaze. Because he knew Devon was right.

'Excuse me.'

Finally. Speech from Dr G.

'What is the concern with the rugby club? I mean, I am familiar with football hooliganism and have witnessed off-colour behaviour in changing rooms, but you are talking about this club as if it is run by mobsters.'

'Nope,' said Emma. 'Just ordinary Kiwi blokes, i.e. right-wing, misogynist, borderline alcoholics.'

'And if you add "yeasty, swag-bellied ratsbane" to that list, you get Rob Hanrahan,' said Gene. 'With a little help from Shakespeare.'

'They cannot *all* be like that, surely?' said Dr G. 'The individual men I've encountered in my surgery have all seemed very decent, though reluctant to book regular medical checkups.'

'That's because they think if you stick your finger in their butthole, you'll release their pent-up homosexual tendencies,' said Devon.

'We do not have to check for prostate cancer digitally these days,' said Dr G. 'The PSA blood test provides effective early detection.'

'That's terrible,' said Gene. 'So many great jokes confined to history by advances in medicine.'

'Why don't you come with us?' Emma said to Dr G. 'See the good ol' rugby club for yourself. Have a beer. Shake your booty.'

Godammit — *typical* Emma. Didn't give a shit what anyone else wanted.

Before a blushing Dr G could respond, Devon said, 'You're going, are you? Screw me, in other words?'

'Dev, there's a band,' she said, calmly. 'A bunch of other young people. Not your usual club night. It'll be fun. And if it isn't, we'll drive to Hampton. Promise.'

Also typical of Emma not to be fazed by his sudden temper. Guess that's what happened when you'd known each other since you were toddlers and played naked in the same paddling pool.

And she had a point. The old geezers hated any music written after 1955. No doubt the band would only play crap covers — another chorus of 'Bliss' anyone? But the nightclub wasn't much better. Where else but in Hampton would you still be dancing to 'Cotton-eyed Joe'?

'All right, okay,' said Devon, hands up in surrender mode. 'But if I get a *sniff* of bullshit, I'm out of there.'

'Wouldn't be worried about trouble,' Gene raised his beer. 'You've got Emma to protect you.'

Gene was dead wrong. Emma was a fat lot of use. Soon as they entered the clubrooms, she spied her old mates from school at a back table and buggered off, leaving Devon, Brownie and Dr G to push their way to the bar. The clubrooms were full — yes, mainly with younger people, Devon saw, though he was surprised to detect a degree of disappointment. Maybe he *did* want the opportunity to stand up for himself? He was fit and a lot stronger than his slender frame suggested, plus he'd recently started Muay Thai lessons with Casey Marshall's boyfriend, Logan. Maybe decking some big dude would show the haters who was *really* the man?

Beers in hand, the three surveyed the room, trying to figure out where to stand. At the front of the clubrooms was a temporary stage, and most of the floor had been cleared, only a few tables up against the back wall. Devon had a quick look for Moana, but wasn't surprised not to see her; it wasn't really her scene. Immy worked Saturday nights at a Hampton bar, and Jase would be at home with his Xbox controller. He found Emma easily enough. She and her mates were in the far corner, overlooked by a stuffed wapati. Table was crowded but she'd nicked a chair from somewhere — no doubt without asking — and shoved her way between two girls Devon vaguely recognised from high school. He hadn't bothered to keep in touch with anyone from those days. They'd all found him tricky to hang out with, didn't like the negative attention he never failed to attract. No one except Emma had ever stood up for him. Devon had been glad to put school behind him and focus on his work with horses, and his university study. His Lighting Tree colleagues were well used to him, plus the clients generally cared more about horses than humans. Distance learning meant limited interaction, and apart from the odd Skype tutorial, none face-to-face.

It suddenly occurred to him that the Boat Shed job was the only part of his life now that exposed him regularly to strangers. And even those wankers who came because they wanted to see the freaky man-girl wouldn't dare give him grief because of Jacko. Since school, Devon saw, he'd made sure his life was pretty damn sheltered.

Well, shit. Guess if he couldn't find a date, he now knew who to blame.

'She is exceedingly popular, isn't she?'

Dr G was staring longingly over to where Emma now held court.

'Doc, if I may,' said Brownie. 'I'd respectfully suggest you set your sights elsewhere. Not because you and she wouldn't make a fine, handsome pair, but because all the signs point to our Emma being otherwise spoken for.'

Now *that* was a surprise. Devon had judged Brownie to be interested in only one person: himself. He wasn't yet ready to completely revise his opinion, but to be fair he should be open to making minor adjustments.

'Yep, gotta second that, Dr G,' said Devon. 'If Emma was available, you'd know. I mean, *we'd* know. It'd be obvious.'

'I have no chance is what you are saying.'

Poor bastard. Sounded like he'd just been told that Father Christmas was actually creepy old Uncle Keith in a red onesie.

'If it's any consolation,' said Brownie, 'I am also currently sans love interest.'

'Ditto,' said Devon.

'And friends,' Brownie added.

'I've got one of those,' Devon said. 'But it's Emma.'

'So we three are the outsiders,' said Dr G. 'The loners.'

'That's small towns for you,' said Devon. 'Only so many aberrations allowed.'

'But don't worry, Doc,' said Brownie. 'You fit the acceptable bill to a tee. After a decade or so, people here will completely forget you're foreign.'

'That is a worry, you know,' said Dr G. 'I realise your comment was a jest, but I am acutely aware that I represent my culture here, and I'm not sure that another, more confident man wouldn't show it in a better light.'

'Dude, seriously, you need to stop running yourself down,' said Devon.

'Correct,' said Brownie. 'And if Gene were here, he'd say: that's our job.'

'There's no point wanting to be someone else.' Devon was getting tired of this conversation. 'You're you. Suck it up. Like the rest of us have to.'

The band was still off stage. Over the club's crappy sound

system, son of Glasgow, Bobby Gillespie, was insisting they should get their rocks off. Yeah, thanks, Bob. Thanks for rubbing it in.

'Ever used Tinder?' Devon asked Brownie.

A firm shake of his head. 'Nope. No point.'

'Because it's a cesspit of douchery?'

'Because there are others more relevant to my circumstances.'

Devon frowned. 'What does that mean?'

But whatever clarification Brownie might have given was lost as Dr G suddenly found his beer pouring down his shirt, courtesy of a large dickhead who, while monstering a space at the bar, had accidentally on purpose knocked Dr G's elbow.

Of course, the usual response to such a provocation was 'Watch it, fuckwit!' To which the provocateur would reply, 'Whadidja call me?' And then it would be all on.

But being unaware of the correct protocol, Dr G said, 'I am *so* sorry,' and, grabbing a towel off the bar, bent to mop up the floor.

Leaving the dickhead at eye-level with Devon. Who saw the boringly familiar sequence of reactions in the dude's pig-ugly face: 'Hey, baby' becoming 'What the fuck?' becoming 'Fuck *this*'. Like Devon was some kind of trick — some prankster's test of gullibility, and masculinity.

Pig Face deliberately looked past him, addressed Brownie. 'Who's your bitch?'

Wow, original. Sparkling.

Devon slipped his beer quietly onto the bar. Best be ready. And best be careful what you wish for — this was a *big* dude, front rower by the look of him. Devon wasn't sure four Muay Thai lessons would be enough.

Brownie said, 'This is my friend, Devon.'

Voice calm, body relaxed, beer still in hand. As if nothing at all was going down.

Pig Face snorted. 'You a couple of bum boys then?'

'Why?' Brownie said. 'Want to make up a threesome?'

Now the warning was neon-clear. As was the message that Brownie didn't give a monkey's whether or not Pig Face heeded it. Devon made a few more upward adjustments to his opinion of Barrett Tahana.

Then, Lord love him, Dr G stood up, and head-butted Pig Face right under the chin.

'Fu-ugh!' Pig Face clamped his hand to his jaw, eyes rolling, like an invisible flock of tweety-birds was circling his head.

'I am so, so sorry,' Dr G said again. 'May I take a look?'

And he reached up to touch Pig Face's hand, which was tentatively waggling his jaw.

That was it. Two bum boys the guy could handle. But three? With a resentful backward glance, Pig Face skedaddled.

'You OK, Doc?' said Brownie. 'You hit a big lump of concrete.'

'I am fine, thank you.' Dr G rubbed the top of his head. 'Yes, no major damage. Unless you count my dignity.'

'Don't knock it,' said Devon. 'You saved us from the ogre. Dr G the giant-slayer.'

Brownie was staring at him. 'Guess that happens all the time, does it?'

'*All* the time,' said Devon. 'When I was thirteen, I thought acne was the fucking worst thing that could happen. Two birthdays later — ta, da.'

Then he said, 'Thanks for taking the heat. Are you any good in a fight?'

'Better than I was six months ago,' said Brownie.

'Oh, right, yeah. Shit . . .'

A whine of feedback made them cringe. Band was on stage, and, judging by the fact they looked like Status Quo, ready to soft rock.

Devon sought Emma. She and her girlfriends had hopped up

and were sashaying their way to the front, where no doubt they'd dance all night. If you didn't know her well, based on tonight, you might decide she was a terrible friend.

But he did know her, and when she had stuff on her mind, this is how she acted. Looked for a distraction, a way to get lost in the moment. Drinking, dancing — who knows, maybe one of these guys would get temporarily lucky? Emma wasn't necessarily a one-man woman. She priced her independence higher than rubies.

A click of drumsticks. Guitarist launched into the opening riff of 'Hard to Handle'. Black Crowes' version. Crowd pleaser. This crowd, at least.

'Twenty bucks they encore with 'Gloria',' said Brownie.

'No bet,' said Devon.

Dr G was watching Emma dance. His shoulders heaved in a sigh, and he turned back to his fellow wallflowers.

'You know they are having a midnight showing of *Blade Runner*, the director's cut, at the Hampton Odeon tonight?' he said. 'In my opinion, it is superior to the original.'

Devon glanced at Brownie, who smiled wryly, and slid his half-empty glass next to Devon's on the bar.

'Best offer we've had all evening, Doc,' said Devon. 'Lead the way.'

CHAPTER 11

Sidney

It cost thirty dollars a year to run a stall at the Sunday morning Hampton Farmers' Market. Not much compared to, say, the American national debt, but if Mr Phipps didn't pay half that fee, Sidney would make no profit (once she deducted costs for ingredients she hadn't grown herself, petrol, jars and labels) for close to a month. Sidney sold 'sticky stuff in jars' — her homemade jam and chutney, along with honey from Mr Phipps' bees. On top of sharing the stall fee, Mr Phipps also let her take a small commission on his honey earnings because talking to the public wasn't his thing. Talking, full stop.

Sidney was happy to man — or woman — the stall on her own. It got her out of the house and gave her a break from the boys (before Kerry, Mac had child-minded; bless them both). And when she chatted to customers, spruiked her products, and totted up the morning's sales, she had an inkling of what it might be like to be a proper business owner. She felt she could be quite good at running an online business — if she had a suitable product to sell, seed funding for manufacture and marketing, and fourteen hours a day to devote to getting it off the ground.

As it was, the only entrepreneurial expansion she'd indulged in lately was selling her home grown seedlings — herbs and vegetables mainly — through the plant collective. They had a regular stall in the old Gabriel's Bay Legion of Frontiersmen headquarters, long since abandoned by the patriots and adventurers for the simple reason that they were all dead. Somebody in the plant collective was descended from the last Gabriel's Bay member, former sapper, Gordon C. Micklethwaite, and had thus gained rights to the hall from the Legion's national body. The collective allowed the hall to be used by other community groups, including the world cinema club and Starchild Music Therapy for the Under Fives. As long as your application fit with their ethos of diversity, inclusion and peaceful collaboration, and you could use 'non-binary' correctly in a sentence, your group's activity would probably be approved.

There were rumours that more subversive activity took place behind the yellow-painted weatherboards, but Sidney wouldn't know about that. Despite taking her expected weekly turn at the Legion stall for some weeks now, she wasn't 'in' with the plant collective. She knew any sense of exclusion was entirely of her own making. In fact, she had much in common with the majority of the members: she survived on a low income, and she'd had a middle-class upbringing. The collective were in the lowest tax bracket now but most hadn't come from poverty. Most were here because, like Sidney's ex, Fergal, they had dreams of a simpler life — self-sufficient, back to nature, part of a supportive community. Unlike Fergal, they had no illusions about the work it took to live that simpler life. Soon as he found out, Fergal had bailed. Sidney had been determined to learn how to stay afloat, and so had these people. Given all that commonality, she and they should form a real bond.

But she couldn't. Not fully. They were lovely people, well meaning, hard working, but some of their ideas were, to be frank, deranged. Sidney knew multiple factors were to blame for her being unable to embrace their theories. She'd grown up in a house where everything matched, elbows were not allowed on tables, and there existed such a creature as a 'nice girl'. That kind of thing left a lasting impression on one's psyche, along with a preference for good personal hygiene and children who remembered to say 'please' and 'thank you'. Sidney had been a bookworm as a child, and while a part of her would still like to believe magic existed, her adult self held the strong opinion that critical thinking trumped blind adherence to faith or fad. She struggled with the concept that atomic interconnection allowed people to turn their wishes into reality, and that milk and white bread were as bad for you as cigarettes. She was also of the opinion that science and medicine had been quite useful to humanity, and that it was rude to tell a cancer patient that their body contained everything it needed to heal if only they focused on the positive and made themselves 'ripe for cure'. If the conversation turned to vaccination, she knew that the most fruitful response was to go outside and beat her head against a wall, rather than to argue against the likelihood of ninety-five per cent of the world's medical community being complicit in a massive conspiracy. She was *so* glad her children were at an age where she didn't have to defend the fact she no longer breastfed. And no one need know that she'd used controlled crying on Rory, and listened to him scream himself to sleep for a week.

She did like crystals. They were pretty. She was also anti using chemicals in her garden and pro saving the bees. So there was that.

Not to mention that if she were living another life, back in her middle-class hood with money, she'd be battling different pressures: why wasn't Aidan reading above his age, was she seriously going to continue with state school, didn't she know everyone was skiing in Japan this Christmas instead of Banff?

So much worse. Apart from the having money aspect. That would be heaven.

'Penny for them?'

Doctor Love was smiling at her in his mildly puzzled way, which everyone who first met him mistook for absent-mindedness.

He soon disabused them of this notion. Man might be seventy-three but he was sharp as a scalpel.

'Or should I deposit one in here?'

He picked up the Littleville donation box that Sidney displayed on her stall, rattled it.

'No you shouldn't,' said Sidney. 'Because those few you can hear are all yours as well. You've given enough.'

Doctor Love — or should she call him Charles now he'd retired? — slid a dollar coin in the slot anyway. Which took the total up to seven dollars, thirty cents and a badge that said 'Kiss me, it's a New Year'.

'Fortunately, we aren't relying solely on this to raise funds for Littleville,' he said. 'I don't wish to raise hopes too far, but I may be close to a breakthrough.'

'Better than my usual state of close to a breakdown,' said Sidney. 'Have you found an investor? Or a rich person to blackmail?'

'A sponsor,' he replied. 'Who may be willing to pay for the privilege of naming rights.'

'No kidding? Local business? Someone with a God complex?'

'As it happens, a national chain of stores,' said Doctor Love.

'Get you!' said Sidney, admiringly. 'Are you allowed to name the namers?'

'Not yet. We're still in negotiations.'

'Get you again with your negotiations! Littleville's own Richard Branson!'

Doctor Love smiled. 'If only I had his hair.'

'His private island would be quite nice, too. If there was no one else on the beach, you'd never have to worry about your body being bikini ready.'

'A worry I'm happy to say I'm rarely troubled by.'

Then he said, 'I've recommended you to Bernard Weston. He is looking to employ an assistant.'

Sidney drew back slightly. 'To assist him with what?'

'Attending to correspondence, liaising with his tenants. Nothing onerous, and the hours are flexible. How would nine-thirty on Monday suit to talk to him about it?'

'Tomorrow? Oh. Well — I guess that would be fine.'

'Splendid,' said Doctor Love. (He could never be Charles. What was she thinking?) 'I'll tell Bernard you will pop round.'

And he left. Having apparently organised for her to be employed, and without giving her a chance to say no.

Whoever was representing that national chain, Sidney wondered if they realised that they'd effectively already written out a cheque.

'Heya, Sidney!'

Emma. Looking, as usual, glowing, and with (not uncommon this, either) a strapping young man in tow. The word that sprung immediately to Sidney's mind was the delectably old-fashioned 'swarthy'. The next was 'villain', as in the damnèd type that smiles.

But she might be judging him unfairly. He looked a little like her ex, Fergal. That was guaranteed to put her off anyone.

'Sidney,' said Emma, 'this is Loko.'

'As in "motion"?'

'As in one of the Haitian *loa*,' he said. 'The spirits of voodoo. Loko is a healer of plants.'

English, well spoken with a hint of West Country. Emma met him there, perhaps?

'And is that what you are?' said Sidney. 'A healer?'

Her question seemed to amuse him. 'You could say that.'

'Loko's joined up with the Wood Sprites,' said Emma, with obvious pride.

'Oh, the lovely Rua,' said Sidney. 'He helps out at the collective. Does the most beautiful wood carving.'

Emma scowled, much like a teenager whose grandmother has just pronounced death metal 'a bit of fun'.

'Their camp's under threat,' she said. 'We're going to do something about it.'

'I assume you don't mean writing a sternly worded letter to the *Hampton Gazette*.'

Emma snorted in derision, but Loko said, 'All means of protest are equally valid.'

Sidney tilted her head in enquiry. 'But some are more valid than others?'

He met her eye, and Sidney's protective instinct surged. Sidney had known Emma since she was a gangly twelve-year-old. She was not a child now, but she *was* — and would always be — Mac and Jacko's daughter. Her best friends' precious girl. And this man, Sidney was convinced, thought life was a game designed for his own entertainment, and all the men and women in it merely playthings.

Mind you, if he even mildly upset Emma, Jacko would nail his head to a wall through his nostrils. If the guy was lucky.

Loko picked up a jar of Mr Phipps' honey, rested it in his palm to read the label.

'The native British black bee was thought to be extinct,' he said. 'Ninety per cent of the population was wiped out by the Spanish flu in nineteen-nineteen.'

'So I'd heard,' said Sidney.

'But now wild hives have been found around the country,' he kept on. 'The bees have adapted on their own to the conditions. Become stronger.'

'Heard that, too.'

Sidney didn't hold out much hope that her declaration of prior knowledge would dissuade him from continuing to educate her.

Loko replaced the jar on the stall. Cheapskate.

'Now, the wild bees need to infiltrate the managed hives,' he said. 'Bring their strength to the rest of the population.'

'Sounds *jolly* good.'

Said in the tone mothers always used when they wanted their children to bugger off. Sidney assumed it wouldn't register.

What did Emma *see* in him? The Emma Sidney had known before had no tolerance for men who were full of themselves. OK, so he was also handsome, and charismatic, and obviously a bad boy . . .

Sigh. Asked and answered.

'Feijoa chutney.' Emma shuddered. 'Urghh.'

'You don't like feijoas?' said Sidney.

'Yuck, no. Texture's like eating a sandy tongue.'

'Jam instead? I have raspberry or blackberry. Homemade.'

'Nope, we're broke,' said Emma, cheerfully. 'Starting tomorrow, got some avocado picking lined up, though, so won't starve.'

'I might have another job, too,' said Sidney. 'My first foray in years into the capitalist machine.'

'Bad *luck*,' said Emma, and linked her arm in her companion's. 'Come on, we gotta go. See ya, Sidney.'

'A pleasure to meet you.'

Loko briefly bowed his head, a gesture that could be seen as courteous, but which felt to Sidney like he was taking the piss.

'Yep,' she replied. 'Sure.'

As they walked away, Sidney saw him extract his arm from Emma's and lay it across her shoulders instead. The better to steer her with, was Sidney's troubling thought.

No. Emma knew how to take care of herself. She wouldn't put up with any rubbish. No matter how handsome its perpetrator.

It was nearly noon. Time to shut up shop. Winter sales were always down on the warmer months but she'd done OK today. Home now to the boys. And Kerry. Fun, affectionate, generous Kerry, who would do anything to make her life easier. Tendency to joke around, sure, but a *good* man . . .

Maybe Mac was right and she did know he was *the one*?

But what would a future with him mean? Did he want to get married? Have a child with her? How would her boys feel about having a much younger sibling, and one who had a dad when they didn't? How would *she* feel? She hadn't much enjoyed being pregnant last two times, and she was glad her boys were long past the baby stage. Did Kerry want to stay in Gabriel's Bay, or take them back to England? What kind of school would the boys go to if they moved? Would they all feel compelled to go skiing in Japan over Christmas?

So many questions. And all of them as yet un-asked. Why? Was it because Sidney was afraid that she *wouldn't* like the answers — or that she would? How attractive would it be to sink into a different life, one with companionship and support, and without daily financial struggle?

A life where she was no longer in sole control. No longer the one who steered.

Sidney packed the unsold jars into her plastic container, stacked the signs and bunting on top and clipped the lid. She put the cashbox in her big tote bag, and picked up the Littleville donation box. The few coins inside clinked sadly.

Without Doctor Love, the project would have no hope of success. Perhaps it was all right to rely on someone? If they were the right kind of someone?

So many questions. Sidney hefted her load, began to trek back to the car.

One day, she might get around to asking them out loud.

CHAPTER 12

Emma

'Are you pissed off at me?'

Emma rested her chin on Loko's bare chest, which was, given his load of dark dreads, almost freakishly hairless. Strong, though. Good pecs. Good abs. Probably some Freudian shenanigans that made her go for bigger blokes. What was the opposite of an Oedipus complex? Didn't matter. It was all BS anyway. Made up by a sad, old bloke who had nothing better to do than to make people feel weird about cucumbers.

'Why would I be?' he replied.

Such a great accent. Made her think of wood smoke and cider.

'For making you go to the farmers' market this morning?'

He lifted an eyebrow. 'Did you make me?'

'Or did you go of your own accord?' said Emma. 'My granddad used to tell a joke like that. Wasn't good then, either.'

'I enjoyed meeting your jam-making friend,' he said. 'She's a sharp one.'

'She won't help us, though. Stickler for the rules, is our Sidney.'

'Most are. When it suits.'

Emma figured sex in the afternoon was probably against someone's rules, but people like that had no fun. Long as they kept the noise down, no one in camp would care. Loko had borrowed a tarp-hut that belonged to a Wood Sprite called Freerange. Freerange didn't like the winters in camp, hiked way up north, came back in November. Emma figured that's how long Loko would stay. Or, maybe, when the camp filled up over summer, he'd meet more people whose company he enjoyed. Find more causes to support.

She never doubted that he'd find a way to protect the camp. That big, dumb farmer was no match for Loko, who knew how to get shit done, knew how to win. How he managed it, Emma didn't fully understand, and she'd never ask. That was how this worked — you got passed a message and you did what was asked. You didn't know who was behind it. Or who else might have been given the same task. No names, no chain, no trail. No chink in the armour, no opening for betrayal.

And Emma *got* that, she did, but it was kind of frustrating. She'd never been good at waiting around for orders. She was an initiator, of ideas and action, an organiser, a do-er. That's why she'd loved being part of the commune, the rural sanctuary for people who needed help. The owners were a young couple, only in their thirties and with three small kids, who, amazingly, were happy to share their home and family time with the kind of people most would prefer enclosed behind a high-voltage barbed wire fence. Damaged, delusional, occasionally dangerous, but all of them *wanting* to be healed, wanting to find some way to gain a bit more control over themselves and their terrible lives. Wanting to know that *someone* cared and thought they mattered. Thought they deserved more than to be chucked on the scrap heap.

Emma had been one of a small team of volunteers, who were given room and board in exchange for working with the residents, teaching them how to grow food, tend animals, cook, clean, build and repair. She had autonomy to manage people, come up with new ways to get them engaged, moving, productive — most had no *clue* how to organise themselves, some didn't even know how to do the most basic of tasks, like washing dishes. She was involved in decision-making, treated like an equal by the owners, who told her she was making a real difference.

They'd been gutted when she announced she was leaving. Pity she couldn't tell them the real reason why. Maybe one day she'd write . . .

Loko had his eyes shut, but he wasn't asleep. He did this form of meditation that was all about defining goals and then visualising yourself achieving them. Was supposed to release all kinds of positive forces that worked on your behalf.

'As Buddha said: "The mind is everything. What you think, you become",' was how he'd explained it.

'I thought Buddhism was about letting go of self and your desire to control, and all that jazz?' she'd replied. 'How does that reconcile with trying to turn yourself into a master of the universe?'

For a second there, he'd looked a bit pissy. But then he'd given her one of his lop-sided smiles. One of the commune residents, Lynda, a former pokie addict, had taken exception to the way he smiled, called him a smug tosser. Guess it could come across like that — if you didn't know him.

'If you don't make things happen, then things will happen to you,' he'd said.

True dat, as she might say if she wasn't a white chick. Yep, that was her problem in a nutshell. She wanted to make things happen . . .

'How about I start a blog?' she said. 'An anonymous one.'

Loko opened his eyes. 'To what end?'

'Gathering support by speaking truth. I could lift the lid on what's going down round here. Overseas developers buying up our land, ruining our waterfront with ugly commercial build-ings. Farmers letting their cows crap freely in the waterways. Authorities persecuting blameless people. All the local news is brave enough to cover is school sports days and the A and P show.

And if the outside world doesn't know, how can they care?'

'It might be harder than you think to make a website anonymous.'

'Actually, it isn't,' said Emma. 'One of the commune residents was a hacker. Also a choof-monster, which was why he was there. Told me how to do it. Long as you can get bitcoin, it's easy.'

'A choof-monster.'

Loko never liked to admit he didn't know stuff, so he'd kind of slide out questions disguised as musings. Fair enough. Emma didn't enjoy looking like an ignorant dick, either.

'Total bong-head,' said Emma. 'We had to kick him out. Caught him smoking in the chicken coop. Next day, swore I heard a hen say, "Yo, pass that shit, man".'

He ignored the joke. Usually did. She *had* to work on her patter.

'How will you bring people's attention to the blog?' he said. 'Last statistic I read put the worldwide blog-site total at over a hundred and fifty million.'

'Search terms,' she said. 'Key words. Meta data bumpf. Plus, I've got a mate in one of the national media chains who's always keen on juicy stories. I can get a burner phone and text her.'

'Like the hardened criminal you are,' he said, and rolled over to kiss her.

'Fine one to talk,' said Emma.

And reached down to prove her point.

'So who's the bloke?' said Devon.

Emma had known full well that when she took Loko to the farmers' market, the news would pass through the good folk of the town faster than Curry Up's legendary Prawns Masala. Even if Sidney had felt it none of her business who Emma was with, others would have spotted her. OK, so she probably should have told Devon about Loko first, him being her best friend in the world and all. Oh well. C'est la vie.

'Just a guy I met in the UK.'

'Who you followed all the way back here.'

Ouch. That smarted. Much as she'd like to think of herself as a free-willed bird, or whatever that quote was from *Jane Eyre*, she *had* upped sticks and hastened off in pursuit. The fact his destination was her good old hometown wasn't really a mitigating factor, because she'd been the one to put that idea in his head in the first place. He'd been looking to move on, go travelling, leave England — and her — and so Emma had dropped the Wood Sprites into conversation. Casting her line out casual-like, cool, while all the time frantically praying he'd take the bait. When he did, Emma had to physically restrain herself from punching the air.

But she'd never admit that to Devon. He'd never let her forget it.

'I was coming back anyway,' she said. Cool-like. Casual. 'I missed the place.'

Devon reached for a chip from the paper packet they'd spread between them on the back steps of the Boat Shed. Emma had missed lunch due to, well, something coming up, so she'd rung Dev and arranged to meet before he started work at five. It wasn't warm but it wasn't windy, either. The sea was teal green, which, along with maroon, was the first choice colour for those stretchy tops worn by the kind of old ladies who called trousers 'slacks' and had an endless supply of zip-up polar-fleece vests.

'Thought you loved working at that commune?' he said.

'I did. But you can't do that kind of work for long stretches. I couldn't, anyway. Too intense. Too emotionally draining. Even for tough chicks like me.'

'Guess so,' said Devon. 'My cousin was a psychiatric nurse.

Got hit and bitten. Had to scrub faeces off the walls. She used to have to take a break every two or three years, go work in a pub, or milk cows.'

He was letting her get away with half-truths because he was a good friend. A better friend than Emma had been for him so far. She should probably do more than leave him the last battered scallop. That was one thing Gabriel's Bay *did* do well — make a mean fish and chips. Pity its fishing industry died — killed by neo-liberal politicians who presented privatisation of vital infrastructure as the way to make New Zealand profitable again, not understanding or caring that the country's true wealth was its people. Communities should be *honoured* — encouraged, supported — not smashed apart like so much quarry rock. Or kicked off some dumb farmer's land.

There she was — doing it again. Putting the big causes first, and her friend, who was right here, second. Focus, Emma.

'So did you score at the club the other night?' she asked.

Devon should have taken that modelling contract — he had that curled-lip look nailed.

'My *score*,' he said, 'is currently zip. Zilch, nada, sweet fuck all.'

'How come?'

He boggled at her. 'Are you *serious*?' Searched her face. 'Shit, you *are* serious, aren't you? You really don't have a clue.'

Emma dipped a chip into the salt caught in the paper folds. Devon had always been prickly. No point in kicking back, just ride it out, cool, calm. She ate the chip, relished its crunchy, salty, greasy perfection. Dusted her hands.

'Some people are hung up on how you look,' she said. 'I get it. But how hard are you trying, really? Are you using it as an excuse?'

'You should contest the world Miss Empathy title,' said Devon. 'You have a real knack.'

'Someone has to ask the hard questions.'

Devon pulled his legs into a cross-sit, began to stab the sand with a piece of driftwood. Emma waited, eyeing up the last scallop. If he didn't hurry up, it'd get cold.

'OK, so I hate it.'

Devon chucked the driftwood hard towards the sea. It crashed pointy-end into the sand, causing a nearby gull to flap.

'I hate being rejected,' he said. 'Hate the stupid arsehole comments, hate the stares and sniggering, hate the hate. *Especially* hate the hate.'

'What if you were a dwarf?' said Emma.

'*What?* Which one — Grumpy?'

'No, a *real* dwarf. Or if you had, I dunno, cerebral palsy, or Down syndrome, or something.'

'All *quite* different. Want to pick one?'

'I did! You're a dwarf, OK.'

'Hi, ho,' said Devon.

'So you could bitch and moan about how typical-sized people don't fancy you — unless you're Tyrion Lannister, of course. Or you could go fishing in a pool that's more your size, if you get me?'

'That's gnomes who fish, but yes, I get your point. Snag is — where the fuck is that pool? And what if there *isn't* one? What if I'm it? *Sui generis*. Dev-only.'

'Where have you looked besides Tinder?'

Dev was also terrific at the side-eye.

'Plenty of niche dating sites,' said Emma. 'There are ones for folk who have food allergies, cat fanciers — not in that way, also probably totally in that way — interpretive dance practitioners, people who like dressing up as furry animals — you name it.'

'How do you *know* this?'

'You learn a lot hanging out with crazies.'

'Shit almighty . . .' Devon dragged his hands down his face.

Emma reached out, lightly punched his arm.

'You could also cut your hair really short, and bulk up at the gym,' she said.

Devon pretended to fend her off. 'No one's touching the hair.'

'Well, then suck it up, girly-boy. We have to find you the right pool.'

The side-eye again. 'We?'

'Hells yes.' Emma held up her palm for a high five, which Devon shied back from in mock alarm. 'What are friends for?'

Then she said, 'Can I have that scallop?'

'How can you be a non-vegetarian eco-warrior?' Devon demanded.

'Because I don't believe in letting others dictate your choices.' She grinned. 'So can I have it?'

Devon leaned back on propped arms. 'Not like I could stop you anyway.'

CHAPTER 13

Patricia

'Come in, Sidney.' Patricia held open the front door. 'You'll find Bernard in the library. Second door to the left down the hallway.'

'Oh, thanks.'

Sidney seemed out of breath and rather pink around the edges. Patricia suspected she might look much the same. It had not been an easy twenty-four hours.

'I'll knock first, shall I?' Sidney asked.

Patricia was about to respond when feet came thundering down the hallway. She'd asked him not to run inside several times already, but on each occasion, he'd stared at her blankly, as if he could not make out what she was saying. This was, as she soon discovered, preferable to the times when he clearly *did* understand her request and objected to it — with loud yells and four-letter words that would make a painting blush. Kicking was also involved, and hitting. Patricia had done her best to remain calm, acknowledge his frustrations and fears, and find a diversion that could reduce the tension. So far, the most successful had been allowing him to kick a football against the back fence. But that was not going to work in bad weather, or in the dark. The boy had not slept well last night, so nor had Patricia and Bernard. Both assumed it was a natural reaction to being in a strange place. Neither wanted to think that it could last the whole four weeks.

The boy did not bother to slow down as he approached.

He hurtled straight into Sidney and threw his arms round her waist. Ah, yes. Patricia recollected that Reuben had been in an after-school soccer team with Sidney's sons. She would be a more familiar face than Patricia or Bernard.

'Reuben!'

Sidney regained her balance, stared down at the small head buried in her midriff, turned in wide-eyed enquiry to Patricia.

'Reuben is staying with us,' Patricia explained. 'While his older sister, Maree, is abroad.'

'With *you?*'

Immediately, Sidney grimaced. 'Sorry, that sounded insulting. I just wasn't aware you knew Reuben's family.'

'We don't,' Patricia confessed. 'I've registered as an emergency caregiver.'

This time, Sidney was more adept at concealing her surprise, but Patricia could see it. Could see she was also mildly concerned. And why not? Why would an elderly, childless woman consider herself suitable for this job? Given how things had gone thus far, Patricia felt Sidney's doubts were entirely justified.

'It's only for four weeks,' said Patricia, as much to reassure herself as well as the boy. 'Then Reuben will be back at home.'

Sidney mouthed 'School?' She'd obviously heard about his recent behaviour.

Patricia shook her head.

'A little break,' she explained, and Sidney shaped a moue of sympathetic regret.

Gently, Sidney prised Reuben from her and squatted down to be at eye-level, though the boy seemed intent on staring at the floor.

'You must be missing your big sister, huh?' she said. 'I bet she's missing you, too.'

The boy lunged forward, as if to wrap his arms around her neck this time, but Sidney deftly kept him at bay, her hands just firm enough around his upper arms. As soon as she saw he'd stay still, she patted his arms and released him.

'This is a really nice place to stay,' she went on. 'You've got a big garden to run around in, and Mr and Mrs Weston are very kind. I know Maree must be very pleased you're here, and I'm sure she would want you to enjoy yourself.'

Reuben's head remained bowed, but Sidney made no effort to lift his chin, as perhaps Patricia might have been tempted to do. Adults often subtly coerced children in physical ways, she realised. Even hugging could be a form of control, couldn't it? Especially if the child did not want to be touched. Yet how could a child feel truly safe if they had no say over who touched them and when? Patricia made a mental note to ask Bernard to refrain from patting the boy on the head. She was certain that a warning not to hug would be unnecessary. Bernard hugged with the air of a man opening up his mouth to the dentist. Verity Weston had a lot to answer for.

'Do you think you could do your best to enjoy it here?' Sidney said. 'Have lots of good stories to tell big sister Maree?'

The small head gave a tiny nod. Sidney smiled, and Patricia released a breath she wasn't aware she'd been holding. Progress, maybe? They would see.

'Good man,' said Sidney, and patted his arms once more as she stood up. 'I have to see Mr Weston now. But I'll say goodbye before I leave.'

'Would you like to join us for morning tea?' Patricia asked. 'I've made a cake.'

'Oh!' Sidney checked her watch. 'Yes, thank you, that would be lovely. I'm due to meet Kerry's parents for a trip to some potter's studio, but that's not until after lunch.'

Reuben tugged on her sleeve.

'Yes, sweetheart?' said Sidney.

His eyes slid to Patricia — at least, in her general direction — and he cupped his hands around his mouth to indicate he wished to speak to Sidney privately. Sidney apologised to Patricia with a glance, and bent to let the boy whisper, no doubt damply, in her ear.

Patricia saw her face briefly crumple, as if the boy's words had both amused and saddened her. Sidney stood, rested her hand on the boy's back.

'I'm sure you could ask Mrs Weston that question,' she said. 'But I'll ask her now if you're feeling shy.' Sidney addressed Patricia. 'Reuben would like to know if he could please have a piece of cake, too.'

How the little things could be the most surprising. Patricia had always intended them to take morning tea together. Obviously, the boy could have milk or juice instead of Darjeeling. But in her mind's eye, she'd already pictured cutting the cake for the boy, hoping that he would enjoy that it was still partially warm from the oven — a rare treat she'd relished in her own childhood, and one only given when her mother was feeling particularly indulgent. Patricia had never imagined for a minute that the boy might feel excluded.

Sidney checked her watch again, and the pink flared in her cheeks.

'Argh, I'm late,' she said. 'Not a good look when you're applying for a job.'

'I'll take you to Bernard,' said Patricia, 'and explain that I kept you.'

As Sidney moved to follow, Reuben clutched her sleeve, his face a rictus of panic. Patricia could not leave it to Sidney to deal with this; the boy was in *her* charge, and she must find ways to make him feel more comfortable, more settled.

'Reuben,' said Patricia. 'Would you like to help me get the tea things ready for when Ms Gillespie joins us?'

Again, that blank look. Morning tea, she guessed, was not a common occurrence in the Coates household.

'You can help me choose which biscuits we should put out,' Patricia went on. 'Because I think we should have biscuits as well as cake, don't you?'

His eyes — huge. As if the concept of biscuits *and* cake was too fantastic to comprehend. But — Patricia's heart leapt a little — he nodded. And let go of Sidney's sleeve.

'Wonderful,' said Patricia. She considered holding out her hand to him, but decided that might be rushing it. Instead, she settled for a smile.

'Let's take Ms Gillespie to see Mr Weston, shall we? And then you and I can busy ourselves in the kitchen.'

Probably the influence of the redoubtable Maree, but Reuben was very good at following domestic instructions. Patricia decided to trust him with tasks that made her a little anxious, such as pouring milk from the container into the jug. But he managed it with only minimal spillage, and she was able to praise him for a job well done.

Patricia had a moment of regret that the biscuits she'd bought were so plain, but Reuben seemed not to mind. After careful deliberation, he chose gingernuts over digestives, and arranged them methodically in a circular pattern on the plate provided. Patricia invited him to pick teaspoons and cake forks out of the drawer, and left it to him to count how many were required. True, the number was only four of each, but he managed the task without hesitation, and Patricia wondered if the classroom environment was partly to blame for his inability to stay focused.

It was possible, given what she'd read about children like Reuben, that an unreliable emotional environment left them in a constant state of high alert, attuned to every movement, every sound, unsure if it signalled friend or foe. A full class of active nine-year-olds would be as quiet and still as rush hour traffic in Bangkok. It would be nigh on impossible for Reuben to keep his mind on his schoolwork. At home, guided by Maree, he had a measure of stability and support. When her presence was removed, so was his sense of safety. And although, right now, this calm domestic activity felt like progress, it might take more than a few weeks for Reuben to overcome years of insecurity.

It was unfortunate that Bernard and Sidney entered the kitchen just as Reuben was removing the container of juice from the refrigerator. The distraction of their sudden presence caused him to leap like a startled faun. He lost his hold on the waxed cardboard and it thudded onto the floor. The boy froze, poised as if to flee, but found his only way out of the kitchen blocked by Bernard.

Bernard's expression was the one he'd worn since Patricia announced Reuben's visit a week ago — pure alarm in the eyes, with the rest of the face contorted manfully into what could, in the right light, be seen as a smile.

He addressed the boy, and while his faux-hearty tone made Patricia cringe, she had to appreciate the intent.

'My goodness, we're both butterfingers today!' said Bernard. 'Earlier this morning, I dropped my concise Oxford English dictionary and it very nearly collected my big toe!'

Reuben was still frozen in a hurdler's start-line position. Only his eyes moved, sliding between Bernard and Patricia, as if wondering who was the greatest threat.

'Reuben, dear,' said Patricia, calmly. 'The juice wasn't open, so it hasn't spilled. Could you pick it up and bring it to the table?'

The boy's eyes now slid to Sidney, who smiled and nodded.

Then, lo and behold, without further ado, he fetched the juice container from the floor and set it on the kitchen table.

'Please.' Patricia gestured for Sidney and Bernard to take a chair. 'Reuben, why don't you sit here, next to me? You can help pass the biscuits.'

She watched, ready to rescue, as Reuben clutched the plate in two hands and held it out to those opposite. But he kept it steady enough.

'Gingernuts! Did you choose those?' Sidney asked.

The boy stared at her, as if she might be accusing him of an error of judgement.

'I *love* gingernuts,' Sidney assured him, taking two to prove her point. 'I love to dunk them in my tea. Which is not done in polite company, so I'll refrain.'

'Oh, we're keen dunkers here,' said Patricia. 'Feel free.'

Having cut the cake, she offered Sidney a slice.

'I shouldn't,' said Sidney. 'But, of course, I will. My rational mind knows perfectly well that if I want to lose weight, I should say "no" to biscuits and cake, and probably run five miles every day to boot. My irrational mind tells the other one to sod—er, get lost because life is short and cake is delicious. And then my rational mind gets its own back whenever I look in the mirror. It's really *quite* spiteful at times.'

'Oh, my dear,' said Patricia. 'You can waste a lot of years self-loathing, and I would heartily recommend that you don't indulge in it for another minute.'

Sidney's cheeks flared pink again, as if she'd realised she might have made a faux pas. Her figure was on the fuller side, that was true, if one was foolish enough to take fashion as the norm. But it would take two Sidneys to make one Patricia.

'I really, truly wish I could heed that advice,' said Sidney. 'But the societal conditioning is *strong* in this one.'

And then her eye was caught by Reuben, who, now that Patricia had been alerted, too, could be observed spitting out cake, quietly and with some care, onto his plate.

'Oh, dear,' said Patricia. 'Don't you like it?'

Caught in the act, Reuben looked stricken, and started to scramble off the chair. Instinctively, Patricia reached for his arm, to prevent him, and he began to bellow in fright.

'Reuben, sweetheart.' Sidney rushed around to his other side. 'It's OK. If you don't like the cake, it's fine. Mrs Weston doesn't mind.'

Sidney met Patricia's eye with a plea. 'Do you?'

'Of course, I don't mind,' said Patricia.

She didn't dare look at Bernard, who had been brought up to eat what was put before him, and expected every child to do the same, despite having shunned tapioca, rice pudding, curried eggs, boiled cabbage, and every variant of offal for the last forty-plus years.

Patricia picked a crumb of un-masticated cake off Reuben's plate to test it. It tasted fine to her, but perhaps the choice of seed cake had not been wise. Just because it was a favourite of hers didn't mean everyone would enjoy it.

'I suppose it's the caraway seeds,' she said to the boy, who, comforted by Sidney's reassuring presence, had resumed his seat. 'They are a bit of an acquired taste.'

With a paper napkin, Patricia removed the spit-laden cake pieces, and cleared the rest onto her own plate.

'Well, now, I think we should make up for this disappointment,' she said to Reuben. 'How about you and I make chocolate cupcakes this afternoon? I have red, yellow and blue food colouring, so we can have a bit of fun with the icing. How does that sound?'

Of course, he turned to Sidney first.

'What colour icing would you choose to make?' she asked him, with a smile.

Slowly, he smiled back, first at Sidney, and then, miraculously, at Patricia.

'Brown!' he said. 'Like a *poo*!'

'O-kayy . . .' Sidney shook her head in mock-despair.

'Welcome to the wonderful world of young children,' she said to Patricia. 'Warning: there may be dirt and many sudden, loud noises.'

Patricia did steal a glance at Bernard, half-dreading what she'd see. But to her surprise, he appeared moderately enthused.

'Scatological humour has a fine tradition,' he said. 'Right back to the Ancient Greeks. I should dig out my Aristophanes.'

Reuben, not unexpectedly, stared as if Bernard had grown another head and the two mouths were now conversing in Moldavian.

'How about Ogden Nash?' Patricia suggested. 'Or Spike Milligan?'

'*Badjelly the Witch*,' said Sidney. 'Always a popular choice in my house.'

'I'm not sure I have that particular work,' said Bernard, which Patricia knew translated to 'I have no idea what you're talking about.'

'Perhaps you could take Reuben to the library?' said Sidney, all innocence. She knew all about Bernard's aversion to well-thumbed, jam-stained books. 'Now that you've so kindly given me a job, you'll have some free time.'

Before Bernard could succeed where Reuben had failed and hightail it out of the room, Patricia said, 'We'll *all* go. Tomorrow morning. I'll use my library card.'

'Wonderful, my favourite place,' said Sidney. 'And now, I must love and leave you. Pottery with my potty in-laws awaits.'

Patricia resisted an urge to beg her to stay. Sidney had the magic touch when it came to Reuben, whereas her own approach seemed to have all the appeal of a wicked witch demonstrating the spaciousness of her oven.

As if sensing her silent plea, Sidney said, 'If you need a hand, you know where I am. Sing out any time.'

The offer was sincere, Patricia knew. But still evident was that hint of concern, and Patricia was surprised to feel it rankle. She wasn't a woman normally given to rankling, so she was curious to know why. Pride, she supposed, and stubbornness. Like a small child, she wanted to do it *herself*. And she did not want to fall at the first hurdle.

But none of that could be expressed out loud, could it? Not without looking like a foolish old woman.

'Thank you,' she said to Sidney. 'Your offer is gratefully received.'

CHAPTER 14

Ash

As she did every Monday morning, Ash's surgery manager, Mac Reid, was readying to drive an elderly bus filled with elderly people over the hill to Hampton. Ash had been told that Gabriel's Bay had once possessed the required amenities, but that when industry and employment opportunity dwindled, so did the population, until such businesses became commercially unviable.

'Town's bloody fortunate to have a doctor,' Mac said, with the clear implication that everyone knew who was to be thanked for that and it wasn't him.

It was eight-fifteen, and the elderly bus passengers were already gathering outside the surgery. Mac left at eight-thirty sharp and anyone who was late or couldn't Zimmer down the street fast enough missed out. Peeping through the surgery window blinds, Ash could see one of his regular clients, Ngaire Bourke, sixty-nine, long diagnosed with emphysema. She was lighting up her second cigarette of the morning, having inveigled both from a passing youth, who gave them to her so she'd let go of his arm. Despite appearing to be made entirely from knotted string, Ngaire had a grip like an eagle. Ash knew now never to let her get too close.

A rasping, grumbling rattle, such as one might hear whenever Ngaire Bourke coughed, heralded the arrival of the bus. The aged vehicle was the legacy of Dr Love, his predecessor, and, as such, was known as The Love Bus. As Mac had presented the weekly bus trip as a fait accompli, no other details had been forthcoming. For example, Ash was unaware how the petrol was paid for — did the passengers chip in, or did Dr Love also provide money for fuel? Ash suspected the latter. Dr Love was, Ash had gathered, a man of simple tastes who did not mind — possibly did not notice — that his house badly needed maintenance and his garden had not been pruned since being planted, somewhere back in the late nineteenth century. Dr Love's passion was tank battle dioramas, and there was only so much one could pay for a set of Medium Mark A Whippets in 1/72 scale. Though now on the pension, the good doctor no doubt had a healthy bank balance.

Mac was herding her passengers onto the bus. Ash got the firm impression she would not be averse to a cattle prod had its use been within the bounds of the law. Whoosh went the door behind the last to board, and with a judder, off the bus trundled, leaving only exhaust fumes mingling with eau-de-Ngaire, to wit cigarette smoke and budget brand gin.

On Monday mornings, Dr Love had made house calls, and now so did Ash. There were a few patients who genuinely could not attend the surgery, but most took advantage of Ash being out and about to avoid a trip into town and/or gain some company. If the majority of Gabriel's Bay elderly had not been on The Love Bus, Ash suspected he'd be spending most of Monday between nine and noon drinking tea that was either weak as water or strong as diesel, while chatting about the weather and far-flung family members who had almost certainly forgotten their aged relative still existed. Though he wasn't at all sure that it was accepted practice for a surgery manager to take a whole morning off each week, he did appreciate that she performed a valuable community service. And saved him from being forced to consume his own weight in dry biscuits.

This morning, he was to visit a patient he had not seen before, one Magnus Torvaldsen, who lived so remotely Mac had instructed Ash to allow forty-five minutes travel each way. This meant he only had time for one more appointment: a young mother with a new baby who, by the sound of it, had an umbilical hernia. Ash would visit that pair on his return from the Torvaldsen house. Assuming he could find his way back, of course. Mac's written directions were very clear, but from his initial forays into the New Zealand wilderness (he could not bring himself to again use the term 'bush'), Ash was aware the dense foliage had a swallowing quality, like some kind of vast Venus flytrap, sucking you in and then closing over you, trapping you forever in a coffin of green. Magnus Torvaldsen lived deep amongst the trees, according to Mac, though she had never been there. Never, in fact, clapped eyes on the man, though he'd been resident of the area for ten years. Magnus Torvaldsen, it seemed, never left the house.

'He's a recluse,' Mac said. 'Either that, or he's horribly disfigured. Dr Love never said, the secretive swine. Well, guess you'll soon find out!'

And will tell all, was the implication. Ash considered sticking to his principles of patient confidentiality, as Dr Love obviously had. Rejected it as a ridiculous notion. He'd have more chance of resisting a waterboard interrogation than he would a demand from Mac. He must remember to set the alarm, too. Not that the surgery contained anything worth stealing, unless one had a fetish for back issues of *Brides* magazine and half-chewed Fuzzy-Felt. But Mac said it was a decent deterrent, particularly as the alarm sounded like the seven bells of hell. Ash knew this because Mac had tested it. Without telling him, because then how would she know how effective he'd be in a real-life evacuation?

Because Mac had told him to, rather than from any real concern about burglars, Ash set the alarm code, locked the door, double-checked that he'd locked the door, and set out for his car. It was a Subaru four-wheel drive, relatively new. Of course, if he were a proper New Zealand male, the kind that would attract a red-blooded woman like Emma Reid, he would have either a much larger four-wheel drive — a mud-splattered utility vehicle — or a much smaller and sportier Subaru with a stereo that pumped up the volume. His choice of car was both staid and citified. Much like himself. Ash started his engine. It purred quietly, in a non-masculine fashion. The radio played light jazz. Dave Brubeck, if he was not mistaken. Emma Reid would not be seduced by the distinctive five-four time signature of Mr Brubeck's greatest hit. She would most likely prefer something with more electric guitar. Ash fiddled with the radio knob. Out of the speakers came 'Waiting For a Girl Like You' by Foreigner. Ash indulged in a fruitless fantasy of slow dancing to it with Emma. Other things, too, until the road became tricky and he had to concentrate.

As it happened, it was not difficult to find the Torvaldsen house. The driveway was where Mac had said, and surprisingly well gravelled. Another surprise at the top — the house. Ash had pictured a crumbling villa or a grim, corrugated shack, the kind favoured by survivalists in Montana. But this was sleek and modern — picture windows and silvered cedar, with verdigrised copper trim. It seemed to be on several levels, the rear of it overhanging the surrounding bush. The entrance was neat and carefully designed — wooden steps winding through a Japanese style garden, leading to a wide front door. This did not look like the house of a man of reduced means, or one who shunned material pleasures. So perhaps Mac's conjecture that Magnus Torvaldsen had suffered some terrible disfigurement was correct? Ash knocked, and composed himself. It would not do to register shock. Good doctors were above all that.

Magnus Torvaldsen opened the door. Ash gasped.

'Ah, I see Charles did not warn you,' said Magnus. 'Will it be a problem?'

Ash summoned all his resources.

'Not at all.'

'Excellent.'

Magnus gestured for Ash to enter, closed the door. 'This way, if you please.'

And Ash followed the tall, blonde, impressively muscled and entirely naked man into the living room.

Which was minimally and tastefully decorated in a style Ash believed was called mid-century modern. Black leather loungers, Scandinavian sideboards, abstract paintings — wait, was that a Rothko? Surely not an original . . .

Magnus indicated that Ash should take a seat in a chrome-framed armchair. From there, he looked out through floor to ceiling glass at the New Zealand wilderness in all its glory, as if the house floated high in the treetops. The room was warm, for obvious reasons, but wooden louvres by the windows were part open, and Ash could hear the distinctive trills and gargles of native birds.

'What a wonderful location!' Ash said.

'Yes.' Magnus sat on a grey wool-upholstered sofa, rested one arm along the back of it and crossed his legs, which made Ash mildly less uncomfortable about where to direct his gaze. 'We are very happy here.'

'We?' Ash checked himself. 'Sorry, I have no right to pry.'

'My partner and I,' Magnus said, with a smile to indicate no offence had been taken. 'She, too, is an immigrant. One of the many things we have in common.'

'Is she—?' Ash glanced towards the adjoining rooms.

'No, she works. She connects directly to the outside world, whereas I choose to interact more — obliquely.'

127

Ash had so many questions. How did Magnus make his money? What was his partner's name, where did she work, and was Ash right in inferring that she also favoured the naturist lifestyle? What on earth did he mean by 'obliquely'?

But Ash was here in one capacity only: a professional, medical one.

So instead, he said, 'And how can I help you today, Mr Torvaldsen?'

'Did Charles not leave you with a file?'

No was the answer to that. Because if he had, Mac would know everything about the man and more. But Ash should have thought to ask Dr Love directly. A stupid oversight.

'It seems Dr Love was keen to guard your privacy. I should have requested the file before this visit. My apologies.'

'Charles is an interesting man,' said Magnus. 'Very open to new ideas.'

Open enough to also get naked? Ash could not imagine his elderly bespectacled predecessor stripping off for a consultation. Oh, look — seemed he *could* imagine it. Ash shook his head to dispel the vision.

'But how can you help me?' Magnus continued. 'I have Crohn's disease. I manage it very well, but a regular check-up is recommended.' He spread his hands. 'Hence your presence.'

Crohn's was a chronic inflammatory disease of the bowel that could be most unpleasant, with diarrhoea, rectal bleeding and severe abdominal pain as common symptoms. It could be medicated, and diet and lifestyle changes also helped, but there was no cure. The cause was unknown, though interestingly, research had shown that people from Northern European countries were more susceptible to it. Magnus Torvaldsen was, Ash gathered, originally from Norway.

Ash felt a need to assert his authority with this man, as he did with every patient who expressed admiration for Dr Love, which was, of course, every patient. And perhaps some time in the next forty years, they would start to take him seriously.

'I am familiar with the condition,' he said.

'That is good to hear,' said Magnus. 'In return, I think you will find me a model patient. Shall we begin?'

As soon as Ash started the physical examination, the nudity became irrelevant. The man was a Norse god! His heart rate, blood pressure, body mass index, muscle strength and lung capacity were all vastly superior to the average. It was astonishing to discover that the man was sixty-one. He had the fitness of a twenty-year-old.

Questions regarding diet and lifestyle revealed only a slight weakness for home baking. Otherwise, Magnus was quite correct: he was a model patient. All Ash could do was congratulate him, and write out a further prescription for anti-inflammatories, as there was no need for anything stronger.

'Now,' said Magnus, 'do you have time to take tea with me?'

'Regrettably, I do not,' said Ash.

His regret was sincere. The calm and beauty of this place were supremely attractive. Ash realised that he'd always been surrounded by bustle and noise. Even growing up in a sheltered, wealthy household, the busy city could never be entirely shut out. It was the same in London, at its quietest an ever-present hum. Perhaps that was one of the other reasons he'd wanted to come to this country? To experience peace? But how could he? No matter how serene his environment, his mind would still be over-active, throbbing with thoughts of Emma Reid.

'Then you will have to return,' said Magnus. 'Soon, I hope.'

Ash's surprise was obvious.

'Ah,' said Magnus. 'You imagine me a misanthrope. Or one who shuts himself away from all contact, like the young Japanese men, the *hikikomori*, who never leave their bedrooms. I certainly

129

value my privacy,' he added, when Ash could only gape, 'but I am not averse to visitors. I have few, it is true, but that is because not everyone is comfortable with nudity.'

He gestured around the room. 'Not everyone is comfortable in a house like this, either. I have had it described to me as more art gallery than home, the implication being that the person was afraid to touch anything for fear of reprimand. Do you play Scrabble?'

The unexpected segue did not help Ash's mouth gape less. But this time, he managed an answer.

'I do, yes. My parents recommended it as a way to improve my English.'

'Is that not your first language?' said Magnus.

Well, yes,' said Ash. 'But, er, our childcare spoke mostly Gujarati, and I spent a lot of time with them.'

'English is the language of the Indian elite.'

A statement, not a question. And not incorrect. Liberal Indians believed up to eighty per cent of the Indian population were oppressed by their lack of English. Those who weren't liberal, i.e. all of Ash's family, felt no need to encourage six hundred million people of lower status to be more socially mobile.

'Hence my parents' desire for me to improve,' said Ash. 'Mastery of language — of everything, really — was expected in my household.'

He did not know why he was being so open with a man he hardly knew (if you did not count being entirely familiar with his physical attributes). Magnus Torvaldsen had a calm command about him. If he so chose, he'd make an excellent cult leader. Who was to say, of course, that he wasn't one? An all-natural wood deity, a green man, a Pan. Spawner of dryads and fauns. Converser with the trees, birds and animals.

Pure fancy. Few forest gods were cited as owning Eames loungers. And expensive-looking paintings.

'Is that — a Rothko?' Ash pointed.

'You know your art?'

'I wouldn't go so far as to say that,' said Ash. 'But I have whiled away many hours in the Tate Modern.'

Ash followed Magnus as he moved to stand in front of the work, its giant squares of orange and ochre practically vibrating off the canvas.

'I was fortunate enough to pick that up in New York.'

Tens of thousands, it must be worth. More. Where *did* he get his money?

'Come for dinner this Saturday,' said Magnus. 'And a game of Scrabble. I will show you the rest of the collection.'

Why not? The man intrigued him, as did the prospect of seeing the rest of his paintings — and his partner. Oh, goodness. Best clarify that particular point beforehand . . .

'Will I, er — do you expect your guests to . . .?'

'I will leave it entirely up to you.' Magnus clapped a hand on his shoulder. 'Whatever feels most comfortable on the day.'

During the drive back, Ash rehearsed conversations with Emma, in which he revealed himself to be a special friend of the famous Gabriel's Bay recluse, and like Magnus, a man who was self-assured and body-confident enough to pay Scrabble in the buff. He would never say these words out loud to her, mainly because he would never get the chance. But he enjoyed how they sounded in his head, enjoyed her imagined look of surprise and admiration.

The new baby did indeed have an umbilical hernia. Nothing to worry about at this stage, he reassured the mother. She seemed quite taken by him, so perhaps some of Magnus' confident charm had rubbed off? That illusion was shattered the moment he entered the surgery and saw Mac.

'So?' was all she said, but it was enough to fluster him.

And he was about to spill every bean, until something rose within and made him pause.

No. If Charles Love could resist, then so could he. To be fair, he did not know exactly why the good doctor had kept his patient a secret, when Magnus seemed unabashedly open about his lifestyle and illness. But Ash had a hunch. In a small town, unusual behaviour could often seem threatening; Ash saw how people looked at *him*, and apart from being dark-skinned and foreign, he was as ordinary as apples. Magnus was not ordinary. He was a *rara avis*, a singular specimen. Dr Love, like all good conservators, most likely wanted to ensure a level of protection. And now it was up to Ash to continue his good work.

'Mr Torvaldsen is doing very well,' said Ash.

'And?'

'And the Haines baby is also fine.'

Ash held up a brown paper bag containing a filled roll he'd bought from the bakery en route.

'I'll have my lunch now,' he said, 'and then I'll be ready for our twelve-thirty.'

He entered his consulting room, closed the door, breathed deeply.

And tried not to imagine the expression that was now, without doubt, darkening Mac's face.

CHAPTER 15

Vic

'If you don't mind my saying so, you're not looking too sprightly there, Vic.'

Bronagh Macfarlane cracked an egg on the edge of the frying pan. The sound cleaved Vic's skull in two.

'Did you get blutered last night?'

If blutered meant shit-faced, then 'yes' was the correct answer, but Vic wasn't quite up to speaking yet. Or nodding, for that matter. Sitting quietly and praying for death seemed the best strategy right now.

He hadn't meant to tie one on. A couple of beers at the club was the plan. Tuesday night, so it should have been quiet. A few club mates to shoot the breeze with, take his mind off Donna, the farm finances, the crap with the Wood Sprites and the Council. No one would ask about any of it because that's not what you did. You talked sport, hunting and fishing, and occasionally you bitched about Federated Farmers or Meat and Wool. No politics, unless it was to bag a Greenie. No religion, because who went to church these days, anyway? No women, past referencing the Missus and rolling your eyes at something she'd done or, more commonly, wouldn't let you do.

And that should have been his evening. Couple of beers, minimal chat, sport on the big screen and then home. But around eight, Rob Hanrahan had strutted in, flanked by his business cronies, and started holding court. Seemed his waterfront industrial development had a buyer already, and before the foundations had even been laid. Some Chinese investor who was talking about using it for aquaculture.

'Fucken *sea*horses!' Rob had smirked.

'What for?' asked a willing stooge.

'Chinks probably eat them,' said Rob. 'Dry them up and use them to get a fucken hard-on, who knows?'

Haw-hawing all round.

'So the profits will go off-shore?'

This from young Brownie Tahana, who should have known better. It was generally agreed that, given his family circumstances and the fact he was quite useful on the rugby field, he should be re-admitted to the club after his stint in jail. But there was also general agreement that this was a favour, and Brownie should be grateful. Questions like that didn't sound like gratitude.

But Rob had been in a good mood. Finding you're about to be rolling in money will do that to you.

'Jobs will be local,' he said. 'And where one Chinese investor goes, others follow. They're like that. Hunt in packs. Gabriel's Bay could see a lot more development next few years. Might even get our fucken service station back.'

The odd, 'Too right,' from blokes who probably still referred to 'Ching Chong Chinamen'.

'And if you're concerned about who has the rights to the widdle seahorses,' added Rob, now with a barb in his tone, 'then tell your *ee-wee* they can take it up with the new owners. We're selling land and buildings only. The Chinks can turn it into a fucken meth lab for all I care.'

Without being obvious about it, Vic watched for young Brownie's reaction. The lad showed none. Maybe jail had honed his poker face?

In any case, Rob had decided he'd given the lad enough airtime. Turned to the barman and said, 'My shout, mate.'

Everyone had cheered. Rob was the man of the hour. Rich, successful, confident, bold. Married for years, and with a grown kid. Hanrahan Junior was in Auckland, selling flash cars to yuppies. His dad, who owned the biggest dealership in Hampton, had pulled strings, sent the boy away. Probably because his best mates had included one Brownie Tahana, and Rob didn't want his son contaminated with the stain of jail.

Vic thought he might say something to young Brownie, but the lad had slipped out. The few blokes Vic had been talking to before were now clustered around Rob and his sidekicks, who were parcelling out the free beers. Vic was already on beer three, which he'd intended to be his final of the evening.

His mate, Otto, touched him on the shoulder. Otto Visser was a well-preserved sixty-something, whose only obvious vanity was hair dyed an unnatural black. He also dressed more like a city bloke than a sheep and beef farmer, with fancy shirts and tailored trousers, but because he was one of the most successful farmers around, and generous with it, the club members let it slide.

'Another beer, Vic?'

What the heck. All this thought of jail and money had lowered Vic's spirits to rock bottom, below even the widdle seahorses. And as Bronagh said, never turn down free. One more beer wouldn't hurt.

After that, the sequence of events became a trifle disjointed. At some point, beer became whisky. There was singing. And vomiting. Hopefully neither of the latter had been perpetrated by him, but given his luck, that seemed unlikely. Did he take a taxi home, or did someone drop him? He had a memory of confessing to Otto that he may have hallucinated a moose, but was that in Otto's car or had he hallucinated the conversation, too? Vic had already peered outside to see if his ute was there. Thankfully, it wasn't. Of course, it could be in a ditch and he'd clambered out and stumbled home. Now there was a happy thought.

Bacon fat was spitting in the frying pan, loud as eighty-eights flakking a British air squadron. The smell, usually one Vic would consider nectar, was making him queasy. More than queasy. Oh, shit—

'S'cuse me.' He ran.

'When you're ready!' Bronagh called after him.

Hunched over the bathroom sink, splashing water on his face and rinsing out his befouled mouth, Vic had a strong desire to crawl back to bed. But he was a farmer, and farmers did not work nine-to-five or take sick days. Obviously, if you lost an arm in the bale feeder, you'd need a bit of time off, but apart from that, you pulled your boots on and did the work. Today, he'd planned to muster the sheep from one paddock to another. With the grass not being up to scratch, due to lack of fertiliser, he had to shift the animals around to ensure what pasture he had wasn't eaten down to dirt. This wasn't a sound long-term strategy, but it was all he had. He should look at the fencing near the river, too. He'd done running repairs, but the rotting posts still needed replacing, and they wouldn't keep at bay several thousand combined kilograms of Angus who decided they fancied a swim. He was supposed to be tending the strip between the fence and the water, too, but bugger that. Bugger all of it, quite frankly.

A tap on the door.

'How're you doing?' said Bronagh. 'Do you feel up to a bacon sanger? Full of amino acids that help clear the head, and lovely carbs in the bread to soak up the leftover booze. I've made Douglas finish up his eggs, so his runny yolks won't send you hurtling back to the jacks. And I've readied a mug of super-strength joe, a big glass of water and fast-acting painkillers.'

Vic emerged.

'I'm an angel, I know,' said Bronagh. 'No need to thank me.'

There was no sign of Douglas in the kitchen. He must have bolted those eggs and hightailed it back to the cottage. Vic should ask him to have a look at the post rammer. It was ancient and lethally temperamental. If Vic had to replace posts, he'd rather it not be his last act on earth.

'Now, Vic,' said Bronagh in a preparatory tone.

God, no, please don't start with the questions. He'd missed last night's round, true, but surely she wouldn't be that cruel? Besides, they'd got right back to his birth the night before, so what more was there to tell? If she thought he'd be willing to describe his own conception, she was *very* wrong.

'What would you say to dinner out on Thursday?'

Was she asking him on a *date*? Ridiculous, no, that was the hangover dulling his faculties.

'Douglas and I have been here a week-and-a-half,' Bronagh continued, 'and we haven't yet dined at Gabriel's Bay's finest restaurant, or indeed Gabriel's Bay's only restaurant, the Boat Shed. We thought Thursday night, because on Friday *The Graham Norton Show* is on telly, and we think the little imp is great craic.'

Vic detested Graham Norton, as before him his father had detested Danny LaRue, Liberace and John Inman. Vic disliked that his feelings went against his general policy of live and let live. But when it came to camp men, nurture overrode nature. Yet another failing for him to work on.

'I know you're barely compis,' Bronagh was saying. 'But Jacko will need to know numbers. So will you join us? Us being myself and Douglas, Kerry and his partner, Sidney. Grown-ups only. Well, if you don't count our beloved son.'

Vic didn't have the strength to say no.

'Excellent,' said Bronagh. 'Is it all right if we go in your ute?'

She peered out the kitchen window. 'What have you done with it, by the way?'

Vic knew Jacko Reid wouldn't kick him out for wearing a Swanndri, but for Bronagh's sake he put on his one good shirt and a pair of chinos that had last been fashionable in 1985. Bronagh wore a silver cardigan over a short green shift that made her look about twenty, and Douglas wore his usual maroon jumper and brown cords. The three squashed into the ute's single cab. Vic had called the club yesterday and been relieved to be told his ute was in the carpark and not a ditch. Downside was having to catch a taxi into town at a rorting cost of seventy bucks, which, when combined with the sum he'd spent on drinks Tuesday night, had blown his budget for this week and next. Technically, he couldn't afford this evening out, but at least the Boat Shed wasn't . . . Vic struggled to think of a famous posh restaurant and had to settle for The Ritz, an establishment he wasn't even sure was still in business.

Upon entering the Boat Shed, Vic was dismayed but resigned to see that their party of five had now grown to include Gene Collins and his wife. Vic knew Gene from the club and generally kept his distance. He wasn't a bloke you wanted to argue with, unless you enjoyed being publicly humiliated. And Gene seemed to be able to suck you into an argument even when you were drinking quietly in a corner, minding your own business.

'I hear Rob Hanrahan's got a Chinese buyer,' Gene said as soon as Vic had sat down.

'Gene, I swear,' said his wife. What was her name? Lee? Lyn? 'If you so much as *hint* at the subject of bloody Rob Hanrahan and his bloody development,' she went on, 'I will stab your hand with this fork.'

'Can a man not show an interest in the welfare of his own community?' said Gene.

'It's not an interest,' said Lyn or Lee. 'It's an obsession. And, quite frankly, it's boring the pants off me.'

She brandished a fork. 'No jokes about women sans pants, either.'

'You know me so well, my darling,' said Gene.

He grinned at Vic. 'Married bliss, eh?'

Bastard. Vic felt his face redden.

The disturbingly attractive young bloke who worked at the Boat Shed came to take drinks orders. His proximity did nothing to reduce Vic's blood pressure. Flustered, Vic ordered red wine, a drink he loathed. Gene ordered a nice, cool glass of beer, and Vic ratcheted his hatred up a notch.

'What's on the menu tonight, Dev?' said Sidney, when the young bloke returned with drinks everyone except Vic wanted.

The Boat Shed served whatever Jacko felt like cooking, and patrons liked it or lumped it. There was less of the lumping because Jacko could make even gristle succulent. It was an unexpected skill in a man who looked like he should be cast as the super-villain who finally did for James Bond.

'Homemade pappardelle with lamb ragu,' said the young bloke. 'With a side of sautéed brussels sprouts and pancetta.'

Vic felt like a dog that could, out of everything its master said, identify only its name. 'Brussels sprouts' and 'lamb' had leapt out at him. The rest may as well have been in Klingon.

'Sounds delicious,' said Sidney, with apparent sincerity. 'Wish I'd ordered red wine, now.'

'Have mine.' Vic pushed it across to her.

'How gallant of you,' said Sidney, with a smile. 'Would you like my sav in return?'

'No, thank you,' said Vic, quickly. Donna had loved sauvignon blanc, but Vic thought it tasted like possum wee.

'You still feeling the after-effects?' Bronagh enquired, before immediately confiding to the entire table, 'Vic got absolutely scuttered on Tuesday night.'

'So I heard,' said Gene with a smirk. 'Otto said he had to pour you out of his ute when he dropped you home.'

Vic's hatred had left the Khumbu Icefall and was now ascending the Lhotse Face. One more crack and it would be right up there at the South Col.

'But not as bad as Kerry after his university finals,' Bronagh went on.

'Oh, dear,' said Sidney. 'Do tell.'

'No need,' said Kerry. 'Let's just say that the police never find it as funny as you do.'

'Douglas refused to bail him out,' said Bronagh. 'Said a night in jail would teach him a lesson.'

'And so it did,' said Kerry. 'It taught me that my parents were as fickle and uncaring as I'd always suspected. And that drunks are truly terrible people to share a holding cell with. That lesson was, of course, imparted to me retrospectively by my cellmates.'

'I'd refuse to bail Gene out,' said the wife.

Liz! That was her name!

'If he lands in jail, he'll one hundred per cent be guilty,' she added, 'so I figure that I should let justice take its course.'

Vic decided he liked her. She had spirit, plus she was extremely attractive. Which made it even more unfair that she should have chosen a bastard like Gene Collins. Nice guys not only finished last, they finished alone, with nothing but a note on the fridge under a Minion magnet.

The young bloke was back. Put a dish down in front of Vic that seemed to contain long strips of pale seaweed under a shredded meat sauce. Nope, it was pasta, and from surreptitiously observing the others, Vic gathered that you were supposed to eat it all mixed up with the meat, which as far as he was concerned, flew in the face of nature. Again, he could only blame his upbringing. At their one foray to a Chinese restaurant, Vic watched his father spend twenty minutes separating every component of his dish of fried rice into piles — peas, corn, carrot, small chunks of unidentifiable meat — and then eat every pile except the rice. They never went back.

Everyone else was chowing down with obvious enjoyment. Oh, well. Might as well be hung for a sheep as a lamb. Whatever the hell that actually meant.

Vic tried the pasta and sauce together. Found it delicious. Perhaps there was hope for him yet?

Only five minutes in, Sidney grimaced, sat back and pushed her part-eaten dish towards Kerry.

'Can't you finish?' he said, surprised.

'You mean: what gives — I'm usually a complete hog?' said Sidney, testily.

'Not at all,' said Kerry. 'It's just that most of Jacko's patrons would rather explode like Mr Creosote than send anything but licked-clean plates back to the kitchen.'

'I've been feeling a bit off lately,' said Sidney. 'Probably — you know.'

'Your period?' said Bronagh in ringing tones.

'God, Ma, could you speak louder?' said Kerry. 'I think some folks on the international space station might have missed that.'

'Paracetamol,' said Bronagh, unabashed. 'And no upside-down yoga.'

'I drink whisky,' said Liz. 'And lie around complaining. Makes me feel loads better.'

'Good tip,' said Sidney.

During this entire exchange, Vic had steadfastly not looked

up from his plate. Donna never spoke like this. If she referred to 'it' at all, she called it her 'time of the month'. And kept all its accoutrements and processes entirely hidden from him.

'Well, don't stay if you're feeling rotten,' said Bronagh.

'God, no, I'm not leaving,' said Sidney. 'I really only came for dessert. Besides, the boys will still be awake.'

'Are the boys with Mac?' Gene asked Sidney. 'Being forced to watch *Project Runway*?'

'No, they're home with Emma,' she replied. 'I had to pay her a bit more than I did when she was sixteen, but the boys still adore her.'

'What's she up to?' said Gene. 'And who's the white Rasta bloke she's been seen hanging around with?'

'His name is Loko,' said Sidney. 'No, not as in crazy, as in some Haitian tree thingy.'

'A *loa*,' said Liz. 'They're the spirits of voodoo. Some benevolent, some very much not.'

'I suspect he's one of the latter,' said Sidney. 'Too full of his own importance for my liking.'

'So what's she doing with him?' Gene persisted.

Vic was interested to hear the answer to this, too. He wasn't sure if knowing that young woman he'd seen at the Wood Sprites camp was Jacko Reid's daughter made him feel more or less secure.

'No idea,' said Sidney. 'Well, apart from the obvious.'

Gene looked thoughtful. Or perhaps 'scheming' was a better word.

'I might pop round to yours after,' he said to Sidney. 'Been trying to pin young Emma down to talk about—' He glanced at Liz '—the thing I'm not supposed to talk about.'

'No way,' said Liz. 'You're tonight's sober driver and I'm not sitting in the car for hours while you yak.'

'I'll tell her to call you,' Sidney said to Gene.

'I forgot all about nominating a sober driver,' said Bronagh. 'Some reputable health professional *I* am.'

'I'm fine,' said Vic.

Not a claim that should be interrogated too closely, he thought. Fortunately, no one was interested in talking further to him, and the rest of the evening passed quickly, and in a relatively enjoyable manner, if you discounted the presence of Gene Collins.

A safe, if chatty, drive home, Bronagh and Douglas decanted into the cottage, and Vic was free to sit and revel in the quiet. He decided to check the computer, see what the weather gods had planned for tomorrow.

His email inbox, usually empty apart from payment demands and spam, said he had forty-five unread messages. He clicked on the first one, from a farmer he knew not far out of Hampton. Clicked again to a link provided, and found a website. A blog site. Vic read the blog.

'Fucking hell,' he said. 'Fuck, fuck, *fucking* bloody hell.'

CHAPTER 16

Devon

'Fuck!'

Oh, man, he was going to kill Emma. How *could* she?

'Didn't you know?'

This from Moana, on behalf of all Devon's Lightning Tree colleagues, who were sitting around the big pine table in the kitchen, smirking at him.

'Do you think I would have said *yes*?' he retorted. 'What am I, some fucking brain dead *masochist*?'

'Whoa, easy there.'

This from Mrs Dickens, the boss, who spoke to everyone as if they were a horse, and occasionally slapped you on the rump to get you moving.

'Sorry, Mo,' Devon muttered.

'All good,' said Moana, with an easy shrug. 'At least you don't have people breaking into song when you introduce yourself, thanks to that shitty Disney movie.'

'What's so bad about it?' said Little Immy.

'Big, fat, funny Polynesians living on Fantasy Island?' said Moana. 'It's blatant cultural appropriation and negative stereotyping.'

'Not the movie, you ning-nong.' Immy tapped the iPad on the table. 'The website!'

'You're kidding, right?' said Devon. '*Find a Date for Dev*,' he read out. '*Are you the right woman for my bestie, this super amazing dude? Send in your cutest pic and tell us why you should get a ride on his horse* — Jesus — *No time wasters, no idiots, no skeezy hoes. Trolls can fuck off, too.'*

He had to close his eyes. It was torture.

'OK, so she's no Virginia Woolf,' said Immy. 'But it's kind of a nice sentiment, don't you think? And who knows? Might work.'

'A *nice sentiment?*' said Devon. 'Humiliating me world wide on the interweb? And how can it *possibly* work? What kind of self-respecting woman would respond to *this?*'

'I met my last girlfriend on the internet,' said Spacy Jase.

'How many times do we have to tell you that Zelda is not a real girl?' said Moana.

'Your *last* girlfriend?' said Devon. 'Not with her anymore?'

'Well, she was going to come over from the States and we were going to meet up, but her dad needed an operation, so she had to stay and look after him instead.'

'*Please* don't tell me you sent her money,' said Immy.

Jase gave her a wary look. 'OK . . .'

'Tea time's over, girls and boys!' Mrs Dickens clucked her tongue. 'Gee up!'

They rose and trekked their mugs and plates to the dishwasher.

On their way out to the paddocks, Moana clapped a hand on Devon's shoulder.

'Chin up, mate,' she said. 'There are over one billion websites out there, so chances are it won't get noticed.'

'*You* noticed it,' said Devon.

'Facebook. One of my friends is friends with Emma and liked her post, so I got to see it, too.'

'Shit. How many friends does Emma have?'

'Dunno. Few hundred probably.'

'And each one of them might have a few hundred more friends, like you . . .'

145

'Huh.' Moana considered his point. 'Still, plenty more interesting stuff out there. Cat memes, for one.'

'Thanks, mate,' said Devon. 'That's a real comfort.'

'No worries.' Moana gave him a wide smile. She had cute freckles on her nose. 'You want Sultan now, or Tatty?'

Sultan was the meanest horse they had, meaner even than the little bastard Shetland. Moana and Devon were the only ones who could handle him. And Mrs Dickens, of course. But she could probably make the 21st Panzer Division half-pass in formation.

'Sultan,' said Devon. 'I mean, day can't get any worse, can it?'

'Are you walking strangely for a reason?' said Brownie, as he took a seat at the Boat Shed bar. 'Or have cowboys come back in fashion?'

Devon handed him a beer and a glass.

'Kicked in the arse by a horse.'

'In the *arse*?'

Brownie was trying not to laugh. Fair enough. It was pretty ridiculous.

'Yeah, well, never turn your back on a maladjusted horse.'

Devon was pissed off. Stupid amateur mistake, but he had no one else to blame.

Oh, wait, maybe he did. Maybe if his 'friend', Emma, hadn't put a tragic and humiliating singles ad online for all to see, he wouldn't have been distracted.

Could you believe she hadn't even rung to give him a heads up? Devon had rung her, though, and left a short, to the point message on her voicemail. An hour later, he'd got a text. It was an emoji of a grinning cat with love-hearts for eyes.

Unlike his own eyes, which were in a permanent squint thanks to the pain in his rear that occurred every time he took a step. He'd phoned to ask Sidney if she'd be his stand-in, but she wasn't well. Stomach bug or something. So Devon had downed painkillers and, humiliatingly, held a pack of frozen peas against his butt cheek, long as he could stand. So far, it had made sod all difference.

Still, at least the injury gave him an excuse to be in a shitty mood. He wouldn't have to confess the real reason to anyone.

'Wa-hay!'

Gene entered the Boat Shed, held wide his arms towards Devon.

'The man of the hour! Gabriel's Bay's own Cyrano de Bergerac. Or Tom Hanks in that bloody terrible Seattle movie.'

Intrigued, Brownie glanced between Gene and Devon. 'What's all this?'

With a grin that was positively shit-eating, Gene pulled out his phone, showed Brownie what was on the screen.

Brownie's eyes widened as he read. He gave a shout of laughter, the most genuinely amused sound Devon had heard him make. If it hadn't been at his expense, Devon might have appreciated it more.

Gene was laughing, too. Devon did not appreciate that at *all*. Prick.

'What genius is responsible for this?' said Brownie.

'Who's this one's "bestie"?' said Gene. 'Emma, of course. See—' He pointed to Emma's contact details.

'Holy David and Jonathan, Batman. Did you know?' Brownie asked Devon.

Oh, what — did *everyone* think he was a moron?

'Yeah, in fact, I dictated it to her word for word,' said Devon.

'Right.' Brownie nodded. 'So no idea at all.'

'That girl has no shame,' said Gene. 'And I wouldn't be surprised if that's not the only online hijinks she's behind.'

Devon slid him a beer. Slowly, in the hopes that might annoy him. No such luck. The man was a human cockroach. Unsquashable.

'Well, go on,' said Brownie to Gene. 'Give us the benefit of your penetrating conspiracy insight.'

'There's a website gone up,' said Gene. 'Anonymous. Ratting out dirty farmers.'

'Dirty, as in "down and"?' said Brownie.

'No! Dirty as in polluting our waterways with cow shit and fertiliser.'

'OK,' said Devon. 'And what's the point of that?'

'Name and shame,' said Gene. 'Prompt the Council to investigate and prosecute. Fines can be *huge*. Tens of thousands.'

'And you think Emma's behind this website?' said Devon.

'Well, I did until I saw your mug online,' said Gene. 'Then I had doubts that she'd do *anything* anonymously. Still, if the accusations are untrue, then the farmers in question would have a right to sue for libel. She might have *some* sense of self-preservation.'

The back door to the kitchen pinged open and banged shut again. A box was dumped on the bench. Jacko appeared, glowering.

'Fucking Otto's selling up,' he announced. 'Saw his name on some online shit-list of dirty farmers and said to hell with it. Not worth the aggravation.'

'Who's put up the list?' Devon said, cautiously.

'Some vegan hippy fucker out to ruin people's lives no doubt,' said Jacko. 'Should be strung up and flogged with a bit of choice leather.'

'And is Otto guilty as charged?' said Brownie.

'Otto Visser's a decent bloke,' said Jacko. 'He keeps his animals in great nick and his farm tidy. But like a lot of farmers round here, his land's tricky to fence, which means money and time. Good farmers like Otto will do what needs to be done, but we can't expect them to do it overnight. And anyway, this isn't about *waterways*. Fucking vegan hippies think meat is murder, and they don't want *any* farmers in business. If they were genuine about preventing pollution, they'd be targeting their so-called freedom camper buddies. Those feral bastards leave muck everywhere.'

This speech included more words than Jacko usually uttered in a day. Devon sincerely hoped that Emma had nothing to do with the website. It could cause a family schism bigger than the Rift Valley. One visible from space.

Mind you, after what she'd done to him, she kind of deserved to have her arse whipped.

'Vic Halsworth's on the list, too,' Jacko said to Gene, who widened his eyes like this was a big surprise. 'Bunch of others.'

'What are they planning to do about it?' said Brownie.

'Club together and get a lawyer, Otto said. Which is, I agree with him, a fat waste of money. They'll never find who's behind it. Probably run out of Kyrgyz-fucking-stan or someplace that sends grandmas and toddlers down salt mines.'

'No salt mines in Kyrgyzstan,' said Brownie. 'Coal, gold and uranium, primarily.' He shrugged at their expressions. 'When I'd finished the Wilbur Smith and James Clavell novels, all the prison library had were the 1995 edition of *Funk & Wagnalls New Encyclopedia* and *The Reader's Digest Treasury of Joy.*'

Front door opened. Dr G. Looking remarkably chirpy.

'So, Doc,' said Gene, as the man took a seat. 'What do you know about Kyrgyzstan?'

'I do not even know how to spell it,' said Dr G, with equanimity. 'I hope it's not important.'

He spotted Devon's limp.

'Have you injured yourself?'

How many times could Devon be humiliated today?

'Horse kick,' said Devon. 'Right on the gluteus maximus.'

'That could cause a nasty contusion,' said Dr G. 'Make sure you ice and rest it. If it continues to pain you, come and see me. Bad bruising can lead to complications.'

'OK, deal. Beer?' Devon bent to fetch one from the fridge.

But Dr G said, 'You know, I think I will have a glass of house red.'

Anyone who thought there could be no such thing as an audible silence would have been proved dead wrong.

'Gone off beer, have you, Dr G?' said Gene in his most casual and thus most dangerous tones.

'I am very partial to a fine ale,' the good doctor replied. 'But this evening, I would prefer red wine.'

He smiled around at the group, who were still looking at him askance. Just showed: scratch the skin of even an intelligent New Zealand male, and you'd reveal a calcified layer of tradition. Accepted customs that defined real blokes, and drew the line between 'them' and 'us'. More often than not, Devon found himself on the 'them' side of that line, even with people he knew well. And now Dr G had put one foot on the dark side, too. Kudos.

'Got an elegant pinot noir from Central Otago,' Devon said, to rub it in. 'If you want to upgrade from the house wine?'

'Why not?' Dr G tapped the bar top with both palms. 'Let us push out the boat.'

'Got cooking to finish,' said Jacko, and left them to go clatter in the kitchen.

He should be happy, not grumpy, Devon thought. The profit on the pinot was a damn sight more than on the beer.

'Celebrating?' Gene asked Dr G.

Gene was also disgruntled. He hid it better, but Devon knew the signs. Gene hated being excluded from any secret, and Dr G clearly had something going on.

'Isn't being alive always a cause for celebration?' said Dr G.

'No,' said Gene. 'It isn't. Have you been inhaling nitrous oxide?'

'Am I not allowed to be cheerful?'

'Only in a low-key way,' said Brownie. 'Even a high five makes

150

us uncomfortable in this country. Anything beyond that, and we think you've been brainwashed by the Moonies.'

'Duly noted.' Dr G picked up his wine glass. 'I was about to say "chin-chin," but I'll desist.'

'Got any plans for tomorrow night, Doc?' Devon asked. 'Want to check out another cult classic movie? Think it's *An American Werewolf in London* this time.'

Last Saturday's cinema excursion had proved to be surprisingly good fun. If you didn't count Dr G sighing about Emma, and Brownie pretending he wasn't on full alert every time some dude came within five miles of them. And it wasn't like Devon had any other options for a social life.

'As it happens, I am otherwise engaged,' said Dr G. 'But thank you for asking.'

'Brownie?' said Devon.

'Sure,' he said.

Well, don't leap up and down with excitement, Devon wanted to say. It wasn't like Brownie was fighting off invitations with a stick, either.

Under the bar, his phone buzzed. Sigh. Let the games begin.

Moana. 'Howz da nono?' she'd texted.

'Lke a Rlling Stne: black and blue,' he texted back, then regretted it as being too obscure. What did Mo know of '70s rock?

'Thx 2 a mean Beast of Burdn,' came her text. She *did* get it. Who'd have thought?

'Oy, lover boy,' said Gene. 'Think you could stir yourself to get me a refill? Or are you too busy checking the teeth of likely contenders?'

Man, he *was* in a bad mood. Which was pretty entertaining. You didn't often get to see Gene Collins behind the eight ball. Do him good.

'I guess Emma plans to do the vetting for me,' said Devon, sliding over another beer. 'Let's hope she gets too busy with whatever else she's got on, and the whole terrible idea fades to nothing.'

'How come you and she never got together?' said Gene. 'You make a super cute couple. Like twins.'

Yeah, yeah. Devon had heard it all before. At school, he and Emma had got called 'the lesbos', 'takatāpui', 'Scissor Sisters'. Emma always laughed and told him to ignore it, and Devon had, back then. But if you didn't call out hate speech, then you were kind of condoning it, weren't you?

Still, there was a time and a place. Gene would keep.

'Spark's never been there,' said Devon. 'We're friends. End of.'

Dr G raised his wine glass.

'To friends!' he said. 'Old — and even more exciting — new!'

Gene's expression was something to treasure, and Devon couldn't help but smile. Dr G was dropping hints but keeping his secret close. Double kudos.

Secrets, though, they could be destructive. Emma mightn't be the world's greatest friend, but she still *was* his friend, and he cared what happened to her. The singles ad he could ride out, as long as it didn't get too crazy. But if she was behind that farmer-shaming website, then that was quite another thing. That bloke she was with — what was his agenda? How much of this was Emma's idea and how much his? No matter how she spun it, truth was she'd followed him across the world. So what else was she prepared to do for him?

He caught Brownie watching him. Now, there was another bloke with secrets. Or at least, one whose outside didn't necessarily reflect what was going on inside. When it came to Brownie, Devon's woo-wah beeped like sonar detecting what could be a submarine but could also be some giant man-eating creature of the depths. Devon wasn't sure whether to be wary or worried about Brownie's state of mind.

'You seen *An American Werewolf in London?*' Devon asked him.

'I haven't.' Brownie gave him an amused, shrewd look, almost as if he'd guessed Devon's thoughts. 'But the ability to release the beast seems mighty attractive at times, don't you agree?'

Devon's woo-wah beeped again. And he was pretty sure the shape below looked nothing like a submarine.

CHAPTER 17

Emma

'No . . . No . . . Hell no . . . What even *is* that?'

Emma had blagged the wi-fi password from the avocado orchard owner, and was sitting cross-legged on the homestead porch, checking her phone.

Loko squatted beside her, handed her a mug of tea.

'Success?' he said.

'In terms of quantity of responses, yep,' said Emma. 'In terms of *quality*, nuh-huh.'

'Your friend is — unusual looking.'

Emma glanced at him. 'Not as open-minded as you thought you were?'

'Oh, the universe is always conspiring to humble one,' said Loko.

Maybe, thought, Emma. But not necessarily the one sitting next to her. He had self-confidence to spare. And that was from another who wasn't lacking. Not that her parents had brought her up to be full of herself. They just didn't believe in being fake. False humility was a lie as much as making shit up, and so was skirting around the truth. If you couldn't say it straight, then you probably weren't living straight. Emma's folks had a healthy distrust of people who weren't direct.

'What I meant was that your friend has a very *specific* look,' Loko went on. 'Which might bring a certain type of person out of the woodwork.'

'Priests and cannibals,' said Emma. 'Prehistoric animals.'

She sensed his puzzlement, and the undertone of resentment that always accompanied it.

'Song by Shriekback,' she said. 'They were big in the '80s. Still big in Hampton nightclubs.'

'I prefer jazz.'

Good thing they didn't have access to a stereo, then. Emma would rather listen to a dentist drilling her own teeth.

'And what news of your other project?' said Loko.

'Huh?'

Emma had got distracted by a photo of what appeared to be a girl with a fur collar. Nope, it was two rats, curled around her neck. Actually, if you looked past all the piercings, the girl wasn't bad looking. She could go in the 'Maybe' file.

Loko reached over, removed the phone from her hand.

'Priorities,' he said. 'Focus.'

'I've *done* my bit,' said Emma, beckoning for her phone. 'Mission completed.'

'We need to gauge the response, too. Find out if and how people are taking action. No measurable effect means the mission is a failure.'

'Someone else should do that,' said Emma. 'If it's me, it'll look suspicious.'

'You were born and brought up in this community. People will expect you to be concerned about what's going on round here.'

Actually, the majority of people round here still saw Emma as Jacko and Mac's little girl. They had perfect recall of when she ran naked on the beach as a three-year-old. They'd seen her drop out of university and flit between part-time gigs. Her mates from school thought she was a laugh, a girl who could party, who could hang. Dev — well, judging from his phone message, he currently saw her as Beelzebub incarnate, though he'd get over it soon enough.

No one in Gabriel's Bay took her seriously, which was partly why she'd left. Seemed that attitude was catching.

'What counts as "action"?' said Emma, trying not to show how irked she was.

'Council investigations, prosecutions,' said Loko. 'But also civilian acts. Organised protests. Other more — spontaneous — demonstrations of disapproval.'

Emphasis noted. Meaning not *entirely* clear, but Emma could make an educated guess as to what fell into this category.

'Anything already planned?' she said.

But the other pickers were coming out from the kitchen now. Break was over. Back to work. The ten of them were expected to pick around twenty thousand avocados over the course of an eight-hour day. If Emma ever felt like eating guacamole again, she'd be smashing those green bastards with extra vigour.

Loko picked up her untouched mug of tea, tipped it out on the ground. Started to head back into the kitchen to put the mugs in the sink.

'Phone?' Emma held out her hand.

'Do you need it?' he said, with a half-smile.

No, but it was hers and she wanted it back. Even in her mind, that sounded childish, and besides, she didn't really want to have this fight. Partly because it was a waste of time and energy, but also, if she were to be totally honest, because she didn't want to find out how far Loko would go to win. Better to be relaxed. Or pretend to be, anyway.

'Nah, stick it in my bag,' she said, and with a backward wave, jumped down the porch steps. 'See you in the forest of denial.'

No way he'd know System of a Down. Put *that* in his jazz pipe and smoke it.

End of the day, Emma drove Loko back to the Wood Sprite camp in her brother's shit-box old Nissan. Harry, knowing he had no chance of selling it on, had on one door painted the top-hatted bluebird from the mega-racist old Disney flick, *Song of the South*, above a flowery scroll that said 'Bluebird of Crappiness.' Never a truer word. But it was a car, and there was no other way Loko could get to work if she didn't drive him. Be nice if he offered to pay for petrol, but Emma hadn't asked outright, so who was she to carp?

Knackered after picking five million effing avos, Emma had slept in Loko's borrowed tarp-hut every day after work, instead of crashing at her parents' house. Since she turned legal at sixteen, her folks had never questioned her about her sex life, trusting her to take care of herself, make sensible decisions. They knew she had a bloke now, and they knew as much about him as everyone else in Gabriel's Bay did — which was only marginally less than Emma knew herself, though she'd be pushing shit uphill to expect full disclosure. They hadn't asked to meet him, again figuring that she'd introduce him when ready. Emma had never had a serious boyfriend before, and she imagined that her folks saw Loko as yet another passing flingship. And she had to face it — that was all it was, all it *could* be, given his choice of life.

Cue refrain from *The Sound of Music*: how could you pin a moonbeam or hold a cloud, or whatever those nuns were squawking on about. Sidney loved that movie, and had brainwashed her boys into loving it, too. Emma had watched it so many times, it bordered on babysitter abuse. But that was the romantic ideal, wasn't it? Find a man, settle down, have a gaggle of singing children . . .

'Do you think we should have picked up curry for the others?' she asked Loko.

'They wouldn't expect us to.'

'We should contribute, though. I'll ask if we can take a few of the bruised avocados.'

'Good luck with that,' he said. 'Even bruised avocados can be sold.'

'Is everyone who owns a business a grasping shit in your book?' she asked.

Loko grunted, as if the question made him impatient. But he answered calmly enough.

'The system allows people to exploit others. Whether they think of it as exploitation or not.'

Emma hadn't told Loko much about her parents, probably for this exact reason: they were white, middlish-class, and as a salaried employee (her mum) and employer (her dad), also cogs in the capitalist wheel. But that didn't mean they didn't care about social inequality and the environment, or that they were anti welfare or tax breaks for the poor. It didn't mean they were the enemy.

'My dad owns a business,' she said. 'He pays an OK wage.'

'But he doesn't get to say what an OK wage is,' said Loko. 'The so-called "market" decides that. The market decides what work is worth remunerating, and how much those workers should be paid. Do you really believe that a person who devotes their life to caring for the disabled is worth less than the CEO of a tobacco company, whose product kills millions every year?'

Emma didn't believe that — how could she? She'd seen first hand how the work her commune team was doing had made a difference, improved society, yet they still struggled for funding. The system *was* fucked up, that was true. But it was hard to see her dad as the system's pawn, its enabler. Hard to see Jacko Reid as anything but fully in charge.

'I'll ask for the avos tomorrow, anyway,' said Emma. 'Don't ask, don't get.'

Following the path from roadside carpark to campsite in the dark was tricky, and required concentration and torches. Usually, the camp was quiet at this time, the evening meal having been eaten early, while there was still light. But when Emma and Loko entered the clearing, the fire was blazing, and all the Wood Sprites were around it, laughing and drinking what looked like cider. More likely, it was Darius' homebrewed nettle beer, which was surprisingly pleasant. The Wood Sprites didn't usually allow alcohol into their camp, but the nettle beer got brought out on special occasions. Emma and Loko had been welcomed with it. She wondered what they were celebrating now.

'Hey! Come and join us!'

A smiling Rua held his arms wide to greet them. Seated on the log next to him was a young woman who looked vaguely familiar. Emma thought she'd seen her at the plant collective stall, or perhaps the farmers' market. She had a feeling the woman had something to do with astrology. Had that look about her. Dip-dyed hair. Lots of beads.

Emma felt uncomfortable eating bought curry in front of everyone, so she quickly stashed it in the tarp-hut and hurried back to the fire. Loko had no such shame; he was eating the curry out of the container with his hands, Indian style, using the naan as a scoop.

'So what's up?' Emma asked Rua.

He put his arm around his companion's shoulders and squeezed. She was pink-faced with fire heat, pleasure or embarrassment. Maybe all three.

'We're pregnant!' Rua announced.

A cheer went up around the group. Mugs were clinked together. Darius uncorked another bottle of nettle beer, and poured a mug for Emma and Loko.

Loko waved his away.

'Thanks, but I'll stick with water.'

To Rua and his lady, he said, 'Congratulations. A child is a very special blessing.'

Emma almost choked on her beer. As far as she'd been aware, Loko thought the world was dangerously overpopulated and would benefit from a good plague. But she couldn't call him out on this now. Rua and his pink-faced baby mama were ecstatic to be creating another drain on the world's resources, and who was she to kill their buzz?

Now she thought about it, it made sense that Loko was only being polite, too. For one, you'd have to be a complete arsehole to rain on these people's preggo parade. Plus, Loko needed the Wood Sprites onside. He needed allies. And followers.

'Do you have a name yet?' Emma asked the couple. That's what you did in these circumstances, wasn't it?

'If it's a boy, he'll be Kale,' said Rua.

'As in "curly"?'

'It's one of Jupiter's moons.' Rua shrugged. 'But the plant's cool, too.'

'If it's a girl,' said the baby mama, 'she'll be Elara. Another of Jupiter's moons.'

'Pretty,' said Emma.

Silently, she wished double-X chromosomes on the foetus. It could thank her later.

'The baby will be birthed naturally?' said Loko.

Emma forbore from giving him a WTF look. Her mum had told her enough stories for her to know that barely any birth turned out as planned, and that labour was insanely painful. You might *want* to give birth in balmy azure seas surrounded by dolphins, but odds were you'd be on your hands and knees yelling for drugs as soon as the first proper contraction hit. All births were different, but the one thing they had in common?

Yep, everyone giving birth was female. Guys could be a hands-on support crew, but ultimately they did *not* have to experience the equivalent of squeezing a pumpkin out of their fundament. Which meant, in Emma's firm opinion, that they had minimal say on how the birth should roll.

'We're keen to try hypno-birthing,' said Rua. 'It gets rid of all the fear and tension, which means no pain. Celeste's mum has a friend who's been training up on it.'

'Beautiful,' said Loko. 'Natural birthing can be profoundly spiritual, for you and your child.'

Good thing about nighttime, Emma thought. No one can see you roll your eyes.

But to be fair, she didn't object to what was being said. How people chose to give birth was none of her beeswax. And if Loko was spouting platitudes to be kind, then what of it?

No, she knew what rankled was that everyone was in agreement. The vibe around the fire was that motherhood was the greatest thing, uplifting, transformative — necessary. It was like it was some great sacred tradition that couldn't be violated.

Emma hadn't given much thought to whether or not she wanted children — she was twenty-three, for Pete's sake. Her environmental friends had all sorts of reasons why breeding was bad: overpopulation, climate change, and the fact Stephen Hawking said humans only had another hundred years, if they were lucky. And Emma had personal reservations, too. She didn't want to give up her freedom, become tied to one spot. She didn't necessarily want to be in a permanent relationship, either.

But what it boiled down to, she knew, was that she objected to doing what was expected. She didn't like being judged, and judgement came with both options. Women who chose not to have babies were seen as dooming themselves to a life of incompletion, of failure. If they did not — or could not — use their bodies to duplicate life, then they died with their work only half done. They were empty vessels.

And women who *did* had to subsume their identities and become Mother with the capital 'M'. Mothers, not fathers, were judged for how their children behaved, how well they achieved, whether they were fat or skinny, bookish or sporty, gay or straight. You couldn't win.

Nope, no one was going to dictate to Emma how she used her body, and she had plenty of time to make up her mind about which way she'd go. And if that certainty came late and she missed the boat, body clockwise, then so be it, tough cheddar. She'd have made the most of her life, lived it to the max.

Emma took another swig of nettle beer. Highlighted by the fire, Loko looked dark and dangerous, and — alcohol on an empty stomach, no doubt — sexy as hell. Emma knew there were plenty of women around the world who'd crawl over glass to be in her position, to jump whenever he lifted his little finger. But she also knew that what drew Loko to her was that she *wasn't* blindly obedient. Sure, she had guts and determination, but more importantly, she showed initiative. The website had been *her* idea, and she'd made it happen. *She* called the shots in her life. *She* was in control.

Emma caught Loko's eye, and nodded towards the tarp hut. He smiled. Invitation accepted. Strategic withdrawal from the celebrations to be executed in five, four, three . . .

She called the shots.

Forget about the future. *This* was living. *This* was exciting. Tomorrow, she'd skip playing yenta for Devon and get stuck back in to the other project. Because Loko was right — the job was only half done. And Emma intended to prove that no one else could complete it better.

CHAPTER 18

Patricia

They'd survived seven days. Nothing had been broken. Nothing valuable, at least. Nerves had been shattered on several occasions, but Patricia was now more familiar with Reuben's moods, and could usually anticipate, and thus forestall, a blow-up.

On Saturday, though, Reuben's sister, Maree, had telephoned from America, which had made the boy happy until two minutes in, when he realised that she wasn't calling from her work and wouldn't be coming around that afternoon to pick him up. Containing that tantrum had required all Patricia's patience. She refused to physically restrain him or shut him in his room — that seemed morally wrong to her. Instead, she'd gently manoeuvred him from the living room into the hallway, and let him throw himself around on the carpet and kick the walls. If paint or plaster was damaged, it could be repaired. Bernard had poked his head out from his library, decided discretion was the better part of valour, and retreated. Patricia had sat on the hallway chair and prepared to wait it out.

'I'm right here,' she said. 'I can see how sad you must feel, how much you miss your sister. I'll be here when you're ready to talk to me.'

She was blathering, but the words had soothed and kept her calm, even if they had precious little effect on Reuben. He was lying flat on his back, circling like a dervish on the hall runner, drumming his heels on the floor or kicking at the skirting. His shouting was, for the most part, incoherent, though the swear words did rather leap out at one. Patricia had pictured Bernard behind his library door, hunching his shoulders as if he were receiving blows to the back.

'I never had a sister,' Patricia continued, 'and I wish I had. I never had a brother, either. I used to imagine having a whole crowd of brothers and a sister. In my imagination, we played games together, and built a tree house, and went sailing. I wanted to be Able Seaman Titty Walker in *Swallows and Amazons*. She was the one who found Captain Flint's trunk. I was so envious when he gave her the parrot.'

It had taken a full few seconds for her to register that the shouting had stopped. Reuben was still lying on his back, his arms and legs splayed like da Vinci's Vitruvian Man. But his eyes were on her, wide as florins.

'What parrot?' he said.

'Her name was Polly,' said Patricia. 'She was green. There was also mention of a monkey named, if I recall, Gibber. And a kitten called Sinbad.'

'Is it a story?'

'It is. A whole book.'

Last week's trip to the library had passed without incident, Reuben no doubt having been trained in correct behaviour by Maree. He'd selected some books to take home, but when Patricia had offered to read them to him, he'd begun to tantrum. Patricia had endeavoured to discover why, but Reuben was not forthcoming, and so she had quietly set the books on his bedside table for him to take up should he choose.

Given this past form, it was with a small prayer that Patricia had added, 'Would you like me to read it to you?'

Reuben had scrambled up off the carpet, run over to the chair and thumped his hands down on her knees. Patricia had tried not to wince.

'Read!' he'd demanded, his nose nearly touching hers.

He was not the most prepossessing child, having a dusty quality about him that brought to mind the Charles Schulz cartoon character of Pig-Pen. His hair was an unruly brown, and his skin had a greyish-yellow tinge, as if he'd spent the last nine years chain smoking. Both his parents *did* smoke, Patricia had been told, so that might explain it. She could see why his classmates singled him out for teasing. It wasn't only his lack of impulse control that made him ripe for winding up. He was a child who looked permanently grubby and could easily be accused of smelling funny, even if he smelled no better or worse than any other small boy.

Forced into close proximity, Patricia realised how easy it would be to draw away, to not look past the sooty outer layer and see the need, the innocence, beneath. She'd felt a rush of affection for the boy, but did not want to startle him with an embrace.

'Can you ask me more politely?' she'd said.

To his credit, he'd given it some thought.

'Read! Please!'

'Very well.'

Patricia had stood and held out her hand, trying not to give the sense she was insisting he take it. But Reuben *had* taken it quite happily, and allowed Patricia to lead him into the conservatory, a room that, due to a preponderance of glass, had previously been off limits. But at this hour, the sun would be dappling the cane chairs with palm leaf patterns, and Patricia couldn't think of a more appropriate setting for the narrating of an island adventure.

Fortunately, her books were not allowed in Bernard's library, so she did not have to disturb him. Her Arthur Ransome collection, including a treasured signed version of *Coot Club*, was in the spare bedroom. She'd asked Reuben to sit quietly while she fetched it, and he had (or at least, he'd been sitting quietly when she returned). Feeling that he was too old for her lap, she sat on the two-seater and invited him to join her. To her surprise, he'd snuggled right up next to her and stuck his thumb in his mouth. An hour later, they were still there, lost in the story, until Bernard coughed gently in the doorway and asked whether she would like him to bring them afternoon tea.

'Surely his sister would have read to him?' Bernard had said to her that night, as they were readying for bed. 'She works in a book shop.'

'She did. He told me,' Patricia replied. 'And that was the problem. Maree was the only one who read to him, and that was their special time. In Reuben's eyes, if it couldn't be Maree, it shouldn't be anyone. Hence our failures thus far.'

'I see.'

Bernard had become silent for several minutes, and Patricia could guess what was in his mind.

'I have no doubt that Maree will continue to care for Reuben until he is old enough to care for himself,' she'd reassured her husband. 'But yes, it is a worry. If something happened to her . . .'

She'd left the thought to circulate in the air and take whatever finished form it might in Bernard's head. She knew Bernard had up until then been counting the days until Reuben left them, possibly chalking each one off on a wall in his library like a prison inmate. Perhaps now he would be thinking a little further ahead, and when the door closed behind Reuben in three weeks, Bernard might not sigh with relief that he could reclaim his usual tantrum-and-expletive-free routine. He might, indeed, want to keep their connection alive.

However, she wouldn't force him to leap so far so soon. And besides, it might not be possible to stay in touch. There might be another child in their house — if the prospect didn't give Bernard the vapours — and another. To emotionally invest in each one could prove exhausting, unwise. Still, that bridge was away in the distance. Plenty of time before it required crossing.

'I wondered if the boy might enjoy *The Coral Island*?' Bernard had said. 'I have a copy somewhere, I think. I'd be happy to read it, if you'd care for a break?'

If not a leap, then certainly a step in the right direction.

'Thank you, Bernard,' Patricia had replied. 'I'm sure Reuben would enjoy it very much.'

Tuesday morning, after breakfast. Patricia and Bernard were doing the dishes, while Reuben, despite being full of Weetbix, was outside energetically kicking a ball around.

'Charles Love will be popping by in half an hour,' Bernard announced.

When you reached a certain age, Patricia reflected, a visit from a doctor, even one who was retired, rang alarm bells.

'Is everything all right?' she asked. 'With you?'

'What? Oh,' Bernard twigged. 'Yes, of course. Hale and hearty. We're having a meeting of the Littleville trustees, plus a general community-oriented discussion. Tai Marshall will also join us.'

'You mean Tai Te Wera?'

'Do I?' said Bernard. 'Is he not Corinna Marshall's husband?'

'He is, but she kept her maiden name,' said Patricia. 'As she tells it, her feminist side had a debate with the side that preferred a Māori surname to a European one. A close run thing, I gather. Their children are Te Weras — that was her compromise.'

'Well, well,' said Bernard, which meant he found the subject both confusing and confronting, and would prefer to talk about something else.

'And what is on the agenda?' Patricia switched to more comforting language. 'Apart, of course, from Littleville.'

'Predominantly this anonymous website accusing local farmers.'

As Gabriel's Bay was surrounded by rural land, news of the site had reverberated to all points as if by jungle drums. Patricia had not looked at it, as it was clearly a scurrilous and cowardly piece of work, but she was aware of what it contained. Knowing the slippery nature of the internet, she doubted that much could be done, but if Tai Te Wera and Charles Love had a plan, then perhaps she'd be proved wrong.

'Is Sidney here this morning?' she asked. 'Or is she still unwell?'

'She said she would come in for an hour,' Bernard replied. 'She assures me she's not contagious. An upset stomach, nothing more.'

Patricia wiped the bench and wrung the dishcloth.

'Knowing how diligent Sidney is, if she had to take yesterday off, then she's rather more ill than she's letting on.'

'Should I suggest she see Charles' replacement?' said Bernard. 'The Indian chap?'

Patricia hid a smile as she hung the tea towels. Bernard's parents had been frightful racists, and he had done his best over the years to overcome this programming. But not having travelled to anywhere but Europe, he saw 'duskier' nationalities as exotic and therefore worthy of note. It was mild in the scheme of things, and given how deep the rot of Verity Weston could penetrate, quite an achievement for Bernard to have evolved that far.

'I suspect Sidney would prefer if you didn't mention it at all,' Patricia advised. 'Being told you look terrible generally makes you feel exactly that.'

Tai and Charles stayed for morning tea, during which Tai kept Reuben entranced with a series of simple magic tricks, the pièce de résistance being the production of a wrapped sweet from behind Reuben's ear.

'I have two small, determined daughters,' Tai explained. 'It takes a lot to deter them once they're on a mission. I had to up my distraction game.'

He eyed Reuben, whom Patricia had given permission to eat the sweet.

'Though it still incorporates a certain amount of bribery.'

Reuben tugged Patricia's sleeve.

'Thank-you-for-my-nice-tea-may-I-leave-the-table?'

The smiles around the table suggested that everyone present remembered parroting drilled-in words of courtesy in that exact same fashion.

'You may,' Patricia said. 'Why don't you take the blue bucket and see how many snails you can find in the garden?'

He needed no more encouragement. As he tore off, primed with mollusc-hunting zeal, Patricia called after him.

'They particularly like to hide in the parsley!'

'Does he know what parsley is?' Bernard enquired.

'Yes, he's becoming quite the junior horticulturalist,' said Patricia. 'We're planting broccoli and beetroot seedlings this afternoon.'

'You're doing wonders,' said Charles. 'I congratulate you.'

'Oh, well.'

Patricia lowered her eyes, embarrassed. Not wonders, surely? Just what was expected of her — providing a safe, pleasant environment for a child.

'Yes, Corinna was thrilled when you decided to become a carer,' said Tai. 'She says some of the people who put their names forward shouldn't be let within fifty miles of a child.'

A chill swept over her. The thought that other vulnerable children might be put in homes where—

A change of subject was mandatory, for her own sanity.

'And how did your meeting go?' she asked the men.

'Well, on the positive side,' said Bernard, 'Charles has secured a promise of seed funding for Littleville from a national chain of plumbing suppliers. I realise that seems an unlikely affiliation, but apparently the founder is originally from Hampton and a dedicated model railway enthusiast.'

He pushed at his glasses. A sure sign that there was a 'However . . .' coming.

'However,' Bernard went on, 'the firm has stipulated naming rights. We could no longer call it Littleville. It would have to be—' He cleared his throat. 'Flange and Ballcock's Miniature World.'

Tai had his eyes averted but couldn't prevent the shake in his shoulders. Patricia guessed this had been a meeting highlight for him.

'It has a certain ring to it,' she said. 'And it is funding, after all. The project will go nowhere without it.'

'Quite right,' said Charles. 'A, er, *distinctive* name is a small price to pay if we want this to succeed. Now that we can count on the Progressive Association's support, Tai and I will present the proposal to the rest of the Littleville trustees.'

Patricia gave Bernard a look. 'You have the whole Association behind you?'

'Of course not,' he said. 'But informing us is merely a courtesy. It's a private project, so we have no right of veto. If Elaine doesn't like it, she will, in the parlance of today's youth, have to suck it up.'

'Wouldn't underestimate her, though,' said Tai. 'She managed to keelhaul the town name-change proposal. Corinna was *spitting*.'

Last year, Corinna Marshall had spearheaded the lodging of an application to the New Zealand Geological Board, proposing that

Gabriel's Bay revert to its original Māori name of Onemanawa. Such a proposal required the support of the Hampton District Council, which had been given but then unexpectedly withdrawn. Though that was no surprise to those who knew the nature of the person who'd lobbied against it — Bernard's rival, Councillor Elaine Pardew. A woman who appeared to be made entirely from pink polyester and spite.

'Corinna won't give up, though, will she?' said Patricia.

'Will the Pope continue to be Catholic?' said Tai. 'No, she's rallying her troops for a renewed action.'

'Holding attack?' said Charles.

'Infiltration, I'd say,' Tai replied. 'And if that doesn't work, she'll go straight to blitzkrieg.'

'Maybe Charles could create a diorama of the battle once the dust has settled?' said Patricia.

'Not out of the question,' said Charles, enjoying the joke. 'I shall have to stock up on pink paint.'

'And after Littleville, we discussed this shameful website,' said Bernard.

He'd always been a stickler for ticking items off the agenda. Patricia had asked about their meeting, and he intended to give her a full and detailed answer.

'I've been asked to represent the farmers,' said Tai. 'Not surprisingly, they want the site taken down.'

'Can you do that?' said Patricia.

Tai rubbed his hand over his head.

'Well, it's not a stretch to say it breaches our Harmful Digital Communications Act. But any complaints under the Act need to be directed to the site host, who must instruct the author to remove the content within forty-eight hours. If the host is not easily contactable and/or the author has concealed their identity, then the complaint simply vanishes in the ether.'

Tai glanced at Bernard.

'So we're trying another tactic,' he said. 'Good old-fashioned dobbing in. We're putting the word out through all community groups, including the Progressive Association, asking folk who have any information to call an anonymous phone line. Again, chances are slim, but if we pitch it as locals helping locals, whom they know and respect, then we might get lucky.'

'What on earth is the moti*vation* behind such a website?' Patricia said.

'Probably a sincere desire to effect change,' said Tai. 'It's a form of protest. Just like chaining yourself to a fence, going on hunger strike, or—' he grinned '—marching for land rights.'

Patricia took his point. But, still.

'Participants in those protests are hardly anonymous,' she said. 'Whereas this seems *cowardly*.'

'Hear, hear,' said Bernard.

'Yet what would we have done without secret agents, or the resistance, during wartime?' said Tai. 'Why do we need undercover police? Don't get me wrong. I don't like this website any more than you do. But I'm also not a fan of double standards.'

'Covert doesn't always mean unscrupulous,' chipped in Charles.

'Yes, I suppose you're right,' said Patricia. 'We're all capable of concealment when we believe it's for the best.'

The front door opened and shut. Bernard had given Sidney a key.

Her face appeared in the kitchen door, and Patricia could see she was still unwell. A wan tinge to her skin and a puffiness about her face.

'Don't go on my account,' she said to Tai and Charles, who had both stood up. 'I'm about to lock myself away for an hour.'

'Tea?' said Patricia.

'Oh, no thank you,' said Sidney, with a small grimace. 'For some reason, tea and coffee taste like used sump oil at the moment.'

As Charles passed her in the doorway, he said, 'Have you seen Dr Ghadavi?'

'No, no.' Sidney waved away his concern. Then she paused. 'Why? Do you think I should?'

Charles tilted his head to one side, his expression, as always, inscrutable.

'He might be able to offer some relief. You don't always have to tough it out, you know.'

Sidney blushed, as if he'd caught her committing a misdemeanour.

'OK, fair call,' she said. 'Truth is, I'm being a cowardly custard. But odds are it's nothing bad. Right?'

A blur of grey and blue outside the window caught Patricia's eye. Reuben, bucket clutched tight to his chest, was racing across the lawn, and Patricia itched to tell him to slow down, lest he trip and fall.

But none of them was truly safe, were they? Not even a strong, capable man like Tai Te Wera, or a determined, smart woman like Sidney Gillespie. They weren't safe from accident, illness or grief, nor from failure, abuse or misfortune. Asteroids could collide with Earth, a maniac might unleash nuclear hell. The sun might roast them all, and they might drown in rising seas.

And children were the most vulnerable of all. Adults could muster strength, intelligence and resources in self-protection. Children depended on adults being kind enough to extend that protection to them.

Charles smiled and patted Sidney on the arm.

'You'll be fine,' he said.

Patricia decided to believe that he was speaking to them all.

CHAPTER 19

Ash

In Ash's experience, patients could react in perplexing ways to his diagnoses. Some laughed upon being told they had a serious illness. Others became angry when the complaint proved minor, or took umbrage that he did not support what the internet had assured them they were suffering from, apparently preferring to have a fatal disease than a temporary atopic rash.

He'd become resigned to being confused by those initial responses, but in this case, he felt he was on firmer ground. When a patient clutched their head and groaned, 'No, no, please God, *no-o*,' he could, with some certainty, assume they weren't entirely happy.

'But I *can't* be.' Sidney Gillespie's whole expression was a rictus of despair. 'We use contraception. Every *time*. Without *fail*.'

'Unfortunately, no form of contraception, bar abstinence, has been proved one hundred per cent effective. So even if you did use prevention without fail,' said Ash, 'the method itself would not necessarily follow suit.'

'God, why *me*?' Sidney expelled the phrase with vigour. 'Was I a truly *appalling* person in a past life? Do I have to be taught every lesson in the book in this one?'

'Forgive me if I'm being obtuse,' Ash ventured, 'but what makes it so catastrophic?'

Sidney looked at him as if he had asked why everyone was so concerned about climate change.

'I already have two children,' she said, enunciating carefully in case he missed a vital point, 'whom I struggle enough to provide for. The youngest is ten, which is a significant age gap, and to be honest, the prospect of returning to sleepless nights, nappies and breastfeeding makes me want to seize your paperknife and stab it through my heart. I have known the father of this child for approximately twenty seconds and have no idea what his plans are for staying in the country, let alone with me. Nor do I know what *my* feelings are on the matter of long-term commitment. I'm thirty-three, and I've been quite looking forward to having grown-up children in my forties. Now, given today's insanely expensive and uncertain world, I'll probably have my gold card before this one leaves home. Unlike more maternally minded women, I found most aspects of toddler rearing mind-numbingly repetitive, and I've been enjoying my children more the older and more articulate they become. I worry about my children's happiness and future every day, and adding in a third might tip me over the edge of sanity. I put on *dramatic* amounts of weight during both my pregnancies, and, as you can see, my body was determined keep most of it, and I was *young* then and much more physically resilient. The father is ginger, so what are the odds this one will face a lifetime of social ostracism and ridicule? My house has only two bedrooms, and it isn't fair to ask my boys to share with a wailing infant. This is all covered under patient confidentiality, right?'

It took Ash a second to realise he'd been asked a question.

'Yes, of course.'

Sidney's eyes narrowed, like a teacher who'd spotted a pupil masticating a spitball.

'And you won't become loose-lipped after a few beers at the Boat Shed?'

'I promise you that I have never discussed a patient with any person at any time, including friends or family.'

Fair to say that he never discussed *any*thing with family.

'What about Mac?'

Ash's sense was that Mac would not let patient information be prised from her cold, dead hands. But, let's face it, Magnus Torvaldsen's was the only file she had not read in detail.

'Mac will not communicate anything that you do not wish her to,' was the best he could offer.

'Shit,' said Sidney.

Ash could sympathise. Knowing Mac was aware that you were wrangling with a tough situation amplified the pressure like a thumb on your carotid artery.

'You do have options,' said Ash.

'Hmm,' said Sidney. 'I guess the point I need to get clear on is whether that choice is entirely mine. How long do I have to procrastinate?'

'To be on the safe side, I'd leave it no more than a week. The, er, termination clinic in Hampton is short-staffed and over-booked, and if you are too close to twelve weeks, then that option may no longer be available to you.'

'Can you give me a plausible cover story? Food poisoning?'

'Unfortunately, most types of food poisoning will last no more than a few days. We could say we are testing for giardia? That can linger in the system, and does cause bloating, fatigue and nausea.'

'Super.'

'However, it is also a notifiable disease, and you would not be allowed around children or your workplace.'

'Not super.' Sidney sighed. 'I'll just have to bluff it out. Say you haven't a clue.'

'I will do my best to bear the slur on my reputation,' said Ash.

Sidney seemed reluctant to leave. Ash could sympathise. Big problems felt smaller when you could share them with people who could offer perspective and reassurance. His consuming infatuation with Emma Reid, for example, shrunk to the proportions of a mere schoolboy crush in the company of Magnus and Oksana. Particularly Oksana, who dismissed anything she considered nonsense with a single wave of her hand and a 'Pfff' — an exhalation she could invest with remarkable scorn.

'Feel free to phone me any time,' said Ash. 'I am not a bad listener.'

'Thanks.' Sidney's smile was wan but grateful. 'Be warned. I might take you up on that.'

'I'll come out to the front desk with you,' said Ash. 'I may be able to distract Mac from asking questions.'

'You're a prince among men, Dr Ghadavi,' Sidney told him as he held the door.

Ash let his chest swell for around two seconds, the time it took for him to see who was talking to Mac at the desk. And then an iron fist punched right through said chest and ripped out his trembling heart.

'Hey, Emma,' said Sidney. 'What happened?'

'She got smacked in the eye by a branch,' said Mac.

'Mum insisted I come here.' Emma held a compress to her face. 'Said I'd be waiting hours at Hampton A and E.'

'Ouch. Hope it's not serious.'

Sidney handed her bank card to Mac, who completed the transaction with speed and without chat, which was probably why Sidney winked at Ash on her way out. At least, Ash thought he caught a wink on the periphery of his vision. Difficult to tell when he could not stop staring at what he assumed was his next patient.

'I know it's your lunch break,' Mac said to him. 'And she's not registered with us but with a clinic in Hampton because she didn't want me knowing her business. But she's here now. You don't mind, do you?'

It was not actually a question. And even if it were, Ash would have only one answer.

'Of course not.'

He gestured to his consulting room, the door of which he was mildly surprised to find he still held open. 'Please. Come this way.'

Ash regretted that he'd not had time to check his breath, but as there was no way to examine an eyeball without being in close proximity, all he could do was keep his mouth shut and try not to exhale until he was back behind his desk.

'Luckily, the corneal abrasion is only superficial,' he said. 'And it should heal within two to three days. I will give you a prescription for antibiotic drops.'

'Hurts like hell,' said Emma. 'Like I've got a chunk of pumice in my eye.'

'Yes, even small abrasions can be very painful. You must do your best not to rub it.'

Ash completed the prescription and handed it to her.

'Do you also require a note for your employer?' he asked. 'I would recommend that you take the rest of the day off. Guard against irritants that could cause infection.'

She screwed up her mouth. It did not diminish her beauty one whit.

'Can't. Have to drive a friend home at the end of the day.'

'The friend cannot take a taxi?'

'We're not *all* on a GP's pay,' she said, with a derision that stabbed him right in the heart that would have been there had the iron fist not plucked it out.

'No, indeed.'

He agreed hastily, while quashing the urge to point out that in terms of doctors' salaries, he could only earn less if he volunteered for Médecins Sans Frontières. And besides, wasn't being a small town doctor an honourable profession? He was a community GP, not some Jaguar-driving Harley Street surgeon.

But now was not the time to quibble. Emma was on her feet, eager, he hoped, to get back to what she was doing, rather than be free of his presence. In a few seconds, she'd be out the door and gone. He hesitated for two reasons, the first professional; an inappropriate relationship could mean the end of his career. But before entering the country, Ash had carefully studied the guidelines, and a one-off minor consultation with a patient who would from now on be visiting her usual doctor was within the bounds of propriety. The second and more troublesome hesitation was purely personal — was he about to make whacking great fool of himself?

In his mind, he heard Magnus say, 'If you're going to make an error, make it one worth remembering.'

And Oksana had once seen a Siberian tiger prowling near her bus stop, and had stayed put because the tiger did not have to earn a living and she did.

Her hand was on the doorknob. Now or never.

'Emma, I, um, that is to say . . .'

He had her attention. Or, at least, she'd turned back with a look of bemused impatience.

'I realise that I am close to being a complete stranger to you,' he pressed on. 'But would you consider coming for a drink with me next Friday evening, and by that I mean not this Friday but the one after? And not at your father's establishment, which is not to say that it is not excellent, but perhaps at a cocktail lounge, if such a thing exists, or upmarket bar in Hampton? Of course, you will undoubtedly have a full social schedule, so if next Friday is too short notice then—'

'Sure.'

'—we could . . .' His brain caught up with his ears. 'Pardon me?'

'I said: Sure. Drink. Not this Friday but the one after. Meet you here at six.'

And she smiled, and shut the door behind her.

Was he dreaming? Ash replayed the words and they seemed supremely unambiguous. Yet, how could she have answered in that way? In the affirmative? Without hesitating?

He pictured her face as she spoke. Was there mockery in her expression? But apart from broken capillaries and wateriness in her left eye, she appeared as open and flawless as always. Unfazed, as if such invitations were ten a penny, which given her beauty, they probably were—

No. He should arrest this unprofitable line of thinking. He had dared to ask, and she had said yes. He should consider that a victory. Completely unexpected and confusing, but a victory nonetheless.

But why? Why had she said yes? What was it that had persuaded her? He was not unsightly, but he did not have the charisma of his older brothers, the confidence that illuminated their handsomeness and drew beautiful women to them like moths, though said women would have done well to heed the simile, as relationships with his brothers tended likewise to be short and brutal.

That, too, could be a perverse part of the attraction. Ash had been told by one girl he'd fancied that he was too nice, as if niceness were akin to having terrible taste in clothes — a flaw that made him embarrassing to be seen with. His mother also viewed niceness as a flaw, but one of character. Boiled down, her advice had been for him to grow a spine. He needed to be more commanding, more certain, more upright and one thousand per cent less apologetic. Stray dogs begging for scraps had more dignity than he did. More authority, too.

Had Emma said 'yes' to be kind, because she felt sorry for him? Felt that, like a stray dog, he needed to be rescued?

And what about the rumours that she was already spoken for? Ash had heard about the man with dreadlocks, but no one had yet confirmed that he and Emma were an item. He would not have asked her out had he been certain she was committed to another. And if she *were* in a relationship, why would she say 'yes'? Perhaps to make the dreadlocked beau jealous? Was Ash only a pawn in an emotional game?

There was no one he could ask. Except Magnus, of course, but any answer he gave would be purely theoretical, not knowing Emma from a bar of Pears.

Mac would know, and Devon, Emma's best friend, but to confide in them would be to invite ridicule. If Ash were to be completely honest, it might also confirm the suspicions that continued to worm away. Emma was a goddess, and goddesses did not fall for mere mortals, especially ones who resembled stray dogs. Emma quite possibly had a boyfriend and might be using Ash for her own ends. Emma might have a whole other reason for wanting to humiliate him that his brain hadn't yet managed to conjure up.

Next Friday. He would know in ten days. And until then, he would have to keep the secret to himself, unable to share his fears or, as he still wanted to, shout about it from the rooftops.

A knock on the door at the same time it was opened — why did she bother? Mac entered, bearing a cup of tea and a sandwich.

Ash's stomach did a nasty flip. Emma would surely have told her mother about his clumsy invitation. All this time he'd been agonising, they'd probably been having a good old chortle.

Mac placed the tea and roll on his desk. Ash could hardly bear to face her.

'Thanks for seeing Emma.'

She sounded sincere. No trace of scorn or levity.

Ash risked it. She looked as she always did — like a short

fluffy-haired prison guard whom even the convicts with tattooed eyelids wouldn't dare disobey.

'You're very welcome,' he said. 'Thank you for bringing me lunch.'

'It's tuna. All they had left. Like it or lump it.'

'I'm fond of tuna.'

'Sheila Swanson's here in ten,' said Mac. 'I thought when Doctor Love retired we'd seen the back of her, but no. Menopausal symptoms for the last decade, apparently.'

'It can happen.'

'Well, you're the doctor,' said Mac. 'But I'd advise you to play it cool. One minute, you're expressing sympathy about a dry vagina, and the next, you have visitors dropping in with cake. Your Sunday afternoons will no longer be your own.'

'Warning heeded,' said Ash. 'I'll, as you say, play it cool.'

An excellent strategy for next Friday night, he thought, as she closed the door.

If only he would work out how on earth to do it.

CHAPTER 20

Sidney

Since she left the medical centre yesterday, conversations had been like something out of Orwell's *1984*, her mind chiming in with the real meaning the instant her mouth uttered weaselly evasions and blatant falsehoods.

'So what did Dr G say?' was Kerry's first question when he arrived at hers after work that day.

'He's not sure yet. *[He's one hundred per cent sure.]* Could be a bug. *[It's not a bug.]* He'll run some tests. *[No need. We already know the result is positive.]*'

Kerry had given her a gentle hug.

'Poor you.'

'Thanks. *[I'm not the one being lied to.]*'

'Do you feel up to hosting my parents for dinner on Friday?' Kerry said. 'They'll completely understand if you'd rather not.'

'No, it's their last Friday here. They have to come. *[I don't want Bronagh within ten miles of me. She's a nurse. She's probably guessed already.]*'

'I'll get takeaways from the chippie. Dad won't have to confess he's once again flouted the "fish on Fridays" rule.'

'Sounds good. *[Shit, I forgot Douglas is a Catholic. They're still anti-abortion. Mind you, any grandparent would object to the termination of their only grandchild. I can't believe I just thought that. Now I want to cry.]*'

'And I'll cook tonight,' Kerry had added. 'You lie on the sofa and rest. You're still looking peaky.'

'Mm. [*It's guilt. And feeling like a terrible person. And panic and fear and darker emotions I don't even want to name. Don't hate me. Of course, you'll hate me. I'd hate me if I were you.*]'

'With luck, it'll only last a couple more days.'

'God, I hope so. [*It'll last a few more weeks. Or six-and-a-bit-months and then a lifetime. No pressure now.*]'

At least she knew she wasn't cut out to be a double agent. The *stress* of keeping secrets and sticking to a made-up story. Always checking that you hadn't contradicted yourself or blurted out a clue. No, her career path, in the unlikely event she'd someday have one, would *not* include espionage.

And then there were the constant reminders, as if the universe thought it hilarious to bop you on the head fifty times a day with a squeaky mallet. Babies *everywhere*! Pregnant women! Men with beer bellies who looked like pregnant women! Ads for in-home nannies in the window of the Four Square! The screaming coming from Starchild Music Therapy for the Under Fives! Old ladies knitting booties!

OK, so there was only one of those and she wasn't that old. Her name was Bea. She'd been rostered on with Sidney at the plant collective stall, and was sitting there, happily knitting away, unaware that she might as well have been driving her single point needles straight into Sidney's heart.

Bea caught Sidney watching her.

'My daughter's due in February.'

'Oh, congratulations. [*Curse her. Curse you. Curse those sweet little booties.*]'

'The baby's a girl.'

'Did she have a scan? [*Please stop talking.*]'

'No, Ianthe read her aura.'

Ianthe described herself as a spiritual alchemist. She channelled an archangel. Sidney found it hard to keep a straight face when speaking with her. Undoubtedly another black mark on her Karmic scorecard. They were totting up.

'Celeste and her partner will be hypno-birthing,' Bea went on.

'Interesting. *[Sounds super dodgy. Don't enlighten me.]*'

'And Ianthe is setting them on a course of pyramid water manifestation.'

'*[OK, no, I HAVE to know more about this.]* What does that involve?'

'You've heard of pyramid water?'

'Remind me. *[And how do you talk and knit at the same time?]*'

'Well, you're given this little pyramid made out of copper wire,' Bea informed her. 'You place the glass of water underneath it, and the pyramid's magnetic resonance enhances the energy and life force already present in the water.'

'Gotcha. *[Ah, ha, ha, ha! Quick, pretend to check on the radish seedlings so she can't see my face.]*'

'Then all you do is place your hands around the energised glass,' said Bea, already finishing off booty two, 'and focus on what you wish for in life. The water records your intent, and then when you drink it, those energy-information particles will tune your body's morphological field and allow it to communicate that intent to the universe.'

'Fascinating. *[And there's a unicorn right behind you! Too late! It flew into the magic rainbow!]*'

'Your hands have twenty-six energy channels, you know.'

'Gives a whole new meaning to taking your future into your own hands,' said Sidney.

'Indeed it does.'

Bea set the booties on the trestle table beside a punnet of Vietnamese basil. They were tiny, soft and yellow, and Sidney could almost see the little feet wriggling inside them. Babies, God, the way they felt, the way they smelled — they were like a drug. Given the effort they required, they had to be, otherwise the exposed hillsides would be stacked with them.

'You can wear the pyramid on your head too,' Bea added. 'The ionisation effect balances the energy field around the endocrine glands and expands your consciousness. Overcomes any mental blockages you might have, and does wonders for your emotional stability.'

'Does Ianthe make the pyramids herself? *[Sod it, I'll give anything a go.]*'

'I think she imports them from China,' said Bea. 'They're around a hundred dollars.'

'Wow. *[Not that thing, then.]*'

Bea pulled yet another skein from her bag. What next? Blanket? Bonnet? Cable stitched spirit animal?

But the wool was coarse and the colour of beetroot peelings. Probably not for the baby, then. Hopefully, not. It looked like it could deflect shrapnel.

'Cardigan for my husband,' Bea explained. 'He's been wearing the same frightful holey thing for years now, and it's time for a new one. I'll finish this and then patch up his old one and donate it to the Sallies.'

'Like the kids' picture book. Grandma donates the cardigan and Grandpa buys it back, not realising. *[My boys loved that book when they were little. Just think, all those sweet, funny baby books could come out agai— Dammit!]*'

'Perhaps the rubbish tip, then,' said Bea, thoughtfully. 'My loathing for that cardigan beats my loathing for unnecessary landfill.'

'Good morning, Sidney. Bea.'

It was Meredith Barton, Kerry's former employer. She was a

coolly aloof older woman whose fine bone structure and upright bearing lent style to the rural gentry uniform of navy jumper over a white blouse. The only flouting of tradition was in the absence of pearls, but she did have on a whacking great diamond ring that was probably worth more than Sidney's house.

Meredith picked up the radish seedlings.

'They're a super variety,' said Sidney, feeling a little like a Cockney barrow boy. 'Just the right amount of heat, and lots of crunch. *[Getchoor luverly radishes here!]*'

'Thank you. I'll take two punnets. And two of your broccoli, also.'

Sidney placed them in the trug Meredith had brought with her, took the proffered ten-dollar note, and recorded the transaction in the ledger. The plant collective took a twenty per cent profit, so that was a whole eight bucks she'd made today. At least the work with Bernard gave her a little more ballast, but if she kept the baby, could she do that work? Could she do *any* work? Gardening took time and physical effort, and beehives and babies were not exactly an ideal combination. She was going to help Mr Phipps after her shift here was over — perhaps she could ask if the bee suits came in infant sizes?

'Congratulations on your impending grandmother status,' Meredith said to Bea. 'Seems I, too, am about to join the ranks. Sophie's pregnant.'

Bea and Sidney murmured appropriate words while the universe wielded its joke mallet. *Bop! Squeak!*

'It was somewhat unexpected,' said Meredith, with a hint of acerbity. 'Especially since she and the father have recently separated.'

Meredith's relationship with her daughter had been what the more charitable might call rocky, though lately there had been a suspension of hostilities. Sidney suspected that truce might undergo strain if Sophie decided her parents were a convenient and free form of childcare.

'Oh, how lovely,' said Bea. 'You can be a hands-on grandmother.'

Judging by Meredith's expression, Sidney's suspicions were well founded.

And how could she blame her? Sidney had meant what she'd said to Dr G — the prospect of re-living the last eleven years with another child genuinely dismayed her. All right, so this time she'd almost certainly have more help. But *eleven years*! It felt like a miracle that she and the boys had got this far without major calamity, and now they'd made it, she had the end in sight. Not that she wanted to push them out the door; that thought dismayed her, too. But for them to be independent and, fingers crossed, mature — that point was only a few years in the distance. Could she really backtrack right to the start and do it all again?

No time to dwell. Here came the replacements to take the afternoon shift on the plant stall. Jill, practical and no-nonsense as her name in polar-fleece vest and gumboots, and the aforementioned Ianthe, in a hand-felted poncho and matching scarf. Exchanging a nod with Jill on her way out, Meredith eyed Ianthe with a lack of appreciation that made Sidney feel more cheerful than she had in days.

Sidney hopped up before Bea could tell Ianthe she was interested in putting pyramids on her head.

'Must be off,' she said. 'Bees await.'

And she hightailed it for the car, and the one person to whom she didn't have to lie for the simple reason that, bless his chunky woollen socks, he was as chatty as an Easter Island statue.

'And how was Titus yesterday?'

Friday, five-thirty. Bronagh had settled herself comfortably at Sidney's kitchen table with a glass of wine. Douglas was in the back garden with Rory and Aidan, possibly showing them how to blow stuff up. He'd make a wonderful grandfather, Sidney thought for the umpteenth time. The kind that transforms ordinary household items such as a piece of hollow pasta (she hadn't asked) into magic. Oh, well . . .

'Mr Phipps was as he always is,' Sidney replied. 'I think they should re-classify him as a geological formation.'

'Like those underground streams in Wales that no one's been able to track,' said Bronagh. 'Hidden depths, has our Titus Phipps.'

Sidney had to smile at the 'our'. After three weeks, Bronagh considered herself an honorary native of Gabriel's Bay. Fair enough; she had insisted on meeting absolutely everyone, and extracting from each of them every last ounce of personal information. Rumour had it she'd even found out why Mac was called Mac, a secret known only to Mac herself and a handful of people who would never tell owing to them valuing being alive.

'And how are the bees?' Bronagh added. 'Busy?'

'Actually, no,' Sidney said. 'Not a lot happening at the moment. It's girls-only in the hive still — poor old drones got booted out months back. So all Mr Phipps and I are doing is getting the equipment ready for spring, and making sure they have enough food.'

'I'd make an excellent bee,' said Bronagh. 'Very fond of routine, I am. And nectar-type fluids.'

She downed a decent glug of wine.

'You're still off the booze?' she said to Sidney. 'No progress in diagnosing your — condition?'

Oh, God, Bronagh knew!!! That slight pause was a dead giveaway.

Unless she was suppressing a burp. Sidney began to pray that it *was* wind, even though the idea of it only made her think of babies.

'No progress yet.'

Sidney kept her expression neutral, even while convinced a neon sign above her head was flashing giant pink words: 'UP THE DUFF!'

Bronagh was about to speak, but the sound of the front door being heaved open by a shoulder (it stuck in damp weather) focused her attention on the imminent arrival of her only son. Sidney blessed Kerry's excellent timing. With luck, he and Bronagh would now chat for hours and she could fade into the background along with Douglas, a man who rivalled Titus Phipps for the world record of fewest words uttered by a human in possession of a functioning voice box.

'Hello, all.'

Kerry dropped a large, greasy paper parcel on the kitchen bench, then stooped to kiss his mother.

'Hitting the sauce already, I see, Ma.'

'I'm on holiday,' she said. 'I'll go back on my strict regime soon as I'm home.'

'Nipping on gripe water in the supplies closet?'

Kerry winked at Sidney, and bent to kiss her, too. He wafted with him the smell of the deep fryer, and Sidney felt her gorge rise. Poor bloke. He didn't deserve a girlfriend who gagged when he came near. He didn't deserve a lot of what she was doing to him. Perhaps she should just spit it out this evening, so to speak? After the boys had gone to bed? Bronagh would be a support, Sidney knew that. Douglas, too, in his way.

But, oh, so many questions still lacking answers. So many hurdles and objections, and no clear way around them. And the *effort* that would be involved in the subsequent discussions. Sidney was hitting the sack before nine these days, but if she spilled the beans, she'd be up till midnight.

No, she wasn't ready. Not yet. Soon.

'The boys are outside with your father,' she told Kerry. 'I'm not sure what they're doing, but it involves a preserving jar, pasta, yeast, matches and a bottle of something Douglas sneaked in with him.'

'Oh, the rocket,' said Bronagh. 'That's a great gas. Occasional loss of eyebrows, but nothing that won't grow back.'

On cue, Rory and Aidan hurtled in through the back door. Sidney checked — two eyebrows each. Good news.

'We made a flame *this high*!'

Rory indicated the ceiling.

'Dur,' said his one-year-older and therefore much more sophisticated brother. 'It was, like, two inches.'

Douglas wandered quietly in, looking exactly like a man capable of making a rocket out of pasta.

'Have you showed them the bouncing egg trick?' Kerry asked him. 'So simple when you know how,' he added, wistfully.

'And undoubtedly a mess when you don't,' said Sidney. 'Right, boys, chop, chop. Hands washed, then straight back to the table. Wait until the adults have helped themselves. And no squabbling over who gets how many chips.'

Mercifully, it was only eight when Bronagh announced she and Douglas should be getting on back to Willow Cottage. The boys were cleaning their teeth, readying for bed, and now Sidney wouldn't have to be far behind them.

'We promised Vic we'd watch Graham Norton with him,' Bronagh explained. 'He does love that show. Watches it wide-eyed.'

'How *is* Vic?' said Sidney.

Everyone in town knew about the website now. But no one yet was saying if they knew who was behind it.

Bronagh's face clouded, an expression so unlike her usual that Sidney's mouth fell open.

'To be honest, I'm quite concerned,' Bronagh said. 'I don't

think he's been entirely frank with me when I've asked how things are going. I suspect his finances are banjaxed, and that it's only going to get worse.'

'How much worse?' Kerry said. 'Riding boxcars and lining up at soup kitchens worse?'

'Don't joke,' said his mother. 'Farming is more than Vic's job — it's his life. If he had to stop doing it, well . . .'

'Sorry, Ma.' Kerry was sober now. 'Is there anything we can do?'

'Keep an eye on him?' said Bronagh. 'Without making it obvious?'

'Easy,' said Sidney. 'Even if Vic does twig, he'll be too polite to tell us to piss off.'

Kerry fetched his car keys, ready to drive them back.

'I might hang round and watch Graham with you all, do a bit of uncomfortable male bonding. You don't mind, do you?' he said to Sidney.

'Of course not. [*In fact, I'd much prefer to be alone with my guilty thoughts.*]'

He kissed her on the cheek. 'I'll give Vic your regards.'

Poor Vic, Sidney thought, after she'd waved them out and shut the door. She hoped Bronagh was worrying unnecessarily. Financial problems were the *worst*. Well, perhaps second worst . . .

Nope, the worst, because a lack of money made *everything* harder. And Vic hadn't struck her as man who was fully in charge of life. He might well let the situation get to the point where he ran out of options. Sidney knew what being down that low felt like, and wouldn't wish it on her bitterest enemy.

But, then again, it was kind of comforting to know she wasn't the only one suffering mental torment. And if she hustled the boys, she could be in bed by eight-thirty.

Yes, indeed, you should take your small blessings where you found them.

CHAPTER 21

Four more days and Bronagh and Douglas would fly back to the UK. The relief that he would once again be alone was diminished by the regret that Vic would, once again, be alone. Despite her nightly interrogations, Bronagh had been a comforting presence. Douglas, too. And who else could fix things like he could? Certainly not Vic.

But there were things he wouldn't miss. Being forced to socialise. Having strangers in his house. Being forced to watch Graham Norton. Vic had done his best to be polite when Kerry had stayed to watch TV with them on Friday, though he was kicking himself for not scarpering to his room before Bronagh and Douglas arrived back. One night of watching a cavorting, camp Irishman was bad enough, but two weeks in a row? All right, the bloke told some good jokes, and the blonde actress he interviewed was very attractive. But that didn't make up for the fact Vic's skin crawled every time Mr Norton opened his mouth.

Thing was, Vic could truthfully say he didn't actually give a toss how people acted or chose to present themselves. Otto Visser dyed his hair and wore floral-patterned shirts and he was a top bloke. Even Jacko Reid wore a frilled apron when he worked. Mind you, not even Rob Hanrahan would dare rib him for that.

Which meant Vic was probably right in thinking he'd learned the cringe response from his dad, who hadn't even liked it when

Dick Emery did his 'Oh, you are awful' skit. Would it have been different if Vic had been brought up by his mother, too? If he'd had a nurturing female influence?

But would he and his mum have been anything like Kerry and Bronagh, who talked like they were best friends as well as mother and son? He had memories of his mum listening to him, her face down low to be on the same level, her eyes and smile genuine, interested, even though it was likely that what he was telling her was childish nonsense. Maybe just the fact he was sharing what he felt was important was enough for it to be important to her. Because she loved him.

Kerry and Bronagh's affection for each other had obviously never faded. It shone in every word, every gesture, even when they were peeved. No wonder Douglas never spoke much; he never had to. His family may have been made from eccentric parts, like a Heath Robinson, but it was a functioning whole. The Macfarlane family didn't need fixing, so Douglas could sit back and let them get on with it. Vic couldn't help feeling envious.

Mind you, Bronagh had been acting like a mother to Vic the last few days. She had been fussing around, making sure his pantry was stocked and his laundry done, and asking him what he'd be working on once they left, who he'd be spending time with, when he intended to do the grocery shopping. If she'd whipped out her hanky and spit-washed his face, Vic wouldn't have been surprised.

Vic gave the kind of answers he always did, short and factual. He was heading up to calving with lambing hard on its heels, so that'd keep him on his toes. Yes, he'd be getting some help in soon. He'd go down the rugby club once or twice a week, see his mates. He was meeting up with the other farmers about the legal action they had planned to take down the website. Yep, the lawyer was hopeful they'd have a result soon.

Bronagh seemed happy enough with what he told her. Vic

guessed she was concerned that he'd become a recluse after they left, foregoing personal hygiene, and subsisting on a diet of bacon, eggs and white bread. Which didn't sound all that bad to Vic, if he were to be honest. But no need to mention that to Bronagh. She wanted to leave knowing that Vic would be busy and reasonably social, and Vic could assure her of that, without even crossing his fingers behind his back.

And because his answers seemed to satisfy her, Vic was also spared mentioning a lot of auxiliary detail. Such as the fact the body condition scores of his pregnant cows were worryingly low. Even though his Angus breeders could survive on pretty poor pasture, thanks to the drought, too many of them hadn't recovered enough of the liveweight they'd lost after weaning. If their scores dropped any lower, they might not be strong enough at calving, which would almost certainly mean more dead calves. But Vic couldn't afford supplementary feed, not even silage. He had hay, but he was worried about how it was keeping in the damp. Mouldy hay had given him trouble before — cows ate fungus that led to abortions. He was probably past the main risk period for that, but still, it was a worry. If the body condition scores dropped any more, though, he'd have no choice. The best pasture he had at the moment was the worst for calving, full of gullies, holes and creeks, all hazards that would claim calf lives. Then there might be a repeat of the rotavirus outbreak. He had no budget for an extra farm hand, and even if he did stay up all night treating sick calves, there's no way he'd save them all. He'd promised the bank he'd meet a certain calving target, but there seemed endless ways the Goddess of Fortune could conspire to bugger up his plans.

Bronagh also need not know of the other fly in the bugger-up ointment — the possible end to his standing arrangement with Otto Visser. Otto had much easier, flatter land, and so he bought young cattle to finish, to fatten up mainly for export, and sold good quality bulls back to farmers like Vic, whose harder hill country land meant they could only run breeding herds. Vic and Otto had done a deal every year, which was one less thing for Vic to have to organise. But Otto, incensed by the bloody website, had put his farm on the market. He'd been thinking about retiring, anyway — like Vic, he had no family to pass the farm to. Despite being Dutch, Otto had always been generous to Vic. With Otto gone, Vic might struggle to get the same price. He was a terrible negotiator. Terrible, too, at picking the right time to sell his lambs. Last lot had finished late, again thanks to the drought, so he had to settle for what he could get — i.e. sweet fuck all. The business of farming seemed to get tougher and more complicated every year, and Vic knew he was slipping behind. He should probably do a course or something. All these smart young grads coming out of Lincoln and Massey with multiple degrees, tech savvy and full of new ideas. Vic knew what he knew from a lifetime of observing his father and then doing it himself. It didn't seem fair that that wasn't enough.

It didn't seem fair that he'd been singled out by whoever the bastard was who'd set up that website. His first conclusion was that it was one of the Wood Sprites, and he'd been all set to go down there and order them off at gunpoint, this time making sure that they *did* leave, instead of ignoring him completely, which seemed to be their preferred response to date. But Tai Te Wera, the young, handsome lawyer, seemed to believe that the Sprites were anti-tech and pro-peace. He suspected a more sophisticated operation of environmental protestors was behind it. Tai had assured the group of farmers that progress was being made, but the website was still up there for all to see.

A further detail Vic could omit mentioning to Bronagh was that every time the phone rang, he assumed it was the council, giving him official notice to clean up his act or pay a hefty fine.

So far, the callers had only been Otto, Tai Te Wera and a foreign bloke who insisted his Windows needed upgrading because it had viruses. Vic felt faulty software might provide a useful excuse of the kind that started with 'a virus ate my emails', so he told the bloke that he was perfectly happy with that situation and hung up.

It was possible that the council was working through an alphabeticised list of the website's 'accused' and hadn't yet got to H. It was also possible they'd be the very next caller. Vic did not think it was likely they'd phone in the middle of the night, but his brain kindly made sure he stayed awake, so as to be ready if they did.

'Are you sleeping OK, Vic?' Bronagh had asked him. 'Thought I saw a light on when I got up for a wee last night.'

'Midnight snack,' Vic replied.

No need to mention it had been two beers. Wasn't like he'd make a habit of it, was it?

Besides, she'd be glad to believe he was eating. During her stay, Vic had obeyed her command to come back to his house for a proper lunch, the makings of which she made sure were in the pantry and fridge, or on the stovetop, waiting to be re-heated. Today, there was split pea soup and two crusty brown loaves, without seeds, Vic was pleased to see. As Bronagh and Douglas were out touring the local arts and crafts vendors, he could always dig out the white bread and mop up the last of the soup with a couple of well buttered slices.

Vic heard a tentative rap on the back door. Shit. The council? Surely, they'd sound more official. Besides, it was Saturday. Only farmers and other minimum wage earners worked Saturdays. Then again, perhaps they liked to catch people off guard. He squared his shoulders, brushed pea soup off his jumper, and went to face the music.

'Hey.'

It was only Rua, the Wood Sprite, squinting as if embarrassed, his dreadlocks dusty in the light.

'What can I do for you?' said Vic, who didn't really want to know.

'Um—' Rua lifted his shoulders. 'Can I come in? It's kind of cold out here.'

As Vic let the young bloke into the kitchen, he wondered how he coped, living in a draughty tarp hut. There was the fire pit, he supposed, and perhaps Rua shared his bed with a warm lady friend? Vic didn't know much about the Wood Sprites' personal lives. He just assumed that everyone but him was attached. Even Darius, who was no oil painting, not even one of those splatter abstracts that looked like the aftermath of Prawns Masala.

'Tea?' Vic offered, as Rua took a seat at the table.

'Is it green?'

'More a very dark brown.'

'No, thanks,' said Rua. 'Too many tannins. They cause cancer.'

Vic leaned against the kitchen bench, folded his arms. 'What doesn't?'

As Rua seemed keen to provide a lengthy answer to that, Vic pre-empted him.

'What did you want? I need to get back out on the farm. Busy time.'

Rua wouldn't quite meet his eye. Started to fiddle with the old Temuka saltshaker that had belonged to Vic's mother. It was the colour of a cowpat, and its hole clogged after one shake, making it effectively useless as a condiment dispenser, but Vic could never think about replacing it. Silently, he wished Rua would leave it alone. If it broke, Vic had no idea how he'd react, and in this case, ignorance was not a comfort.

Rua squinted up at Vic, even though the light outside the kitchen window barely made it through the glass.

'Um, look,' he said. 'We — well, Darius, me and a couple of the others, we wanted to let you know we're not responsible for that website. It wasn't us.'

He paused, but Vic had nothing to say. What difference did it make who was behind it?

'I mean, we support keeping the water clean, and not ruining the land and all that, but we would never—'

'Hold on.'

Vic's brain rewound until he found the phrase that troubled him. 'Ruining the land?'

'Yeah, you know.' Rua seemed surprised to have to explain. 'Wiping out native vegetation, and killing the native species that live in it. Deforestation and changing the course of rivers and all that. They reckon all this new intensive farming is creating the worst bio-diversity crisis since European colonisation.'

'My farm's been here since 1849,' said Vic.

'Yeah, since then,' said Rua.

Vic had to be quite sure. 'You think I'm ruining the land?'

Rua screwed up his face, as if he'd finally realised he might be giving offence.

'Well, maybe not your farm so much because you're quite small, aren't you? You haven't got as many animals, or as much grass to fertilise, so your impact isn't that big, I guess. But those big corporate farms, they don't give a shit about the environment. It's all about production targets and profits. And more and more of our farming is going that way these days. It's not sustainable.'

Vic was torn. Part of him felt deeply insulted. In fact, he felt insulted on behalf of every one of his antecedents, back to the very first Halsworth who emigrated from somewhere in Sussex. This whippersnapper, who'd never done a hard day's work in his life, was tarring them and every other good farmer with the same sticky, black brush. The folk whose output still formed the backbone of the country's economy were being treated like pariahs by yuppies and lefties, labelled callous opportunists motivated only by short-term greed.

Not all farmers had integrity, sure, but the ones Vic knew cared deeply about the land. They, as he did, saw themselves as guardians of it, taking the baton from the past and handing it to the future. Many were ardent conservationists, doing their best to preserve and protect, because their land was a part of who they were. Defined them as much as they'd shaped it.

But another part of Vic agreed with the lad. Farming *was* more commercial these days, and smaller operators like him *were* being pushed out and under by those big corporate enterprises, who could do everything faster, better, cheaper. No matter how hard he worked, Vic would never be able to farm as successfully as his forebears, and that felt like letting them down. Part of him knew he'd been hit by bad luck — weather, disease, events not entirely under his control. But the rest, well, the buck had to stop somewhere and that could only be with him. The farm's failure was his failure, and his alone.

'So, yeah.' Rua finally set the saltshaker back on the table, nudged it carefully back into position. 'We just wanted you to know we didn't have anything to do with it.'

He wasn't a bad lad. How could Vic blame him for lamenting that bare paddocks had usurped lush native bush? What was wrong with caring that snails and lizards and species of grass were disappearing, never to be seen again? That the majority of our rivers and streams were no longer fit to drink? Vic didn't like that, either.

'Thanks for letting me know,' said Vic. 'I appreciate it. Are you sure you don't want a cup of something? I might have some Milo in the cupboard.'

'Nah, that's OK. Better get back. Stuff to do.'

Rua stood up, tugged his sleeves down over his hands in preparation for going back out in the cold. Vic felt a stab of disappointment. He wouldn't have minded a chat, a chance to ask what the lad meant by 'stuff', how he lived, day to day. The Wood Sprites' philosophies might be alien to Vic, but when you boiled it down, they were just ordinary folk who wanted to live decent, wholesome lives, free of the hustle, bustle and stress of the modern world. A lot like Vic, in fact.

But fair enough. Vic was ruining that life for them. Or at least forcing them to shift it elsewhere. Coming here was a generous gesture, but that would be as far as it went. The Wood Sprites would not visit him again. With luck, they'd be true to their word and not protest, but pack up and go peacefully, before Vic even had to show his face.

'OK, well, thanks again,' said Vic.

And he shut the door behind the lad, who had a good half hour's walk back to his camp, over paddocks that still contained untouched stands of native bush, should he care to observe them.

The silence was as much a presence in the air as the yeasty smell of pea soup. And Vic finally understood what really bothered him about Graham bloody Norton. It wasn't the skipping and shiny blazers; he didn't give a damn about those. No, it was the unquestioning acceptance of openness and intimacy. Even though any idiot could see that no real secrets were being spilled, you were still given an impression of friendly collusion. Graham and his chums, was how it came across, chatting easily, frankly, humorously and without shame about personal stuff. Vic had never had a conversation like that in his life, with anyone. He wasn't sure he could.

Even Bronagh, who had extracted his entire life story in all its mostly boring detail, didn't know how he felt about events in his life beyond the standard reactions of sad, angry or disappointed.

Vic had been brought up to believe there was no point in harping on about your emotions. What good did it do you, other than to prolong the discomfort? And make other people think you were losing your grip? Failing? Most of the rugby club already saw him as a bit of a saddo — Vic No-Wife. How would they look at him if he suddenly poured out his heart? They'd back away, clutching their beers, and quietly instruct the barman to turn up the stereo.

When Bronagh and Douglas left, Vic would have no one to talk to at all. No one who would lend a friendly ear, and offer advice without judgement. He'd be alone in the house, with only ghosts for company. The last of the Halsworths. End of the line.

Looking back, he could see them all, his father, grandfather, and sepia-toned ancestors. Big men, hard working, determined to succeed. Looking ahead, all he could see was a black void, an abyss of nothingness that was only a step away, waiting for him to make his move.

CHAPTER 22

Devon

'God-*dammit*, Emma! Just — gahhh!'

Devon shook the newspaper at her, too angry to form words.

'I didn't ask her to write it,' Emma replied. 'She picked it up off my blog site, ran with it all on her lonesome.'

'For fuck's sake, isn't that some breach of privacy?'

'Sorry, man. If it's online, it's fair game.'

'But it says where I *work*. How did she find *that* out?'

'You're on the Lightning Tree website, doofus. Under "Our Team". Plus, you're in the photo that went with that restaurant review of Dad's place. Don't need a Deep Throat to help bring those facts to light.'

'If you weren't her friend, though, she wouldn't have seen that stupid online personal ad, would she? You told her!'

'Might have mentioned it in passing. As you do when an old pal says, "So what've you been up to?"'

'An old pal who's a *journalist*!'

'Dev, seriously — chill,' said Emma. 'It's one small article in a weekend paper full of crappy stories. It'll be lining cat litter trays by tomorrow.'

'It's not an article about *you*, goddammit!'

Devon jumped to his feet — a rash move that made his still-bruised glute muscle twinge — screwed up the offending newspaper, and shoved it in along with the empty fish and chip wrapper in the Boat Shed's wheelie bin. It took some effort, the bin being already full, and the exertion helped work off some of the steam. Only some, mind. Didn't help that his so-called friend appeared in no way apologetic. *And* she'd made him pay for the fish and chips, too, even though she'd been the one to invite *him*.

Devon was too shitty to sit back down with her on the Boat Shed steps. He stood looking out at the ocean, arms folded tight, because he was tense and because it was bloody cold.

'Why are you so ticked off?' she said behind him.

Unbelievable.

'Oh, *I* don't know,' he said. 'Maybe the five million gleeful texts and calls that are probably queuing up right now in my phone. Maybe the smirks and wise-ass comments I'll get for the next three hundred years. Maybe the fact I'm enough of a public curiosity already without this shit. Now, I'll be freak of the freaking century.'

'And then again, maybe it will do what it was intended to — find you a Ms Right.'

He couldn't fault the relentless quality of her optimism. Couldn't share it, either.

'Yeah? Any likely candidates so far?'

'A few.'

He turned to face her, held out his hand for her phone.

'Let me see them, then.'

She shook her head.

'No way, José, I'm still whittling down the shortlist. You'll see them when I'm ready. Who knows? Might get a whole bunch more now the article's out.'

'Ferrrk . . .'

Devon breathed out and tried not to picture how it'd go down at work this evening. Gene Collins wasn't a Saturday regular, but no doubt he'd make a special effort. And Brownie would be in later on — another movie night planned, mainly because the two of them couldn't think of anything better to do, and movies meant they didn't have to talk to each other for a couple of hours, which suited them fine. Tonight's classic '80s movie was *Cherry 2000*, about a guy in the future searching for a replacement sex android because his one fried its circuits. Thirty years on, Japanese were making pretty lifelike sex dolls — some dudes even took them out to the park or the beach. Maybe he should save up for one of those. Be way less complicated, if you didn't count getting the thing serviced.

Devon felt Emma's hand slide around his waist and her head lean against his shoulder. He could shove her away but what was the point? Emma deflected anger like she was surrounded by an anti-rage force field. Words, vibes, shirty looks — they all bounced off, ping, pong, pyow! Nothing penetrated. All you did was waste breath and energy.

And she genuinely believed she was doing him a favour, being a good friend. She was convinced she'd find Devon's perfect match — and maybe she would? He wouldn't hold his breath, but he also couldn't deny that Emma had a way of getting what she wanted.

'So what are you up to besides turning my life into a circus?' he said. 'Everything OK?'

'Everything's great,' she said. 'Got paid work for another couple of weeks. Shitty job, but you know. Harry's car hasn't shat itself. Mum and Dad are in fine form. My eye healed up, thank God. Having a drink with Doctor G next Friday.'

Devon jumped from her as if she'd jabbed him in the ribs.

'You *what?*'

He scrutinised her face for telltale signs of wind-up. 'You're shitting me, right?'

'Nope. He asked me. I said yes.'

'But — you've got a bloke. Or has that gone kaput?'

'We're not exclusive,' she said.

'Yeah, but does Dr G know you're shagging someone else?'

'Who says I'm going to shag Dr G?'

He'll certainly be hoping, thought Devon, but decided to keep schtum.

'It's just a drink,' Emma went on. 'He's cute, but a bit soft and squishy. Not really my type.'

'Why'd you say yes then?'

Translation: why did she get Dr G's hopes up?

'He's cute. It's nice to be asked. I'm a free bird and all that jazz.'

'Where's he taking you?'

'Somewhere flash, I hope. I'll have to dig out a dress. Or borrow one.'

'Is this public knowledge?'

'Yeah, I guess,' said Emma. 'I mean, I don't think he's told Mum, but why would you? Who needs that kind of pain and humiliation?'

Honestly, her ability to un-see screaming irony was almost cute.

Devon checked his watch. 'Time for work.'

'Bit of a sigh there, buddy,' said Emma. 'You over the old hospo biz?'

'Nah, just been working an extra evening while Sidney's off sick. Tiring, plus it plays merry hell with my study. Got a three thousand word assignment due end of next week. Haven't started it.'

'You'll nail it.' Emma clapped him on the shoulder. 'You always were the smart one.'

Yet as he said goodbye, Devon knew he wasn't the one who took risks and made things happen. He'd noted she hadn't fessed up to the farmer-shaming website, but then, why would she? It was probably top secret work for some top secret activist group, and even though he was no fan of extremists and considered their anonymous palaver a bunch of self-important wank, for a moment, Devon felt envious. Even if Emma's activities were of questionable merit, she still lived a way more interesting life.

Oh well. Devon pushed open the Boat Shed back door. Maybe some amazing chick would come out of the woodwork and make his dreams come true. Yeah, and maybe Gene Collins wouldn't give him shit for the rest of his natural life.

He checked what Jacko had in the ovens. Pigs. No wings visible. Devon went out front and braced himself for what would no doubt be a very long evening.

———

'So I'd appreciate it if you didn't say one word about a certain article,' Devon told Brownie, on the drive to Hampton's cinema. 'Or I might be forced to punch you in the face.'

'How *are* those kick-boxing lessons going?' said Brownie.

'Apparently, I have issues achieving a state of calm.'

'Don't we all?'

Devon gave him a sideways look. 'What's up with you?'

'Nothing that wouldn't be fixed by a hammer blow to the temple.'

Devon didn't know whether he meant himself or someone else. Decided he didn't want to find out.

The queue for movie tickets was short, comprising as it did of just him and Brownie. Then a hand tapped him on the shoulder.

'Hey there,' said Moana. Her eyes checked over Brownie. 'What are you two fullas doing at a feminist classic?'

'Is that what it is?' said Devon.

'Nah, not really,' said Mo. 'But Melanie Griffith is pretty bad ass.'

She stuck out her hand to Brownie.

'I'm Moana. Devon's favourite colleague.'

Brownie shook her hand, amused. 'I'm Barrett. Devon's barely tolerated acquaintance.'

Moana smiled wide, as if her evening had suddenly got way more interesting.

'I'll sit between you jokers then. Keep the peace. Good thing I got a large popcorn. Might even let you share some.'

And she linked arms with Brownie, much to Devon's irritation, and led him into the cinema. Devon followed, face like a smacked bum, as his mum would say.

The movie was shit. Soon as the credits started to roll, Devon exited. Didn't wait to see if Mo and Brownie were ready to go, just went. Hung outside on the street, waiting for them, even though it was dog bollock freezing.

'OK, you ready?' He jinked the car keys in his palm, soon as Brownie appeared.

'What's the rush?' said Mo. 'Night's young, and so are we.'

Yeah, and she just wanted to get with Brownie. Devon didn't know why that irked him so much. Perhaps because Brownie was on the right side of handsome, whereas he was way over on the freakish far side? Perhaps because he considered Mo *his* friend? OK, sure, they never hung out, but they got on well at work, didn't they?

'What did you have in mind?' said Brownie.

'Well, despite my night is young promise, nothing exciting,' said Mo. 'Cuppa at my place?' She hooked her thumb. 'I'm five minutes' walk thataway.'

Brownie caught Devon's eye.

'What do you want to do? You're the one with the heavy workload.'

Goddammit, he was being thoughtful. Probably doing it to impress, smooth bastard, but still, Devon couldn't be shirty in return without looking like a total arse.

He shoved the car keys back in his jacket pocket.

'Yeah, OK.'

Instinct made him duck as a vision of his Kuia Agnes appeared, hand poised, instructing him to remember his manners.

'Thanks, Mo,' he added.

On the way to her place, Devon realised he had no idea where she lived. Or with whom. In fact, when it came down to it, all he knew was her name, her age, and that she'd been living in the King Country before coming to Hampton, but her iwi was further north. He had no idea about her family or where she'd spent her childhood, because that wasn't what they talked about at work. All they'd discussed was horses, obviously, and subjects like if Jase got kicked in the head, would anyone notice, and could Immy lift a car off a person if she had to? They traded the usual insults. Fun stuff. Nothing personal. Nothing intimate. Why? Did Mo not trust him or like him enough to talk about her life?

Devon wondered if Mo would tell Brownie her life story. Probably. Because Brownie was handsome, and *thought-ful*. His brain pronounced it in a spiteful little singsong, which made him immediately ashamed. He really was being a prize Grinch. Why was that? Oh, yeah. He'd now been humiliated in the mainstream media as well as online.

'Here we are,' said Mo. 'Tāku kāinga.'

''Pai tō whare,' said Devon.

Switching between English and te reo Māori happened all the time at home. Though you had to be mindful of which was expected when, or you might get a swift, exquisitely painful reminder in the form of one of Kuia Agnes' infamous ear-tweaks.

Mo's house was a cute villa. In the porchlight, Devon saw a pale grey front door with white trim, and what should become roses on either side, unless the owners liked pots full of jaggy brown sticks.

Inside, it was warm, tasteful and tidy. Lots of art — good stuff, too. Nice thick rugs, and furniture that had definitely not been bought from the Sallies Family Store. Devon's family were comfortably off compared to others, but he knew real money when he saw it. And he hadn't expected to see it in conjunction with Moana, who generally looked like she'd slept in the stables. But maybe she knew the owners?

'This must cost a bomb to rent,' he said.

'Who says I rent it?'

She was smiling at him.

'Lucky you, then. Owners friends of yours?'

'You could say that.'

Devon followed her into the kitchen. Old-fashioned with modern touches. Miele appliances. Le Creuset pans above the stove. A shiny coffee machine. The proper kind. Not a Nespresso.

'Tea or coffee?' Mo asked him. 'Or beer? I think I've got some in the fridge.'

'Tea, thanks. Gotta do some serious assignment writing to-morrow.'

'You?'

Mo was talking to Brownie, who, of course, was still with them. He'd been so quiet, Devon had forgotten for a sweet half a second.

'Same.' Brownie sounded subdued. 'Thanks.'

Mo got the tea out of the cupboard. Leaves, not bags. With flash packaging. The teapot she fetched looked Japanese and matched the mugs. Devon would bet the beer she had in the fridge was craft stuff with a weirdo name. Certainly not good old Lion Brown. Owners of this place probably ate homemade muesli for breakfast, too, the kind with Super-seeds and Bat-berries that cost fifty bucks a gram.

'Miraka, huka māu?' Moana asked.

'Miraka noa iho,' said Devon.

'He aha māu, "Mister Acquaintance?"'

Brownie didn't answer. Like Devon, he'd taken a chair at the kitchen table, but he was sitting half on, half off, as if preparing to leg it. He wasn't looking at them, either, but out the window, where there was nothing to see owing to it being two am.

Moana snapped her fingers. Did the trick.

'Apologies,' said Brownie.

Might be the light, but he looked kind of ill.

Mo obviously thought so, too. 'You OK?'

Brownie righted himself in the chair, chest expanding as he breathed in.

'I don't speak it.'

'What?' said Mo. 'Te reo?'

'My mother did, but my father didn't,' Brownie replied. 'That's why she never taught me. She didn't want my father to feel excluded. Or like he was a failure.'

Devon's woo-wah pinged again, but the warning was redundant. He knew exactly what was swimming below the surface, because it'd been his own constant companion for too long. Brownie wasn't upset or ill. He was furious.

But he wasn't about to let it out any time soon, because that was Brownie's thing wasn't it? Being Mr Cool.

'Why can't she teach you now?' said Mo.

Ah, shit. But there was no way Devon could have warned her.

'She's dead,' said Brownie.

Mo nodded. 'Aroha mai, ka aroha. Losing your māmā is *hard*.'

Then, with a breezy tactlessness that reminded Devon of Emma, she added, 'Do you still want to learn? I'll teach ya.'

Devon bristled, but Brownie was shaking his head.

'Thanks, but it'll take more than that.'

Typical reply. Brownie was like one of those annoying Facebook friends who post some cryptic comment about not wanting to talk about it, forcing everyone to ask if they're OK.

'Take more than that to make you feel like a real Māori?' said Mo.

Yep, she definitely reminded Devon of Emma. Zero tolerance for BS. Try it on and you'd get called out, and if you didn't like it, too bad.

Brownie didn't like it, Devon was pleased to see. First time his smooth façade showed signs of cracking.

'Is anyone a real Māori these days?' he said to her. 'Or are we all mongrels?'

'Bro, what does *that* matter?' said Mo, with a laugh. 'I might have whiteys in my whakapapa, but far as I'm concerned, I'm Hori through and through. Anyone who thinks blood dictates identity is a racist fuckwit.'

'We get smacked for saying Hori in my house,' said Devon. 'Except for when Uncle Hori comes to visit. Still usually just call him Uncle, though.'

'High *five*, my brother.'

Moana's palm connected with his, and Devon felt a ridiculously over-the-top sense of gratification.

'And I guess Devon here's living proof of your point?'

Brownie's remark might have sounded offhand, but Devon could clearly hear the snap of angry jaws below. Devon understood. Whānau, whakapapa, te reo, tikanga — how would he feel if they weren't an integral part of his life?

And he'd sympathise with the dude — if Brownie weren't being so goddamn patronising.

'You listen to the gossipmongers, do you?' he said.

Brownie had the grace to look embarrassed.

'There's goss about you?' said Moana, for whom embarrassment was a foreign concept. 'Is it juicy?'

'Nah, it's pathetic,' said Devon. 'You know — I was swapped at birth. My mum shagged around.'

'And?' said Mo.

'Seriously?'

'We're fighting a war against fact-deniers, man,' she said. 'Gotta play your part.'

'Facts, OK . . .' Devon breathed deep. 'One: I wasn't a hospital mix-up because I was born at home surrounded by whānau doing the full haputanga. Had eyes on me until I was big enough to walk to school on my own. Two: Mum is staunch about fidelity. She thinks having affairs is a sign of a weak character. If Dad ever played away, she'd kick his sorry arse to the kerb. That enough for you?'

Moana grinned, delighted. 'Your whānau sound like they totally rock,' she said. 'Can I come meet them?'

Shit, she was *just* like Emma. No way you could stay angry at her. Plus, his family loved Emma, and he didn't doubt for a second that they'd love Moana, too.

'Sure. Any time.'

Then he almost choked on his tea as Moana said to Brownie, 'You should come, too. You need more Māori friends than just us.'

'I'm flattered you consider me a friend,' Brownie said, in his superior way. Devon's hackles were up and down like a rough sea. 'You might want to actually get to know me before confirming that.'

'Nah, I've got good instincts,' said Mo.

Devon could *not* let this pass.

'His mates have all left town,' he said. 'Gone to better lives in the big cities. Oh, yeah, except Deano. He's in witness protection.'

'Witness *protection*?' Mo was agog. '*Hard* out. Whaddid he do?'

'He testified against a gang drug syndicate,' said Devon.

Knife was in. Might as well wiggle it around.

'How come *you* got prison?' he said to Brownie. 'Why didn't you get the same deal?'

'Wait, *you* were involved with a drug gang, too?' Moana's lip (finally!) was curling. 'Why the heck would you be that stupid?'

Brownie gave Devon a steady look that made him feel instantly ashamed. The guy had needed money to look after his sick father when his mother died. OK, so he'd chosen a dumb way to get it, but that didn't make his intention any less worthy. Devon should stop being a total arse.

But then Moana reached out and fist-bumped Brownie's arm. Gently. Like she cared about him.

'Come on,' she said. 'Tell me it's all in the past, and you're living the good life now.'

'Sure,' said Brownie. 'I've got a job and a place to live. For now, anyway. My father's in fully subsidised care. So really, the only downsides are a criminal record and the ever-present threat of violent retribution.'

'Sarcasm sucks, bro,' said Moana. 'And, OK, you've been a dick, but you're young and you're cute, and if you stopped talking like you had a white-people's dictionary shoved up your arse, you could be like a super Māori.'

Brownie's smile was hitched up, like he couldn't decide whether to continue being pissed off, or give in and laugh out loud. Devon found he was wishing for the former. Moana would soon lose patience with a pissed-off Brownie.

But, of course, the dude laughed. 'You've got it all sorted, haven't you?'

'Shit, no,' said Moana. 'I'm making it up as I go along. But so far so good.'

She lifted her mug of tea as if it were a wine glass to toast with.

'Here's to friends, making it up, and not being a dick.'

As the three of them clinked mugs, Devon saw Brownie and Moana lock eyes.

Goddammit. The realisation shot through him like an arrow. Brownie wasn't the man for Moana. *He* was. *That's* why he'd been so shitty.

But because he'd been *so* stupidly damn slow to work it out, it was already too late. Mr Right-side-of-handsome had won the girl, and Devon was out in the cold again. A loser before he'd even realised he was in the game. God*dammit*.

And just to rub it in, now he had to chauffeur the smug bastard home.

CHAPTER 23

Emma

'Hey, there.'

Gene pulled out a chair at the corner table Emma had commandeered at the Crown, otherwise known as the worst pub in the universe.

He peered at her.

'Wow, looking sour. Wanna turn that frown upside down?'

'Were you born annoying?' Emma said. 'Or did you take lessons?'

'Are you referring to my Honorary degree from the Academy of Arse-Hattery?'

Despite her mood, Emma had to smile. She'd known Gene all her life, and admired how he could push the limits of people's tolerance and yet remain on their good side. He and her dad had met at primary school, and although Gene made her dad's neck veins bulge at least twice every conversation, they remained firm friends. Perhaps it was true, and opposites did attract? In that case, she and Dr G should have a wild old time this Friday. But even if the evening was a dud, it couldn't be worse than the rest of her week was shaping up to be.

'Why did you want to meet in this dump?' Emma asked.

She glanced around the Crown's so-called lounge bar. Dark wood, faded signs for beer brands that were last available in 1973 (Leopard Continental Lager, anyone?), a pool table with baize so torn it was more like a mini-golf course, and a carpet that looked and felt underfoot like the inside of a long-discarded pizza box. At five-thirty, the employed punters were starting to shuffle in, taking their places beside those who'd been there since the doors opened at eleven that morning. Emma could just see outside to the smokers' area — a square of concrete with a broken trellis and plant pots filled with a crop of cigarette butts. Ngaire Bourke was out there, which spoke volumes about the desperation levels of anyone else who used the space.

'I didn't want us to be seen together,' said Gene.

'Seriously?' said Emma. 'Why? Are you planning to sell me drugs?'

'Nope. But I can give you some Tic Tacs that look like Minions. My girls bought them, then decided they tasted like monkey vomit.'

'Mm, tempting.'

'Beer instead? My shout?'

'Make it a vodka,' said Emma. 'Hopefully the alcohol content will kill any bugs.'

'OK, so I know you're wondering why I called you here today,' said Gene, as he placed two glasses smudged with best-not-know-what on the table.

'Tell me off?' said Emma, glumly.

Gene looked genuinely surprised.

'No. Why? What have you done?'

'Devon called me this arvo and ripped me a new one,' Emma said. 'Seems the newspaper article over the weekend triggered the online ad to go viral, and now he's being hounded by flakes and trolls, and worse, media. He's had to shut down all his social media accounts, and his parents might have to disconnect their phone. Reporters from all over the bloody *world* are calling anyone even remotely connected with him. His folks' address got shared and now they've got reporters and nosy-parkers on the doorstep as well. And people have started sending stuff to him, love tokens, or their idea of a love token, anyway. One crazy couriered a gift-wrapped pack of thong undies. Used.'

'Hoo boy.'

Gene ran his hand down his face in an attempt to smooth out his grin. Failed.

'He was *so* shitty with me,' Emma said. 'I said I'd take the ad down, but he said it was too fucking late and hung up. I took it down anyway, but yeah, I guess he's right.'

'You weren't to know it'd spread.'

'Well, I didn't help it *not* spread. I was the one who told my journalist mate.'

In exactly the same light tone, Gene said, 'Did you also tell her about the dirty farmers?'

Emma jumped. Couldn't help it. But being a Reid, she'd had plenty of practice maintaining a poker face. School principals, cops, petty bureaucrats — she'd bluffed them all like a pro. You weren't much use to Loko and his crew if you were going to crumble soon as a man with a badge said 'Boo'.

'She's pretty resourceful, my mate,' she replied. 'Can do her own digging.'

'No doubt.' Gene sucked in his bottom lip. 'Is she interested in other stuff like that?'

'Such as?'

'Corrupt councillors, dodgy foreign investment, coastal damage, stealing rights from the local iwi?'

'Is any of that true?'

'Does it matter?'

Emma laughed.

'Dad said you had a burr up your butt about the waterfront development. He didn't say "butt", of course.'

'Of course.'

'Why are you so against it?' she went on. 'I mean, I'm no fan of the project, but you seem to be *really* anti. Which is ironic, seeing you've always given me shit for being an eco-warrior.'

Gene sipped his beer, made a face, set it down again. 'I have my reasons.'

'You'll have to do better than that if you want my help,' said Emma. 'Which you obviously do.'

'OK, so I hate Rob Hanrahan's guts and I want to see him fail,' said Gene. 'I didn't say I had *good* reasons.'

'What did he do? Make a move on Liz?'

'He'd never stand upright again,' said Gene. 'Nope, more simple than that. He's an arrogant prick who doesn't give a shit about this community. Everything he's doing is, on the face of it, perfectly legal — and I've certainly investigated a bunch of avenues. And, sure, a factory might create employment. But where's the long-term benefit? We won't see any of the profits. What if seahorse farming turns out to be a crock and the owners cut their losses and quit? We're back to empty buildings and people out of work. People who've probably got financial commitments like rental leases and hire purchase, which they can no longer pay. When the fish factory shut down, we had a social bloody crisis that only got partially solved because folk were forced to move to find work. Now, if *new* workers come in, we haven't got the infrastructure to cope. And Rob Hanrahan doesn't give two hoots about that. He's got his money. He's fine.'

'So do you just want to make his life a misery?' Emma asked. 'Or do you actually want the development to fail?'

'Do I have to choose?' said Gene. 'They both sound enormously appealing.'

'Former's a lot easier than the latter, but short-term. You know, order a thousand pizzas to be delivered to his house, set a paper bag full of dogshit on fire on his front step, pour fish oil into his car radiator . . .'

'Fun times. But I take your point.'

Gene sucked in his bottom lip again.

'All right,' he said. 'I choose failure. Or at least not-immediate success. I want the Chinese scared off, the deal to die. I want Rob to sweat while he scrambles to find other buyers in time to meet his commitments to the bank. I want to use that time to see if *we* can find buyers, ones we *know* would have the long-term interests of Gabriel's Bay at heart. They could be foreign, too. Chinese, even,' added Gene. 'But they'd be *our* Chinese, on our side. What do you think?'

'What would it take to scare off the buyers?'

'Delays in construction? Revelations of one or more of the developers' criminal dealings? Massive earthquake? Fire, flood, pestilence?'

For all his jokes, Emma could tell Gene was dead serious. Must be more to his loathing of Rob Hanrahan than he'd said. Or maybe not: ol' Rob wore alligator skin cowboy boots and (so he claimed) had shot an elephant in Africa. With luck, there was a special hell reserved for men like that.

And, besides, this could be another way to prove she was an asset. Loko hadn't been that impressed with the response to her farmer website. Her mate's coverage in the newspaper had been tiny. Even the Wood Sprites were complaining about the call to action she'd added after Loko said he wanted to see more happening. All right, so 'Let's show them they can't get away with this' might sound aggressive, but what were people actually going to do? Form a mob and torch farmhouses? Hardly.

Of more concern was Tai Te Wera, who'd be asking for people to come forward anonymously if they knew anything about who'd created the site. She'd have to be careful about how she approached this particular side project. Best plan would be to suggest it to Loko and let him take it from there.

'Delays in construction might be doable,' Emma said. 'But hang on — aren't you doing the concreting?'

'Concrete's laid,' said Gene, with a truly evil grin. 'My work is done. Billed. Paid for.'

'How did you swing *that*?'

'Lure them in with competitive pricing. Seal their fate with a watertight contract. And remind them of their obligations via the subtle presence of Reggie, my foreman, who makes The Rock look like a Subbuteo player.'

'So you could afford a donation,' said Emma, 'to a worthy group of helpful people?'

Gene mock-winced. 'Is it tax deductable?'

He clinked his smeary beer glass against the edge of Emma's untouched vodka.

'Thanks, mate,' he said.

'Don't thank me yet,' said Emma. 'And given how my other plans have been working out lately, you might want to save some of that money for bail.'

―――

The tarp hut was empty. Emma had told Loko that her meeting meant she couldn't drive him back from work to the camp. He'd shrugged like it was no big deal. Which it shouldn't be, should it? He had other friends. He had money from the avocado picking, despite telling Emma he didn't. When she'd finally asked him to contribute to her petrol costs, he'd made her request seem petty, like driving him around was the least she could do, and wasn't even that important in the scheme of things. Apparently, he was donating every cent he didn't need for food to the group, whereas she was frittering hers on going out for drinks with her mates. Plus she got a weekly free dinner from her folks and child-minding money from Sidney and Kerry, so really it was pretty selfish of her to even think about asking for a contribution.

He'd made her feel like a spoiled brat, who would never be fully committed because she could run home to Mummy and Daddy soon as life got tough. There was just enough truth in this to sting, and maybe Emma had sulked a bit. Maybe she'd been a bit offhand and last minute in telling him she couldn't drive him back from the avocado orchard. Maybe she should have invited him to meet Gene, too, or got him to hang around in town until she was done. As it turned out, looks like she'd made it back to camp before him. If he had a phone, she could have found out where he was, swung by and picked him up.

The camp was in twilight, a few figures still sitting around the firepit. Rua and his baby mama, Celeste, Darius, some of the others whose names Emma should know by now but didn't. Weren't their real names most of the time, anyway. Rua's birth name was something super middle-class and white like Oliver. OK, so *she* could talk, but at least she hadn't stolen a name from a whole other culture. Or called herself Solstice or Cascade.

The group around the firepit greeted her in a low-key, slightly reluctant way. Emma knew they didn't really consider her one of them, which was fair enough; she wasn't. They were nice people, but their hippy-dippyness drove her crazy. She could well understand the impulse to retreat from the world. It *was* harsh. It favoured the rich, and it chewed up and spat out the poor and the vulnerable. But running away never solved anything, as her folks might say. If you see a problem, don't wait for someone else to solve it — get stuck in! Don't moan and complain from the sidelines — act!

Emma's time with the English commune had cemented her view that Utopian society was a pipe dream, that people were their own worst enemies, and that real progress, societal and personal, required effort and struggle. Sure, rub crystals, meditate, think happy thoughts, grow organic veges — all good. But if you think you can shut out the world then you're no smarter than a little kid with their eyes closed who believed that if they can't see anyone, then no one can see them. The world was there. It was coming for you. You'd better be ready.

'Hi guys,' Emma said. 'You seen Loko?'

'Not this evening,' said Rua, as the others shook their heads.

Darius muttered something that sounded like, 'Good riddance.'

He wasn't a fan, Emma knew. Thought Loko's presence would bring them bad luck. Oh well, too bad. If the Wood Sprites had any gumption, they'd kick him out. If Loko stuck around, they had no one but themselves to blame.

No point in Emma sticking around, though. The tarp hut was too cold to sleep in without another body to keep you warm. She'd crash at her folks, help her dad out in the Boat Shed kitchen. Maybe she could take over from Devon so he could go home early? One tiny step on the long, grovelling road of apology.

As she started up the Bluebird of Crappiness, it occurred to Emma that Loko might be finding another body to keep him warm tonight. There was more than one chick among the picking crew who'd made it bloody obvious that they fancied him. And today, she'd left the door to that opportunity wide open for them.

It shouldn't bother Emma — if she was a free bird, then so was he — but, of course, it did. Not that she wanted to be exclusive, she honestly did not. Then what *did* she want?

To be his equal was the answer. To be his trusted ally, his teammate, Black Widow to his Ironman. To be the one he admired and respected above all others.

She was competitive, that was her problem. Emma wanted to win. She wanted to stand on the podium in triumph, and see Loko gazing up at her in admiration.

The Bluebird's headlights lit up an empty gravel road. Emma was the only one here, alone, but with *her* hands on the wheel. She wouldn't tell Loko about the meeting with Gene. She'd organise the action herself *and* she'd use the opportunity to rark her team up against the farmers. Loko was supposed to be the main contact, but she knew when they met, and where. She had enough cred to have earned the right to make her request. And she had what it took, she knew she did, to lead the charge.

Oh, yes, she loved it when a plan came together.

Wonder what her dad had on the menu for tonight?

CHAPTER 24

Patricia

Patricia had been called to the headmistress' office only once during her time at school. It had been a case of mistaken identity — not her but some other pupil spotted by the headmistress smoking on the street, in uniform, no less. Despite that, Patricia had still felt like a criminal. Now, fifty years later, sitting across from what one must now call the principal or head teacher, Patricia repressed an urge to pull her skirt down over her knees.

'Thank you for seeing me, Mrs Dundy,' Patricia said. 'I appreciate how busy you must be.'

'Please. Call me Jan,' said the woman behind the desk.

The name suited her — short, spare and practical. She was in her thirties, with the sinewy physique of a long distance runner. In Patricia's limited experience of sporting people, they tended to be rather intense and lacking in conversational sparkle. Though, to be fair, if one regularly ran hundreds of miles across mountainous terrain, one might consider sparkling to be an unnecessary use of energy.

Jan Dundy, however, had warmth as well as intensity. Being principal of Gabriel's Bay Primary School could not have been an easy job, but she seemed to enjoy it. She'd certainly been most sympathetic in her previous discussions with Patricia, and sincerely apologetic about her decision to keep Reuben out of school until his sister returned. Patricia had sensed that if it had been entirely up to Jan, the boy would have been able to stay. But she had teachers and other children to consider, and Reuben's outbursts were not conducive to a peaceful, positive learning environment. Or any other environment, for that matter.

Still, Patricia believed they had made progress, which was why she'd made the appointment. She knew it was out of her remit as temporary caregiver, but it was important for her to try and plead Reuben's case.

'Thank you, Jan,' she said. 'I thought you might appreciate knowing that Reuben has been doing very well with us. We have had some tricky moments, particularly at the start, but his behaviour lately has been excellent.'

'That *is* good to hear,' said Jan. 'Out of interest, what strategies have you been putting in place?'

Patricia was temporarily thrown by the word 'strategy' being applied to childcare, but she supposed there were indeed military aspects to it. Discipline, for one, mainly to regulate her own responses and temper. Anticipation of another's actions, so you could execute a pre-emptive manoeuvre. It might be a stretch to compare it also to bomb-disposal, though choosing the right words to neutralise a tense situation might well be every bit as stressful as deciding which wire to snip.

'I'm not sure if this is what you mean,' Patricia ventured. 'But, for one, we have been clear about our expectations around his behaviour. A few simple rules, which we repeat, so that he knows what we find acceptable in our home and what we don't.'

Jan was nodding, so Patricia felt confident enough to continue.

'We've also had a bit of a breakthrough — in that Reuben is now eager for Bernard and me to read to him. We now have not only an incentive for good behaviour but also a consequence if he behaves badly. We use it most often as the former,' she added.

'I imagine it works better that way,' Jan said, with a smile.

'I've also made a point of observing the general pattern of his energy levels — when he needs to run around and when he needs to rest. We've discovered that he responds well to routine, and to being asked to help with simple household tasks. For example, gardening has proved a hit, although I have to say, Reuben's talents lie more towards putting plants in than weeding them out.'

'Bit too enthusiastic, is he?'

'I left him to it, and when I returned, the beds looked like they had been hit by a small, localised tornado.'

'As good a description of Reuben as I've heard.' Jan compressed her lips. 'And believe me, I've heard a few.'

Patricia had no need to ask for details. Still, her heart rate elevated and she knew the cause was anger. She wondered what she might do if she ever heard one of the aforementioned adults being cruel about — or to — Reuben.

'Was there anything else, Mrs Weston? I appreciate the update.'

Jan spoke politely, but she clearly wanted to get on. Now was the time for Patricia to come to the point of her visit.

'I wondered,' Patricia began, 'seeing we feel we've made progress with his behaviour, whether Reuben could return to school? He has been completing the assignments you provided very diligently, and I think it would do him good to feel included again.'

The look Jan gave her was one of sympathy and pity, and Patricia knew what her answer would be.

'I'm sorry, but I can't go back on the agreement I've made with staff, and the Board. And personally, I think the work you're doing with Reuben will be of more benefit to him than being back in this environment.'

This environment. The words struck Patricia like blows, and she realised what her true fear had been all along. It was not that Reuben would suffer from being excluded from school. It was that, if he did not find a way — was not given the *chance* — to fit in when he returned, then the rest of his childhood would be a misery.

Patricia realised she'd hoped to present Jan Dundy with a new, improved Reuben — but not for the school's sake; for the boy's. She'd hoped that in just over a fortnight, she'd taught him skills that would miraculously transform him into the kind of child who impressed teachers and attracted friends. Because she could not bear the idea that, no matter how hard he tried, Reuben's fate had already been sealed. He was a pariah, and that label would follow him forever. No amount of care or attention from her, or his sister, would alter that. And unless a miracle occurred, Reuben would only grow more removed from society, until — well, the few paths that would be left to him led nowhere positive.

Patricia became aware that her hands were clenched on the wooden edge of the chair. If she'd been in anyone else's presence, she might have felt embarrassed, but Jan Dundy was not a woman who judged. She probably did a fair bit of chair clenching herself.

'Is there anything we can do to smooth his passage back into school?'

Patricia felt sure all would be done that could be, but she'd be remiss not to ask.

'I've been thinking about that,' said Jan, and, noting Patricia's expression, added, 'Don't thank me; it's my job.'

She picked up a pen and began to tap it on the desktop. A kinetic thinker, Patricia decided. One who learned better when allowed to move part of their body. Like Reuben.

'There are a couple of tried and true ways to encourage good behaviour,' said Jan. 'One is to reward, with praise or the old favourite gold stars, and another is to give the student a responsibility, a task such as tidying the classroom or feeding the class pet. Trouble is, Reuben being only nine, and an immature nine at that, there have been few opportunities for either of the above. He reacts violently to any teasing or taunting, which, of course, only encourages the taunters to goad him further. And his reactions almost always mean he's disrupted from appropriately executing his allotted task, and our agreed consequence for not meeting your responsibilities is to have them taken from you.'

'A vicious cycle,' said Patricia.

'Certainly not a productive one.'

Jan dabbed the pen end on a pad of sticky notes, making a series of black dots.

'But it's not as if Reuben's our only problem child.' She glanced up. 'You know Sidney Gillespie, don't you?'

'I do. Sidney works part-time for my husband.'

'Well, her eldest, Aidan, had a rough start to the year. But for the last couple of months, he's been taking martial arts lessons in Hampton. Free ones, courtesy of Casey Marshall, whose partner is the instructor.'

Jan's smile was knowing. 'I suspect a condition of being Casey's partner is that you're expected to carry out an element of social work, whether you were planning to or not. My point is that Aidan has benefitted significantly from the lessons — and I was wondering if Reuben might too?'

'Learn martial *arts*?'

Patricia couldn't conceal her surprise. Surely, *less* violence not more was the answer?

'It's not about learning to fight, or even to defend yourself,' said Jan. 'It's about physical and mental discipline, understanding how your mind and body work together, positively *and* negatively. It's learning where your strength *really* lies — in self-control rather than impulsive reactions.'

As if Patricia were about to protest, she hastened on. 'We've seen a measurable change in Aidan Gillespie — he's calmer, happier and more focused on schoolwork. He's always been a competitive boy, but he used to be a sore loser, and a terrible team player, critical of others because he saw their failure as reflecting badly on him. Now, his competitive instincts are channelled constructively, and he is building up his own *internal* standards of assessment — becoming self-directed rather than caring about what others do or say.'

There was no denying the persuasive nature of her argument. But still, something in Patricia balked.

'Aidan is eleven, going on twelve,' said Patricia. 'Do you not think a nine-year-old is too young to absorb the same lessons? You said yourself that Reuben is not especially mature.'

Jan looked her in the eye. 'Would you be prepared to help him find out?'

Patricia put her doubts aside. Chances were they were her own issues and nothing to do with Reuben.

'Of course,' she replied. 'If you let me have the details, I'll organise it immediately.'

Patricia arrived home to find Bernard and Charles Love in the kitchen, and Reuben out on the back lawn with Tai Te Wera, playing — if her eyes did not deceive her — croquet.

'It was an old set that belonged to my grandmother,' Bernard explained. 'I thought it might amuse.'

Through the open kitchen door, Patricia observed Reuben whack one of the faded wooden balls. It knocked a hoop clean over and he cheered. Tai Te Wera gave him a thumbs up.

'None of us could remember the rules,' said Bernard. 'So we invented our own.'

'Bernard and I were eliminated quite early on,' added Charles. 'Left the young ones to battle it out.'

On purpose, Patricia suspected, so Reuben would not have to wait too long between turns. She watched Reuben strike again, with all his might. The ball ripped the last hoop from the ground and rocketed into the shrubbery, taking a low branch off a daphne that had just begun to flower. Observant Tai picked up both ball and stricken bloom, and handed the latter to Reuben with a nod in the direction of the kitchen door. Noticing Patricia for the first time, Reuben beamed, dropped his mallet on the grass and raced towards her.

'For you!'

He thrust the daphne at her. The muddy grass on his shoes was now on the floor and his hands were *filthy*, but what did that matter? Patricia held the sprig up to inhale its scent.

'Thank you, dear,' she said. 'I'll put it in a bud vase. Take your shoes off outside, and wash your hands at the sink. Then we can all have afternoon tea.'

Reuben rushed to obey, causing Tai to have to swerve and nearly lose his armful of mallets and balls.

'I'm not sure your grandmother would approve of our adaptions to the game,' he said to Bernard.

'She's been dead for forty-five years,' said Bernard. 'Her days of disapproval are long past.'

'One tick for European descent.' Tai washed and dried his hands at the kitchen sink alongside Reuben, discreetly towelling up the puddles the boy created. 'No ancestors to judge you from on high.'

Patricia resisted remarking that Verity Weston's ghost was guaranteed to continue to make its malign presence felt. Poor Bernard was haunted enough by her alive.

She set a plate of chocolate biscuits on the table, and saw Reuben reach out then snatch back his hand and shove it under his leg, as if to prevent it escaping and embarrassing him with its bad manners.

'I know it seems unfair to wait for the grown-ups,' she said to him, 'but it *is* polite, so well done.'

She offered him the plate, and he slid a biscuit off it, carefully ensuring not to touch any of the others. His fingers were still grass-stained, but a little dirt never hurt anyone.

He ate the biscuit quickly. 'MayIpleaseleavethetable?'

'You may,' said Patricia. 'And as it's past four, you may watch television if you like.'

A beaming smile, a dash from the room. A head popping back round the door. 'Thankyouverymuch.' And disappearing again.

'The lad has better manners than some adults in our community,' said Bernard. 'Although after that telephone call, I'm not sure that my sympathies don't lie with the vandals.'

'Vandals?' said Patricia. 'Have we a graffiti epidemic again?'

'Worse than that, I'm afraid,' said Tai. 'The phone call Bernard referred to was from Rob Hanrahan. The waterfront construction site was broken into last night and considerable damage done.'

'By whom?'

'Unknown at this stage,' said Charles. 'So for now, there'll be no public lynching, despite Mr Hanrahan's express wish for same.'

'Why on earth did he phone *you*?' Patricia asked Bernard, and felt an immediate need to qualify what sounded like an insult. 'I can understand him wanting to complain, but surely it's a matter for the police, not the Progressive Association?'

'Apparently Councillor Elaine Pardew intimated that if the town had a better organised Neighbourhood Watch, then criminals would not feel so free to roam.'

'I see,' said Patricia. 'Did the site not have its own security measures? Barbed wire fences, Doberman Pinschers and suchlike?'

'A "Keep Out" sign and some cameras,' said Tai. 'But our vandals seemed to know about those and kept their faces averted.'

'Indicating the attack may have been organised,' said Charles, 'rather than spur of the moment. The damage also seemed deliberate, which would support that theory.'

'But why that site?' said Patricia. 'Were the motives personal?'

Bernard looked enquiringly at Charles, who smiled in his usual enigmatic way.

'I doubt the person you're alluding to would go to such extremes,' he said.

'Perhaps not,' said Bernard. 'But the man is a professional mischief-maker whose antipathy towards Rob Hanrahan has been publicly stated.'

'Gene Collins,' said Tai, for Patricia's benefit. 'Close friend of Jacko Reid, whose daughter Emma is a known environmental activist, and may also, sources suggest, be the person behind the dirty farming website.'

'Little Emma?' said Patricia in surprise.

'She's twenty-three,' said Tai. 'Not little any more.'

'I suppose not . . .'

From the living room, Patricia could hear the television. Reuben was watching *Ben 10*, a programme he loved. In a year or so, he would most likely outgrow it and move on to cartoons with more violence, darker storylines, stranger animation. Soon, he might feel too old to watch cartoons at all.

She glanced up to see Tai smiling at her, his brown eyes full of sympathy.

'When I was sixteen, I read *The Catcher in the Rye*,' he said. 'I remember none of it now — except the part where Holden explains the title, when he talks about standing in a field of rye on the edge of the cliff and seeing thousands of little kids who are running through the field towards him, not looking where they're going, and it's his job to catch them before they fall off. I thought: "Yeah, I could do that job, too. Easy".'

He paused, and the smile rose in one corner to become wry.

'But now, with my work and Corinna's work, and just watching people around me grow up, I know that some kids will be determined not to be caught, and some we simply won't reach in time. And I have to find ways to come to terms with that truth, or I, and everyone close to me, will suffer.'

'Is it enough, then, to know that we tried?' said Patricia.

'No one could try harder than you, my dear,' said Bernard gallantly.

'I agree,' said Charles. 'The effort you've put into Reuben's care has been exceptional.'

'Effort's not the same as doing the right thing, though, is it?' she said. 'And, unfortunately, I'm beginning to suspect that we can only know what the right thing is after the fact. When it may be entirely too late.'

CHAPTER 25

Sidney

Kerry had got up at crack of dawn to drive his parents to Hampton airport, so they could catch the first of many flights back home to Blighty.

'If we were loaded,' said Bronagh, 'we could get there in three hops. But, no — cheap tickets mean we bounce around the world like jewel thieves eluding Interpol.'

The Macfarlane seniors had come round for their farewell Gabriel's Bay takeaways, Kung Pao chicken, yesterday evening, but to Sidney's relief, hadn't stayed long. She was so certain that Nurse Bronagh must have spotted her 'condition' that she spent the whole dinner with hunched shoulders, preparing to be publicly outed, or, at the very least, pulled aside and whispered to loudly in the hallway.

But if Bronagh knew, she chose to keep schtum. And when the last hugs, goodbyes and promises to look after Vic were over, and Kerry had driven his folks back for their final night at Willow Cottage, Sidney realised how much she'd miss having them around.

So, it seemed, would the boys.

'Is Grandpa Douglas coming back soon?' said Rory, once she'd kissed him goodnight.

Sidney decided not to correct him. It wasn't as if the boys had a real grandfather anyway. Fergal had been estranged from his parents. And her own mother and father — well, the fact she thought of them as that instead of Mum and Dad said it all. They were her parents and she loved them, and she knew they loved her, as best they could. But the way she lived was so foreign to them. They'd visited once when the boys were small, and it was clear her mother considered their living conditions only one step up from dossing beneath an overpass. Her father didn't understand why she needed to stay on the benefit. She could be a secretary, surely? In a firm filled with eligible lawyers or accountants?

There'd been no point trying to bridge the gap of under-standing; it was too large. And until now, Sidney had put it out of her mind. The boys had not bonded with their grandparents on that first visit, and never questioned why they did not come again. She spoke to her parents by phone once a month for all of ten minutes. Her mother sent money for Christmas because she did not know the boys well enough to know what they'd enjoy. Sidney sent a card and a pot of jam or honey. And that was the relationship complete.

What a shame, Sidney now thought. What a shame that we didn't make more of an effort. She was pretty sure her father had no idea how to make rockets out of yeast, but perhaps he had other skills that would appeal to boys? He certainly knew some whiskery-old jokes about books and authors (including such classics as *Tragedy on the Clifftop* by Eileen Dover, and the positively risqué *Eating Asparagus* by Major P. Smellie).

She should invite them for Christmas. That was months away. Plenty of time to cultivate an inner calm.

Then again, no one would be calm if she stayed pregnant. If she was, say, two months gone now, then the due date would be middish-February. No way she could disguise the bump at Christmas, unless she convinced everyone it was the new way to defrost a turkey.

God, she *had* to make a decision. And, yikes, it was nearly nine.

The boys had headed off to school half an hour ago, and left her dreaming over her toast. She'd be late for work.

'You're looking much better,' said Patricia, as she invited Sidney in.

'Feeling it, to my relief.'

It was true. The sickness had suddenly stopped, and Sidney's energy had returned. Her mind was still in crisis, of course, but that was easier to hide than a green face and sweaty brow.

'Come and have a cup of tea,' said Patricia. 'Bernard is just on a call. He absent-mindedly answered the phone, and it was his mother.'

'Does he usually avoid her calls?' Sidney asked.

Patricia switched on the kettle. 'Like a triskaidekaphobian avoids the number thirteen.'

'Oh, well, I can't cast aspersions,' said Sidney, glumly. 'I was just thinking about what a crap daughter I've been. Mind you, my parents are pretty crap, too. It's like we're pressing on with a bad date because we're too polite to say no.'

She glanced around. 'Where's Reuben this morning?'

'Doing his school work,' said Patricia. 'Mrs Dundy supplied us with assignments. If he completes them to the best of his ability then he gets an extra half hour of story time.'

Sidney watched Patricia pour hot water into the teapot and swirl it around. There was something nice about this ritual. It was calming. Gracious, even.

Patricia placed a tray of tea things on the table. Porcelain cups and saucers, a sugar bowl, milk jug and silver teaspoons.

'So civilised,' Sidney said, wistfully.

'I confess, I only make pots for guests,' said Patricia with a laugh. 'Personally, I'm quite happy with the terrible teabags.'

'Thanks to a present from Kerry, I now drink from a mug that says Coffee Makes Me Poop,' Sidney admitted. 'Which the boys find newly hilarious each morning. As they're wont to do.'

'Speaking of boys, I thought you might like to know that I've signed Reuben up for martial arts lessons with Casey Marshall's partner,' said Patricia as she passed over a teacup. 'It was Jan Dundy's suggestion, and I'm not entirely convinced of its merit. What do you think?'

'It's been marvellous for Aidan,' said Sidney. 'And Casey's partner, Logan, is terrific, if a little on the earnest side. I think the only issue with Reuben will be ensuring he uses his powers for good not evil. No chop-chop hi-yaa in the school grounds, for instance.'

'I've been reading him *The Phantom Tollbooth*,' said Patricia. 'And I think *James and the Giant Peach* will be next. I'd like him to become acquainted with imaginative, gentle boy characters, who use their intelligence to solve problems. With luck, that will counteract any unhelpfully macho models he may be drawn to, and open his mind up to a less confrontational way of being.'

Sidney felt a rush of tearful affection that was probably hormonal. But, golly, could Reuben have ended up with a better carer? And to think she'd had doubts.

'You're amazing,' she said. 'I'm so pleased Reuben's here.'

'Oh.' Patricia blushed. 'Well, thank you. We've enjoyed having him.'

'You didn't want children of your own?'

The question was out before Sidney realised how tactless it sounded.

'Sorry, none of my business,' she added hastily. 'Forget I spoke.'

'Yes, it's a tricky subject,' said Patricia. 'But I don't mind you asking.'

Now Sidney was blushing. 'Don't feel compelled to answer, though. Really, it is none of my business.'

'I think it does me good to talk about it openly. I wasn't able to talk about it for many years.'

Patricia picked up her tea. She liked it dark as teak, Sidney observed. Strong.

'We couldn't have children,' Patricia said. 'I'll spare you the medical details, but it was a combination of issues. Bad luck, really, when you came down to it. And nothing to be done. Not in those days. Now, with IVF, the story might have ended differently.'

Bad luck, thought Sidney. That's how she felt about her own situation. Was she being selfish? Was she not appreciating her natural advantages, the ease with which she could achieve what women like Patricia wanted so badly but couldn't, through no fault of their own?

Or was it her right to choose, as the old protest posters used to say? Maybe, but was it her right to choose on her *own*?

Bernard entered. He looked green, and sweaty across the brow. Sidney felt it safe to assume the conversation with his mother was the cause, and not morning sickness.

'Tea?' asked his wife. 'I could put a spot of brandy in it.'

'The only piece of information I can bear to relay,' Bernard pulled out a chair and sank into it, 'is that, apparently, the home is considering naming a new wing after her.'

'They have those sets of rooms in castles, I believe,' said Patricia. 'Though they more commonly call them dungeons.'

'Ouch,' said Sidney.

'You have no idea.' Bernard dunked heaped spoonfuls of sugar into his teacup. 'Torquemada was a rank amateur.'

'It's a bit of a lottery who we end up with for parents, isn't it?' said Sidney. 'Some get lucky, some don't.'

'Your boys are fortunate to have *you*,' said Bernard.

Kind of him to say, though Sidney suspected that next to his own mother, even Joan Crawford would look like Florence Henderson.

But, of course, then he added, 'Pity more solo mothers don't follow your example.'

'I think you'll find most of them do,' Sidney said. 'Or they would if they could. The system doesn't exactly work in our favour.'

'Really? I can appreciate that the benefit payment might be inadequate in some cases, but surely you've proved that with prudent financial management and a willingness to find outside work, it's possible to make ends meet?'

Sidney snuck a glance at Patricia, who, to her surprise, winked. Which Sidney interpreted to mean that her husband had a good heart, but was clueless. And could she please be gentle while setting him straight.

'Well, I have a very good support network,' said Sidney. 'And a food-producing garden. And use of a car. And a tertiary education, good health and white skin. All of which helps tremendously. But regarding my willingness to work — for every dollar I earn over a certain amount, the government clips my benefit accordingly. And if I needed to take out a loan to pay for unexpected expenses — that could also be counted as assessable income. If that loan exceeded my benefit, then the government could deem that I'd been overpaid, and take me to court to claim it back.'

Bernard's mouth was agape. 'A loan counts as *income?*'

'If I use it for what they call "income-related purposes", i.e. day-to-day living expenses, then yes. If I bought *investments*, such as shares, then no.'

'That's positively Orwellian,' said Bernard. 'I had no idea.'

'Yes, it's almost enough to make you believe that reading, writing and arithmetic are *not*, in fact, the skills we should be teaching our children,' said Patricia. 'Instead, we should be teaching them how to survive in a world that favours only a privileged few.'

'That's you and me, dear,' said Bernard.

'I know.' Patricia reached out and patted his hand. 'Aren't we lucky?'

Getting in her car at noon, Sidney checked her phone. Two texts. One from Jill at the plant collective, asking if she could fill in for the next couple of hours as the person rostered on had fallen sick. She texted back in the affirmative and began to drive towards the Legion of Frontiersmen headquarters. The other was from Dr Ghadavi. It was very polite, but prompted an immediate recurrence of sweaty-browed nausea. The message was: the Hampton clinic had rung to tell him that their next free appointment was in three weeks' time, but that they would only hold the booking until tomorrow morning. The timing meant she would also be required to have a scan to ascertain how close she was to twelve weeks. Could Sidney let him know what she wanted to do?

Sidney knew that if she had a scan, she would keep the baby. Not because she'd see a living foetus on the screen, but because, to her, scans and radiographers signalled the start of a process that had twice ended in labour and a baby. Once the warmed gel was squirted on her stomach, it would be impossible for her not to project forward to that end result. She'd feel the baby in her arms, smell its iron-and-yeast scent, see its eyes flutter open. She'd fall in love with her future baby then and there. And there'd be no going back. She texted the good doctor and said she'd have an answer for him by the end of the day. She didn't know what that answer would be, but that was the end of the day's problem.

As she parked opposite the plant collective, she saw her stall partner was Ianthe. Sidney considered turning the car around and pleading some emergency, such as an allergy to felt, but decided today was not a day for wimping out. And maybe Ianthe could suggest some herbal drink that boosted willpower and didn't taste like it had leaked from a rusty leaf-filled gutter.

Ianthe had on a tiered skirt, ruffled blouse and a bright green felted waistcoat that looked to have been formed from play-dough by a toddler who'd lost interest halfway through. But who was she to judge, thought Sidney? She herself had on an old Superdry hoodie of Kerry's over a striped women's work shirt she bought at the op shop in Hampton so she'd have something suitable to wear to Bernard's. He didn't seem to notice she wore it every time.

'Hello.'

Sidney nodded at Ianthe, pulled her folding chair in closer so she could check out what was on the stall. Helped to be familiar with what you were meant to be selling. 'A plant' was not usually appreciated as the answer to the question 'What's that?'

She glanced over to see Ianthe gazing at her with a slight frown on her normally round, cheerful face. That did not bode well.

'How *are* you, Sidney?' she said.

'Much better, thanks.'

'Things have been weighing on you, haven't they?'

Sidney resisted giving Ianthe a sidelong glance, like a suspicious dog in a cartoon. What things did she mean, exactly?

'Have they?'

'It's in your aura.'

'Is it?'

Ianthe did not seem at all deterred by Sidney's clipped tone. But then, she hadn't got where she was today by being embarrassed about talking bollocks.

'I see brown, which signifies confusion, or opposing forces in your life. And a hint of maroon, which means either potential or abrupt change. I expect the latter is causing the former.'

'Auras come in maroon?' said Sidney. 'What else? Puce? Eau de Nil?'

Clearly, Ianthe's superpower was an ability to un-hear sarcasm.

'Would it help to chat?' she asked. 'I realise we don't know each other well, but sometimes that can make it easier. Despite my haphazard appearance, I'm actually the soul of discretion.'

Dear Lord, she'd sounded for a moment like a normal person. A *nice* normal person. A kind large-bosomed auntie who'd stroke your head while you let it *all* out—

'I'm pregnant,' said Sidney. 'And I have to decide whether or not to keep it by five o'clock today.'

Ianthe was unfazed. She'd probably heard worse. People who'd chanelled bad energy through their chakras and suchlike.

'And fear is getting in your way.'

A statement, not a question. Was it that obvious?

'Multiple fears,' said Sidney. 'A roiling rat's nest of them.'

'Well, I'm not one who believes fear is an illusion,' said Ianthe. 'It's real and very often a valid warning. But it also grows over-large if we feed it, like that plant in the musical.'

'*Little Shop of Horrors?*'

'That's the one. And our struggle is often to determine what size the fear should rightly be. To see it clearly, so we know whether we need to heed it or not.'

'By five o'clock today,' said Sidney.

Ianthe beamed. 'Nothing like a deadline for motivation. Have a sniff of rosemary.'

'Rosemary who? Oh. Right.'

'Clears the mind and improves concentration. Not as effectively as Madagascan periwinkle, but, as you won't be astonished to learn, that's not as readily available round here.'

Sidney glanced upwards, half expecting to see God wagging His finger at her, telling her off for being smug and judgemental.

'Thanks, Ianthe,' she said. 'That *did* help.'

'Any time,' said Ianthe. 'It's what I do.'

Kerry came round after work, at six-thirty. In time to check the boys were still doing their homework in their bedroom, and peel potatoes. As Aidan and Rory had no after-school activities today, Sidney had had time to make a chicken pie. Jacko had given her the meat in exchange for broccoli, cauliflower and rhubarb. She was a lucky girl to have such good friends. She slid the pie in the oven.

'Bronagh and Douglas get off OK?'

'Mm-hm,' was the slightly strangled response.

'Oh, dear.'

Sidney moved behind him, slipped her arms around his waist.

'You miss them already,' she said, hugging him tight.

'Rubbish,' he said. 'These tears are caused by onions.'

'You're not chopping onions.'

'Very pungent potatoes, then.'

'I miss them, too,' said Sidney. 'So do the boys. They should come back and live with us.'

Kerry turned to face her. 'Us?'

Now, it was Sidney's turn. 'Mm-hm.'

'This is new.'

Kerry's tone was, fair enough, somewhat guarded. Thus far, Sidney had been unambiguous about her feelings on co-habitation.

'Yes, well . . .'

The boys could emerge any minute, and a four-way conversation on this subject would be tricky. Difficult enough with just the two of them.

'After the boys' bedtime, let's sit down,' she said. 'I have something to tell you.'

CHAPTER 26

Ash

Sidney's phone call should have pleased him. Instead it plunged him into a depression, in which voices that sounded like those of his family members took turns to enumerate his failures. While Sidney was now on her third child, and Kerry his first, Ash, at a similar age, was not even partially attached, and the ever-present threat of his mother resuming her efforts to wed him loomed large. His career (if it could ever have been so termed) had gone backwards, and he would accumulate no wealth or assets besides the clothes he stood up in. His predecessor being so beloved, he was unlikely to ever attain the same status in the community. Maybe they'd say nice words after he'd died? No, who was he kidding? They'd build a statue to Dr Love, whereas Ash would be lucky if they spelled his name correctly on the death certificate.

Such self-castigation did nothing to improve an already fragile state of mind, made so by the looming reality of his date with Emma, now only a day away. The week since he'd asked her had passed like school holidays used to when he was back in Ahmedabad — long periods of boredom enlivened only by moments of panic and dread. In one of those moments, he'd phoned Magnus, who'd suggested they bring forward their weekend Scrabble evening, so that Ash could get everything off his chest that he needed to before Friday night. Ash suspected he'd need more than a few hours to peel back all the layers of his insecurities, but then again, Oksana was ruthless in her lack of toleration for wallowing, so it was quite possible he'd get down to the nub in the time it took to say Triple Word Score.

It was Oksana who opened the door. Ash had become used to being in the presence of a nude Magnus, but he was still grateful that Oksana chose to cover up when he visited. Not that he had any issue with naked women; he'd be no kind of doctor if that made him uncomfortable. No, it was more that Ash found Oksana overwhelming even when clad in a pink velour wrap patterned with Hello Kitty faces. In her mid-sixties, the beauty of her youth was still visible in her brown eyes and lush blonde locks, and thanks to a physical job, she was in fine, strapping shape. If she were to stand before him in all her naked glory, it might have the same effect as looking directly at the sun.

'Why slapped bum face?' was Oksana's greeting. 'You are here for free wine and food, plus waste-of-time English word game. What to complain about?' For Oksana, this was comparable to a kiss on both of his cheeks. She'd told him she was a Tatar, descended from Genghis Khan, a man whose idea of diplomacy was to make pyramids out of the severed heads of his enemies.

'I am in need of relationship advice,' Ash replied, stepping inside.

'What is point of advice? You do not have relationship.'

'Precisely.'

Ash made space for Oksana to sweep past him into the living room, where Magnus was standing at the picture window, glass of red wine in hand, giving native birds and possibly the odd possum an education into the ideal male physique.

'Spring is coming,' Magnus said. 'The tūī are in the kōwhai.'

Ash was still getting his ear and tongue around Māori pronunciation. It didn't help being filtered through a fine gauze of Norse.

'Two-ee?'

'They love the nectar.'

Magnus pointed at a tree in which a black and iridiscent blue feathered bird with its distinctive white wattle plume bobbed among yellow bell-like blooms.

'I planted those to bring the birds in. I like to encourage the wildlife to visit me.'

'Free wine.'

Oksana handed Ash a glass of pinot noir, poured lavishly from a bottle open on the round glass and wood coffee table.

'Thank you,' he said, and received a wave of her hand in response, a gesture that could mean 'No bother' or 'If it were up to me, you'd get dry bread and gruel'.

She settled onto the Eames lounger with her own glass and a book of what appeared to be Russian poetry.

'I have not seen as much of the wildlife here as I would like to,' Ash admitted to Magnus. 'I had plans of tramping excursions, but I have only been on a few short walks. Which is a shame, as I had a particular interest in investigating the rumours of moose.'

'Did you?' Magnus smiled. 'Now that *would* be interesting.'

'And Jacko Reid, Emma's father, offered to take me hunting when the weather improves, but—'

'You would kill innocent animals?'

Magnus, now very much unsmiling, fixed on Ash eyes the exact blue-green of glaciers. Ash imbibed a large slug of wine before replying.

'Er, well, I was under the impression that the deer here are introduced pests, and cause great damage to the native environment.'

'They are still living creatures, with brains, blood and hearts. I would have thought that you, being a doctor, would know we have no right to take a life.'

'I suspect Emma would agree with you.'

All subjects led around to Emma, Ash found. Deliberately so in this case, as he was keen to change tack. The only reason Magnus was not a vegan was because Oksana refused to use substitutes for egg, butter or honey in her baking. But he was a committed vegetarian, and adhered to a life philosophy that was, as best Ash could tell, a combination of Buddhism and Stoicism. Ash had become used to the experience of bumping up against Magnus' certainty about what was ethical, what served the higher good, and what was to be endured and what opposed. It would be like bumping into Magnus himself, and being sent flat on your rear by a wall of corded muscles and raw Nordic bones. Better to chart a course around.

'Ah, the exquisite Emma,' said Magnus. 'That is tomorrow night, yes?'

Ash took another slug of wine.

'I am terrified,' he said.

'Is she a Gorgon, who will turn you to stone with a look?' Magnus enquired. 'A siren, who will lure you to your death with song?'

'Can one die of embarrassment? Or does it only feel like it?'

'What have you to be embarrassed about?'

Ash glanced sidelong at the Eames lounger. Oksana was no longer in it, having gone, Ash assumed, as Magnus appeared not to cook, into the kitchen. He lowered his voice, nonetheless.

'I fear that I will not live up to her expectations of what a real man should be. I am not the strong, silent type; neither am I an adventurer of the Bear Grylls kind or a risk-taker. I am not a fighter, and I would make a terrible military leader. I am moderately good at sports but probably the wrong sports, for example, football and tennis. I am, in short, nothing like her father, a man I respect and admire but cannot hope to emulate. I fear that I will bore her or talk her into a stupor as I am doing now with you.'

Outside, the tūī emitted a gargling, honking call that to Ash sounded like a circus clown celebrating his fellow jester's pratfall. The fellow jester, of course, being him.

'And why is it so important to impress her?' said Magnus.

Good question. A few more mouthfuls of excellent pinot noir might help him form an answer. Ash had been smitten immediately by Emma's beauty, but physical attraction alone was a poor basis for a lasting relationship. Her breezy confidence appealed, as did her no-nonsense frankness, both family traits. Ash's own family members were also forthright, but they wielded it like a sharp, cruel weapon, whereas the Reid family used it to expose hypocrisy, or at least give it nowhere to hide. No wonder Emma had grown up confident. She'd never had to second-guess motives or suffer intentional malice. She'd had love and support, and been encouraged in her boldness. She'd been given the freedom to grow wings and fly.

'I want to learn from her,' said Ash. 'I want to discover what it takes to become fully yourself, to live without shame, guilt or fear.'

'That is a large undertaking for one person.'

Before Ash could ask whether he meant Emma or Ash himself, Oksana announced from the living room doorway:

'Food ready. I make dumpling. *Pel'meni*. Stick to your ribs, so you can last until next free meal.'

'She loves having you here,' Magnus murmured to him as they made their way to the dining table. 'I haven't heard her sound so cheerful in years.'

Which only went to show, Ash decided. *What* it went to show, he felt unqualified to speculate.

———

The restaurant he'd chosen was attached to a winery twenty kilometres out of Hampton. Although, originally, Emma had agreed only to have a drink with him, she'd not objected to accompanying it with food. Ash had selected the restaurant because it had excellent reviews and was only just above his price range. He'd also heard none of his acquaintances mention it, and assumed that meant it was a place they were unlikely to frequent. A bonus if you hoped for intimate conversation.

Now he and Emma were here, though, Ash felt he'd made a mistake. The main dining area was cavernous and the décor severe in its minimalism. All to make a statement, Ash assumed, if staring down one's nose qualified as a statement. Their waiter was, like all the staff, dressed in black, with manners that could best be described as formal. Or by Emma, after he'd left to fulfil their wine order, as, 'That guy has a cruet set up his jaxie. Not that I'm down on hospo. No shame in serving people, as Dad rightly says. Then again, Dad's got no tolerance for anyone who's rude or who acts like they're superior to the staff. Whereas I think these jokers are used to sucking up big time. Poor bastards.'

Ash was trying not to stare at her too much. Emma looked amazing, in a deceptively simple sleeveless dress that enhanced her athletic figure and revealed, by dint of a side split in the skirt, one smooth leg up to mid-thigh. The old-gold shade made her blonde hair glow. She wore hardly any makeup, and didn't need to, her colour being naturally high and her skin without flaw. She was the most beautiful woman Ash had seen outside of magazines or movies, apart from the one time he'd spotted Cheryl Cole coming out of Selfridges. He felt he should compliment her, but did not want to seem pushy, or worse, creepy.

'That is a very lovely dress,' he settled for saying.

'Thanks,' she said. 'You're looking pretty sharp yourself, Doc.'

It was the only suit he owned. His mother had commissioned it from a tailor in Savile Row and presented it to him, less as a gift and more as a rebuke. Ash's brothers wore custom Brioni suits and casual wear from Dolce & Gabbana. Ash shopped at H&M, or if he was feeling flush, Zara for Men. He'd worn this suit twice before: at a family wedding and a friend's birthday party at Windsor racecourse, and had felt like a pretender both times. It was a suit that belonged to a more successful, self-assured man who could flaunt a cerise silk lining with aplomb. None of the above, of course, could he tell to Emma. She probably considered him enough of a sad case already. Certainly, she was looking at him right now with a rather strange expression. Quizzical, with a hint of amusement.

'So what's the deal here?' she said. 'Are you trying to make a new friend, or are you hoping to get into my pants?'

People were under the misapprehension that dark skin concealed blushes, when all it did was make one go a darker red. Ash's blush extended from his clavicle to the roots of his hair.

'It's no biggie if it's the latter,' Emma went on. 'I'm not saying that's a "Yes", mind, but it's better to be straight with each other than to waste time pfaffing around, don't you think?'

The waiter returned with their wine, and unfurled a notepad.

'May I take your order?'

'Sure can,' said Emma, blithely, as if she had not rocked Ash to the very core of his being. 'Steak and chips, thanks.'

She smiled at the waiter, as if daring him to point out that what she had ordered was, in fact, grass-fed grain finished signature prime rib with truffle oil béarnaise accompanied by triple-cooked hand-cut pommes frites.

Nary a flicker of irritation. The man had the iron self-control of a seasoned professional.

'And for sir?'

The words on the menu swam before Ash's eyes, which left him with only one option.

'Fish of the day, thank you.'

He handed the man his menu, and chugged down a fortifying mouthful of Tempranillo.

'Are you not used to women being direct?' Emma was still smiling.

The face of Ash's mother floated across his inner vision, followed by his aunties, several of his lecturers and colleagues at medical school, the interchangeable cast of his brothers' girlfriends, and last but most definitely not least, his office manager, the mother of the woman sitting opposite.

'Oh, yes,' he said. 'But not usually about that subject, nor so quickly into a conversation.'

'Well, I figured you didn't need time to think about the answer. You being the one who asked me out tonight.'

A fair point. But would it pay to answer honestly? Or was being forthright something only the genuinely bold could get away with? Something, like dancing, that you needed to practise daily, or you'd look like a fool when you tried it?

Only one way to find out.

'I am attracted to you,' he said. 'I think you are beautiful, and exciting, and unlike anyone I've met. But I realise very well that I am not your type, and so I will not pursue any contact past this evening if my attentions are unwanted.'

'Not my type?' said Emma, with narrowed eyes. 'What's my type, then?'

Ash hoped he could never be accused of sexism, but it did seem to be a particular trait of women, to pluck out one part of a sentence and use it to shunt the conversation onto a new track entirely.

'I, er, I have assumed it would be a man not unlike your father.' Ash suppressed an urge to crawl under the table. 'Masculine, adventurous, practical, no nonsense . . .'

·'And that's not you?'

'Well . . .'

Emma propped both elbows on the table and leaned forward. 'You know what *I* think?'

'I daren't guess.'

'Exactly!'

She sat up, slammed her palm on the table, causing the silverware to shiver and the other diners to stare.

'You need to back yourself! Stop worrying so much about what people think of you, or how they'll react. Stop worrying about what you *ought* to be doing, because you'll never please everyone, no way.'

Magnus had given Ash similar advice, though in a quieter voice. He'd suggested that Ash would benefit from a healthy detachment, from people, status and things. Less looking outward for validation, more looking within.

Intellectually, Ash could see the sense in this. He shouldn't let others dictate the measure of his worth. But surely that didn't mean he should focus *only* on himself?

'It's better, though, wanting to please rather than displease, isn't it?' he said. 'Otherwise, I'd end up with no friends at all.'

'If people aren't pleased, that's *their* problem, not yours,' said Emma. 'It's not *your* responsibility to make others happy.'

'I suppose not. But don't you think we should at least *consider* potential consequences before we act?'

'Did you know exactly how this evening would go when you asked me out?' demanded Emma. 'Did you know how I'd behave, what I'd say? What if I turned out to be a psycho bunny boiler who stalked you for the next ten years?'

'I think that's hardly likely . . .'

'But you didn't know for *sure*.' Emma smacked the table again. 'And if you'd started thinking about all the possible scenarios, all the things that could happen this evening, then you'd never have asked me out, would you?'

Ash felt as if he were on the last carriage that had been decoupled from the rest of the conversational train, now merrily steaming off into the distance.

'So, you're saying—?'

'I'm *saying* that there are a million and one factors that can determine what happens after we make a decision, so why bother worrying about it? If shit happens, deal with it. But don't drive yourself nuts second-guessing how to avoid it.'

'Steak and chips for you, madam.'

The waiter deftly set a plate in front of Emma, who grinned up at him.

'I'll bring more wine, shall I?' said the paragon, as he placed the fish.

'Bless you.' Ash made a mental note to leave a generous tip.

Emma pointed a triple-cooked pomme frite at him. 'Do you get what I'm telling you?'

'If you could summarise, I'd be very grateful.'

'OK, in short: who gives a flying fuck if you're my type or not?' she said. 'Even if I did have one, I could change my mind. You asked me out because you wanted to spend time with me. I said yes because ditto. If it leads somewhere, then great. If not, we had a fun evening.'

Ash forked fish into his mouth in order to arrest the nervous questions that threatened to burst forth. Emma was right; he did drive himself nuts second-guessing, worrying. He should take her advice, and Magnus', and be in the moment. He was having an excellent dinner in stylish surroundings with a beautiful, intelligent companion. He should just relax and enjoy it.

'So,' said Emma. 'Tell me about your family.'

CHAPTER 27

Devon

'Do you feel like your personal safety is being threatened?'

Casey Marshall addressed the question to a kitchen full of Devon's whānau, while he cringed in one corner. If only Emma were here and could see how *pissed* they all were, might teach her to pause for half-a-second next time she decided to do him a so-called favour.

'Can't get out the bloody gate without tripping over one of those pōrangi. Soon as I say I'll set the dogs on them, they bugger off.'

This from Devon's dad, Hutana, senior health and safety inspector. No one would dare point out any irony in that.

'So that's a "No" from you, Mr Pohio-Ladbrook.' Casey glanced round the room. 'Any of the rest of you felt in danger?'

'In danger of unleashing an arse-kicking.'

That from Awi, one of Devon's two older sisters, who both played in the front row of the Hampton women's rugby team.

As the rest of the room muttered agreement, Casey said, 'Can I be assured that no one here has lightly smacked, accidentally bumped or been aggressive in any physical way towards these people?'

'Why are *we* the ones who need to watch out?' said Devon's cousin, Joel, who subscribed to magazines with titles like *Reps* and *Flex*. 'They're invading *our* privacy, interfering with *our* lives.'

'I appreciate that,' said Casey. 'But there's a difference between civil and criminal harassment, and I need to work out which we're dealing with before I can act.'

'Dad hasn't actually set the dogs on them,' said Devon. 'As you might have guessed.'

Casey's mouth twitched in acknowledgement. The Pohio-Ladbrook family canines were a pair of golden retrievers named Lolly and Dolly. Lolly was currently lying on her back under the kitchen table, having her belly rubbed by the toe of Casey's shoe. Dolly was sprawled on the living room couch, asleep.

'Have you found any of these people loitering on your property?'

To her credit, Constable Marshall was exploring all angles.

'Not likely,' said Devon's dad. 'They know they'll get a bloody good hiding.'

'So am I right in concluding that none of these people have been trespassing, and that you see them as more of a nuisance than a danger?' said Casey.

'Does moral danger count?' said Devon's mum, Jasmijn. 'The mokos have seen some nasty stuff come through the mail, and one of the girls outside lifted her top right up and showed us her poho!'

'Not ideal,' said Casey. 'But not easy to prosecute — unless you took photos?'

'What am I?' said Jasmijn, outraged. 'Some kind of pervert?'

Casey drew a line through a note she'd made in her book. 'Anything threatening in the mail?'

'After the used undies, we stopped looking,' said Awi. 'Chuck the parcels and letters straight in the bin now.'

'OK, why don't you start dropping them off to the station,' said Casey. 'Give me something educational to do on lunch break other than the crossword.'

'If you do spot a likely match for our tama here, can you pass on her name?' Awi deflected Devon's glare with a grin. 'He's been Mr Pukuriri for days now. Maybe some good loving would improve his mood.'

'Yeah, cuz,' said Joel. 'Pick one, eh? Put us all out of your misery.'

Devon wanted to raise his middle finger to them both, but couldn't deny they spoke the truth. If he'd insisted Emma take down the stupid online ad right away, then his family would never have been caught up in this farce. If he'd twigged to how he felt about Moana sooner, he wouldn't be in a shitty mood 24/7. He needed to suck up the teasing, and pray that these fruitloops would lose interest in him soon and leave them all alone. As for Moana — well, the power of prayer only went so far. And murdering Brownie was *probably* out of the question.

Slotting the notebook into her top pocket, Constable Marshall stood to address the room.

'As nothing you've described qualifies as trespassing or criminal harassment,' she said, 'best I can do is drive by each day and have a stern word with whoever's hanging about.'

A murmur of discontent. Casey held up a placatory palm.

'I know that's not ideal,' she said, 'but if they're basically harmless they should be easily scared off. Let me know immediately if anything changes. And drop off those parcels and letters, so I can keep an eye on the contents.'

'Better wear protective gloves,' said Awi. 'Maybe a whole hazmat suit.'

'What about the phone calls?' said Devon's mum.

'If you're getting regular calls from the same people,' said Casey. 'Then log the times and dates, and tell your phone company. They can bar them from calling you.'

'So basically you're saying we just have to put up with it?' Joel stepped forward, arms tensed. 'People can ruin our quality of life and we can't do shit to stop them?'

Devon mentally rolled his eyes. Joel always had to be the tough guy.

But Casey was well used to young men with too much testosterone.

'You've done the right thing and called me,' she said. 'Anything beyond that will almost certainly *not* be the right thing. Am I making myself clear?'

Sighs and feet scraping round the room. 'Ye-es.'

'Thanks for coming out on a Saturday morning,' said Devon. 'And I'm sorry for letting this get out of control.'

Casey nodded. 'You and Emma still on speaking terms?'

Despite everything, Devon's whānau still believed the sun shone out of Emma's bum, so there was no point in slagging her off in front of them. If she set their house on fire, they'd probably compliment her on how evenly the flames were spreading.

'She's apologised,' he said, with a shrug. 'And I guess it's not like she had any real clue how crazy this would get.'

Constable Marshall picked up her car keys, jinked them in her hand.

'Personally,' she said, 'I'm amazed how often people believe "I didn't mean to" is all the excuse they need.'

Devon arrived a half-hour early at the gym, intending to work off some steam on the punchbag before his two o'clock session with Logan. He was surprised to see Casey's partner with a small boy, whom he vaguely recognised. And wasn't that Bernard Weston's wife — Patricia? — on one of the seats along the wall? Devon didn't know they had a grandkid.

He had to pass her on the way to the changing room, so he nodded and said hello. She'd been concentrating on the boy and

Logan, and took a moment to focus.

'Devon, isn't it?' she said. 'Do you train here, too?'

Though she sounded fine, Devon could tell she was anxious about something, keen for reassurance. In his mind, he kissed goodbye to punchbag time and sat down next to her.

'I imagine you're very good at it.'

'Kind of you to say,' he said. 'But to be good at this sport, I need way less aggression and way more self-control.'

'You've always struck me as entirely self-possessed,' said Patricia. 'But I suppose we all react differently depending on the situation.'

'Maybe that's my problem.' Devon lent forward, rested his elbows on his knees. 'Bottle it up too much. Need to release it more often, so it doesn't burst out in one go like a geyser.'

Patricia's attention was on the boy again. Logan was helping him put on kick pads and gloves. The kid was impatient, raring to go, but Devon knew Logan would never let him start to spar until he was calm. Devon should teach the kid a few tricks about pretending to be calm, except that Logan knew him well enough now to see through his ruses.

'That your grandson?' he said to Patricia.

'No.' She sounded amused and sad at the same time. 'Bernard and I have registered as respite caregivers for children in need. Reuben is with us for only another six days.'

'Reuben, yeah.'

Devon recalled Sidney talking about Reuben. Problem kid, caused by problem home life was what he'd gathered. Not everyone was as lucky as he was, Devon reminded himself. There are a lot worse things a family can do than piss you off.

'So why Muay Thai?' he asked.

'Do you think it's a bad idea?'

Again that need for reassurance. Devon watched Logan guide

Reuben into the starting positions. Saw that the kid was already getting frustrated. Little man just wanted to kick the shit out of something. Devon knew how *that* felt. He felt it right now watching Logan.

Devon liked the guy; he was a good teacher and not in the least bit arrogant. He also had the kind of chisel-jawed athletic looks that could model expensive jeans or underwear. Lucky bastard.

Shit. This had to stop before it destroyed him, and pissed off everyone else. The lady was waiting for an answer and it better be a fair one.

'It might not turn out to be the right sport for Reuben,' said Devon. 'But he couldn't be in better hands.'

As if to confirm it, Logan gave up on trying to coach positions. Instead, he held out the sparring pads and let Reuben flail at them with all his might. Why not? If the kid didn't have fun, he wouldn't want to come back.

Fun. Devon tried to recall the last time he'd had fun. He loved riding Tiu, but only if the beach was empty, no one there to stare or yell insults. He relished the challenge of studying, but he'd hardly call it fun. Work? The Boat Shed crew, Jacko, Gene, Sidney — they all accepted him, but they weren't his friends. Lightning Tree felt like a second home when he was there, but his colleagues had their own lives and social circles that didn't include him. He'd missed the boat with Moana, and Brownie had nailed it with the phrase 'barely tolerated acquaintance', so who did that leave? Emma, he guessed. Emma, who, right now, embodied the phrase, 'With friends like these, who needs enemies?'

Reuben hurtled up to Patricia, red-faced and beaming.

'I went smack, smack, *pow*!' His demonstration required Devon and Patricia to move their heads out of the firing zone. 'Pow! Wham! Pow!'

Logan approached, smile apologetic.

'We'll work on the discipline aspects,' he said to Patricia. 'After another couple of lessons, I'll include him with a group of kids in his age-range. A little competition does wonders for motivating them to learn proper technique.'

Patricia, Devon observed, didn't look entirely convinced. But she thanked Logan politely, and began to encourage a still air-kicking Reuben away.

'Goodbye,' she said to Devon. 'Thank you for indulging me.'

'Sure,' he said. 'Any time.'

Reuben stopped suddenly mid-hi-ya, fixed his big eyes on Devon.

'You look like a girl,' he said.

'Reuben, dear, that's not polite,' said Patricia.

'Are you a girl?' said Reuben, undeterred. 'With a deep voice?'

'No, little man,' said Devon. 'I'm all dude. One hundred per cent. Don't let appearances fool you.'

'I'm sorry,' said Patricia.

Devon shrugged. 'He's a kid. Asking questions is what they do.'

'POW!'

Seemed Reuben was done with biology, and was keen now to explore the laws of physics by kicking over a chair.

'Time to go,' said Patricia, firmly. And they went.

Devon could feel Logan staring at him. No doubt with a pitying expression. He forced himself to meet the guy's eye.

But Logan's face was Shaolin monk impassive.

'Five minutes', warm-up on the punching bag,' was all he said. 'Make it count.'

No problem with that, thought Devon as he headed to change. He was going to smash that sucker into oblivion. Wham, *pow*!

Waited tables all evening like he was on autopilot. Gene wasn't a Saturday regular, and, usually, Devon liked having a break from being roasted, but tonight, he could have done with the stimulation. Jacko didn't notice that Devon was barely present. None of the customers did, either. Perhaps he was good at pretending everything was hunky dory?

Last table was ready to leave by nine, and after clean up, that'd be Devon done. No movie later on with Brownie. He'd received *that* call before he started work.

'Moana and I are going out tonight,' Brownie said. 'Is that all right with you?'

'Why wouldn't it be?' said Devon.

'Because she was your friend first?'

Brownie didn't sound like he was taking the piss. But then this was a bloke who'd led a secret double-life for months.

'My friend, not my property,' said Devon. 'I've got no say over what she does.'

'So you don't mind?'

'Wouldn't go that far.'

A short pause.

'Noted,' said Brownie. 'Well, see you round, perhaps?'

'Sure. Yeah.'

He'd hung up, and shut down, and that was how the evening had rolled. Now, he was holding the front door open for the last table. Jacko had already gone home to Mac, King the dog, and a well-earned beer in front of whatever TV programme Mac let him watch. Devon, as per routine, would do the final clean and lock up alone.

Or not.

'Room for a little one?'

Dr G stood outside, making room for the last customers to pass.

'Kitchen's closed.' Devon let him in, shut the door. 'But you can have a drink if you want. Might join you.'

'Yes, better not to drink alone. Although, of course, that was exactly my intention.'

Devon brought out a bottle of pinot, poured two glasses as Dr G settled at the bar.

'Your date cancel on you?'

Dr G's eyes widened. 'My, er — Oh! You mean my regular Saturday engagement. Yes, this week, we brought it forward to Thursday.'

'You're never going to spill the beans, are you?' said Devon, with a grin. 'Be careful. Nature and small towns abhor a vacuum. What they don't know, they make up. And then they convince themselves it's all true.'

'That is no doubt excellent advice.'

Devon envied his composure. Seemed everyone he knew had some core of certainty that kept them solid. Some were more rock-solid than others, of course.

'So how'd last night go with Emma?' he said. 'Unless you're keeping mum on that subject, too?'

If Dr G *had* been about to tell all, the moment was lost. Front door clattered open. In walked some dude.

'We're closed,' Devon called out.

The dude strolled up to them. Devon's woo-wah began to ping.

'I was told to meet someone here.'

White man with dreads. Dressed like some kind of combat anarchist, though he wouldn't last two seconds in the Crown. Handsome, if you liked the type. Which was, and Devon was never mistaken, Class 1 Arrogant Wanker.

'You can meet them outside,' said Devon. 'We're having a private drink.'

The bloke leaned one hip against the bar, one elbow on it.

'You must be Devon. Emma's told me all about you.'

Devon's woo-wah went into hyperdrive.

'And you are?'

'Loko.' A pause for obvious effect. 'Her lover.'

Devon couldn't help a quick glance at Dr G. Poor guy looked like he'd been freeze-framed, which meant, God damn her, that Emma had failed to mention she was playing the field.

Unless, of course, this whakahīhī arse was doing the equivalent of pissing on a doorway, marking Emma as his territory. Something he'd never dare to do if she were present, owing to it guaranteeing him a swift kick in the nads.

Devon *really* wanted Emma to show up soon, and for completely contradictory reasons. He wanted to see her embarrassed and apologetic about how she'd strung poor Dr G along, but he also wanted to see her put this dreadlocked douche in his place. Because he was seriously making Devon's shit itch.

'Emma showed me your photo,' said Loko. 'You're even more distinctive in person.'

Devon's adrenaline began to pump. But no way was he going to react.

'Emma thinks you should leave town,' Loko continued. 'She could be right. Conservative communities like this one don't make it easy to be non-binary, do they?'

Now, that was some patronising fuckery right there. Couldn't let that pass.

'Non-binary?'

'Does that term make you uncomfortable?'

'I don't give a fuck about gender. And I don't care if people are queer, straight, bi, or if they reproduce by fucking parthenogenesis,' said Devon. 'But in the words of Popeye, I am what *I* am. And that's the full hetero-normative. Sorry to disappoint.'

Loko nodded, slowly. 'Your stance is completely understandable.'

'What does *that* mean?'

Dude spread his hands in faux conciliatory fashion.

'No judgement,' he said. 'It's typical of small rural communities to privilege the cis-male, so it's no surprise that you'd prefer to present as one.'

This douche-tard had a *degree* in patronising fuckery. Time to step it up a notch, and take a leaf out of the Pohio-Ladbrook 'no one messes with us' playbook.

'So you're saying if Gabriel's Bay folk weren't a bunch of backward shitheads, I could stop putting on a show?'

'Devon, could I trouble you for another glass of that excellent wine?'

Being a medical man, Dr G had no doubt observed Devon's blood pressure rising.

Without taking his eyes off Loko, Devon slid the bottle along the bar.

'Help yourself, Doc.'

Then he rephrased his previous question less ambiguously.

'So you're dissing not only me but my friends and whānau? My kāinga?'

Loko wore a tiny smile, like this was where he'd wanted the conversation to head the whole time. Maybe he was pissed off at Emma for two-timing him, and because she wasn't here, her childhood friend became the next-best target? Or maybe he was a borderline psycho, who got his rocks off from getting under people's skin?

'May I also offer *you* a glass of wine, sir?'

Dr G, the peacemaker. The good guy, trying to do the right thing and defuse the situation.

'No, you can't,' Devon told him. 'Wine's for friends only.'

Loko laughed.

'I can see why Emma likes you,' he said. 'You're loyal. And — what's that word you all love to use here? Staunch. You'll see off anything that threatens your familiar world, so you can keep your little circle safe. In its way, it's admirable.'

The barbs were subtle. Nothing you should really take offence at. Unless you'd already hit peak pissed off . . .

'Fuck you, man,' said Devon. 'We're all good here. I'm good, he's good — we don't need your shit stirring, more-PC-than-thou blah blah. Why don't you take your condescending bullshit and fuck off?'

'Oh, I'll be leaving soon enough.'

The dude's smirk, the way his gaze swept over Dr G like he was of no consequence; Devon's fists started to spasm.

'I didn't have high hopes for this place, so I can't rightly say I've been disappointed. A few minor successes, but as I'd suspected, shifting attitudes in such a narrow, culturally repressive frame is like prising limpets off rocks without a knife.'

Loko kept his eyes on Devon.

'So I'll be heading away to where I can effect real change. And *you* can retreat safely back into your delusion that this place has anything to offer you.'

Slam of the front door. Emma hustled in, breathless.

'Hey, so sorry I'm late.'

Douche-tard swivelled to face her. You could *see* him swell with self-importance. As far as he was concerned, he'd crushed Devon and his fellow small-town retards like a bug, and now he was being apologised to by his 'lover', an abasement which put him high in the catbird seat, preening. Far as he was concerned, he was king of the world, and he no longer had to pretend to be a compassionate, thoughtful guy.

'No problem,' said King Loko. 'I've just been giving your friend some advice. Sadly, it seems he's not man enough — so to speak — to take it.'

Devon wasn't sure how he got out from behind the bar. He couldn't remember the first punch, or how many came after. The geyser had blown, and he was a creature of boiling steam. An avenger from the molten abyss. Kia kīia ai!

And then his arms were pinned behind him, and someone was shouting. And gradually, his vision cleared and it was Dr G who held his arms, and Emma shouting, and Loko was on the ground with a bloodied face.

All Devon could think of to say was, 'How come you're so strong?' to Dr G.

Who replied, 'Treating meth addicts. The orderlies are not always close by.'

Emma was staring up at Devon, eyes wide and angry, tearful.

'What the hell, Dev? What the *hell*?'

And he knew he'd have to come up with a better answer than the one in his mind right now. Which was: I didn't mean to.

CHAPTER 28

Emma

'Call an ambulance?'

Emma's mum waved her phone at Dr G, kneeling on the floor beside Loko, who was sitting up now, but not exactly being the ideal patient.

'There appears to be more blood than damage.' Dr G had given up trying to swab Loko's face. 'Most of it due to nosebleed, though the nose appears to be unbroken. He was unconscious for only seconds, but I can check later for concussion. I observed also that he sustained a few hard blows to the torso, so he may have broken ribs. And I should examine his abdomen for—'

'Don't touch me.'

Loko said it through gritted teeth.

'A ruptured spleen can be fatal,' said Dr G, mildly. 'I would strongly advise undergoing a CT scan.'

'Ambulance — yes or no?' said Emma's mum.

'No!' said Loko. 'No quacks anywhere near me.'

Grimacing in pain, one hand holding his ribs, he tried to stand. Emma stepped forward to help him, but he threw up his free arm to ward her off. The furious expression on his face stopped her protest mid-utter.

On his feet, breathing hard, Loko demanded, 'Bring the car to the door.'

Emma was acutely aware that everyone was waiting for her

response. Dr G, now stripping off his latex gloves. Her mum and dad, who'd come as soon as she'd phoned them. The only one missing was Devon, sitting on the back steps, having taken himself out of the way.

'I'll drive you,' said Emma's dad.

'Not necessary.' Loko replied. 'Emma — we're leaving.'

Another order. But he was in pain, humiliated — who behaved well under those circumstances? And how else would he get back to camp?

'No can do, buckaroo.'

Emma's mum. Stepping in. Sorting shit out.

'Unless you want to crawl home,' she told Loko, 'you'll go with Jacko. Emma's got family matters to attend to.'

Loko's smile wasn't nice. It said, 'That's right. Hide here with Mummy, little girl.'

If Emma had been in her usual state of mind, she would have flipped him the bird, and good riddance. But seeing Dev like that, insane with rage — it had knocked her sideways. And then his *expression* when she'd yelled at him: a mix of misery and challenge, like he was telling her, 'Welcome to the real me.' That wasn't Dev. That wasn't how her world *worked*.

'It's the Wood Sprites camp, Dad,' she said. 'Thanks.'

And she walked to the nearest window, pressed her cheek up against the cold glass. Kept her back to the door, so she couldn't see Loko hobble out.

'Need any help?'

Her mum, asking Dr G. Another person Emma didn't want to face right now.

'I'll take the gloves and swabs, dispose of them at the surgery,' he replied.

'Good thing Jacko keeps the first-aid kit topped up,' Emma's mum remarked. 'Or you'd have been making do with torn strips of frilled apron.'

'This floor will need cleaning, too. Obviously. And where is Devon now? I'd like to examine his hands for fractures.'

Dr G sounded oddly cool and detached, but Emma assumed that was because he was still in professional mode. He'd been quite the superhero tonight, holding Devon back until he'd settled down, ordering him to fetch the first-aid kit and then doing the full A&E action on Loko, calm, purposeful and efficient. Whereas all she'd done was yell at Dev and phone her parents in a panic. Like a little girl.

She should speak to Dr G. She should do *something* useful.

Too late.

'I'll fetch him,' said her mum. 'He's on the back steps — should have brought him in earlier. Shock and cold air could give him hypothermia.'

Twenty seconds later, she rushed back in. 'He's gone. Driven off. *Bugger.*'

Her mum was genuinely upset. Why not? Dev was like a son to her.

'I'll call him.' Emma's mum pulled out her mobile.

'He won't answer if he's driving,' said Emma.

Devon had always been the sensible one when it came to cars and phones. The sensible one full stop.

'Crap.' Her mother shoved the phone back in her jeans pocket. 'Well, no point mooching around here. Let's sling a bucket of bleach on that bloodstain and head home. Tea and a biscuit at ours, Doc? Something stronger if you like.'

'Thank you.' Dr G was putting on his jacket. 'But I'll say goodnight.'

Shit. Time for Emma to woman up.

'Hey.' She hurried over to stand in front of him. 'You were pretty amazing, how you dealt with all that.'

'Thank you.'

Where was the kind, funny Dr G she'd been out with only the night before? The Dr G who'd turned out to be a way better kisser than she'd expected? For all the spark in his eyes, the dude in front of her might as well be reading the newspaper on the train.

'Look, I know I didn't mention Loko,' she said. 'But why would I? He's not my boyfriend. We're not a thing. He's just a guy I—'

'No need to explain.'

He'd started doing up his buttons. Navy wool pea coat. Classy.

Emma wanted to fold her arms, but she knew it looked defensive. She shoved her hands in her jacket pockets instead.

'So?' she said. 'Does that mean we're cool?'

'Oh . . .'

He ran a weary hand over his head.

'Cool is what I have never been, and never will be, I'm afraid.'

In his apologetic half-smile, she saw a hint of the man from last night.

'Take care, Emma.'

And with a nod to her mother, he exited.

They all had. Dr G, Devon and Loko. Exited stage left.

'Grab a bucket and brush, Em,' said her mum. 'It looks like a slaughterhouse in here.'

When her dad got back home, Emma and her mum were still up, sitting in the kitchen, drinking tea and eating Krispies. Well, her mum was eating Krispies. Emma had no appetite.

Her dad retrieved a beer from the fridge, joined them at the table. King scrambled up from his prone position on the floor, rested his head on his master's leg.

'Is he going to press charges?' said her mum.

'Doubt it.'

Her dad removed the bottle cap with his hand. Chances were it wasn't a twist-top.

'He hates the pigs more than he hates quacks. I received quite the lecture about the evils of our neo-liberal fascist regime. Until I told him to shut up.'

'Did you stop the car before you let him out?' her mum asked.

'Camp's over a mile from the road. Long walk when you're sore as hell is probably punishment enough.'

Her dad reached down to fondle King's ears.

'Bloke's an A-grade arsehole, Em.'

'I know,' she said.

'Was it serious?'

Emma was touched. Her mum wanted to know if she had a broken heart.

'I wasn't in love with him,' said Emma. 'But I liked hanging around with him. He wasn't an arsehole *all* of the time.'

'Use of past tense noted, with some relief,' said her mum. 'Onwards and upwards.'

They were great like that, her parents. If she'd hooked up with a douchebag, then that was a mistake, sure, but they knew she knew that; she didn't need their censure on top of her own. Their priority was to support her, not tell her how to live her life.

Maybe she should have done the same with Devon? If she'd just lent a friendly ear and not pushed him — more accurately, ridden roughshod over him — then he wouldn't have got wound up to breaking point. He might still be grumpy and alone, true, but he'd be grumpy and alone *his* way, on his terms.

No reply yet to her messages and texts. He'd probably gone home, Emma decided. His family would look after him. Wouldn't ask too many questions, either. Devon had always been a good kid. Honest, clean living, reliable. They trusted him.

Like her parents trusted her.

Should she tell them? About Loko's group? About what she'd done? Her dad always said you had to live by your principles. Talk was cheap — it was your actions, not your words, that counted.

He'd also given her the advice she'd passed on last night to Dr G — that how other people reacted was their responsibility, not yours. But now Emma could see that it wasn't so simple when you were the one having the reaction. When it was *you* feeling threatened, fearful or rejected. She could see the sense now in what Dr G had said — that we should at least *consider* the impact of our actions on other people. We might still choose to act, but we couldn't rightly plead ignorance when the shit hit the fan.

Thing is, she *hadn't* fully considered the knock-on effects, and now it was too late; what she'd done she couldn't un-do. So Emma guessed she had two choices: fess up and face the music, or keep schtum and hope it all went away.

If she did the former, how would her parents react? Her dad would be angry about the website because it had hurt people he liked and respected. Her mum would be worried that Emma might fall foul of the law. Both would think her moral compass had gone awry; no matter how noble your principles, your actions should never cause harm. It was possible neither would ever trust her wholeheartedly again.

And if she kept schtum, she'd have to live with the deceit all her life.

A real dilemma, the kind with horns. Ha ha — an Emma-dilemma. Pity it didn't feel all that funny.

Her mum was yawning behind her hand.

'God,' she said. 'Feels like three a.m. but it's barely gone eleven-thirty. Time for bed.'

'Heard from Dev?' her dad asked.

Emma shook her head.

'I'll pop round to his place tomorrow morning,' she said.

'Tell him he can take tomorrow night off. I'll ask Sid if she can step in.'

'Might be out of luck there,' said her mum. 'Sidney's got a bit of drama happening.'

'Aidan acting up again?'

'No, and I've been sworn to secrecy, so stop guessing.'

'You're the boss,' said her dad, and pulled his wife to him, so he could kiss her cheek.

They loved each other so much, Emma thought. Better than that, they were friends. Best mates. Had been for nearly forty years, since her dad was seventeen and her mum fifteen. Unbelievable, really, but the evidence was right in front of her, had been since she was old enough to see it.

Usually, her parents' happiness made *her* happy, too. She'd always loved how well they treated each other, the mutual respect, the way they showed affection by helping each other out, having each other's back. All Emma's life it had felt like a point of pride. A place of safety, too; it reassured in the comfortable, familiar way of a favourite soft toy.

But tonight, it made her miserable. With everything she'd done to screw up people's lives, did she deserve affection or respect? If she couldn't be honest or generous or caring, why would anyone want to get close? No wonder Dr G had cut her dead. For all his professed self-doubt, he knew what was good for him. And that wasn't a person like Emma.

'Your bed's made up, Em,' said her mum. 'Stay as long as you like.'

'Night, kid,' said her dad. 'It'll look brighter in the morning.'

And the pair of them headed off to their room.

It'll look brighter in the morning. Said with love, and because that's what her dad believed. No problem that couldn't be solved if you put your back into it.

Better start stiffening her spine now. Because of the two choices, fess up or keep schtum, Emma knew there was only one she could live with — even though it would come with a world of hurt.

Tomorrow morning, however, her top priority was Devon. She'd get up early, head round at breakfast time. And hope that's where he was, because the alternative didn't bear thinking about.

The Pohio-Ladbrooks lived on the other side of Gabriel's Bay, in a neat thirties roughcast bungalow that had always housed however many whānau members were in need of a place to live. Extra accommodation included a pop-top caravan and converted shed in the back garden. Beyond that was farmland. The farmer was an old family friend who let Devon graze Tiu on his paddock, stable him in the old stalls when he wasn't at Lightning Tree, keeping other horses company.

Emma had fond memories of playing in the fields, and in Devon's garden, which, in those days, seemed enormous, with mature fruit trees and a vegetable garden that was out of bounds lest they incur the wrath of Devon's granny, who could be found stooped over it every day.

Kuia Agnes was dead now, as were Devon's other set of grandparents, but despite having smoked for the first sixty years of his life, Koro Tama kept on keeping on. The old guy must be nearly ninety now, Emma thought, as she took the corner into Devon's street. Still sharp. Still liked to tease.

What the hell?

Emma brought the Bluebird of Crappiness to a more abrupt halt than she'd planned. Who the heck were those people sitting on the footpath outside Devon's house? On blankets and an old sofa

275

that had been dragged from God knows where. At eight o'clock on a freaking Sunday morning!

As she approached, Emma could see the group was made up of youngish women, and one dude. Holy shit, these were Devon's stalkers! The diehard last-standers who hadn't been chased away by the fiercer Pohio-Ladbrooks. Which was pretty much every Pohio-Ladbrook to be fair, so this lot were either not easily frightened or nuttier than squirrel dung.

'What are you *doing* here?' she demanded of a girl aged around twenty, sporting green hair, rainbow leggings and a Powerpuff Girls T-shirt.

'Why do *you* want to know, bitch?'

The dude. Slim, dark-eyed, camp. And soon to be dead meat.

'Cos I'm Devon's number one honey,' said Emma. 'His main squeeze.'

'Oh, *please*,' said the dude. 'He's not even *into* women.' He waved his hand dismissively at the others. 'Which I've *tried* to tell them.'

'Uh huh,' said Emma. 'Because you know him so well, right?'

'Better than you, Coyote Ugly.'

Emma got out her phone.

'Calling police, mama?' The dude laughed. 'She drives by, we just smile and wave.'

He ducked his head back as Emma thrust the phone in his face. On it was a photo of her and Devon, arms around each other's waists, taken at Emma's leaving party.

'Me and my man,' she said, turning it so the whole group could see. 'Later, losers.'

Insults of variable quality followed her as she walked up to the front door.

'Emma!'

Devon's mother looked thrilled to see her, even though Emma

hadn't been to visit them once since she'd been back.

'Hi, Mrs Pohio-Ladbrook. Is Devon home?'

'Come in, come in!'

Devon's mum opened the door wide.

'You get past those pōrangi youngsters OK? They give you any trouble?'

'No trouble,' said Emma, hoping the group had noted her warm welcome, the kiss on both cheeks from Devon's mum. Losers.

'Go knock on the boy's door, wake him up,' said Devon's mum. 'Don't know what time he got in last night. Then come in the kitchen and have a cuppa with us.'

Emma knew the house as well as her own. Had spent many an afternoon in Devon's bedroom, doing homework, listening to music, talking shit. It had always been super tidy, even when he was a teenager. Self-discipline. Dev had it in spades. Usually.

She knocked. No answer. Could he have hurt himself more than he let on last night? She tried the door.

'Dev?'

The room was empty. Bed was made, neat as if he were at military school. Shit.

He wasn't anywhere else in the house; his mum would know. Come to think of it, Emma hadn't seen his car parked on the street. Double shit. Where *was* he?

His mum was waiting for her in the kitchen. No way she could stay. But no way to leave without saying goodbye.

Popped her head round the kitchen door. Only Devon's mum and dad, and the two dogs.

'Emma!'

Devon's dad was just as pleased to see her as his mum. Judging by the amount of slobber now on her hands, so were Lolly and Dolly.

'Hi, Mr Pohio-Ladbrook. So sorry, I can't stay — something urgent's come up.'

'Devon still in bed?' His mum frowned. 'That boy is usually up with the sun.'

'He's not home,' said Emma, trying to sound cool. 'Maybe at a friend's?'

'You could try Barrett Tahana,' said Devon's dad. 'He and Dev have been spending time together lately. I wouldn't be so keen except Millie was a wahine mārohirohi. Hope her tama has learned his lesson, got back on the straight and narrow.'

'Thanks, I'll do that,' said Emma. 'Nice to see you both. Sorry I can't stay.'

'Next time, hey? Don't be a stranger.'

God, they were so nice to her. If only they knew . . .

'Planning the wedding,' she told the group on the footpath, as she strode past. Felt rather than saw the raised middle fingers.

In the car, she dialled Gene. Barrett worked for him.

'Emma.'

Gene didn't sound like his usual chirpy self. Probably hadn't woken up properly yet.

'Hi, have you got Barrett Tahana's mobile?' she asked. 'Want to see if he's with Dev.'

'I'll text it to you,' said Gene, briskly. 'Listen, Emma, you know that stuff you — arranged — for me?'

'What about it?'

'You haven't arranged for anything similar to happen in other places?'

'What other places? What do you mean?'

'Otto Visser had his barn set on fire last night.'

'So?'

Emma was impatient to get on, find Dev.

'So were you behind that?'

'What the fuck, of course not! Why would I be?'

'You sure?'

'Jesus, Gene, I know what I've done and what I haven't!' said Emma. 'A fire in Otto Visser's barn is *nothing* to do with me!'

'OK, OK! Just checking.'

'Text me Barrett's number, please. I've got to go.'

'Coming your way,' said Gene. 'You be careful out there.'

The phone beeped, and then it rang. Her mum.

'Hi?' said Emma, hoping it wouldn't take long.

'I've got Tai Te Wera in the kitchen,' said her mum. 'He came to see you, but we've all had a very interesting chat. And now we'd like to hear *your* side of the story.'

Emma closed her eyes. Breathed in.

'I'll be home in five minutes.'

CHAPTER 29

Vic

'Now, are you eating more than white bread and bacon?' said Bronagh.

It was Saturday evening in the UK, and Vic could hear the occasional Scottish-accented imprecation in the background. Douglas'd be watching the news, then.

'Because you know what happened to Elvis, don't you, Vic?'

'His baby left him?'

'He died! At forty-two!'

Three years younger than Vic.

'With over thirty pounds of faecal matter backed up in his colon,' Bronagh elaborated as only a nurse could. 'The majority quite probably comprising the masticated remains of his favourite food — peanut butter, bacon and banana sandwiches deep-fried in lard.'

Vic made a mental note regarding peanut butter and banana. He'd always rated Elvis.

'Do you have any more guests booked in?'

Should he tell her he hadn't opened his email for over a week? Or his actual mail? There was quite a pile of it now on the sideboard, weighed down by a docking tool Vic had forgotten to ask Douglas to fix.

'Can't,' he said. 'Too close to calving — and lambing.'

'And you've got help coming in for those?'

'Yep.'

Dogs counted as help, right?

'Did Sidney bring you round some of her jam?'

Sidney had. She'd looked, as his father used to say, like the Ghost of Killiecrankie, and had declined Vic's invitation to stay for a cuppa. Which was what Vic had been hoping she'd do, so that worked out well.

'Blackberry,' said Vic.

Bastard of a weed. Grew like topsy around the edges of streams. He should spray it, but that would mean spending money he didn't have on brushkiller.

'Oh, lovely,' said Bronagh. 'And are you getting off the farm, seeing other folk?'

'Been down the clubrooms.'

Drove into the carpark on Friday night. Sat in the truck. Drove home again.

'Grand.'

Vic crossed fingers that Bronagh had reached the end of her 'Is Vic OK?' checklist.

'All righty, then,' she said. 'Douglas and I are having a day out in Victoria Park tomorrow. After all those weeks in your winter, we need to top up our vitamin D. I'm eager to have a go on the rowboats, though Douglas is more of a pedalo man, himself. If you don't hear from me next week, it means we've drowned.'

'OK,' said Vic.

He wouldn't hear from her if his phone line had been cut off, either. Mind you, that would also put paid to the calls from the bank. Vic didn't answer the phone these days. Or check his voicemail. Bronagh had got through because she'd rung ten times in a row until he picked up. He'd known it was safe to answer. With that kind of persistence, it could only have been one person.

'Take care of yourself, Vic,' she said. 'You know Douglas and I are here if you need us.'

'Yep.'

Unsually, there was silence on the other end.

'Er — bye?' said Vic.

'Bye, now,' said Bronagh. 'We'll talk next week.'

Vic put down the phone and wondered if she were worried about him in particular, or whether, being a nurse, she had a general concern for people's welfare. It should be comforting to know that he mattered to at least one person in the world, but, all told, good wishes were of limited practical assistance.

Bronagh's desire for him to take care wouldn't, for example, help him set up the calf shed or build the extra pens he could really do with. It wouldn't pay for the calf tags, electrolytes, new feeding teats and a pump so he didn't have to bucket milk. It wouldn't buy fertiliser, or magnesium, or the aforementioned weed spray, or 5-in-1 vaccine for the ewes, or feed supplements. It wouldn't put diesel in the truck or petrol in the quad bike. It wouldn't help him keep an eye on all his stock at this crucial time, and spot sick animals or abortions or down cows or cast ewes. It certainly wouldn't help him manage any scours outbreak in the calves.

The weight of his obligations hung on Vic like a sodden Swanndri. He'd been brought up to believe that any problem could be solved if you worked hard enough. That's what farmers did — because *not* doing it meant you were lazy, a poor show, second rate. Meant you should be ashamed . . .

Hell, the phone. Ringing, and ringing again right away. Bronagh forgotten to remind him to chew his food properly?

'Vic, it's Otto. There's an emergency meeting at the clubrooms. Get here quick as you can, yeah?'

'Meeting of—?'

But Otto had gone.

Vic glanced around the room. Sunday morning. Should be out checking stock, fences, water supply, pasture growth. Reviewing his budget, his payments due, his cash position . . .

Clubrooms it was, then.

Carpark was full. Vic had to park a way up the road and walk. Inside, he found about fifteen blokes, a few of whom were farmers he recognised, in a standing cluster facing the area where bands performed. Only at the microphone wasn't some wannabe Bono but Rob Hanrahan. Red-faced and furious.

'These are fucking terrorist acts,' he was saying. 'Committed by scumbags who don't give a flying fuck about the law — so why should we? Police investigation could take weeks, and in the meantime, how many of us will be victims? How many of us will suffer irreparable damage to property. *Our* property. Which *we* should have the right to defend!'

Vic had spotted Otto's over-black hair. Sidled his way through to where he stood.

'What gives?' he whispered.

'They burned down my barn last night,' Otto told him.

'*What*? Who did?'

'Same buggers who vandalised Rob's building site.'

'How d'you know that?'

Otto nodded at the man at the mike.

'Rob found out.'

No point in asking how. Money could buy you various methods of extracting information. Rob wouldn't care if some included extracting fingernails as well.

'So who are they?'

'Your mates by the river,' said Otto.

'The *Wood* Sprites?' said Vic in disbelief. 'No. They're not—'

'What d'you say we pay the dirty fucking scumbags a visit? Show *them* what it's like to be on the receiving end!'

Rob's exhortation was met by a resounding roar of approval.

Hell, thought Vic. No one would listen to him now. He ought to scarper and warn Darius and co.

No, what he *ought* to do is ring the police. Trouble is, his mobile was defunct, couldn't afford to top it up. And he could hardly borrow one from Otto, who was cheering with the rest of — well, you had to call them a mob, didn't you? Rob's mob, with shotguns instead of pitchforks.

There was the clubrooms phone. Maybe he could—

'Come on, Vic, my friend.' Otto grabbed him round the shoulder. 'You ride with me.'

Vic sat in Otto's Land Rover and tried to think how he could get to the camp quicker than anyone else. But Otto was last in the convoy. Rob's Porsche Cayenne had sped away up front. It'd have ten minutes on them by now. The nearest phone booth to make an emergency call was back in town.

There were probably blokes like Vic at key moments in history — Kristallnacht, the October Revolution, Klan lynchings — who'd just popped along because they had nothing better to do, and found themselves swept away on the tide, unable to sneak off or make excuses about having left a pot on the stove. They'd committed atrocities because they'd happened to be there, not necessarily because they wanted to. An excuse, Vic reflected, that wouldn't cut much ice in the final reckoning.

But could he stand up to this lot? Stand between them and people he was *sure* were innocent. Would anyone listen to him? To sad, useless, wife-less Vic?

Soon as Otto pulled up along the river road, Vic could tell he'd get no chance to find out. Three vehicles in front of them, all empty. A dozen big men gone down the path, armed with weapons and righteous anger. Vic felt like throwing up. God knows what he'd see when he got to the camp.

Fuck it. He began to run.

Events got a bit hazy then, due in large part to a lack of oxygen; he really should be fitter. Darius was sitting on the ground holding his head, and the dreadlocked bloke and Jacko Reid's daugther were nowhere in sight. But Vic was relieved to see that all the others, including Rua, his arms round a weeping girl, were huddled under the riverbank trees, watching wide-eyed and mute as the homes they'd built were smashed to pieces, their few possessions strewn around, stamped into the dirt. One bloke was taking to the food store with a tyre iron. Vic watched a bag of chickpeas explode, small beige missiles hurtling.

No one had spotted him arrive; too intent on their task. Vic jogged up to the group under the trees.

'Rua,' he said. 'Get out of here. Go the back way, up to my place.'

The young man blinked at him, dazed.

'They shoved her,' he said, holding the weeping girl tighter. 'She's *pregnant*.'

'Vic?'

Otto, wondering what the hell he was up to.

'Go on, fuck off,' Vic said in an urgent whisper. '*Do it!*'

'What's going on?'

Otto was right there, not angry, just puzzled. All Vic could do was stand firm and face him, and hope that the Wood Sprites were getting their arses into gear.

'They aren't the vandals, Otto,' he said. 'I guarantee it.'

He could see Otto glance over Vic's shoulder, and then back at the camp, where there was nothing much more to destroy, though that didn't seem to be deterring anyone.

'Then who is?'

'Dunno,' said Vic. 'But—'

'Oy!'

The fleeing Wood Sprites had been spotted. Now Vic had a

285

dozen men converging on him, not one of them looking in the mood for a reasoned debate.

But what else could he do? Vic stepped forward, put his hands out. 'Let them go.'

Then Rob Hanrahan was in his face. Six foot four of belligerent beef. A police riot baton in his fist.

'What the fuck's this, Vic?'

Inadequate at the best of times, Vic's ability to articulate fried like an ant under the magnifying glass of accusation.

'I just . . . that is . . .'

'Vic says they're not the vandals.'

Otto to the rescue. Or dropping him right in it. Could go either way.

'And what makes *Vic* suddenly a fucking expert?'

'There's another bloke.' Vic had to try. 'English. He's not here, though . . .'

'So the real culprit's the invisible man?' said Rob. 'Fucking brilliant, Victor. Top work. You bleeding heart *muppet*.'

'Hey, Rob.'

One of the other blokes, whom Vic knew vaguely, directed Rob's attention back to the camp, where Darius was now lying on the ground, unconscious. Or worse.

Rob shoved the baton under Vic's chin.

'If any of your little friends say one word about this, I'm coming for *you*, Halsworth, you fucking prick. And don't show your face at the club again. You're not welcome.'

He jerked the baton upwards, clipped the edge of Vic's jaw. Which bloody hurt.

Rob turned his back, began to stride off. The others followed him, but not before giving Vic the evils and muttering variations on the theme of 'Prick'.

Otto laid a hand on his shoulder in passing.

'Ah, Vic,' he said.

No way of telling whether he spoke out of sympathy or pity. Not that it mattered.

'Call an ambulance, Otto?' Vic said. 'I don't have a phone on me.'

Otto shook his head, apologetically. Too risky, Vic supposed. Trace the call.

He should check on Darius right away, but he couldn't bring himself to until the last of Rob's stormtroopers had left the camp. He knelt, felt for the older man's pulse. Found it, went dizzy with relief.

Darius' eyes began to flicker open.

'Sorry, mate,' said Vic. 'You had a bit of a knock.'

The man spat in his face.

'Go to hell.'

A breathless rasp. Darius wasn't in good shape, and Vic shouldn't leave him. But he wasn't a doctor, either, and if Otto refused to call an ambulance, then Vic would have to.

Vic stood, wiped off the spit with the hem of his Swanni. He didn't blame the bloke. The camp was munted, looked more like a refuse tip than a place people had once lived in. But he managed to drag out a couple of blankets. Laid them over Darius, who was still prone, eyes closed again, breathing ragged.

'Help's coming, mate,' Vic whispered. 'Hang in there.'

Across the river, forty-five minutes uphill; he *really* should be fitter. The dogs were barking as he approached — strangers on the property, he guessed. But what was that smell? Smoke? His house was never locked. Had the Wood Sprites got in and lit the fire? But the crackling noise. So loud . . .

Not the fireplace. The house. *His* house, his family's home for generations. All of it ablaze.

'Vic . . .'

Rua, approaching cautiously. Vic hardly had the energy to turn his head. The Wood Sprites were in the distance, in the middle of a paddock; this hadn't been their day. They were stuffed if they needed transport into town. Vic's truck was back at the clubrooms.

'It was on fire when we got here,' said Rua. 'I called the fire department.'

'I thought you shunned technology?' was all Vic could think to say.

'Um, I got a mobile just in case, you know — Celeste. The baby.'

Guess the couple would be moving back in with family. Because, like Vic, they didn't have a home any—

'Hell,' said Vic. 'Darius. We need to—'

'Called the ambulance, too,' said Rua. 'And the police.'

'Good,' said Vic.

The dogs were howling now. Really going for it.

'Um, should we let them out?' Rua asked. 'They sound distressed.'

'No.' Vic shook his head. 'They're safer in their kennel. Fire won't spread that far.'

The blaze had taken out all the walls and most of the roof, and the house was a black skeleton of framing. The flames were enormous, bursting out beneath a stormcloud of smoke. The heat was blistering, even though they were a good fifty metres away.

'I'm really sorry,' said Rua. 'We didn't see anybody here when we arrived. I don't know who did this. None of us does. I swear.'

'Not your problem,' said Vic.

Suddenly, his legs didn't want to hold him up. So he sat down on a macrocarpa stump and watched the flames crackle and roar. Watched his life disintegrate into blackened splinters.

CHAPTER 30

Sidney

There was something to be said for being surrounded by drama. For one, it turned everyone's attention away from you. And it made *your* problems seem minor by comparison.

No, that last bit was utter bullshit, thought Sidney. Her problems still felt as insurmountable and hideous as ever. They felt like the end of the world.

Kerry hadn't reacted the way she'd expected when she told him about the baby. She'd figured he'd be a combination of thrilled and terrified, as you are when you first find out you're going to be a parent. But after getting past the shock, he'd retreated into a cool silence so much unlike his usual manner that Sidney had started to panic.

'How long did you say you'd known?' he'd asked.

'A week.'

Kerry nodded. His mouth was set in a line. Even though he often made jokes at inappropriate moments, Sidney wanted very badly for him to smile now.

'And you couldn't tell me then because — why?' he said. 'Did you think I'd freak out?'

'Maybe,' Sidney hedged. 'No. I don't know. I needed time to think.'

'About?'

'*Everything!*'

The boys had only just gone to bed, so she should keep her voice down. But God damn him. *He* wasn't the pregnant one!

'About the age gap, how the boys will react, how it'll affect my finances, how I'll find time for paid work and gardening and the market and the boys and all their commitments with looking after it — him, her, whatever! How hard I found the last two pregnancies — I'm no earth mother, that's for sure! And about how much it *sucked* being a solo parent of babies! You and I have been together eight months, not even a whole gestation! How do *I* know you'll stick around?'

'And you couldn't discuss that with me?'

'No, Kerry, I couldn't.'

She shouldn't be so defensive. Snapping might be temporarily satisfying, but it was a useless de-escalation tactic. She *shouldn't*, but—

'It's my body, and my life, and I needed to get *my* head around it first.'

'It's my child.'

This was ineluctably true. And hearing it stated so baldly, Sidney felt ashamed. Keeping it from him for a couple of days might be deemed reasonable. A whole week was a slap in the face. She knew that. She just wasn't ready to concede.

'*My* body.'

'Fuck.'

He'd said it quickly, under his breath. And then he'd stood up, grabbed his car keys from the kitchen bench and walked out. Hadn't even slammed the door, just shut it firmly behind him. Sidney would have felt better if he'd given it a hearty slam. Blazing anger she understood, but this reaction left her floundering. Was it temporary? Or was that it? Over, red rover? Had she blown it completely?

That had been Thursday night, and now it was Monday

morning, and she and Kerry hadn't spoken. He wouldn't answer her calls or texts, and on the one occasion she'd summoned the courage to drive round to his house, his car wasn't outside. She had no choice but to wait until he was ready to talk. If he ever would be.

Mac, as usual, had lent a willing ear. After Sidney's tearful call on Saturday afternoon, she'd popped round with King the dog to keep the boys amused outside, and a packet of Toffee Pops. ('Figured Krispies wouldn't cut it.')

But there was only so much comfort she could give. Sidney was still pregnant — 'It's too late now' — and Kerry was still absent.

'Do Bronagh and Douglas know?' Mac asked.

'God, I hadn't even *thought* about *them*,' Sidney replied. 'Probably not. I suspect Bronagh would have been straight on the phone if Kerry had told all.'

There were her parents to tell, too, when she could find the strength. The domino effect of being pregnant was quite extraordinary, Sidney reflected. So many people with a connection to the child-to-be, so many people prepared to love it. She probably should have thought of that earlier . . .

'Should *I* call him?' said Mac. 'Tell him to stop being a big baby? If you'll pardon the expression.'

It was tempting. Mac knew how to get action. But—

'I suspect he feels isolated enough already,' said Sidney. 'And he's not the villain here.'

'Neither are you,' said Mac.

'I could have handled it better,' said Sidney.

'Well, baby Gillespie's not going away,' Mac reminded her as only Mac could. 'Kerry needs to stop sulking and make up his mind about whether he wants to be a father or not. It's not all about *him*, is it?'

No, Sidney thought as she pulled the car into Bernard and

Patricia's neatly gravelled driveway. But that didn't mean it had to *include* him.

In the driveway's wide circular end were parked two other vehicles. Doc Love's Skoda and Tai Te Wera's Audi station wagon, complete, she observed as she passed by, with the detritus one associates with children under five: empty raisin packets and a half-eaten banana, wet wipes, three unmatched shoes, and a My Little Pony whose green mane had been given a drastic trim. It was a lot tidier than *her* car had ever been when her boys were that age.

That was another issue — the car. If Kerry buggered off, he might want it back.

Well, she'd cross that bridge when she came to it. Hopefully not on foot.

Sidney knocked on the door. The Doc and Tai were here for their regular Littleville trustees meeting, but she'd bet anything that wasn't the current topic of discussion. She had no doubt they'd heard the news. Given the effectiveness of the small town rumour mill, space aliens orbiting Jupiter probably knew by now. Otto Visser's barn had been torched by unknown arsonists, and a group of vigilantes had blamed the Wood Sprites and smashed up their camp. No one knew who the vigilantes were. Well, the Wood Sprites obviously did, being there at the time, but their evidence hadn't yet filtered down.

Of course, that didn't stop there being lots of very firm opinions. Small towns were superb at declaring they knew exactly what was going on, even if it was based on nothing but a someone-heard-from-someone rumour or a feeling they had 'in their waters'. The prevailing, and dispiriting, view was that even if the Wood Sprites weren't the arsonists, they'd had it coming. They'd had the gall to cock a snook at society, claim they were better off apart from it. And if you turn your back on your community, don't expect to come crying back when it all goes up the boowai.

However, as she kept reminding herself, all this fuss was a useful diversion. It stopped people looking too closely at her.

'Good morning, Sidney.'

Usually, Patricia answered the door. Today, it was Bernard.

'Patricia has taken Reuben into Hampton,' he said, as he let her in. 'To the library and then, I gather, the moving pictures.'

Sidney bit her lip to prevent a smile. Bernard was a dear man, really, but he should have been born in 1886. The modern world must terrify him at least ten times a day.

'Won't this be his last week with you?' said Sidney, as they headed down the hall.

'Yes. His sister, Maree, arrives back on Friday.'

Bernard's reply had a hint of ambivalence about it. Sidney guessed he'd delight in having his sanctum returned to him, but that he'd also become quite fond of Reuben and would be sad to see him go.

'I think that's why Patricia wanted to give him a treat today,' Bernard added. 'I was to join them but, unfortunately, events of the hour have rather taken precedence.'

And Patricia would miss the boy even more, wouldn't she?

The sheer unfairness, the *randomness* of fertility! Why couldn't those who desperately wanted children have as many as they liked? Why did women like Sidney get pregnant even when they were using contraception?

Oh, well, at least she could get stuck into a bit of work. Take her mind off it for a couple of hours.

At the door of his study, Bernard paused.

'Sidney, your parents-in-law stayed with Vic Halsworth, is that correct?'

'They're not—' Too hard. 'Yes, they stayed in Vic's cottage. Got on like a house on fire, according to Bronagh.'

'Ah, ha, yes.'

Bernard gave a nervous little bray.

'And would you say *you* know Vic reasonably well?'

'We're friendly enough, I suppose.'

She could almost see Bernard's mental cogs shifting. What on earth was up?

'Could you join us in the kitchen?' said Bernard. 'I think you could be of some assistance.'

Doc Love and Tai greeted her as she entered. Both men were unsmiling, serious, particularly Tai, who was positively grim, and hollow-eyed as if he hadn't been getting much sleep. She'd seen an identical look in her bathroom mirror this morning. Must be all the rage.

'I guess you've heard about Otto Visser's barn, and the attack on the Wood Sprites camp?' said Tai.

'I've also heard that Elvis runs the local pirate radio station,' said Sidney, 'so I've taken the news so far with a pinch of salt. Is it true or not?'

'True,' said Tai. 'One Wood Sprite was injured in the attack, but he's recovering in hospital and doesn't want to have anything to do with the police. Nor do any of his friends, so looks like we'll never officially know who was behind it.'

'I heard those inverted commas around "officially",' said Sidney. 'You *do* know?'

'I do.' Tai's face suggested he wished it were otherwise. 'Vic Halsworth arrived on my doorstep yesterday afternoon and told me.'

'Vic? How did *he*—?'

'Sidney, I know you'll keep what we say here in confidence.'

This from Doc Love. Of course she would, now that he'd told her she had to. Doc Love was a person whose good opinion you never wanted to lose. Besides, she was good at keeping secrets, wasn't she?

'Vic was part of the attack on the camp,' Doc Love began.

'*What?* No! He's Gentle Ben!'

'Unwillingly,' Doc Love pressed on. 'Seems he was dragged into it and couldn't extract himself.'

'He didn't hurt anyone, or damage anything,' said Tai. 'He helped the Wood Sprites escape, to his place.'

'There's a giant "But" coming isn't there?' said Sidney. 'Because that all sounds like good news so far, and none of you has a good news face on.'

'They arrived to find his house on fire. It burned to the ground. Nothing saved.'

'God, no!'

Sidney's mind did what everyone's does when they hear about another's catastrophe: after a brief burst of empathy, it descended into an anxious recitation of what *she* would do if the same thing happened to her. Would she manage? How bad would it be? What had she put in place to prevent it being a *complete* disaster?

'His insurance should cover it, though? Right?'

'He'd let his premium lapse,' said Bernard.

'Oh, *Vic*!'

Sidney wanted to slap him. How *could* he? The big doofus!

She knew the answer to that. He did it because he had no choice. Because, financially, things *were* as bad as Bronagh had suspected. She had good instincts, did Kerry's mother.

'I guess he can live in Willow Cottage,' she said. 'There *is* only Vic, after all.'

With those expressions, the men would be a shoo-in if Death ever needed to recruit another three Horsemen of the Apocalypse.

'Come on! He hasn't lost *that*, too, has he? Did the fire spread?'

'I started making calls on Vic's behalf first thing this morning,' said Tai. 'It went from bad to worse. First, the lapsed insurance. Second, the Hampton District Council has fined him for polluting waterways. They'd tried to contact him, but seems Vic has been somewhat incommunicado lately. The fine is over forty thousand dollars.'

'Forty *thousand*? Holy moly.'

'The bank was number three on the shitty calls list,' said Tai. 'There's no way they'll help; he's in too much debt. Vic'll have to sell his land, and his stock. If he declares bankruptcy it's the same result, only he'll get nothing and his life from then on will be immeasurably tougher. He has no choice.'

'But couldn't the council let him pay it off over time?' said Sidney. 'Surely, they'd be open to allowing for mitigating circumstances? I mean, they're bureaucrats, but they're not *Nazis*.'

'Seems they're keen to make an example of Vic,' said Bernard. 'Well, *one* councillor is, at least.'

'Don't *tell* me,' said Sidney. 'Evil Elaine! OK, I take back the comment about them not being Nazis.'

'Honestly,' said Tai. 'I know she almost scuppered Littleville, and that Corinna spits tacks every time her name's mentioned, because of her putting the kibosh on the name change to Onemanawa. But until recently, I had no idea how many *other* people's plans she'd meddled with. I think it's because she never fronts anything, just machinates behind the scenes.'

'She's Sauron behind a net curtain,' said Sidney. 'But why Vic? What has he ever done to *anyone*?'

'Well, that ties in with one of your earlier questions,' said Tai. 'About who attacked the Wood Sprites camp.'

'And?' said Sidney, as he hesitated.

'This is *strictly* confidential,' he said. 'We can't have this going wider. Vic needs all the allies he can get, but it will have to be a tight group. OK?'

'I won't breathe a word.' Sidney crossed her heart. 'Although if Mac senses something's up, I can't guarantee I'll withstand her interrogation methods.'

'We'll allow Mac into the fold,' said Doc Love with a smile. 'History proves the benefit of keeping the Gurkhas onside.'

Sidney met Tai's gaze as she waited for him to spill the beans. Poor sod looked shattered. Unlike his wife, he was more of a peacemaker than a fighter. But sometimes, you had no choice but to take up arms.

'Rob Hanrahan instigated the attack on the Wood Sprites camp,' Tai told her. 'But the Wood Sprites resolutely refuse to press charges. They don't want anything to do with the police or the courts. Even the bloke who ended up in hospital won't sue for assault. I'm impressed,' he added. 'There are precious few who are able to resist Casey when she's got the bit between her teeth.'

'Can't she press charges anyway?' Sidney asked. 'And use Vic as a witness? Surely, it's a serious enough crime.'

Tai rubbed a weary hand over his face.

'It is,' he said. 'But Vic's backing out, too. He believes Rob Hanrahan will take revenge on him and the Wood Sprites if he speaks out, names names. One of the young Sprites has a pregnant girlfriend, apparently, and Vic feels a need to ensure they're protected. And with no witnesses at all . . .'

'No luck making the charges stick,' said Sidney, with a sigh. 'Bugger.'

'Vic also believes Rob's behind the council digging its toes in regarding the fine, as a way of keeping Vic in check,' Tai said. 'Mr Hanrahan and Councillor Pardew certainly seem to be, er, *fans*, of each other's work.'

'Like Rosa Klebb and Ernst Blofeld.'

That raised a smile from Tai and Doc Love. Bernard was clearly at sea when it came to James Bond. She might slip him the DVD of *From Russia with Love*. Maybe not.

'Do we know who set fire to Vic's house?' Sidney asked. 'Same people who torched Otto's barn, I assume. But why the hell would anyone do that in the first place?'

She hadn't thought Tai could look any more despondent. Seemed she was wrong.

'Casey *does* have someone helping her with those enquiries,' he said. 'I can't tell you who it is this time, I'm afraid.'

Someone he knew, Sidney guessed. Someone he heartily wished wasn't involved — a friend or maybe even family? How tough would *that* be — knowing a person you cared about had not only put people's lives at risk, but might also be facing a lengthy jail sentence?

Yes, other people's problems could certainly put your own into perspective. Hers still loomed over her, gargantuan and terrifying, like Godzilla. But she was healthy, her boys were safe, she had a roof over their heads and masses of support. She could handle it, just like she'd handled it for the last ten years.

'So what's the plan?' she said. 'How can we help Vic?'

CHAPTER 31

Patricia

The week was flying by far too fast. Friday was only two days away. Two short days and then Reuben would be gone. No more reading in the conservatory. No more 'hi-ya' in the hallway, or kicking a ball endlessly on the lawn. No more snail hunts or kneeling side-by-side planting annuals. No more 'PleasemayIleavethetable' or 'Thankyouformylovelytea'. No more mud traipsed inside. No more boys' clothes to wash, dry and fold, each soft, child-sized item a poignant reminder that this was a moment in time that would not recur. Reuben would grow, and become whatever kind of man his life circumstances and his own decisions would allow. Patricia tried not to let pessimism cloud her vision of his future. There was always hope for the young.

She knew that filling this last week with treats and special outings was more for her sake than his. On Monday, they'd visited the Hampton library, happily sat in on story time with the under fives. Taken out more books than could be read in the coming week. Patricia might pass them on to Maree, if returning them to the library wasn't one task too many for her. The young woman must have relished the freedom of this trip. How wonderful to be surrounded by people her age and in clean, bright surroundings. No ill parents. No disintegrating house. Was there a chance that Maree might choose to stay away, or give up her responsibilities and start afresh somewhere new? No. Maree was purposeful and resolute. She'd set herself a goal: buy a house of her own, accommodate her parents, and Reuben until he was ready to leave. She would see it through.

After the library, Patricia and Reuben had gone to a film — a rather strange Japanese cartoon adaptation of *Howl's Moving Castle*. Patricia had first read Diana Wynne Jones when she was in her twenties, more than a decade past the intended reading age but not too old, it transpired, to adore the magic. Over the coming years, she read every book the author wrote. Patricia wasn't sure Reuben understood everything that happened in the film, but the magic grabbed him just as it had her all those years ago. He was particularly captivated by the castle itself: a flying beast that resembled a Victorian inventor's scrap heap crossed with Baba Yaga's chicken-legged hut. Patricia tried not to think about the boy returning to the decrepit gloom of his family home. Maree would be there. She'd provide the light.

Coming home late Monday afternoon, Patricia had been caught up by Bernard on the news of the weekend, and the plight of poor Vic Halsworth, a man she knew only vaguely by sight but would soon know better, as he was apparently due for dinner at their house the following night, along with Doc Love, who was one of a team, including Sidney, Tai Te Wera and Mac Reid, who were keeping an eye on Vic, supporting him through this crisis.

'I'm sorry it's short notice,' said Bernard. 'You don't mind, do you?'

'It's the least we can do,' Patricia had replied.

Not being familiar with Vic, Patricia had been unable to tell whether his lack of conversation was normal or a result of shock and grief. He'd eaten everything that was put in front of him, which might be a reassuring sign or could simply have been his habit. No farmer worth their salt left food on the plate. Doc Love had kept the conversation going, in his gently humorous, comforting way, and then drove Vic to Willow Cottage. Bernard and Patricia had washed the dishes in contemplative silence, and gone to bed.

Now it was Wednesday. At breakfast, Reuben had begged to go to *Howl's Moving Castle* again, but, alas, it had been replaced by another Japanese cartoon that looked far too frightening. So she'd suggested instead that they visit the Hampton adventure playground. The place had all manner of climbing frames, swings, tunnels, turrets, and even a flying fox, which Patricia hoped Reuben wouldn't need her assistance with. Running up a slope (or, indeed, down) was not her forte. They could spend the morning there and then go to lunch at the Kozy Kettle. Reuben, who'd picked up early on that this was a special treat week, might make a plea for McDonald's. But after an energetic morning at the playground, Patricia knew she'd be craving the dusty calm of the Kozy Kettle and, most likely, one of their jumbo-sized sausage rolls.

As it turned out, the only one expending energy at the playground was Reuben. Farsighted planners (no doubt parents themselves) had placed comfortable seats all around, each with excellent visibility of the equipment, so you could avoid those moments of panic when your child went out of view. Patricia had a book in her bag; she always carried one, in case a quiet (or deadly dull) moment presented itself. The playground designers, bless them, had also put safety first, and as other children his age were all at school, Reuben only had to share with a handful of toddlers, who were unable to compete for the monkey bars and preferred to cluster around the sandpit. Patricia was considering that it just *might* be safe to take her eyes off him and spend a few blissful minutes reading her book.

'Hello,' said a voice at her side. 'I saw you through the fence on my way to the park. May I join you?'

Patricia was surprised to see Sidney's partner, Kerry, in one hand a full paper bag covered in grease spots.

'Of course,' she told him. 'Are you on an early lunch break?'

'No.' Kerry sat rather heavily on the seat. 'I've taken the week off. Needed some time to think. Hard to do that when you're having trouble localising strings in nested non-determinative view stacks.'

'I can offer no help with that, I'm afraid,' said Patricia with a smile.

'No one with a soul could.'

Kerry gave her only the briefest smile in return. Normally, he was a buoyantly cheerful young man, full of gab and charm. When Patricia had first met Kerry, she'd described him to Bernard as having a whiff of the snake-oil salesman about him. But he'd put his heart and soul into Littleville until he'd been forced to find full-time employment, and he was devoted to Sidney and excellent with her boys. Patricia's opinion of him had measurably improved.

'Is that young Reuben over there?' said Kerry, in surprise. 'Swarming across that climbing edifice? If a single child can constitute a swarm, which evidence would suggest they can.'

'It is,' said Patricia. 'He'll be pleased to see you. He still talks about your football coaching.'

'God, does he?'

Kerry seemed dispirited by the news.

'I wish I'd been able to continue,' he said. 'I feel I let those children down.'

'Sidney's boys have now found alternative coaching in Hampton, I gather?'

No reply. Kerry bent forward, swung the paper bag listlessly between his knees.

'Is everything all right?' Patricia enquired.

'I am troubled.' Kerry exhaled the words as he sat up. 'Troubled with a capital T that rhymes with B that stands for—'

He clipped the end off his sentence. His tone had begun to shift,

Patricia noted, from half-hearted towards angry.

'May I offer a confidential ear instead?' she said. 'Reuben and I are having lunch at the Kozy Kettle, but we won't leave here for at least another half hour.'

He screwed up his mouth as if embarrassed. But his expression when he faced her told her he intended to accept her offer.

'You may regret this,' he warned.

'Oh, I think it's important to do things you may regret,' said Patricia. 'Because if you don't, you miss out on far too much.'

And Kerry told her everything. About Sidney keeping her pregnancy from him. (And them, Patricia reflected; but then, she had never been pregnant herself, so how could she have spotted the signs?) About how Sidney might have terminated the baby without even consulting him, without giving him any say in the matter whatsoever.

'It's my child, too,' he protested. 'How could she *do* that to me? To the baby? *Our* baby.'

In Patricia's experience, it was better not to attempt an answer to these questions at this point. Like all those wrestling with resentment, fear and hurt, Kerry didn't want quick solutions imposed by others. He wanted to talk it out, expel it in words, shift it round and around, until, like one of those picture puzzles with the moveable squares, the right course of action finally became evident.

'I've never *been* so upset, so *furious*. I've never felt so *betrayed*. I'm *still* furious. I can't—'

His voice lowered to a near-whisper.

'I don't think I can forgive her.'

Reuben was on the flying fox now. He was used to playing on his own, and did so quite happily. When he bumped to a stop, he slid off lithe as an eel, grabbed the rope end and pulled it all the way back to the start. Like a mini Sisyphus, was Patricia's thought, but happy, contented. If only we could face all our obstacles like that.

'Thing is, I love her.'

Kerry was moving the squares.

'She's the first woman I've ever truly loved, and my greatest wish has been to marry her and have children. But how can — I can't work out how to let this go. It's *killing* me. I'm reduced to sitting in parks, eating terrible potato-top pies and fantasising about drinking myself into a stupor. Which I've only done once, by the way,' he added. 'Still feel queasy, though that might be the pies.'

The pressure had been released, and he was perking up. Now it was safe for Patricia to offer a small amount of advice.

'Loving somebody doesn't mean you'll never be hurt by them, or vice versa. Hurt is, I feel, almost an esssential aspect of a relationship, because it forces you to decide whether or not you wish to continue. And if you *do* wish to, you must put that hurt behind you. Let it go, as you say. You must forgive, and move on.'

'But *how*?' Kerry demanded. 'How can I forgive such a *huge* betrayal? How can I ever trust her again?'

'By choosing to,' said Patricia. 'Forgiving someone doesn't mean condoning their behaviour. It doesn't mean hiding how you feel. What it means is deciding not to dwell on that past behaviour or bad choice, not to let resentment and anger fester and poison your present life together.'

'And all I have to do is make that choice and the bad thoughts magically disappear?'

Kerry sounded both cynical and hopeful.

'No, you have to work at it on a daily basis,' said Patricia. 'As I can attest. For my part, I try to focus on what I like, and what I'm grateful for, and that seems to counteract the bulk of ill feeling. And also, it's so much *nicer* being in love, and knowing that you're helping and supporting someone. Without wishing to emotionally blackmail you, Sidney has been on her own for years. Giving, not receiving, is what makes you truly happy. Why *wouldn't* you want to choose that?'

Kerry was quiet for a full minute before he spoke.

'Have you ever considered getting a job as a guru?'

'I'm not built for sitting on the peaks of mountains,' Patricia replied, with a smile.

'Yes, I've often wondered whether they suffer from piles. Deep vein thrombosis, too, from all that leg crossing.'

'Kerr-eeee!'

Reuben had spotted him and was sprinting over, beaming from ear to ear.

'My man!'

Kerry held up a palm and the pair high-fived. Then he had to move both hands into a defensive position as Reuben aimed a 'hi-ya' kick at his head.

'Woah, there, Jackie Chan,' said Kerry. 'Mind the fizzog.'

'What's a fizz-hog?'

Bernard had got so excited by Reuben's keenness to understand new words that Patricia had overheard him once attempting to explain how to identify the ablative in a Latin phrase. Reuben, to his credit, had been giving him his full attention.

'It's a nonsense word for your face,' explained Kerry. 'Like this is your gob.' He pointed at Reuben's mouth. 'And—' His nose '—this is your snot.'

'Snot!' Reuben fell about, giggling.

'Or you could call it your "boat",' Kerry continued. 'That's Cockney rhyming slang. Boat race is your face. Scotch eggs are your legs. Chalk Farm's your arms. And the Queen Mum is your—'

'BUM!'

Reuben was laughing so hard, he fell into Kerry, who was laughing, too, caught by the contagious nature of a child's unfettered hilarity.

'Football!' said Reuben, when he could speak again.

'Sorry, matey,' said Kerry. 'I didn't bring a ball with me. Only a potato-top pie, and while they can be quite satisfying to punt, you can only do it once.'

'Would you like to join us for lunch?' Patricia asked. 'And if you don't have plans for the afternoon, how about a kick around in our back garden?'

'Yesyesyesyesyes!'

Reuben jumped up and down clapping his hands.

'Much as I'm tempted to stick to my original plan, which was to go home and lie around in a darkened room feeling sorry for myself,' said Kerry, 'I think I'll accept your kind invitation. Thank you.'

Kerry left at five o'clock, after lunch, back garden football, and an afternoon tea that included a lecture from Bernard about the progress of Littleville. Bernard still harboured reservations about what he referred to as 'young Macfarlane's organisational inadequacies' and blamed him for allowing Elaine to nearly put an end to the project, though it was only Kerry's purchase of an old farmhouse, complete with barn, that had enabled Littleville to live on.

'With all the delays,' Bernard said, 'it's been generous of Charles Love to allow his war game dioramas to be housed in the barn. And it's *very* fortunate that he has continued good relations with Meredith and Jonty Barton, otherwise we might have lost their commitment to provide the dolls' house and miniature railway. I gather Jonty is still to be fully convinced, so let's hope Charles can succeed where you could not.'

The Bartons had been Kerry's first employers, the job the

reason he'd come to Gabriel's Bay. It had not ended on a high note, and from Kerry's quick wince, Patricia could tell Bernard's foil had made a palpable hit.

'I agree that we're in Doctor Love's debt,' said Kerry. 'Though occasionally, I have to say, his war gaming cronies can be quite rowdy. I could overhear heated debate during the recent re-enaction of the Battle of Kursk. That's the danger when you mess around with history. HG Wells was quite right.'

Bernard ignored this.

'And, of course, Charles has successfully secured a generous sponsorship. Which means, once the funds clear, that work can begin on turning the barn into an appropriately equipped visitor facility. I assume you're prepared for this?'

A startled glance at Patricia showed that Kerry was about as prepared as medieval Europe had been for the bubonic plague.

'Bernard, dear,' she said. 'Poor Reuben is dropping with exhaustion. Could you take him into the living room and set him up in front of the television?'

Her husband blinked, then observed that Reuben was, indeed, nodding in his chair, too tired to even finish the biscuit he still held in one hand.

'Of course, dear.'

Gently, Bernard coaxed the biscuit from sticky fingers, and led Reuben away.

'Thank you,' said Kerry, when they'd left. 'I have to confess my mind has *not* been on creating Gabriel's Bay's number one tourist attraction.'

'I imagine not.'

'I have big decisions to make, don't I?' he said.

A smile was as much reassurance as she could provide.

He stood, ready to leave, and bent down and kissed her on the cheek.

'I wish I were just like you,' he said. 'All serene and Zen-like. Able to do the Kipling thing of keeping your head, and forcing heart and nerve and sinew to keep on serving. I suppose, as usual, I'll just have to work harder at it.'

After seeing Kerry to the door, Patricia walked to the living room to check on Reuben, found him asleep on the sofa with his head in Bernard's lap. Bernard looked up from his book, smiled at her to say, 'All is well.'

He was right, but he was also very wrong. Patricia retreated to the kitchen, busied herself clearing dishes, wiping crumbs, trying to deflect the pain of her breaking heart.

What were those other lines from Kilping's 'If'? 'And so hold on when there is nothing in you / Except the Will which says to them: Hold on!'

Kerry had been wrong, too. She gave only the impression of being serene. When Reuben left, day after tomorrow, it would feel like there was nothing in her. She'd feel stripped, barren, bereft and, despite Bernard's company, alone.

And she did not trust that she could hold on. She did not know how she would bear it.

CHAPTER 32

Devon

What was happening? It was like his punch-up had caught hold of some metaphorical thread and now everything around him was unravelling. On Sunday afternoon, Jacko had left a message on his phone to say he was shutting the Boat Shed for a week and going bush. Devon didn't know if the punch-up was the cause, and he sincerely hoped it wasn't.

On Monday, Devon had phoned Sidney.

'No idea,' she confessed. 'All I know is that, since yesterday, Mac's been a bit — tense.'

'She and Jacko aren't having woes? I thought they were tight for eva.'

'Doubt it. More likely something to do with Emma. Maybe she and the pirate boyfriend are getting engaged. Really hope not. Have you met him?'

'Uh — briefly,' said Devon.

'Have you called Emma?' Sidney asked.

'Left a message,' Devon lied.

'Oh, well, Emma's not backward about coming forward, so she's bound to tell you. If it's not a big secret, let me in on it. I could do with the distraction.'

'You OK yourself?' said Devon.

'Peachy,' she replied. 'You?'

'Yeah, good.'

It was much easier to lie over the phone.

'Well, fingers crossed Jacko re-opens next week,' said Sidney. 'I need the dosh. But then, sigh, what's new.'

But that wasn't true, was it, Devon had thought when he'd hung up. Everything had changed. He'd smashed the shit out of a guy — and who knows how far he would have gone if Dr G hadn't pulled him off?

He'd lied about his hands to his parents; told them it'd happened sparring at Muay Thai. Since then, he'd been avoiding everyone — hadn't returned Emma's calls or texts, used study commitments as an excuse to stay in his room when at home, and a wish to steer clear of the crazies when he headed off early or came back late. Most times, he didn't go out the front door, anyway, but out the back garden gate, across the paddocks to Tiu. The horse was restless, wanted to go riding — he knew the signs. But that felt like a pleasure he didn't deserve right now. He whispered an apology in Tiu's soft, twitching ear, and hoped the horse would forgive him.

He'd called in sick to Mrs Dickens at Lightning Tree. Couldn't face Moana. More accurately, he couldn't face the prospect he might get angry again. None of this was her fault, but just seeing her would remind him of what he'd lost, and how he'd lost it. Even if he kept his cool, Moana would spot his bruised, scabby knuckles and demand he tell all. He probably would, too, even though he knew he wouldn't be able to bear her inevitable scorn.

He'd spun some line about being ill to Logan, too, to get out of his Muay Thai lessons. Logan was another person who'd want to know about the marks on his hands. Another who'd look at him with scorn . . .

At least the hounding had died right down. Story was old now — journalists were onto new shit, such as crims with absurdly handsome mugshots. Get out of jail, score a modelling contract.

Good luck to them. Phone didn't ring off the hook any more, and the parcels and letters had stopped coming. The last little group of crazies was still out there, sitting on the footpath, but Devon got the impression even they'd got new interests now, and were hanging around because they liked each other's company. They used to shout and wave frantically whenever they spotted him coming or going. Now, they often didn't even look up from the phone they shared between them. He ought to be relieved, but, of course, it felt like another rejection. Emotions were like banana skins in bad cartoons — sent you flat on your arse to guffaws of canned laughter.

Now it was Thursday, the week was nearly over, and he'd done sweet fuck all except hide. His excuses about study were actually true — he had an assignment due in five days, on speciation, but he hadn't even started his research. Instead, he was sitting on his bed, rolling his phone over and over in his hand, working up the courage to finally call Emma.

Fuck it. Phenotypes and polyploidisation would have to wait. He hit the call button on Emma's contact.

'Hey, stranger.'

Though she'd answered immediately, her voice sounded flat, tired.

'Hey,' said Devon. 'Sorry I haven't got back to you. Sorry for — yeah, well, everything.'

'Over and done,' said Emma. 'No lasting damage.'

'Your man OK?'

'Not my man. And who cares?'

'And — are you OK?'

'Fair to say I've been better,' she replied.

'Want to tell me about it?'

'Thanks, but it's my mess. I have to clean it up all on my own.'

'What kind of mess?'

He could hear her breathing. Shallow, rapid.

'Gotta go, Dev,' Emma said, and hung up.

Shit. What was going on?

He lay back on his bed. Man, his room stunk. Time for some fresh air.

Sneaking quickly out the back door, he headed for the far end of the back garden, where there was an old seat one of his uncles had made from slabs of macrocarpa. Devon had never smoked, and neither did his parents, so this was where his nicotine-addicted whānau escaped to. The seat was out of sight of the house, behind the shed. Good place when you wanted to be alone—

'Eh, boy.'

Koro Tama, sitting back, cigarette in hand. Devon didn't know whether to be outraged or entertained.

'Thought you gave up years ago?' he said.

'Gunna be ninety in a month,' the old dude said by way of explanation. 'Figure I've earned the right to the odd hikareti.'

'Can't argue with that,' said Devon.

'Don't tell your mum, eh?'

Seemed Gabriel's Bay bred all its women tough. Even his grandfather was scared of Devon's mother. It was like she channelled the spirit of all the feisty female ancestors.

'You off to take care of your hōiho?'

'Nah, done that already. Tiu's good.'

Koro Tama patted the wooden seat.

'Come sit then. Talk to your Koro. Tell me why you've been so ririwhakariuka these past days.'

That obvious, huh? But then it would be, wouldn't it? Devon had always been a creature of habit, steady, reliable, predictable. Skulking round, restless, unsettled — that wasn't him. His parents would have noticed, too, but they'd trust him to sort it out because he always had. He'd never let his whānau down. Until now.

But, as he'd said, Koro Tama was nearly ninety. Could anything shock him now? Devon sat down next to his grandfather.

'I got in a fight,' he said. 'Completely lost it. Hurt a guy pretty badly.'

Koro Tama blew a wisp of smoke up into the sky.

'Did he deserve it?'

'He insulted me, but I should have shrugged it off.'

'What'd he say?'

Devon was embarrassed. Even before he'd grown into his current looks, he'd been the only one with lighter skin and blonde hair. But his whānau had never, *ever* made him feel like he wasn't one of them. They'd *never* focused on his appearance, always on his character. They had no tolerance for others who made remarks, singled Devon out. And he knew how fortunate he was. Knew it was perhaps why he'd always worked so hard — he wanted to pay his family back for everything they'd given him. Wanted to make them proud.

To tell Koro Tama about what set him off was to admit that he wasn't happy. That he was the only one of his loyal whānau who *wasn't* OK with how he looked. That he was an ungrateful, precious, discontented loser.

But he'd started the story now. Was kind of obliged to finish.

'He questioned my manhood,' said Devon.

Close enough.

'Ah.'

From the raspy chuckle, Devon knew Koro had seen right through him.

But all he said was, 'You know that movie, boy? The one with that John Travolta and the rock-and-roll songs?'

What the hell?

'You mean *Grease*?"

'*Grease*, that's the one.'

'Yeah, I've seen it on DVD. Why?'

'The lady actor—?'

'Olivia Newton-John.'

'She starts off all sweet and innocent, but to get her man, she decides to dress up in the leather, and the high heels.'

'Koro, no offence, but what are you on about?'

The old man stubbed his cigarette on the ground. No doubt he'd do what the other smokers did — pick it up before he left and put it in the outside bin, well wrapped in newspaper so Devon's mum didn't spot it.

'You could stick to your guns,' said Koro, 'or you could try a few changes. Adapt. Maybe make it easier to get what you want. That Olivia-John was still the same on the inside.'

Right. Got it.

'You're talking about me cutting my hair.'

His family had always teased him about his hair, sure, but Devon thought they supported his wish to keep it long. And now, here was Koro suggesting otherwise.

Was he right? Devon had studied enough about adaptation to know it was common, natural, to every living thing from mammals to parasites. Species adjusted to survive in changing environmental conditions and, of course, to dominate in the sexual attractiveness stakes. Devon knew this subject very well; he'd have a whole frigging *degree* in it in a couple more years. It had been right in his face the whole time.

'Fuck,' said Devon without thinking. If it had been Karani Agnes next to him, she would have clipped his ear.

'Too true, too true.'

Koro Tama shook his head, pulled the cigarette pack out of his pocket, flipped open the top, held it out.

'Want a smoke?'

Devon took a walk, all the way to the beach. Sat on the cold sand while the wind whipped around him, and the gulls squawked and squabbled amongst the kelp.

He had other options. He could take Emma's advice, given what seemed like an eon ago, and leave town. He could go where there were people even more unusual looking than he was. He hated the city, but perhaps noise and crowds and cramped indoor spaces were the price he had to pay?

Maybe he could seek out that model agency again, see if they were still interested? Living in the city might not be so bad if you had money . . .

Phone beeped. A text from Moana.

'U in 2moro?'

Was he? Or would he be getting on a bus, hitting the highway, catching the midnight train to any-the-fuck-where?

He balanced the phone in his palm for a moment, staring at her name.

'Yep,' he texted back. 'CU thn.'

'GR8 xx!' was her instant response.

Ridiculous, the effect of two little xes. Meant nothing but everything at the same time.

Devon got up off the sand, dusted off his damp pants, shoved his phone in his pocket and walked home.

Where he sought out his mother's sewing scissors and his dad's razor, and locked himself in the bathroom. How long would he be in there? He didn't know. He'd never done this before. He'd probably make a pig's ear of it.

He picked up the pair of scissors. Its gold handle flashed in the mirror.

Time to adapt.

CHAPTER 33

Emma

It wasn't until things didn't go your way, Emma reflected, that you realised how much they always had up till now. In twenty-three years, she'd had very little to distress or frustrate her. She'd had a loving, stable, free-range childhood and an adolescence untroubled by acne, weight issues or broken hearts. She'd been academically able across the board, sporty, popular with school friends and liked by the teachers who weren't threatened by her desire to question everything. (The principal was one of these, and Ms Kelly and Emma had come to an agreement early on about how Emma would behave in the classes of the teachers she did *not* respect.) Her parents hadn't been concerned when she dropped out of university to go overseas. Neither of them believed there was some straight path to success; in their view, you'd be better off climbing trees and mountains than a so-called career ladder. Emma and her brother had been raised to be independent in spirit, thought and action, and under no illusion that the world owed them anything. Whatever they wanted to have or do, it was up to them to figure out how, and be determined enough see it through.

Which was entirely sound advice — *if* what you wanted didn't turn out to be a steaming pile of destructive doo-doo that fucked up your life and the lives of everyone you cared about, not to mention a bunch of people you hardly knew. Consequences, eh? They were right pricks.

And the worst by far was the reaction of her dad. When Emma had confirmed Tai Te Wera's claim that she was behind the dirty farming website, and that her group was probably responsible for the arson attacks, her dad hadn't yelled at her or even given her a stern telling-off. In fact, he hadn't uttered a single word, just got up from the kitchen table and left the room. Next thing they knew, he'd packed his hunting gear and supplies into his old red ute and taken off for the bush. Left King the dog at home, so they knew he'd be a while. Emma didn't dare ask her mum how long. Her mum had expressed her disappoinment with Emma in a few choice words and some testy slamming of cupboard doors as she fetched another packet of Krispies. But when Emma's dad had driven off, her mum'd gone horribly quiet. Retreated to her bedroom and stayed there for the rest of Sunday. Got up super early on Monday morning and went to work. Emma cooked dinner for them both — least she could do — but conversation was sparse and strained, and she didn't have the right to push it. That was how it'd been all week, and she had no choice but to suck it up. As she'd said to Devon (who, thankfully, unbelievably, was still speaking to her), it was her mess. She had to clean it up.

How, though? When Casey Marshall came round, all Emma could tell her was how she'd met Loko, and what kind of group he was involved with. She couldn't name names because she'd never known them; that wasn't how these groups worked. She couldn't even be sure they *had* been behind the arson attacks, though odds were high. Loko had kept Emma in the dark; she hadn't even been privy to the real name on his passport. She could have spun Casey some sob story about him using her, but in truth, she'd been a willing participant. She'd believed in the group's cause and, to some extent, their methods — marches and signs were pretty futile forms of protest; if you wanted real change, you had to force it. But, again, that was OK (maybe) when you were

317

acting against corporates and organisations with resources and insurance. When it was ordinary people in your community who suffered loss — that was like robbing your mate's family home. It was a callous betrayal.

Emma had always admired Casey. She'd babysat Emma and her brother Harry often, and even though she was only six years older, she had an absolute knack for maintaining order. No shouting, pleading or bargaining; just a quiet, unyielding presence that tapped into some primitive wolf-pack urge to obey. When Casey asked you to turn the TV off now, you turned it off. Emma had responded the same way when Casey had interviewed her. Told her what she knew and what she'd done without once trying to justify or explain. No point. Casey would only wait until you were done blathering and press on with her next question. She'd noted Emma's answers without a single flicker of judgement, which made Emma feel worse, not better. This was Casey in professional mode, a police constable doing her job; not the person Emma had known since she was little. This Casey was not Emma's friend. Highly likely that Emma would have zero friends when her part in this got out, as it must in a small town. Oh, well, she should have thought of that earlier.

Well, there *was* Devon, who, yesterday, to her surprise, finally returned her calls. He'd asked if she was OK, too, so he must still care at least a bit. Emma hadn't been in the mood to chat — she'd just found out that Vic Halsworth had no insurance and would probably have to sell up — but today, she could do with some company. Devon worked mornings at Lightning Tree, but maybe he could come round for lunch? The kitchen felt so lonely without her dad banging around as he did, talking to suppliers on the phone, planning menus, experimenting with new dishes, talking to the dog, yelling at some 'plonker' on the radio.

Emma knew he'd be perfectly safe out in the bush, and that

when her dad came home, he would have worked his frustration and disappointment out of his sytem. But she also knew that their relationship would never be the same, that a vital, glowing thread had been severed, undermining forever the strength of their connection.

She could shrug off the criticisms of the townsfolk — had plenty of times before — but the prospect of a reduction in her parents', particularly her dad's, esteem was a whole other stinking fish kettle. They'd always love her, no doubt of that, but unconditional love was part of the natural parent-child bond. It didn't mean your parents had to respect you — or even like you. The thought of even the slightest coolness in her dad's eyes when he looked at her filled Emma with nauseated dread. She'd have to leave town, for good this time. She wouldn't be able to bear it.

Crap. That sucked so much she wanted to cry. Crying alone sucked too. Emma bit her lip, picked up her phone and called Devon.

'Not answering right now,' said the voice that was so familiar, so dear to her. 'Leave a message.'

'Guess you're working,' she said to no one. 'Call me if you have time. Nothing urgent. Just—' She had to take a breath, bite her lip harder. 'Like to catch up is all.'

And she ended the call, and wiped away a tear that had annoyingly emerged. Emma was like her mum — she didn't see crying as a weakness, but there were many more practical things you could expend your energy on when it all went tits up.

The tear was followed by another. Fuck it. She let it slide down her cheek.

A knock on the back door made her jump. Voice outside. 'Hello?'

Gene. What did *he* want? To give her shit like he always did?

'Hey.' Emma opened the door only a crack. 'Dad's not here.'

'I know,' said Gene. 'It's you I've come to see.'

'I don't need *your* opinion, thanks. Got enough of those to be going on with.'

'I'm not here to offer an opinion,' he said. 'I'm here to apologise.'

'For what?'

Gene's shoulders sagged, as if he didn't have the strength.

'Em, will you just let me in? Let me talk?'

'Fine.' Emma opened the door. 'But if you want a cup of tea, you can make it yourself.'

Emma had known Gene for all her twenty-three years, and while she'd seen him angry and fed up, she'd never once seen him in despair. Gene was like one of those toys that bounce right up again when you try to knock them over. He never, ever, let life beat him down, which is probably why he and her dad had stayed friends all these years. Neither of them messed with Mister In-Between.

But across the table from her now was a man she hardly recognised. Gene looked grey, worn, penitent. Emma wondered what on *earth* he was about to tell her.

'I did a bad thing asking you to — you know — with the building site,' he said. 'It was out of order, unfair on you, and puredee wrong. I want to make amends. But I can't fess up to Casey, because that would drop both of us in it, wouldn't it?'

'Oh, yeah,' said Emma. 'I've been shown the relevant section in the Crimes Act. Anyone who incites another person to commit an offence is party to and guilty of that offence. Whether you were there or not.'

'Shit.' Gene's eyes went bushbaby. 'I've only been thinking about the vandalism. What about the arson? Do the cops consider you party to that?'

'The wording on the website doesn't actually *say* burn down someone's house. But, you know, if they wanted to make an example of me, then they probably could claim it was inciting *some* kind of violence.'

'Shit . . .'

Gene brought his mug of tea up to his mouth, set it down again without drinking.

'I'm really sorry, Em. I mean, it's not as if I consider myself a particularly responsible adult, but I *did* think I was a decent human being. But entangling you in my petty revenge fantasy — that was low. Despicable, scuzzball low.'

'I had a choice,' she said. 'I could have told you to sod off.'

'You're a better man than I am, Gunga Din. If I were you, I'd blame me big time.'

Gene's face went from grey to green. Looked like he was about to throw up.

'I mean, Christ, you're my best friend's *daughter*. What kind of rat fink *dirt*ball would—'

'Don't tell Dad,' said Emma, hastily. 'Ever. Please.'

Gene made a rueful face. 'I have to, don't you think? I can't hide it from him.'

'Yes, you can,' said Emma. 'Dad's barely coping with my shenanigans. If he finds out you're involved, too, another person he cares about, that he trusts, his world will crash down in pieces. Don't do that to him. Please?'

'So I get off scot free?' said Gene. 'No blame, no shame? Public, at least.'

Emma's tea was cold, and the milk was scummy. She stared down into it anyway. Even though you knew life wasn't fair, it felt bad when you encountered actual proof. But making amends had been top of *her* mind, too, and there was an idea she'd been toying with . . .

'Could you — I don't know — set up some kind of fundraising effort?' she said. 'For Otto and Mr Halsworth? Help them out that way?'

A tiny gleam returned to Gene's eye.

'Otto had insurance, so he's covered,' he told her. 'But Vic — he *does* need help. Big time, poor bastard. Not that this community has a lot to give, but every bit will be better than nothing. Tide him over until he sells the place.'

Gene straightened up, animated now.

'I could rope in some volunteers to help with calving and lambing, get some people to donate food, too, clean his cottage, that sort of thing. Practical assistance as well as financial.'

He looked over at Emma.

'You want to help?'

'Will he let me anywhere near the place?'

The old shit-eating grin was back. 'Soon find out.'

Her phone beeped with a text. Devon. 'U free@5? Irsh pub Hmptn?'

'Wow, mega smile,' said Gene. 'New boyfriend?'

'Hell no.' Emma typed her reply. 'Someone *way* better.'

———

'Holy shit.' It was all she could say. 'Holy shit-a-fucking-brick. It's gone.'

'Can't deny it.'

Devon wasn't one for blushing, but there were definitely spots of colour on his cheeks. Probably why he'd chosen the Irish pub. Lighting was dim, and you could hide in the booths. Plus, no one they knew went there. No one under eighty-*five* went there. They'd had to manoeuvre around three mobility scooters to get in the front door.

Emma craned her neck, so she could view him from all angles.

'It looks *good*. Truly. You've left just enough on not to look like you've had lice or something. And your head's not a weird shape, either.'

'Thanks. I think.'

'Why'd you do it?'

Emma knew it was none of her business, but she needed to be sure he was OK. That this was a positive move, not the onset of a crisis.

Devon leaned back against the padded booth, raised his eyes to the nicotine-stained ceiling. A weird twisted smile appeared, and Emma began to worry.

But then he looked back at her, and his smile was now only a smidgeon wry.

'Why else do you make major life changes?' he said. 'I did it for love.'

Emma's heart lurched in panic. Did he mean her? She loved Devon, but she wasn't *in* love with him. Was their friendship about to crash and burn? With her rejecting him?

'Trouble is,' he went on, 'she's got someone else.'

'Yeah . . .?'

'Yeah, I was a dick and didn't realise how I felt until it was too late.'

The tension was *killing* her.

'What's her name?'

Dev fixed her with his best slitty-eyed glare.

'If I tell you, will you *swear* you won't interfere?'

Emma held up her palm.

'Swear,' she promised. 'My match-making days are over and *done*.'

'Good,' he said. 'Because if not, I'll — I'll think of something *ultra* bad to do to you.'

'Sure, sure,' said Emma, impatient. 'So-o — what's her name?'

Only a slight pause; he wanted to tell her. Even though the signs seemed to point to someone other than her, Emma had been wrong a *lot* lately. She braced herself.

'Moana,' said Dev. 'Works with me at Lightning Tree.'

Felt like melting into a puddle, every limb loosening with relief.

'And who's she hooked up with?'

'Brownie,' said Devon, with a hint of a sulk. 'Handsome Barrett Tahana.'

'Yeah, he *is* pretty handsome,' said Emma. 'Super sexy smile.'

'Always the comfort,' said Devon, dryly.

Emma grinned. He knew how she rolled.

'Is it serious?' she said. 'Are they in *lerrrv*?'

'Only had one date, far as I know. And Mo's super level-headed. Not one to rush into things. Brownie's, like, three years younger, too, so—' Devon emitted a bitter huff. 'Shit, listen to me,' he said. 'Trying to rationalise my wishful thinking. What a saddo.'

'You should tell her how you feel,' Emma said. 'You'll never know what *her* real feelings are until you do.'

Devon rubbed the bridge of his nose as if he had a headache.

'I almost did today,' he said. 'But I bottled. I'd like to say it was because we were shovelling horse shit at the time, but it was actually because she hardly even reacted to my hair. Immy and Mrs Dickens and even Jase went totally gaga, but Mo just kind of nodded once, all cool-like, and that was it. I figured she wasn't interested enough in me to comment.'

'Devon, my friend,' said Emma. 'You *have* to stop over-thinking. Just *talk* to her!'

He knew she spoke the truth. She could tell by his resentful expression.

'What about Brownie?' he said. 'I mean, he's not my bosom pal, but there's such a thing as bro-loyalty. I'd feel bad going behind his back.'

'Uh, newsflash, "Bro" — Moana doesn't belong to either of you. Only *she* gets to decide who she goes out with.'

'It's still shady as fuck.'

'Your call.' Emma spread her hands. 'But as Mum always says: don't ask, don't get.'

'And if I do ask, there's only a ninety per cent chance of total humiliation.'

'Welcome to the world, my friend,' said Emma. 'Only the tough survive.'

Devon gave her a look of both amusement and solidarity.

'And we're the toughest of them all, right?'

Emma lifted her glass of Guinness and clinked the edge of Devon's own.

'*Damn* right,' she said. 'We get knocked down, we get up again. No way the bastards are getting the better of *us*.'

CHAPTER 34

Ash

It was here. The email he'd been dreading. And as expected, it sent shivers, ones not limited to the area of the vertebral column.

'The girl is 25,' wrote his mother. 'Slim and of fairish complexion. Traditional family with numerous business interests. Her father was at first put off by your non-veg habits, but decided your qualifications would compensate. Needless to say, we have not mentioned your current location. The introduction will take place on the 30th inst. at our home. Arrive in enough time to look rested.'

No details about the 'girl', Ash noted. Such as education level, hobbies and interests, or even that inconsequential detail known as a name. Reading between the lines, he concluded it was not a daughter of any family his parents knew, so how did they find her?

With trembling fingers, he googled his full name and qualifications (so important) and scrolled the search results. And found his profile, complete with photograph of him at his graduation from medical school, on a website called happymatrimony.com.

His mother had been busy. If Ash's brothers were intractable, then Ash must be the lucky winner of the status wedding. Oh joy.

Ironically though, as a doctor, Ash was a more desirable commodity than either of his financier brothers. Indian parents still aspired to marry their daughters only to doctors or engineers.

Any other profession was newfangled and risky. Ash, to the vast majority of parents, was a catch. And his mother's seemingly casual reference to 'business interests' meant that the girl's family was wealthy, and though dowry was illegal now, that did not preclude the concept of lavish gifts. His parents had not become wealthy through altruism. They didn't care about other people. Or Ash, for that matter.

What to do? How to respond? Should he simply ignore it and plead ignorance? If he didn't turn up for the introduction, the girl's family would be offended, and would surely call off the whole arrangement. He would apologise from afar, from the location that was not to be mentioned, and with luck, his mother would give him up as a bad job.

Yeah, right, as the local saying went. When Ash's mother had a goal in mind, she was never deterred by trivial concerns, such as what anyone else wanted. If she'd decided Ash would be married, then pressure would be brought to bear. Holding a small child hostage, that sort of thing. Or worse, flying all the way here and refusing to leave. The people of Gabriel's Bay might have their faults, but no one deserved *that* level of punishment.

'Morning.'

Ash had long admired how Mac managed to tap on the door just after she'd opened it, thus rendering the tap redundant while giving the impression that she'd tried to be polite.

'Good morning,' he replied, as she placed the obligatory cup of milky tea on his desk. Doctor Love had enjoyed his tea with lots of milk, so Ash would, too.

Mac gave him a hard stare.

'You're looking peaky. Hit the turps last night?'

'No, but I could happily hit it right this very moment.'

He indicated the computer screen, where the email sat, square and deceptively innocuous as a slab of Semtex.

Mac chuckled, or perhaps cackled was more the *mot juste*.

'No photo of the bride to be,' she said. 'That a bad sign?'

'Not necessarily,' Ash said. 'My mother does like everything to reflect well on her, so it's unlikely she would choose a girl who is—'

'A huckery mole?'

'I have no idea what that means, but I can guess. She'll be no Priyanka Chopra but, yes, my mother would most probably balk at huckery mole-ness.'

'So are you going?' said Mac. 'To be "introduced"?'

'I really don't want to,' said Ash, with a sigh. 'But I doubt my own wishes enter into it.'

'Well, don't dilly-dally,' said Mac. 'End of the month is short notice to find a locum, so we'd need to get onto it pronto.'

'Duly noted.'

Ash closed his email, opened his calendar, frowned.

'Bronagh Macfarlane is my first appointment? I thought she and her husband had jetted back to the UK?'

'Phone call. She wants to talk to you about Vic Halsworth.'

'He is the farmer whose house burned down?'

'The very same.'

'I'm not sure I can discuss him without his consent,' Ash called after Mac. 'He *is* listed as a patient on our books.'

'Course you can,' was Mac's parting shot. 'Bronagh's a nurse. She won't say a word.'

Not scrupulously accurate, Ash thought. Ten minutes into the phone call and he'd managed to utter approximately half a sentence. Bronagh had many concerns about Vic, predominantly regarding his mental stability, and was using the conversation to successively relay them to Ash and talk herself into being less worried. The outcome was a call and response solo act, in which Ash had only a bit part.

'Now, of course, your rural type male can be terribly stoic, which doesn't help,' said Bronagh. 'They'd rather eat bulls' testicles than talk about emotions. Which is actually a dish, did you know? Served deep-fried or in a demi-glace, apparently. Though I suppose, being Hindu, you're vegetarian?'

'Well, actually—'

'But even if they *do* regularly snack on bulls' balls, they won't be any more likely to fess up if they're feeling down in the dumps. And our Vic, Lord love him, is locked tight as an oyster, if you'll pardon the spree of food analogies. Getting him to comment on the weather is chore enough. And I just think that with all he's been through, he'll be storing up the grief something terrible. He'll be like a peat bog, packed full of dense, smouldering matter that could burst into a raging fire at any time. Poof!'

'Yes, depression in farmers can be—'

'On the plus side, I hear he's got a lot of folk checking up on him. I know Sidney pops in regularly. She's pregnant, did you know? Of course you did, you're her doctor. I'm going to be a grandmother! And me only a youthful fifty-eight.'

'Congratu—'

'And that Gene fella's arranged some volunteer workers, so there will be folk on the farm during the day. I think someone should remove his guns, though. To be on the safe side. I'll see if Gene can whip them away when Vic's not looking. He strikes me as the sort of man who wouldn't shirk from a bit of trickery. Gene, not Vic. Vic wouldn't know how to lie if he were given a script to read out loud.'

'If you suspect Mr Halsworth is suicidal, we should ring the police,' said Ash.

'Way ahead of you, big guy,' said Bronagh. 'That young police constable is frighteningly efficient, isn't she? She says if anyone has the *slightest* concern, they're to phone her immediately.'

'That's goo—'

'But I'm still bothered. The man needs *counselling*. And no doubt a generous dose of anti-depressants. Is there any way you can coax him in to see you?'

Not really was the correct answer, but hardly the one Bronagh would accept. Not that it mattered—

'I'll give it a go,' she said. 'He trusts me. And he knows I'll jump on a plane and give him *what* for if he does anything stupid.'

'I can also visit him,' said Ash. 'In a neighbourly rather than a doctorly way.'

'Good man,' said Bronagh. 'Well, it's been great to chat. Take care now.'

And she hung up, leaving Ash conflicted. He'd successfully not compromised patient confidentiality, but only because he hadn't been given the chance. Bronagh had got it all sorted without him. Seems that was to be the theme of the day.

It was time for his next patient. A six-year-old with impetigo. To be followed by a pensioner with, according to Mac's note, an impressive case of haemorrhoids. Ash wondered how his mother had described his medical career to marriage candidates. Probably she ommitted the school sores and piles.

A calendar alert reminded him that tomorrow night was his first Scrabble evening with Magnus and Oksana since — well, how *would* he describe to them the events of Saturday last? Devon's unexpected pugilistic proficiency had not been as shocking as the revelation of the man with dreadlocks, though, if he were to be entirely honest, Ash should not have been in the least surprised. Emma had agreed to one night out with him, not an exclusive lifetime commitment. He had not asked about other attachments, so she had not lied. She was young, beautiful and independent, so what could he rightly expect? That she'd fall for him over the pommes frites, follow him home and never leave?

Delusional fantasising. It should be a recognised condition, with its treatment a large dose of reality, for best results administered in suppository form.

But first, Kayden Briggs and his rampant school sores.

'Message for you.'

Mac handed him a note as he passed her desk on his way to greet Mrs Briggs and her highly contagious son.

'Not urgent,' she added.

Ash thrust the note in his trouser pocket without looking. Anything labelled 'non urgent' could be safely ignored. Unlike his mother's email, which would glow like nuclear waste in his inbox until the last patient of the day had left, and he'd have no more excuses for postponing his response.

'And what did you tell her?'

Magnus and Oksana had listened in polite silence to Ash's tale. Mostly; Oksana had given the odd snort of derision, though as none were followed by explanatory comment, it was hard to tell who or what had elicited her scorn. Ash assumed it was he. It usually was. Oksana shared his view about delusional fantasies, but her cure, no doubt, would involve castor oil and ice baths, and quite possibly leeches.

'I told my mother I would have to organise a locum before I could commit to a date.'

Ash shifted around the Scrabble tiles on his rack and observed that he'd managed to spell A BLOUSE. As in 'a big girl's blouse', a phrase he'd first heard uttered by Jacko Reid. It meant 'milksop', apparently. Devon, the only one who would thus dare, had derided it as sexist, and instead of tearing him a new one (another phrase

Ash had learned), Jacko had agreed and altered it to 'woofter', whereupon Devon had given up.

'But you are hoping for an excuse to avoid the trip altogether?'

Magnus, perceptive as always. Yes, woofter, girl's blouse, milksop, fraidy cat — all would apply to Ash. He shifted the tiles again, and singled out U LOSE.

'A part of me wishes to accede,' said Ash. 'But I know that could be fatal to what exists of my self-esteem.'

'Many arranged marriages work well,' Magnus pointed out. 'In fact, evidence would suggest arranged couples are happier than those who chose each other.'

'My parents are quite satisfied,' Ash agreed. 'Although my father does like to joke that because he'd only met my mother once before the wedding, he couldn't be entirely sure it was the same woman at the altar.'

'In Russia, groom get fake bride and have to pay ransom for real one.'

Oksana, who pffted at Scrabble, was in the Eames lounger reading a translation of Erica Jong's *Fear of Flying*.

'Everyone laugh at fun trick,' she added. 'Then we have proper ceremony, and get drunk for whole week.'

'We also play games,' said Ash. 'And have weddings that last for days.'

'Not same as Russia,' said Oksana, crushingly and no doubt correctly.

'Of course, a legal marriage ceremony is not mandatory for an enduring relationship.'

Magnus had finished placing his tiles on the board. QUIXOTIC. Twenty-six points plus the X and C on triple letter scores.

Don Quixote. Now *there* was a man in the thrall of delusion.

'Oksana and I pledged our troth in the woods,' Magnus continued. 'With crowns of leaves and the birds as our witness.'

Nude, Ash imagined, and then immediately tried not to. Oksana was in a very brief pink kimono wrap this evening, and its waist tie had become rather loose. When she was younger, she would have been goddess-like: tall, blonde and athletic. A physique a lot like Emma's . . .

'How did you meet?' he asked, by way of distraction.

'I petitioned the universe, and she appeared.'

Was that a twinkle in Magnus' eye? Hard to tell — they did glitter so.

'Ripe Singles,' said Oksana from the lounger. 'Sexy dating site for over fifties.'

Who was Ash to judge, when his profile was probably still active on happymatrimony.com? (His mother was never one to count unhatched chickens, and without a qualm would discard the current prospect if a better — read wealthier — one came along.)

His turn. It wasn't the greatest word, but it did attain him two double letter scores plus the use of Magnus' Q and, below it, his Y from YTTRIUM. (It was a rare earth element, according to the dictionary, atomic number 39.)

'Queasy,' said Magnus. 'Fine descriptive word. From the Middle English "coisy". Twenty-six points. My turn — last tiles.'

Down they went, in parallel to Ash's previous. XYLOGRAPH.

'An engraving on wood,' said Magnus. 'Thirty-five points, plus a fifty point bonus for using all seven tiles. That takes my score to six hundred and fifty. And you are at two hundred and six.'

U LOSE, thought Ash. With this game, as with everything else in his life, he should be used to it by now. And to be fair, he *had* learned about yttrium.

It occurred to him that if Emma were telepathically privy to his inner monologues, then she would, in Bronagh Macfarlane's words, give him what for. (A phrase that meant a sound scolding; Ash was forever grateful that he was not living in a pre-internet time.)

He could hear Emma now, telling him to back himself and appreciate the qualities he had instead of hankering for those he did not. *You* are all you need to be, she'd told him, before they'd entered into a clinch, the memory of which still made Ash's extremities tingle.

But Emma was no longer in his life, and that was undoubtedly a good thing as they were hardly compatible. He was not her type, or her speed. Emma blazed through life while he had all the brilliancy of a Christmas lightbulb.

She would have told him off for that, too. *Everyone* loves Christmas lights, she would have said . . .

'Another glass of wine before you go?' said Magnus.

Ash stretched his arms above his head, de-kinked his neck and shoulders.

'Thank you, but I'd better not,' he said. 'I still need all my concentration for these rural roads.'

Magnus began to pack up the Scrabble set. His was a luxury edition that came in a burled-walnut case and had gold-plated racks and leather pouches. One day, Ash would summon the nerve to ask him how he made his money.

'You have plans for Sunday? Apart from, of course, contemplating the response to your mother.'

More nerve required. Ash had calculated that he could put her off until Tuesday. After that, he had to poop or get off the pot, as Jacko would very nearly say.

'I might take a bush walk,' said Ash. 'Peace and quiet and exercise could help me think.'

'You have given up all thought of hunting, I hope?'

'Oh, that was never for me,' Ash confessed. 'I will never be a so-called man's man. A cool sophisticate, neither. And I accept that. Hopefully, I will meet someone who accepts that also.'

Someone he couldn't quite imagine yet, owing to his mind

being still full of the unsuitable Emma. He needed to rein that in, let his rational brain take control. No use hankering after what we could not — *should* not — have.

Oksana looked up midway through Erica Jong and subjected him to scrutiny.

'You are handsome boy,' she said. 'Any girl in right mind should be happy.'

'Thank you,' said Ash, in surprise. Oksana had never once complimented him, and he wasn't quite sure how to take it.

'But she will have to see you when you not look like startled rabbit. Otherwise — pfft.'

With a wave of her hand, she settled down once more to whatever the Russian was for 'zipless fuck'. Ash's earth tilted back onto its normal axis.

Outside, Ash reached into his trouser pocket for his car keys and felt at the bottom a piece of paper. That's right, the note Mac had given him yesterday. If it hadn't been urgent then, it might have become so.

Inside the car, he switched on the roof light and uncrumpled it. The message was, with Mac's usual brevity, only a number and a name, but a name that immediately undid all of his resolutions to be rational.

Emma.

He checked the clock. Ten-forty. Late. But perhaps not *too* late.

Emma had already waited more than a day, so could no doubt wait until the morning. And she probably only wanted something trivial, like a prescription for more eye drops, though her eye had looked fine last time he'd . . .

Nerve, Ash. If she didn't answer, no harm done. If she did, he'd find out what she wanted.

He dialed the number. And waited.

CHAPTER 35

Sidney

'I'm sorry,' Kerry said again. 'I should have made more effort to step into your shoes. Considering what a big Jessie I am about even small physical inconveniences, like hangnails, I should have realised how hugely daunting it must feel to be pregnant.'

Sidney snuggled into him. Since Kerry had arrived back on her doorstep on Wednesday evening, arms full of flowers, eyes full of remorse, they'd had a satisfyingly large amount of make-up sex, made even more pleasurable by the fact they could now throw birth control to the wind. It was only eight on Sunday morning, and they'd already done it twice. The boys, up since six-thirty, had been well-trained not to barge into the bedroom, and now that they were old enough to work out what was going on, they didn't want to anyway. Aidan had pronounced the cause of Sidney's pregnancy 'disgusting'. Kerry suggested that he might feel differently once adolescence truly took hold, though they both agreed that connecting the sexual act with one's parents remained beyond the pale no matter *what* age you were.

Apart from that, the boys were thrilled by the prospect of having a sibling. Again, once reality hit, their enthusiasm might wane, but that was six months away. Plenty of time to prepare them for the outrages of crying, soiled nappies and regurgitated sour milk. Not to mention the possibility (not considered by them at this point) that their sibling might be a girl.

'No, *I'm* sorry,' said Sidney. 'It was wrong of me not to tell you earlier. We get all indignant about fathers who won't take responsibility and sod off to Aussie to avoid child support payments, and here I was not even giving you a *chance* to step up. I turned all *my* fears into barriers, when I could have dispelled them immediately by simply asking how you felt.'

Kerry kissed her, and smiled.

'We're being sickeningly generous with each other, aren't we?'

'Positively oleaginous,' agreed Sidney. 'Don't worry. I'll soon get exhausted and cranky and we'll be back to sniping in no time.'

'Good to hear. There's nothing so comforting as a familiar routine.'

There was silence as both of them absorbed the import of that quip.

'I think I'll skip the farmers' market today,' said Sidney. 'So I guess we could start discussing plans?'

'We don't have to immediately,' Kerry offered. 'Though I confess I base that on no prior knowledge of planning for such events.'

'Part of me wants to put thinking about the practicalities off for as long as possible,' said Sidney. 'But, yes, let's start while I still have some vestiges of energy. When I'm the size of a whale, *everything* will seem too hard.'

Kerry propped himself up on one elbow and looked down at her. Sidney hoped the baby would have his eyes, because they were such an attractive shade of brown. The red hair was nice, too, certainly better than her beige non-colour. And let's face it, if your only worry about your child was that they might be teased for being a ginger, then you were blessed indeed.

'You *do* want us to do this together, don't you?' Kerry asked her.

'Yes,' she said, firmly. 'I do.'

'Is that "I do" in the sense of—?' He paused. 'I'll pop off and make breakfast, shall I?'

'Good call,' said Sidney. 'Pancakes get my vote, with plenty of syrup. If I'm going to get whale-sized, I might as well enjoy the ride.'

Early Sunday afternoon and Sidney was feeling a little like a Victorian vicar's wife on her obligatory round of visits to the needy. First stop was Mac, who'd been without Jacko for almost a week now. Sidney knew how much Mac worried about Jacko's health, and also how much Mac hated that she worried. Jacko was an experienced, savvy bushman, and a crack shot, so there was little in the wild of threat to him. And over the new year, he'd given up smoking and let Doc Love give him a check-up, which had revealed him to be a generally healthy fifty-six-year-old male who would benefit from more regular exercise and less beer. Jacko, to no one's surprise, ignored the latter, but to everyone's absolute astonishment had taken up slow jogging along the beach, King the dog in boisterous tow. Devon joked that you always knew when Jacko was pounding the sands because the water in your glass started to ripple, like the scene in *Jurassic Park*.

Nonetheless, Mac worried.

'It's not Jacko so much as other people,' she told Sidney. 'Moron hunters who shoot first and gibber excuses later. Wild pigs, too. Unexpected crevasses.'

She cracked a Krispie in half with an air of snapping its spine.

'When I was young, I never turned a *hair*,' she said. 'He could be hanging out of a helicopter netting deer, driving stunt vehicles at absurd speeds, sailing miles out in deep water on a fishing boat, or flying a tiny top-dressing plane, dodging power lines and trees — and I never *once* doubted that he'd come home safe. It's only now that we're heading into our golden years that I see him as anything but ten-foot-tall and bulletproof. Probably projecting my own fears of mortality onto him,' she added. 'Getting older is a pain in the butt.'

'Mac, you've only just turned fifty-four,' said Sidney. 'Hardly old.'

'Emma's gone bush-walking with Doctor Ghadavi.' Mac was obviously keen to change the subject. 'I think they're an item.'

'*Are* they now?'

Sidney was intrigued. It seemed an unlikely pairing, but then on the surface, so did Mac and Jacko, and they were perfect for each other.

Mac was glowering into her tea as if it had scam-called her.

'She'll probably marry him and make me a grandmother before I'm ready.'

'You'll *adore* being a grandmother,' said Sidney. 'And I think it'll be safe to wait a *few* more days before you start planning the wedding.'

'Are you and Kerry getting hitched? Is he making an honest woman out of you?'

'One step at a time!' Sidney protested. 'We haven't even agreed on a name yet.'

'Meredith Barton told me Sophie's having a girl and calling it Kusama after that Japanese artist who covers everything in polka dots,' said Mac. 'Jonty will have an aneurysm.'

She dipped the Krispie in her tea. 'Fingers crossed.'

Seeing as that thought had perked Mac right up, Sidney took her leave. Next on the list was Vic, and even though neither he nor Sidney found the visits anything less than excruciating, they were in thrall to a higher power known as Bronagh Macfarlane, who had made Vic's wellbeing her zealous personal mission.

Bronagh rang Sidney every few days now, as part of checking up on everyone who'd promised to check up on Vic, and to talk about the baby. Unlike Mac, Bronagh was more than ready to be a grandmother, and had already started amassing a layette.

'I found a onesie that says, "If you think I'm cute you should see my grandma",' she'd informed Sidney. 'Though I was very taken by another that said, "I only cry when ugly people hold me".'

'Kerry found one with the AC/DC logo,' said Sidney. 'Only it says AB/CD. This child is going to feel like a living internet meme.'

'I did discard the one that said, "All Mummy wanted was a back rub".'

'And the unborn and I will be forever grateful.'

'Now, I've talked to Gene and he's managed to whip away Vic's guns,' said Bronagh. 'Also the big, sharp kitchen knife.'

'Won't Vic notice?' said Sidney.

'Well, he never cooks, and if he does, it's bacon and eggs which require, at most, tongs and a fish slice. And it's not forever,' Bronagh had emphasised. 'Just while he's in the mental danger zone. Another month or two and he should be back to his usual self.'

Which was not dramatically different from Vic's current self, Sidney reflected, as she drove up the road to his farm. Even at his best, he hadn't exactly sparkled with vivacity. But, poor man, he was doing it tough, despite the help that Gene had organised, including some of his own staff, who, once the fire brigade had deemed it safe, had helped clear the charred remains of the house. Nothing had survived intact bar a silver teapot, a few coins and the docking tool Vic had left on his sideboard. The guns Bronagh had mentioned were locked away in a luckily unscathed shed, along with the other farming tools. The garage had also been spared, as had Willow Cottage, where Vic was now ensconsed, looking, Sidney thought, rather like a giant who'd been forced to live in a gingerbread house.

He wouldn't be there long, however. A plea to the Hampton District Council from a group of townsfolk fronted by Tai Te Wera *and* Corinna had failed. The Council would not forgo or delay the fine. The farm was going to auction in two weeks. If it sold, Vic would have nowhere to live. There were no Halsworths who could put him up; all his relations were distant, both physically and kinship-wise. Gene was on the case of sourcing alternative accommodation, apparently. Sidney must ask him why he'd taken such an interest in helping Vic. Perhaps Gene, too, was feeling the pressure of his own mortality, and wanted to redress his Karmic imbalance before it bit him on the arse.

Sidney found a note taped to the door of Willow Cottage. The notepaper had Minions on it. Bronagh had observed several similar touches about the cottage, and concluded that Vic's ex-wife was a daft spanner, and he was better off without her.

The note said: 'Gone for a walk.'

Should she be concerned? He didn't have guns anymore, according to Bronagh, and she would have grilled Gene mercilessly on this point. The local trees had branches that were too slender or too high for slinging nooses over, and Sidney couldn't envisage Vic filling his pockets with stones and wading into the river, à la Virginia Woolf.

It was a lovely day. He'd probably craved fresh air and solitude, and who'd blame him? Sidney would phone him this evening, and if she got no reply, *then* she'd start to worry. She dug a pen out her bag, added 'Hope you enjoyed it, S' to the Minion note. Left on the doorstep a jar of tomato chutney that Vic might, but almost certainly wouldn't, consider adding to his eggs and bacon.

Sidney pulled out her phone, texted Kerry that she'd be back early. He'd taken the boys for a kick-around at the Hampton rec centre, after which they'd go for milkshakes at the new diner that had opened. Sidney had advised he regulate the speed of their intake, otherwise he'd find the milkshakes would re-appear on the drive back over the hill, adding a non-standard decorative feature to the interior of his car.

She ended the text with, 'Don't rush home'. It would be nice to have an hour to herself, though the irony of that did not escape her. Only a few short days ago, she'd been a miserable wreck convinced she'd be alone forever.

God. Sidney clutched her phone. Patricia. Reuben's sister would have collected him by now, taken him away.

She'd meant to pop in yesterday, see how Patricia was coping, but since Kerry had come back, she'd been distracted. She should do it now.

Of course, she really shouldn't arrive unannounced, especially on a Sunday, but only Bernard would be bothered. He and Patricia were quite different, when you peered past the pair's genteel, middle-class façade. She was calm when he was easily agitated, and adaptable while he had no intention of budging from his well-worn groove. She liked detective novels and he read nothing but literary classics. But, to be fair, Bernard *did* have a similar core of determination and integrity. Perhaps that was the key to an enduring relationship — not shared interests, but shared values? Sidney hoped that what she'd seen of Kerry's values meant that he and she could also go the distance. And that it wouldn't matter if she confessed she found football a giant snore.

Driving through Gabriel's Bay, Sidney had to smile. The sun was out, and people were strolling around, some in optimistically light clothing. Spring was officially still three weeks away, but on a day like this, you could be convinced it had arrived. Her baby would be born in summer, and the warmth would make it all seem a little easier. Kerry would have time off, and they could relax — as much as anyone can relax with a newborn. Stop that, she scolded. Focus on the positive. Focus on—

Good grief, was that *Devon*?

Sidney slewed the car to a halt, hopped out and onto the footpath in front of what was *definitely* Devon, apart from—

'Wow,' she said.

'Yeah, I'm getting that a lot.'

A more civil reply than she rightly deserved.

Devon brought forward his companion — a tall girl, fresh-faced and attractive, with an amused glint in her eye.

'This is Moana,' he said. 'Mo, this is Sidney.'

'Who's not usually this crazy and rude,' said Sidney, holding out her hand.

'It's like walking around with a tame tiger or something,' Moana said, as she returned the handshake. 'Everyone's freaked out and fascinated all at once.'

'Yes, it's a small town,' said Sidney. 'A giant lump of tallow washed up on the beach a decade ago and people still talk about it.'

'Oh, *yeah*,' said Devon. 'All us kids thought it was cheese.'

'Pity anyone who tried tasting it. Be like tucking into what you thought was crumbed schnitzel and discovering it was tripe.'

'Speaking of,' said Devon. 'Have you heard from Jacko?'

'Nope, but Mac reckons he'll be back tonight. He said a week when he left, and he's a man of his word.'

'Hope he's forgiven Emma,' said Devon. 'She was gutted about him taking off.'

'I know.' Mac had told Sidney all about it. 'But she's finding ways to keep her spirits up. Gone on a tramping date with Dr G.'

Devon gave a shout of laughter. 'No shit!'

'Let's hope they don't get too preoccupied and fall off a cliff,' said Sidney. 'We don't want a repeat of last year.'

'Brownie,' Devon explained to Moana. 'Had a major fall out hunting and got lost. Everyone figured he was a goner, but Jacko and Gene found him. Saved his life. Only downside was he had to go pretty much straight from hospital to jail.'

'Brother hasn't had it easy, has he?'

Moana gave Devon a look Sidney couldn't interpret, but which caused Devon to hunch his shoulders in an impatient, embarrassed shrug.

'I *did* call him,' he said. 'Didn't answer. I'll try again later.'

'Barrett's probably gone for a walk, too,' said Sidney. 'Sunny Sunday afternoon — what else would you want to do?'

Both of the young people suddenly froze, like students praying the teacher won't single them out to give the answer.

'Ha!' said Sidney, to their instant mortification. 'Well, nice to meet you, Moana. Looking good, Devon. Enjoy the rest of your day.'

And she chuckled all the way to the Westons.

'Sidney, hello?'

Bernard opened the door, novel in hand — *The Way We Live Now*, Sidney observed. Published, as she recalled, in the 1870s, a decade Bernard would no doubt prefer to now, despite incurable consumption and dentistry performed by barbers.

'Sorry not to forewarn you,' she said. 'I just came to see how you both are now that Reuben's gone home.'

'I see. Well, er, the house is very quiet,' he said. 'Which is not unpleasant, but—' He adjusted his glasses. 'You do become *used* to a certain level of, er, energy about the place . . .'

'Is Patricia in?' Sidney said to rescue him.

Bernard opened up the door.

'Yes, yes, feel free to go through. She's out in the garden.'

The ideal spot to be on a day like this, Sidney thought, as she made her way to the back door. She'd tended her own garden yesterday — staked her broad beans, planted some beetroot, spinach and strawberries, pruned her apple trees and her feijoas, divided her rhubarb and squished some early season aphids. All very satisfying

— and even better, chores done meant she could lie slothfully out in the garden later today, reading or, more likely, napping.

Patricia's garden was beautiful, and robust enough to have survived the routine assaults of Reuben's football. It reminded Sidney of Patricia — calm and serene, nothing clashing or clamouring for your attention. Nothing too formal, either, just a relaxed, comfortable space that welcomed you and buoyed your spirits. Sidney knew how much effort it required to achieve that effect, and admired Patricia all the more.

It was also a large garden, and Sidney could not immediately spot her. There she was, on one of those kneeler things that Sidney always associated with 'proper' gardeners, along with lawn rollers and trugs.

Patricia had her back to Sidney, and so it wasn't until she was upon her that she noticed. Patricia's face was in her hands, and she was sobbing. The fat, shaking sobs that only come from a broken heart.

Sidney didn't hesitate, but dropped to her knees and hugged her. There was no need to say anything, and besides, what comfort could she give? Patricia, she knew, was not grieving only for the loss of Reuben, but for all the children she never had, and who had been wanted so very badly. It was bereavement at a level Sidney had not experienced, and so she responded in the only way she could, by holding this kind woman tight until the worst of her hard, fresh grief had eased.

CHAPTER 36

Vic

Vic's dad, for reasons best left unknown, had been very fond of the kind of humorous music hall-style songs that hadn't stood the test of time, though most probably hadn't been all that hilarious in their day, either. Vic had memories of listening to Gracie Fields, Flanagan and Allen, and Stanley Holloway, and it was a number of the latter's that was currently refusing to leave his mind. It was entitled, in that cringingly quaint way, *My Word, You Do Look Queer,* and was about a bloke going for a walk and being told by everyone he meets how unwell he looks until he becomes convinced he genuinely is at death's door.

After a week of being surrounded by well-meaning, solicitous folk, Vic knew exactly how the bloke felt. He couldn't take a step without someone offering to help him, or asking how he was. Seemed like every eye was upon him, as if he were a small child near open water. Initially, he'd thought it was just because of the fire — people wanted to help him get back on his feet. But then he'd realised it went way beyond that. They weren't just worried about how he was managing practically; they were concerned about his mental state as well. Everyone, even Bronagh, Vic had belatedly realised, was convinced he was about to do something daft.

At first, he'd been perplexed — the thought had never crossed his *mind*. Then he'd been offended. He wasn't a loony — how dare they? And then he'd started to wonder if they didn't have a point. Maybe he *was* a bit mentally skew-whiff? Maybe it *wasn't* normal to box on, figuring he'd eventually come right? Maybe some deep-rooted psychological force was in charge, and Vic would suddenly find himself in the ute sucking a vacuum pipe full of exhaust fumes, or in the barn chowing down on a box of rat bait. Vic generally assumed that other people were smarter than he was about most things, so they could well have picked up on clues that he hadn't. Trouble was, he definitely did *not* want them to be right.

That morning Vic had opened the front door of Willow Cottage and drunk his tea standing in the first rays of the sun. Sunday. A week since Ron Hanrahan and his mob had gone berserk. Had he been right refusing to dob the man in? He'd said no because he was worried about the Wood Sprites. Rob was vindictive, as he'd proved, and even if he chose to keep a low profile this time, he had money to pay professional revenge-takers. Rua and the others were field mice, with neither the disposition nor the resources to defend themselves. Whereas Rob was a bloody big vengeful hawk.

But now he'd time to think, Vic wondered if perhaps the Wood Sprites weren't his first concern after all. Was it possible fear of his *own* inadequacy was holding him back? If the Wood Sprites wouldn't testify, it would be Vic's word against Rob's. Inarticulate, bumbling Vic versus a slick, confident, successful bloke with plenty of high-powered supporters. Vic had supporters, too, and he was grateful, but they were ordinary folk, not business and civic leaders, people with money and influence.

And if he testified against Rob, he'd also be dropping Otto in it. The man had done him plenty of favours in the past, and Vic owed him. Far as he could tell, Otto hadn't taken part in the actual damage-fest, but he'd be guilty by association. He'd been one of the wrecking gang — as had Vic, for that matter, and saying he hadn't meant to only made him sound even more incompetent.

The morning sky had a shimmer to it that boded well for a beautiful, sunny day. Forecast said it might get up as high as fifteen degrees. Good news for the new animals that would soon be standing wobbly legged on his land. Thanks to Gene Collins — though Vic still held some suspicion about his motives — the calving and lambing would not be the nightmares he'd envisaged. The blokes, and women, too, that Gene had roped in were all experienced contract farmworkers. Vic didn't know how or what they were being paid, and when he'd asked had been told not to worry about it. Given what else he had to worry about, Vic was happy to comply. He was also happy to ignore the irony that the worst time in his life was also the first time he'd felt like everything was under control.

Couldn't ignore reality, though. He was about to lose the farm, and he had no idea what would come after. Who would he be if he weren't a farmer? What job could he do? How the hell would he explain this to his dead ancestors when he arrived at whatever after-life the Halsworths were destined to frequent?

Vic closed his eyes and let the surrounding smells and sounds permeate. The bass chorus of cattle, the strident bleat of sheep, a bellbird, a fantail, a distant kingfisher with its one-note summoning call. Grass, leaf mulch, pine sap and Bell tea. Wafts of the vanilla plug-in air freshener that Donna had insisted on. Bronagh had switched it off, saying it made her feel like she was trapped in a cake tin, but Vic quite liked it. He particularly liked the fact it no longer made him sad. He hoped Donna was enjoying life in Coonamble, and that her new bloke wore the right kind of underpants.

Right overhead, the clown-horn honk of a tūī. Vic opened his eyes to see it zooming, Spitfire-like, into the far trees. The bush would be terrific on a day like today; tranquil, sweet smelling and completely devoid of helpful people.

Bugger it. Sidney was due to visit this afternoon, but she'd understand. In fact, she'd probably be thrilled. She was a nice woman but he wasn't quick-witted enough to keep up with her in conversation, and more often than not, they just sat there, sipping tea, in embarrassed silence. He'd leave her a note, so she wouldn't worry. Then he'd pack a small rucksack and head off for a decent tramp.

The bush out the back of Vic's — well, whoever's — farm was a combination of broadleaf and podocarp, mature and remarkably untroubled by pest species such as hawthorn, old man's beard and ivy. New saplings were coming through on the forest floor, and big roots and supplejack vines were prevalent, but the ground was dry and so walking was relatively easy. It had been a while since he'd taken this route, but Vic had always had a good sense of direction, and if that failed, he had his compass to fall back on. These days, hunters had GPS devices and all manner of technology, but on this fine morning, Vic didn't envy what he lacked. A stout pair of boots, Swanndri and compass were all he needed. Peanut butter, bacon and banana sandwiches (thanks, Elvis) and his dad's old metal water flask. The only thing he *could* do with was a slightly higher level of fitness, but no one was around to see him pause for breath on the slopes, or grumble about his knees on the downward side.

He was heading for a clearing about an hour in, where he intended to sit, eat his sandwiches and listen to the birds. He hoped he might spot a kākā, a bird that always amused him. It screeched like a fishwife, and, if you weren't vigilant, would steal your food. New Zealand birds were often prone to thieving. Last time Vic had gone on a hunting trip, a weka had stolen his fork, and he'd had to eat his eggs and bacon with a teaspoon. Vic had read somewhere that most native birds hadn't actually evolved in New Zealand but had blown across from Australia. Which would explain their light-beaked habits.

A sudden cracking of branches to one side reminded Vic that deer might be venturing out from cover to eat the new grass that was coming up now because of the warmer weather. Feeding time — and thus good hunting — was generally early morning or later afternoon, and besides, he hadn't brought a gun. Couldn't have even if he'd wanted to; he'd given Gene the keys to the tool shed, the ring with the gun locker keys on it, and the bugger hadn't given them back yet. Oh, well, he wasn't in the mood for shooting anything. And with his current luck, he'd probably only see pregnant hinds. Only dropkicks and complete bastards shot those.

Speaking of — he was still unsure if he'd done the right thing not naming Rob Hanrahan. The Wood Sprites might have decided to drop out of society, but that didn't mean they should be excluded from its system of justice. Darius almost died, and the whole group had lost everything: homes, food, clothes, all their meagre possessions, most of which they'd made by hand. That wasn't fair and it wasn't right.

But then, there was Otto, his friend. Maybe Vic should talk to him first, and if Otto got on board, then the two of them would be more convincing.

It could wait until Monday, though. Right now, he'd enjoy this walk, this last bit of freedom and peace . . .

Vic stopped short. He was near the edge of the clearing, and in it, through the trees, he could see a dark shape. A deer? Looked from this angle more like a large brown dog, or a small bear, sitting hunched over, with its back to him. Unlikely, but you never knew. He'd seen some strange things in these woods. Maybe they *had* been real.

He approached as quietly as he could, skirting the periphery to get a better look at whatever it was.

Jesus! Vic's heart began to hammer, and his breath came in rapid, shallow puffs. The shape was a man, sitting on the ground, legs bent up and out, and between them, held in outstretched arms, a rifle, its barrel propped against the bloke's forehead.

Not just any bloke, but one Vic recognised, even though he couldn't believe what he saw. Young Barrett Tahana — handsome, confident, outspoken Brownie. Unless Vic's eyes deceived him, about to do something daft.

Before he could worry about startling him, Vic yelled out, 'Don't!'

Brownie dropped the gun fast as if Vic had been the one to shoot him, and scrambled backwards along the ground like a rat putting hasty distance between it and a snake. One elbow gave out, causing him to lurch sideways, and then he just stopped moving, and lay there on the ground like a broken doll.

Vic ran. Instinct made him check the gun first and engage the safety, and then he dumped his rucksack and dropped to his knees beside Brownie, panting out, 'You OK?'

Stupid question. The bloke had been about to top himself, so he was as far from OK as you can get. Brownie was curled in a near foetal position now, his hands over his face. Not crying but shaking all over. Shock. Shame. Whatever. It didn't matter — the lad was alive. Vic refused to think about what he might have found if he'd arrived later. He hadn't, so no point in dwelling. His focus now was getting this young man out of the bush and into care. Ironically, now that his cellphone was operational again, there was no coverage out here, but Vic would get him back to his farm, even if he had to semi-carry him.

'Hey.'

Vic placed a hand on the lad's shoulder, and as if he'd pressed an off switch, the shaking began to subside. Vic shifted his hand to Brownie's back, patted it, half-ashamed that his touch was so hesitant. Coming from a long line of physically undemonstrative men tended to do that to you. But maybe a full-blown hug might not be what the lad wanted; Vic should let him take the lead.

Brownie's hands slid down his face to expose his eyes, wide and aghast; Vic couldn't tell whether he was horrified by what he'd almost done, or by the realisation he'd failed and was still here, still alive.

One eye slid to Vic, who said, 'It's OK. You're OK.'

It might be nonsense, but times like this, people needed comfort, reassurance. They didn't need to hear the truth.

'Come on, sit yourself up.'

With a few gentle nudges, Vic coaxed the lad into a sitting position, or a bedraggled semblance of one. Brownie's back was bent, his head hanging low, both arms limp on his legs as if he'd been rescued from a shipwreck and had barely the energy to breathe.

Vic got off creaking knees and sat beside him. Ridiculous phrases circled in his mind, such as 'Well, here's a to-do', and 'Did you see Taranaki's taken the shield?' Fortunately, his mouth didn't let them out, and the pair sat in silence while the birds carried on singing around them.

Beside him, there was a ragged intake of breath and Brownie lifted his head. Didn't look at Vic, but stared into the trees. The sun was shining on them, and Vic had nowhere else to be. He could sit with the lad all day.

But then Brownie spoke, his tone flat, subdued.

'I suppose you want to know why.'

'Only if you want to tell me,' said Vic. 'None of my business, otherwise.'

More silence. Vic hoped he hadn't put him off.

'Happened when I saw the gun,' Brownie eventually resumed. 'I imagine the idea had been in my mind before then, but it wasn't until I held that rifle that it fully formed. It seemed so obvious, the answer to everything. Took the gun and the bullets and got up here as fast as I could.'

'Pretty final answer,' said Vic. 'Problems must have been big.'

'Or else I'm *stupid* for not being able to solve them. Stupid and *weak*.'

The bitterness made Vic's heart thump anew.

'I didn't mean that, mate,' he said, hastily. 'I know what it's like to feel stumped by life, up against a wall that you can't see round or over. It's not your fault. Sometimes we can't sort it out no matter *how* hard we try.'

Not the best comparison, because young Brownie was smart and Vic wasn't. But Vic hadn't much else to offer.

Brownie sunk his head in his hands again, and this time, he *was* crying. Bugger it. Vic put his arms round the lad and hugged him. Awkwardly, owing to the position, but not tentatively. It was a great big man hug, and the lad leaned into him, even though Vic's Swanndri must scratch like hell. Bit whiffy as well, but too late now.

'I'm just so *tired*,' Brownie said against Vic's chest. 'So fucking tired of being *afraid*, and *pretending*, and being *alone*.'

His voice dropped to a whisper. 'So fucking tired . . .'

'Yeah, loneliness is a bugger all right,' said Vic. 'Makes you wonder what you did to be so unlovable.'

Brownie sat up, smeared the tears from his face with dirty hands.

'It's not what I did,' he said. 'It's who I am. Who I *really* am, not this — sham persona I put on. But I'm too cowardly to find out how the real me will get on. People look at me sideways enough now. They don't trust me or like me, and why should they? I was a stupid, arrogant, criminal idiot. Why give them one more reason to hate my guts?'

Vic had lost the thread — if he'd ever had it in the first place.

'What would be worse than you being a drug dealer?'

Not terribly tactful, but there didn't seem a better way to put it.

Brownie uttered a short, despairing laugh.

'What do you *think*? Honestly, I've no idea why nobody's spotted it before now. Well, to be fair, the odd one has, but they have the same vested interest in keeping mum.'

'Uh . . .'

Vic was truly struggling. The upside of this was that Brownie was very nearly amused.

'I'll give you a hint, shall I?' he said. 'I'm extremely neat.'

'OK?'

'And I've never had a girlfriend.'

'*Oh* . . .! Oh, *shit*.'

Brownie shot him a challenging, sideways look.

'Regret touching me now?'

Vic's struggle was now of a different kind. He *did* find gay men, especially the camp ones, off-putting, and the idea of man-on-man sex was just — no. Vic couldn't even contemplate that kind of, er, rear positioning, with a *woman*. But this lad here, what was he, nineteen, twenty? If Vic had got his act together earlier in life, he might now have a son that age. Brownie was a boy, a deeply unhappy boy, and if he *had* been Vic's son, Vic would not have hesitated to hold him and comfort him. His own father might have balked at even a pat on the back, but Vic could still well remember the joy and reassurance of his mother's embrace. Why should that kind of physical affection, those gestures of love, be the sole province of women?

And so he put his arm around Brownie again, pulled him close. And Brownie once more buried his face in Vic's chest and cried, possibly this time out of relief as well, that he'd finally been able to tell someone.

'Sorry about the Swanni,' Vic said, when the fresh bout of tears had abated. 'Didn't realise how much it stinks until now.'

He felt the lad's shoulders briefly shake with laughter, and had to steel himself not to sag with relief.

Brownie sat up, smeared more dirt on his damp face. 'I'm not exactly cool-mint fresh myself.'

Vic reached out for his rucksack, retrieved the flask of water. Offered it to Brownie, who drank as if he'd just crawled out of the desert.

'Thanks,' he said, handing it back.

Vic drank, too, without wiping it off. Seemed a small but important gesture.

He became aware of the rifle, lying a few feet away. Never a good thing to leave a weapon unguarded. He should fetch it, but he didn't want to upset the boy.

Cracking of branches again, behind them. Vic turned his head, but whatever was there was keeping out of sight.

'Deer?' said Brownie.

'Most likely. They come out for the new grass. Good time to go hunting,' he added.

There was a silence, during which Vic mentally kicked his own stupid, tactless arse.

'I've never killed anything,' Brownie said. 'When I went to prison, I thought I was going to *be* killed, but turns out the guards aren't stupid. They separated me from the gang affiliates, and stuck me in with the sex offenders, lawyers and accountants.'

'Accountants, huh?' said Vic.

'We played poker for biscuits. They were the worst cheats by far.'

'Gang given you any trouble since you've been out?'

Brownie hung his head again.

'Not yet,' he said, 'and that's part of it, too. Waiting's a worse torture than any beating. Can't go out without looking over my shoulder. Can't stop worrying about Gene and his family staying safe. The only bright spot is that I don't have any family around — or anyone else who's close to me . . .'

'You know, my mum died when I was six,' Vic told him.

'I didn't know that.' Brownie raised his head, met Vic's eye. 'I'm sorry.'

'Miss her every day.'

The lad said with a sigh, 'Oh, yes.'

Branches cracking again, to their right this time and much, *much* louder. Both men instinctively scrambled to their feet. Vic risked it, stepped forward and snatched up the rifle.

Jesus, what was *in* there to make a commotion like that? An *elephant*?

At the edge of the clearing, it appeared. Stood there gazing at them, untroubled.

'Holy—'

Vic couldn't finish. He was conflicted. Either this was good news and he *had* seen that mother and calf. Or else he was hallucinating a second time, which meant all the recent shocks had permanently addled his brain and everyone was right — he *was* a loony.

'It's *real*.' Brownie tone was questioning, as if he needed Vic to confirm he saw it, too.

'I guess.'

Vic wasn't quite yet ready to commit.

'It's *huge*,' Brownie whispered, voice nearly an octave higher in awe.

The moose calmly bent to graze. Guess it knew it didn't have to be afraid. One swat from that head or kick from those hooves and Vic and Brownie would be two jellied sacks of broken bones. Nothing to do but keep still and watch it eat grass. If it came towards them — well, hopefully, Vic would be able to come up with a Plan B.

'God, it's beautiful,' said Brownie. 'Like something out of another time.'

Absolutely correct. Vic felt a surge of elation. How fortunate he was. How privileged. As if to make up for handing him a pile of shit, God, nature, fate — who or whatever — had given him this. It had given him Brownie, alive, and now a second miracle. A joyous, liberating vision that made anything seem possible.

And then a low, horribly familiar voice in his ear, said 'Don't move a fucking inch.'

Of course. How could Vic have imagined for a *second* that he was lucky? He was the winner of the booby prize. Haw, haw, haw.

'No *way*,' hissed Brownie, and he made a lunge for Rob's rifle. Rob, with surprising agility for a bloke his age, booted the lad right in the guts, and Brownie sat down heavily, too winded to even gasp.

Without a second thought, Vic raised the rifle in his hand and aimed it at Rob's head.

'Put it down,' he said.

Rob didn't flinch, didn't even glance at him. Kept his gun trained square on the moose, and quietly scoffed.

'Sure, Vic. You're going to shoot me. Right.'

'You're not going to kill that animal, Rob,' said Vic.

'Can't now,' Rob agreed. 'It's facing me. Need a broadside shot.'

Then he muttered, 'Come on, you fucker. Turn to the side.'

Brownie was on his knees now, clutching his abdomen, trying to suck air back into his lungs. Vic could yell at the moose, try to startle it, but soon as it turned to run, Rob would shoot it. Why couldn't it have been a normal animal that vamoosed at the first sight of humans? It was almost as if it was *used* to them.

Oh, shit, it was ambling around to reach a fresh patch of grass. Vic saw Rob tense in readiness. But the bastard was right — Vic wouldn't shoot him. Even if he aimed for an arm, at this distance the shot would most likely do mortal damage. The rifle was a .243 calibre Remington. Powerful and accurate. Vic had one exactly like it.

Vic had read books where dramatic events seemed to unfold in slow motion, but turned out that was complete bollocks. The ensuing sequence played out so fast, he couldn't follow it. Far as he could tell, the moose turned and Brownie leapt up, just as a bullet twanged with an unholy thunk against the stock of Rob's rifle, sending it flying out of his hands. The moose reared and skedaddled, Rob swore and made a dive for his rifle, whereupon he tripped over Brownie, now lying on the ground, and sprawled flat next to him. And then, somehow, Jacko Reid was there — did he kick Rob in the head? Vic wasn't sure, but Rob seemed to be unconscious now, and Jacko was on his knees next to Brownie and yelling at Vic to help him.

Shit. The lad had been shot. The bullet — Jacko's, Vic could only assume — had bounced off Rob's rifle and hit Brownie in the upper arm.

'Only nicked him, thank fuck.'

Jacko handed Vic his rifle, slung the pack off his shoulder and began rummaging in it. So many weapons; Vic dithered about what to do, and decided to sling them all over his shoulder. Rob was moaning on the ground, and Vic was sorely tempted to kick him again. But it was two of them against one now, and the moose had gone. Rob would kick up a fuss but too bad. Nothing else he could do.

Brownie was sitting up now, grey-faced and sweaty, while Jacko expertly wrapped his arm in a bandage. From his first-aid kit, he plucked painkillers, a bar of chocolate and one of those silver foil blankets.

'Get these down you.' He handed Brownie the painkillers and a bottle of water, and then wrapped the blanket round the lad's shoulders. 'Shock,' he explained, and broke off squares of chocolate for him to eat. 'How're you feeling?' Jacko said, when the chocolate was gone.

'Hurts,' said Brownie, succinctly.

'Yeah, it does,' Jacko agreed. He got off his knees, sat down with a whoosh. 'Jesus. Nearly had a fucking heart attack when you leapt up like that. You are fucking lucky, my friend. Could have been the end of you.'

Brownie and Vic's eyes met, and Vic could read the message there, clear as day. He nodded, smiled to reassure. Their secret.

'Count our blessings, eh?' Vic said.

Rob, still moaning, had rolled over and was clutching his head. Jacko gazed upon him with distaste.

'Think you can walk?' he said to Brownie. 'Vic and I will prop you up. It's just the air's getting a little rank around here. And I badly need a beer.'

'Sure,' said Brownie. 'I think . . .'

'Oh, and you know that thing we saw?' said Jacko. 'We never saw it. Did we, Vic?'

'Nothing but birds out here,' Vic said.

Jacko chuckled.

'That's the story. Come on—' He helped a shaky Brownie to his feet. 'You need to see the doc. But first, cold beer and a sit down at Vic's place. I'll get Dr G to meet us there.'

'On a Sunday?' said Vic.

'Why not?' Jacko said. 'It's not like he has anything better to do.'

CHAPTER 37

Ash

The prairie vole of North America, unlike most of its promiscuous rodent kin, mated for life. Science put this down to the presence in the vole of a particular hormone known as vasopressin, which in its less romantic capacity also controlled thirst. Vasopressin was the reason prairie voles indulged in more sex than was strictly necessary for the purposes of reproduction. The hormone was also, Ash guessed, the reason why he and Emma had not ventured even a step out into the bush, but had flung themselves at each other like — well, not prairie voles, some other less fluffy wild creature — and had not left his bed for the past four hours.

There were other hormones, too, at play in the field of sexual attraction — serotonin, dopamine, adrenaline, oxytocin — but as far as Ash was concerned, his medical knowledge could go hang. Sex with Emma was a sublime encounter, akin to a mystical awakening. It was an experience, as a Hindu guru might say, unable to be grasped by mere intellect alone, numinous but unclouded, a moment where perception and sensation fused in one supreme, perfect union.

'Where do you keep your bog roll?' Emma called from the lavatory.

'Er, is there none on the handle of the toilet brush?'

'Nup. All out.'

'One moment.'

Ash pushed back the covers and resumed contact with reality. Pulled on his boxer briefs and trotted off to open up the twelve-pack of Plush in the hall cupboard.

The toilet door was ajar, but he knocked anyway, before pushing it open just enough to hand over the roll.

'Thanks, man,' said Emma. 'Hey, triple ply. Nice.'

'I, er, I'll go and take a shower,' he said, clearly less comfortable than she was about conversing through a toilet door.

'Yeah, we're both pretty funky,' said Emma. 'I'll hop in after.'

Which was a relief, as Ash had lost his taste for shower sex some years back, after an incident involving a soap-on-a-rope that he shuddered to recall.

The bathroom was next door, but as Ash reached to turn on the shower, he heard his mobile. He considered letting it ring, but after a swift calculation, realised it was the small hours of the morning in Ahmedabad. Even if someone had died, he'd be the last to be rung out of a long list, so it was safe to assume the caller was not a relative. Must be someone who needed an emergency after-hours visit. He jogged back to the bedroom and answered.

'I see,' was all he could say in response to the information imparted. 'I'll be there in twenty minutes.'

Emerging from the bedroom, he found Emma gloriously naked in the hall, and had to suppress the regret (and hormones) that instantly arose. But there would be other opportunities. He hoped.

'That was your father,' he said.

'Dad?'

Emma rushed up.

'Is he OK? Why's he ringing you? Is Mum OK?'

'Yes, yes, they're fine.'

Ash embraced her, kissed her temple.

'Barrett Tahana has been shot—'

'*What*? Fuck!'

'He's also fine. But your father would like me to take a look at the wound. He's at Vic Halsworth's cottage. I said I'd drive up now.'

He hesitated. Emma had told him everything that had transpired over the past week.

'Would you like to come with me?'

'Definitely,' she said, though he could see the anxiety in her eyes. 'Probably should put some clothes on, though, huh.'

Any room, including the hundred thousand square-metre London Millennium Dome, would feel small with Jacko Reid in it. But as Willow Cottage was designed for two average-sized people comfortable with each other's proximity, the word 'cramped' could be aptly applied. Barrett had been laid on the sofa, and when Ash and Emma arrived, Jacko and Vic were forced into the narrow galley kitchen, from whence could be heard the occasional muffled curse as one or other of them knocked his head on the rangehood.

Ash, in professional mode, went straight to Barrett and began to inspect the arm. Glancing up, he noted that his patient's attention was elsewhere directed, and in a manner that must be described as riveted. Swivelling, Ash saw that Emma had remained in the doorway. She had eyes only for her father, and her expression was one of pure poignant woe.

'Come here, you.'

Her father held out his arms and she launched herself into them, wrapped her own arms around his neck (he'd bent to allow it) and sobbed on his shoulder.

'I'm so-rry,' she said, each syllable a damp hiccup. 'I was stu-u-pid.'

Ash observed Vic looking perplexed. As far as Emma was aware, only her parents, Casey Marshall and Tai Te Wera knew about her involvement with the website, and anyone else they may have told could be relied on for discretion. Vic had suffered enough, in Ash's opinion. He could be spared an explanation.

'It's OK.' Jacko held his daughter tight. 'You're still my best girl.'

Words that sent Ash's nerves a-flutter. Dear Lord, what if Jacko did not approve of Ash and Emma? There'd be no other option — he'd have to leave town. Most sensibly in the dead of night.

'Ow, Doc,' came a gentle protest.

'Sorry.'

Ash released his vice-like grip on Barrett's wrist. His own pulse was pounding too hard for him to get a reading anyway. Best take the blood pressure instead.

Examination over, Ash pronounced his verdict.

'You're extremely lucky. It is a flesh wound only and not that deep. Nowhere near the brachial artery. Jacko's first-aid was excellent, but I will give you these painkillers to tide you over, and these antibiotics to ensure there is no residual infection. Are your tetanus shots up to date?'

'I've no idea,' said Barrett, without enthusiasm.

'Come to the surgery tomorrow, and I will give you a booster.'

'Oh, joy.'

'Do you also need a ride home?' Ash asked. 'To Gene's house?'

'He's welcome to stay here.'

Vic stood by the sofa.

Barrett glanced up at Vic, and his smile overlaid gratitude with regret.

'Thanks,' he said. 'But I'd better get back. I've got a bit of explaining to do.'

'They'll understand,' said Vic.

'Yes, they probably will,' said Barrett, softly. 'Bogeymen tend to disappear when you turn the light on, don't they?'

Now it was Ash's turn to be perplexed, but whatever was passing between the two was none of his business.

He straightened up and turned to Emma, whose apologetic expression told him that she would not be returning to his bed today.

But she did move close and kiss him on the mouth in lingering fashion. Ash didn't dare glance at *any*one to see how *that* had been received.

'Sorry,' she said. 'Dad's parked down by the river, and I'll walk with him. I need some quality family time.'

'Of course,' said Ash. 'Call me when you're ready.'

She gave him such a radiant smile that every hormone in his body fully activated, even the ones that regulated cell apoptosis and circadian rhythm. Ash hoped fervently, as he farewelled the pair, that Emma would be ready soon.

'Would you like to leave now, too?' he asked Barrett. 'Or wait a while? I don't mind.'

'Now, please,' Barrett replied. 'Before I lose my nerve.'

'You should chat to the doc,' said Vic. 'On the way.'

Barrett swallowed. He'd become increasingly hollow-eyed, and Ash was about to suggest they wait after all. He could use the time to compose an email to his mother. One that was courteous but unambiguous in every respect.

But then Barrett eased himself, wincing, off the sofa, and gave Ash a wan grin.

'OK, Doc, let's hit the road. How are you at driving and listening?'

'Oh, you know, on a day such as this,' said Ash. 'I feel capable of mastering anything.'

CHAPTER 38

Devon

'Are you going to almost die *every* year?'

This from Jenna, Gene's youngest daughter, aged ten. The Collins clan, including Brownie, was gathered in their kitchen around a stack of food that could feed them all twice over. Devon had been invited as Brownie's mate, and he'd accepted, despite feeling like a fraud.

(And a cuckolder, let's not forget *that*, even though Moana assured him that nothing had happened on her and Brownie's date.

'Yeah, no chemistry,' she'd said. 'He's cute, but — nada, zip.'

'Cute as me?' Devon couldn't help himself.

'Don't be a dick.'

(Yep, Mo had zero tolerance for Devon's bullshit. Good thing, too.)

Brownie had taken Jenna's question in his stride.

'Not planning to make a habit of it, no,' he said. 'But then, I didn't plan to fall off a mountain or get hit by a ricocheting bullet, either, so who knows?'

'Jen-*na*,' said Gene's eldest, Billie, fifteen and Ninja-level eye-roller. 'You're such a *spaz*.'

'Girls,' said their mother, Liz, in a tone that brooked no denial.

'Did getting shot hurt?' said Frankie, twelve, the middle daughter.

'Yes,' said Brownie.

'More than breaking *heaps* of bones?'

Frankie's role model was apparently Wednesday from the Addams Family.

'Guess whose bones *I'm* thinking of breaking right now?' said her mother, cheerfully.

'That's child abuse,' said Jenna, picking minuscule traces of egg yolk out of her potato salad. 'We can report you.'

'See what happens when you teach children to think for themselves?' remarked Gene. 'Should have stuck to the old ways — lifelong psychological scarring and repression never hurt anyone.'

Devon saw Brownie's eyes flicker briefly in his direction, and wondered what that meant. It was exactly a week since the shooting, details of which had not been divulged by any of the participants. Hunting accident was the official verdict, and if Casey Marshall knew any different, she wasn't saying, either. Why Jacko, Vic Halsworth and Brownie had happened to meet in the same part of the bush and whose gun had fired the shot would remain matters for speculation. As would the cause of the livid bruising down one side of Rob Hanrahan's face.

Gene knew, Devon could tell. But then Jacko was his best mate, and they didn't keep secrets from one another. And Brownie was sort of his unofficial ward. Devon's woo-wah wasn't giving him any specific clues, just an all-purpose signal that something big had gone down and its repercussions were still vibrating in the airwaves.

As the last of the dessert was being scraped from plates, the front door bell rang. Jenna hopped off her chair.

'I'll get it!'

'If it's Jehovah's Witnesses,' Gene called after her. 'Ask them how much they'd pay to take you girls away with them.'

After an inaudible interaction at the front door, Jenna re-entered the kitchen.

'It's a man,' she announced, got back on her chair, and reached for the ice-cream.

'Name?' said her mother.

Jenna licked the serving spoon. 'I forget.'

'Duh, you *spaz*,' said Billie.

'It's probably a *murderer*,' said Frankie. 'And Jenna's let him *in*.'

Sighing heavily, Liz got up. Seconds later, she was back. Trailing sheepishly behind her was Vic Halsworth.

'Vic!' hailed Gene. 'Have a seat.'

Vic looked like he'd been invited to give a scorpion a lift across a river, but then, he always *did* look like he'd just been bitten on the bum.

'Coffee?' Liz offered. 'Or would you men like to retreat to the den?'

'The man cave,' said Gene, smugly. 'Complete with minibar. Shall we?'

'We should help Liz clear up first,' said Brownie.

Liz blew him a kiss.

'Thank you, Barrett, but I won't be clearing up, the girls will be.'

Jenna's reiteration of, 'That's child abuse,' coincided with Billie's complaint of '*Mu*-um' and Frankie's dark muttering of, most likely, some ancient hex.

Gene rose and gestured for Vic, Brownie and Devon to quickly follow him through the laundry and out the back door. The so-called den was actually the extended back half of the garage, which had been equipped with a La-Z-Boy suite, wide-screen TV and beer fridge, and decorated with the obligatory bad-taste posters.

Opening the fridge, Gene pulled out a six-pack.

'Women,' he said. 'Gotta love 'em. Even in hordes.'

His expression suddenly froze.

'Sorry, mate,' he said to Brownie. 'You know what I mean.'

Brownie's wry half-smile and Vic's anxious eyes said that *they* both knew why Gene was apologising. Devon hadn't a frigging clue.

'Beer, Dev?'

Gene held out a can. Devon accepted. So did Vic. Brownie abstained.

'Still on antibiotics,' he said.

'That's a myth, you know,' said Devon. 'Doctors lied about patients not being able to drink because of syphilis. It took a while to clear up, so they didn't want guys getting shit-faced and spreading it before the drugs had time to work.'

'No kidding?' Gene extended the footrest of the La-Z-Boy and cracked open his can. 'Any chance they lied about alcohol making you fat, too?'

Devon ignored him. All his attention was on Brownie and Vic, who'd been exchanging coded glances — a silent Q&A session that Devon, to his now immense frustration, still could not interpret.

'What's going on?' he said. 'You all know something I don't. Care to share?'

Gene and Vic immediately looked at Brownie, Gene in enquiry, Vic a-flutter with nerves.

Brownie screwed up his mouth, but then the wry half-smile appeared again. He leaned forward on the other La-Z-Boy, preparing to speak. Devon heard a slight crunch as Vic's hand contracted around his beer can. What the hell was Brownie about to declare?

'I'm gay.'

For a second, the word did not compute. Then it became the key that activated the lock, and all the parts of the tumbler clunked into place. So *that's* what his woo-wah had been signalling about Brownie's hidden side — shadows could be bad or sad, and they could be ashamed and afraid, too. Yeah, well, Devon knew a bit about that, only *his* reaction wasn't to flee but to fight — or at least be super shitty pretty much 24/7.

'Got it,' said Devon. 'Sorry, man, should have twigged *way* earlier.'

'Why?' Brownie said. 'I only rid myself of my last doubts a couple of weeks ago.'

'Really? What, when you and Mo—'

'Interesting evening.' Brownie nodded. 'I thought — *may*be. But all it did was confirm that I'm one hundred per cent not straight.'

'Mo doesn't know,' said Devon.

Brownie laughed. 'Of course she does! I asked her not to tell you.'

Devon bristled. Of all the people who should understand about sexual identity issues, he'd be number *one*, right? Why couldn't—

'And then I had a crisis,' said Brownie, now subdued. 'Monumental one. I'll tell you about that later, OK?'

'You don't have to.'

Devon's mental lock gave one final clunk, and now the *whole* picture was clear. Poor bastard. Shit, *lucky* bastard. Who'd stopped him there out in the bush — Vic? Jacko?

Hardly mattered. When miracles occurred, it was churlish to demand details.

'Your Mum must have known?' Devon said. 'She was a smart lady.'

'No.' Brownie tilted his head to one side. 'Well, maybe. She would have known Dad wouldn't cope, and she never kept secrets from him, so perhaps she decided it was best not to ask.'

'You're sure about your dad?' said Gene, gently.

'I witnessed him often use "faggot" as a term of abuse,' said Brownie. '"Poofter", too, occasionally. Mainly on the sporting sidelines, to be fair . . .'

He rubbed his hands roughly on either side of his face, as if trying to wake up.

'I don't *know*,' he said. 'I can't tell where my insecurities end and reality begins.'

'Your dad and I, our generation's not that — comfortable,' said Vic. 'Don't forget, it wasn't even legal when we were growing up.'

'Explains a lot about Otto,' said Gene.

'What do you mean?' Vic's voice went all squeaky.

'Vic, did you not realise? Otto's *totally* gay.'

'No, he isn't!' Vic glanced helplessly at Brownie. 'Is he?'

'As the day is long,' said Brownie. 'He was the first to — broach the subject with me.'

'*What*?' Vic hopped in his seat. 'He didn't — you didn't—?'

'Otto has a Chilean boyfriend by the name of Eduardo,' said Brownie. 'He's twenty-nine.'

'Eddie the *farm* manager?'

Gene was wiping away tears of mirth.

'Vic, Vic, Vic.' He tossed over a can. 'Have another before you burst a blood vessel.'

'He wants to meet with me tomorrow, Otto does.' Vic's eyes were practically revolving with anxiety. 'Didn't say why.'

'Vic, your belated discovery of his sexual preference doesn't change a thing,' said Gene. 'You won't have to suddenly wear a necklace of garlic. Otto's the same old Otto. Just gayer than you'd thought.'

As the conversation had progressed, Devon became aware of an undercurrent in his own psyche, and not one he was proud of. Brownie might have had a hard time coming to terms with being gay, but he was handsome and *normal* looking, which meant he'd have no trouble getting laid, whereas—

'Whoa, Dev,' said Gene. 'Someone plot spoil *Game of Thrones* for you?'

He really *must* do a better job of keeping his feelings out of his face.

'Nah, just — thinking.'

'About?'

The desire to know was sincere; Devon could always tell with Gene. And he could hardly complain that people didn't take an interest if he clammed up and refused to answer their questions.

'About what next,' Devon said. 'Whether I should leave or stay. What I should do with my life. That kind of thing.'

'Join the club,' said Vic. 'Farm goes to auction this Saturday.'

OK, universe, message received. *Everyone* had bigger problems than Devon did. He needed to shake off this self-pity cloud once and for all, count his *multiple* blessings, and do something useful.

'Have you got somewhere to go?' he asked Vic. 'I could put the word out around the whānau, see who's got a spare room?'

'Thanks,' said Vic, in surprise. 'But I'd like to hang in there till the last minute. Don't know if the farm'll sell yet.'

'Might be some corporate farm owner who'll want you to stay on as manager,' said Gene. 'Could you cope working for someone else?'

Vic's gaze flickered between Gene, Devon and Brownie, and alighted on the beer can resting on his knee.

'Last few weeks have taught me that a lot of stuff I thought was important isn't,' he said. 'And I don't really give a toss what anyone thinks of me any more, because most of the people who judge you are arsewipes.'

Gene saluted with his beer. 'Preach it.'

'Plus beggars can't be choosers,' Vic added. 'So, yeah, if such an offer came my way, I'd consider it. Get to do what I love with half the worry. Steady wage. Maybe accommodation . . .'

He sipped from the can, and his temporarily brightened expression became glum again.

'Be too good to be true, wouldn't it?'

'Now, Vic, don't lose heart,' said Gene. 'It's a big, old goofy world, and you *know* stranger things have happened.'

He raised his beer again.

'Here's to serendipity, synchronicity and magical woo-wah. May they smile down on all of us.'

'To woo-wah,' said Devon, and drank the toast. 'It's never *completely* failed me yet.'

CHAPTER 39

Patricia

Everyone had been so kind: Sidney, Charles Love, Tai and Corinna and, especially, Bernard. Once he'd realised the extent of her unhappiness, he'd been loving, attentive and, at times, overly helpful. Bernard's ability to execute domestic tasks was limited, and often it was less trouble for Patricia to refuse his offers. But she could accept the flowers, the embraces, the gifts of books and small tokens he thought she might appreciate. Bernard wished her to be happy, and Patricia wished she could oblige him.

She should have known, perhaps — should have anticipated such a reaction. But there was no point in berating herself. It had happened. Now, she must get through it and out the other side.

Corinna had asked whether she wanted to continue as a respite caregiver, and Patricia had given an honest answer: No. She knew she would become attached to even the most troubled child, and the prospect of suffering the same pain of loss made the whole idea out of the question. As she'd said to Bernard only a few short weeks ago, it was an experiment — and now that she'd failed, there was no need to try again.

'That's such a shame,' Corinna had said. 'Good caregivers are like gold dust. And you did *so* well with Reuben. His sister can hardly believe it's the same boy.'

Corinna had paused, before adding, 'Maree wanted me to ask you if you'd be interested in having Reuben for one or two days after school — or a weekend morning. No obligation; it's certainly not something the team would expect, or even encourage. But if you were keen, I don't see the harm.'

Patricia had told her that she'd think about it. It was quite a commitment, and Bernard would agree only to please her. She could not put him in that position.

He was in the kitchen now, with Charles and Tai. Tai seemed considerably happier than he had been over the past fortnight. The farmer-shaming website had been taken down, and the eco-terrorists seemed to have departed, though rumour had it that the police had arrested one at an airport, so Vic and Otto might get justice yet. No charges had been laid regarding the attack on the Wood Sprites camp, but as Tai said, you can't win everything.

She popped her head around the kitchen door.

'Everybody all right?'

'Yes, yes of course,' Bernard hastened to assure her.

'Delicious cake, Patricia,' said Charles. 'Thank you.'

Yes, Patricia had much more time now for baking, gardening and reading.

'Tai has a piece of very good news,' said Bernard. 'Otto Visser has hired Vic.'

'I thought Otto was selling his property?' said Patricia.

'Decided against it,' said Tai. 'But he wants to retire, travel the world with Eduardo, and so he's asked Vic to manage the farm in his absence. Vic can even bring some of his own stock over if he likes, there's enough pasture. *And—*'

He paused for effect, and to relish the pleasure of the revelation. 'Otto has also endowed a part of his property to the Wood Sprites, for them to set up a permanent camp, or for however long they need it. Vic will ensure it meets safety standards, and even Gene Collins has offered to help them reconstruct. Vic's not sure if they'll take up the offer yet, but he's hopeful. Says he enjoys their company.'

'That *is* good news,' said Patricia, and added politely, 'Who is Eduardo?'

Tai's face lit up with amusement.

'Otto's boyfriend. The clubrooms are in *quite* a flap.'

Patricia shared his smile. 'I can imagine.'

'And in *less* positive tidings,' Bernard continued, 'Flange and Ballcock have decided to defer their Littleville sponsorship agreement until next year. Some business arrangement with China fell through and they need to cover the shortfall.'

'Shame that couldn't be said for the waterfront development,' said Tai. 'All systems still go there. Seahorses for Gabriel's Bay.'

'Well, who knows?' said Charles, who could see a silver lining in a raging tempest. 'That might add to the attraction of Littleville. Miniature horses as well.'

'When I was eight, I ordered sea monkeys from a comic book,' said Tai. 'They are *not* as much fun as they look in the picture.'

Patricia began to close the kitchen door. 'I'll leave you to it.'

She could feel Bernard's anxiety emanating, but Charles would manage that. Patricia and he had spoken and he'd given her good advice. Everyone had been *so* kind.

It had re-surged, that overwhelming feeling of loss and despair. As it did, randomly, cruelly. The best place for her to be was the garden, and that's where she went. The garden was so assiduously tended these days that she was reduced to sitting and waiting for weeds to pop up, like a hawk poised over a rabbit burrow.

Sitting, however, allowed her to enter a sort of meditative state. The late winter weather had been positively balmy, and Patricia appreciated the warmth on her back, and the scents of daphne and wintersweet that wafted on the gentle breeze. The bulbs were surfacing — hyacinth, narcissus and daffodil. T.S. Eliot had described the start of spring as cruel because it gave one hopes that could only be dashed. Patricia was not so self-pitying as to believe this dark period in her life would endure. She also knew that there was no point in fighting it. It would be over when it was over, and, if she were vigilant, would never recur with the same intensity.

'Patricia?'

A hesitant request roused her from her not unpleasant languor.

'Sorry,' said Sidney. 'I can bugger off and come back later if you like?'

'No, no,' said Patricia. 'I'm only daydreaming.'

Sidney joined her on the Lutyens bench. Its paint was peeling quite badly, Patricia observed. This would be a perfect time to refresh it.

'I resent it deeply when people interrupt my reveries,' said Sidney. 'It always seems to happen just as I've got to a good bit.'

'I was thinking about bulbs,' Patricia admitted.

'Yes, well, not a *million* miles away from my dream themes,' said Sidney.

Patricia prompted her. 'Did you need me for something?'

'Oh. Gosh . . .'

Ever since Sidney's pregnancy had begun to agree with her, she'd been looking, as the cliché ran, positively blooming. Now the apples of her cheeks flushed an even brighter pink, and Patricia wondered what on earth she'd come to declare.

'It seemed such a good idea when it was all in my mind,' Sidney said. 'Now, I'm worried you'll be offended.'

'Despite my middle-class appearance,' Patricia told her, 'I'm actually very rarely offended. Try me.'

'OK.' Sidney inhaled a deep prepatory breath.

'Patricia,' she began, with the air of a suitor proposing marriage. 'Would you consider being godmother to our baby?'

Goodness. That she had *not* anticipated. And instantly, a midge swarm of conflicting emotions rose inside her. She was flattered, terrified, thrilled, reluctant, tearful, joyful and entirely at sea as to how to respond.

'You don't have to answer right now,' added Sidney, blush deepening. 'I know it's probably terrible timing, and maybe even a terrible idea, but—'

'I'd be honoured to,' said Patricia. 'How lovely of you to ask me.'

'*Really?*'

Sidney looked as if she were about to cry. Patricia knew exactly how she felt.

'I can't think of anything I'd like more,' she said. 'Although I'm not sure I'm entirely suitable to direct the "God" aspect of the role.'

'Oh, just teach it 'Jerusalem' and a few of the more rousing Christmas carols.'

Sidney was smiling now, but had to reach up and wipe her eyes.

'Here.' Patricia reached into her skirt pocket and pulled out a handkerchief.

'See,' said Sidney, as she took it. 'I *knew* we'd made the perfect choice.'

CHAPTER 40

Sidney

'And I couldn't resist the dummy that makes the baby look like they've got a gold grill.'

'A *what*?' Sidney said.

'You know, like a rapper?' said Bronagh. 'A whole front row of gilded choppers.'

'I thought nurses were supposed to be against dummies and bottle-feeding and all that?'

'Oh, pish. As long as you don't fill the bottle with Fanta, you're grand.'

'I don't really *need* a bunch of new stuff,' said Sidney. 'I kept a few of the boys' clothes, for reasons of both supersition and sentiment, and there's a thriving market in secondhand baby gear round here.'

'So you wouldn't be keen for the infant pillow that looks like a giant pair of stuffed hands?'

'How about a nice set of Mothercare onesies? In purple or yellow or some other non gender-specific colour?'

'Are you not going to find out before the day?'

Bronagh sounded disappointed.

'I'm convinced it's a girl,' Sidney told her. 'And I've always wanted to know if I have any vestige of psychic power.'

'A granddaughter,' said Bronagh, wistfully. 'Wouldn't that be lovely?'

'I will refuse to treat her any differently from the boys,' Sidney chided. 'So Douglas better be prepared to make yeast rockets with *everyone*.'

'Will you be OK to put us up in February, for the birth? We could stay with Vic in his new digs, if that suits you better?'

'Vic's agreed to that?'

'Not yet,' said Bronagh. 'But you know how much he adores us.'

'The farm sold for a cracking price,' Sidney said. 'He paid off his debts as well as the fine, and even had a fair chunk left.'

'I know! He should watch out.'

'Why?'

'The gold diggers will come flocking,' Bronagh asserted. 'And you know what a babe in the woods Vic is. Next phone call, I'll make him swear not to go on any dates until we get there, so I can vet the candidates.'

'No dates for nearly six months? Seems a bit harsh.'

'Better safe than sorry,' said Bronagh, cheerfully. '*Some* folk out there are madder than a box of frogs!'

The Moose

It must be more vigilant. The incident in the grassy glade had proved that not all men could be relied upon to stand mute and motionless. The gunshot — so loud. It had awakened all the survival instincts that the moose had foolishly suppressed. Men were dangerous. It would never again forget that. The cow was halfway through its pregnancy, and convinced the calf was male. All the more reason to keep the little herd safe.

So it was with trepidation that the moose approached the glass house in the trees. The man without clothes had always been kind and gentle, but men were dangerous. What if he'd hidden his real nature all along, and today was the day he'd finally do the moose harm?

Peering through the trees, the moose saw that the man sat in his downstairs studio, clad only in a pair of headphones. He sent music out into the air, the man had once explained.

'Into the universe, perhaps,' he'd added. 'Wherever those with open senses will receive it.'

The music sounded to the moose like the squeak and crunch it made when it walked over the old tin and bricks of a long-abandoned bush shack. It much preferred the wail of a female in season, but it supposed every being was entitled to its personal taste.

The moose could not see the woman. She must be out, wearing her pink, sparkly clothes. But, as it neared, it caught smells that belonged to *other* humans, strangers, and it halted immediately.

If that had been the only smell coming from the house, the moose would have turned back, but overlaying the human scent was the aroma of fresh-baked Russian buns. Cheesy, jammy, delicious. The moose had not eaten a bun in many days.

Taking care with every step, the moose drew closer to the house. The buns were on a table outside on the lower patio. It could see them there, on the corner, *almost* within reach.

But wait — the humans it had smelled were there also. A man and a woman, clothed, reclining in the egg-shaped seat that hung from the joists of the deck above. How the two could be comfortable in that tight space, the moose had no idea. They were both slender, true, and the position they were in suggested closeness was not an issue. The young man, with his dark skin and hair, made an attractive contrast to the young woman, whose hair shone gold as aspen leaves in autumn. The moose's DNA remembered aspens.

Neither human had noticed the moose, but then that was understandable as their faces were mashed together in a way that surely must risk damage to their teeth. Quietly as a mouse, if a mouse weighed four hundred kilograms, the moose sneaked to the side of the table, and with its prehensile lips, eased a bun from the plate and into its mouth.

It could eat it here and now, and consume a second, but the moose now knew better than to take such complacent risks. Besides, buns always seemed to be in season at the man's house.

The moose trotted off to eat the bun in the safety of the trees. It would come back another day.

Acknowledgements

To make Gabriel's Bay seem like a real place, I had to write about cultures that aren't my own. A little knowledge being a dangerous thing, I decided to get expert advice. Thank you Rijula Das and Matariki Williams for your time and your invaluable suggestions, translations and corrections. Any errors that remain are my own.

Thanks also to the following people who have made my life immeasurably easier and much more fun:

Harriet, Abby, Rachel and Rebecca at Penguin Random House; Barbara, copy-editor and provider of Swedish moose art; my agent, Gaia, and her lovely assistant, Alba.

My talented writing group: Whitney, Alisha, Fiona, Helen, Simon, Finn, Ruby, Sarah, Penny, Redmer, Meryl, Libby, Fran, Stuart, Pallas, Rijula and Johnny.

Elisha and Juliet at Vic Books, Pipitea; Gareth and Lou at Wardinis; and Carole and her team at the Women's Bookshop for championing *Gabriel's Bay*. Hope you like this one, too.

Peter and Mary Biggs, David Hedley, Claire Mabey and Andrew Laking, Marty Smith, Anne O'Brien, Catherine Wallace and Gail Pittaway, Rachael King, and Mark Cubey for inviting me to their brilliant book fests.

To John Campbell, who said (I have witnesses) that *Gabriel's Bay* was an important New Zealand novel.

And David, Callum and Finn, my Robertson clan.

PS: Those who know about agriculture will spot that avocados are unlikely to be grown in a place where the lambing season is as late as Vic's. But Gabriel's Bay is a deliberate amalgam, and wherever you think it is, you'll be correct.

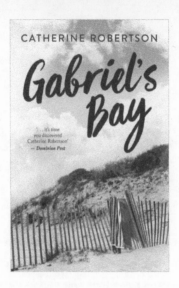

A heart-warming, thoroughly entertaining novel about a whole community.

Kerry Macfarlane has run away from his wedding-that-wasn't. He lands in coastal Gabriel's Bay, billed as 'a well-appointed small town' on its website (last updated two decades ago). Here Kerry hopes to prove he's not a complete failure. Or, at least, to give his most convincing impression.

But Gabriel's Bay has its own problems – low employment, no tourists, and a daunting hill road between it and civilisation. And Kerry must also run the gauntlet of its inhabitants: Sidney, single mother deserted by a feckless ex; Mac, the straight-shooting doctor's receptionist; a team of unruly nine-year-olds; a giant restaurateur; and the local progressive association, who'll debate apostrophe placement until the crack of doom.

Can Kerry win their respect, and perhaps even love? Will his brilliant plan to transform the town's fortunes earn him a lasting welcome in Gabriel's Bay?

'Gabriel's Bay *is a rich, layered, affecting view
of life in a small New Zealand town.'*
— **Maggie Trapp, NZ Books**